# Quail Fried Rice

# Quail Fried Rice

## Rice

Jill Carroll

# Acknowledgments

Thanks to the people in my writing group and to my beta-readers for their invaluable input. Thanks to NaNoWriMo for the structure and support. Thanks to Joanna Penn (www.thecreativepenn.com) for her advice and encouragement. Thanks especially to Nishta Mehra—my love, my key—for everything.

# Chapter One

The old hotel had ceased to function as a hotel, or as anything at all. The beige stucco walls were cracked and the wire backing showed through in places where the mud surface had deteriorated. Exposed raw beams of the roof protruded where the red tiles had fallen away and been covered over by the desert sand. Crumbling and crooked bricks lined the ground along the front of the building, once a border for landscaping. The only thing that looked alive in the garden bed now was a rambling cactus about to spread over the entrance's walkway and across to the matching bed on the other side. Weathered plywood covered the front door and the windows of the building, two on each side of the front entrance. Rusty brackets and deep gouges in the stucco stretched across the front doorway and extended in a line across the front of the building.

Tori Reed stared at the building in front of her as she sat in her black sports car. Dust clouds from her wheels swirled forward and spread across the building's façade and disappeared with the wind around the its corners. She shut off the engine and sat quietly, sinking into the leather seats, folding her hands in her lap. She took a deep breath.

She owned the building now, and the ten acres on which it stood just off the main highway that ran through Logan. And the twenty sections of West Texas desert behind it, for a grand total of 12,810 acres. She had owned it for nearly two months, but had not been able to get away from Houston long enough to come see the property. The total of it all, the sheer immensity of space and distance, overwhelmed her. She was only ten years old the last time she had been here; she had not seen any of this land for nearly thirty-five years. Never did she think she would end up owning it.

She knew that the building as a whole was horseshoe-shaped and that from her place in the car she could only see the "bottom" of the U. Two wings stretched out behind the front structure south toward the low mountains in the distance. She sat still in her car. It was cold and windy, she was not dressed warmly enough, and her sweater and jacket were packed in her bag in the trunk. She wanted to take a few more minutes to absorb the shock of the front of the building before seeing any more.

Tori looked out her passenger window to the west, squinting into the late afternoon sun even through her car's tinted glass. The main road, visible on the right edge of Tori's field of vision, ran like a line into invisibility, disappearing into low mountains and mesas many miles removed. No buildings dotted the landscape, only grasses the color of almond, bronze and rust, and cacti of various heights and styles, some tall and skinny, others thick and sprouting low to the ground. Other small bushes and trees—mostly scrub brush—grew randomly across the desert vista, their stubby branches stiffly shaking in the blowing wind. Tori thought she recognized a juniper about a hundreds yards away.

To the east, the vision was not much different. More desert plain, cactus, scrub brush, some low hills and mountains rising in the distance, behind which she knew stood the buildings of Logan about five miles back. She imagined its structures would seem tiny and inconsequential against the enormous expanse of desert that surrounded it.

Tori looked at her watch—five o'clock straight up. With a deep breath, she opened the car door and stepped out. The cold wind chilled her ears almost immediately, before she could even get to the trunk of her car. She unzipped her leather bag, grabbed a gray sweater and pulled it over her head and her black turtleneck t-shirt. She threaded one arm into her lambskin jacket as she closed the trunk. She zipped the jacket to the top, stuffed her hands into the pockets and began walking toward the corner of the building.

She moved down the east side of the building, noticing the cracks in the stucco, stepping on crumbled pieces of roof tiles as she walked. The half dozen windows were boarded up, so she could not see into the rooms. With every step she took alongside the eastern wing of the dilapidated hotel she took in more of the land behind it, hundreds of acres at a time, at each step. Once past the end of the wing, she stepped from the shade of the building into its so-called backyard. The full measure of the land—of *her* land—hit her in the face as hard as the biting wind. In the nearest foreground of a few dozen acres, a desert plain stretched out from the hotel, occupied by various plants and brush scattered randomly. This plain gave way to several clusters of larger rocks all in a broken line on the edge of what looked like a ravine or gorge. Across the gorge, the plain continued to a rise of small hills, the lines of their rounded tops pressing upward to peaks of jagged rocks. Beyond them were more small mountains and hills divided by sandy strips of land that were, she would learn, traversed with winding creek beds and natural trails that cut through the brush. Clusters of hills and mountains arose and then gave way to long stretches of land, which themselves played out and submitted to new risings of mountains and hills, all of them mottled by the golds, browns, auburns, and occasional dark greens of the desert's winter foliage.

This alternating landscape pattern repeated itself, vista after vista in the distance. Tori began walking toward the gorge and the expanse of desert across it. She picked her way through the small rocks, low cacti, and other mysterious thorny and funny-looking plants that covered the plain behind the hotel. From a distance, the ground on which she stood appeared flat, but walking upon it now she felt the unevenness of the terrain. She placed her boots carefully with each step in order not to fall.

She reached the edge of the gorge and peered into it. Jutting rocks and cliffs comprised its sides, which sloped sharply downward for a few hundred feet before finishing in a sandy bed at the bottom. Scraggly trees and other brush lined both sides of the bed that, Tori surmised, must indicate that the bed was a runoff channel for rainwater. Across the bed, the sides of the gorge re-formed and climbed upward until leveling into a flat plain that matched the one on which Tori stood. The flat plain extended several hundred yards before dissolving into the first group of low hills.

Tori scanned the length of the gorge in both directions. To the left, it extended eastward curving slightly and disappearing from view, then reappearing again as a gash on the landscape that finally disappeared from her view behind a hill. To the right, it cut through a group of mountains, and meandered snakelike across the desert, far past Tori's vision, around other hills and mesas until it crossed from her property into other lands and finally played out near the Rio Grande a hundred miles away.

Tori heard a door slam. She turned and saw a man in jeans, a khaki jacket, and a cowboy hat standing by a red pickup truck parked beside the hotel's east wing. He waved at her. She waved back and started toward him. His name was Ken Honeycutt and they had arranged to meet in front of the hotel. Tori had a good feeling about him. He had left a phone message at her office about three months ago, introducing himself as the executor of her uncle's will and saying he needed to speak with her about an inheritance in Logan, Texas. Since then, she had talked to him a few more times on the phone. He seemed reliable, warm, friendly, regular; he had a nice phone voice.

"I hope you haven't been waiting long," he called as she came nearer. He took a few big steps toward her and stuck out his hand as they met. "Hello, Tori. I'm Ken. It's nice to finally meet you in person." He looked directly into her eyes with a big smile. She smiled back at him.

"Yes, finally!" She shook his hand, noticing his firm grip and the dry warmth of his palm and fingers. "I haven't been here long at all. I was just looking over things."

"Well, this isn't much to see, I don't imagine, coming from the big city like you do." He motioned behind him to the hotel. "Course, I guess ya'll have run down buildings in Houston, too, huh?" He smiled again.

"Yes, we certainly do." She turned to follow him as he walked past her toward the gorge. "Of course, I don't *own* any of the ones in Houston."

He laughed and looked back at her, slowing so that she walked beside him. He was only a little bit taller than Tori, standing just short of six feet. He was thick from the neck to his hips, and his strong leg muscles stretched the legs of his jeans as he walked. He zipped his jacket to the collar and adjusted his hat brim to shade his eyes from the late afternoon glare. He thumbed through a folder of papers he held until he found what he wanted and pulled it out. He handed it to Tori.

"We've just got a half hour or so of daylight left, so we can just see the basics of the building and the property." He talked slowly, but deliberately, not as easy or free as when he first greeted her. *Getting down to business now,* Tori thought.

"This right here is a topographical map of the property. You can keep that—I made you this copy." He took the map from her, turned it, and handed it back to her. He stuck his finger on a spot on it. "Here's where we are. See the road?" She did. "And here's the building—I marked it on there for you to see." He pointed again. "And here's where we're standing, on the edge of this small gorge. See?"

She did. She looked at the map and back up at the lines of hills and mountains across the gorge. The place where they stood was at the very bottom edge of the map, right near the margin of the paper, and was a tiny little dot. The rest of the map, what looked to Tori to be two feet on all sides, was covered in topographical detail. A black boundary line rimmed the property on the map, mostly straight, but never more than a quarter-inch from the margins. According to the line, nearly everything they could see from their place on the gorge edge belonged to her.

"Is this the property line?" She spoke trying to minimize whatever incredulity might be in her voice at the immensity of the acreage. To read or say `twelve thousand eight hundred and ten acres' sounded big enough. But, to see it on the map was even bigger.

"Yes m'am—that's it," he said calmly and matter-of-factly. "It's a real nice piece, too, if you ask me." He paused for a few seconds. "Your uncle took a long time buying it. He was really proud to own it."

They both looked out across the expanse. The sun was orange as a pumpkin above the western horizon and gave everything a rich, golden hue that was turning more auburn every minute. The beige desert sand took on a kind of glow and even the gray rocks appeared infused with vigor and light.

"I'll take you on a drive of the property tomorrow, but for now, see that far peak just to the left of where the road disappears from view?" He pointed to the west. "That's the far edge of the property on that side. Now, here in the middle, if you can imagine looking past that last line of mountains back there…" He squinted and pointed. "See that last little line back there, right through that first crevice?" She did. "Just behind that is the line at that point." He turned to the east. "See where that first section of gorge ends? Well, move your eye to the right of until it's about even with that little clump of bushes there, then look up and back into the distance and there's little flat-top hill way back there. You see it?"

Tori moved to his side and positioned herself so she could look down the length of his arm as he pointed. "Yes, I see it," she said.

"Well, that's near the line on that edge. It's actually a little bit past that little hill, but…it's pretty close. That'll give you an idea until we can go look at it more close up tomorrow."

He turned to look out over the gorge again, then looked at Tori. "You want to take a look inside the building before it gets dark?"

"Sure, I'd like that," she replied and started toward the hotel. He walked alongside her. Rocks crunched under their boots. She reached up and touched her ear because she could no longer feel it. Ken noticed.

"That's the thing about having short hair, huh? Your ears can get pretty cold in this wind. Hazel always tells me to wear ear muffs or something over my ears." He paused for a few seconds. "I don't think I'd look too authentic wearing earmuffs with a cowboy hat, though, do you?" He grinned and looked down at her. She laughed.

"Oh, I don't know," she replied. "It could be the start of something big, you never know." She liked him. He was easy to be around.

"How long have you lived in Logan?" she asked.

"A little over ten years fulltime. We bought property here back in the early eighties while we were living in Austin, thinking we might retire down here. I came down on weekends, or for several days at the time. Mainly to hunt. Then I made a few friends down here, got involved in a few real estate deals, guys wanting me to sell their land to people I knew up in Austin."

As he talked, he guided them between the wings of the hotel to the back door of the front part of the building that Tori had faced while sitting in the car. She noticed some bricks or cobblestones loose in the packed sand between the wings. *Must have been a courtyard*, she thought. A broken piece of a concrete garden structure leaned against the wall of the west wing.

"Finally, I got to where I didn't want to go back to Austin so much. I preferred it down here. Hazel, my wife, asked me flat out if I was having an affair, but I said, no, I just really didn't want to live in Austin anymore." He fished a key out of his jeans pocket and inserted it into the lock of the metal door. He opened the door, but finished his story before entering. "So, we moved our real estate business here, and that was it."

He turned to go into the building, holding the door behind him for Tori. She stepped past him into the darkness. She thought it seemed they were standing in a hallway or back entrance area—she could make out a wall about eight feet in from the door.

"Hold on a minute," he said, reaching into his jacket pocket with his free hand to retrieve a small flashlight. "This'll help a little," he said as he snapped on the light. He pointed the beam toward the floor, scanning the area around them. "I don't think there's anything in here that we could trip over. Be careful just the same."

He started walking along the wall toward the left, with Tori following. As they neared the west wall, he turned to the right again, toward the front of the building that faced the road. Tori followed without really looking at the surroundings until he stopped at the front door and turned around.

"Okay, this is the front entrance." He shined the light around the room. It was a spacious room with a large console style desk along the back wall. *The check–in desk*, Tori thought. A few musty looking chairs stood along one wall, arranged around a couple of coffee tables. On the opposite wall was a dingy overstuffed couch with an end table and lamp that looked too small next to the couch. A few slivers of light came in between the cracks in the plywood that covered the two western windows. One of the slivers illuminated the wall behind the check-in desk. It was covered over in wallpaper, but Tori thought she could make out a stone pattern in places where the paper was torn away.

"This is the lobby, as you can tell," Ken continued. "I've not found any water damage anywhere in this building, so even though the top roof is deteriorated, I think the lower roof is sound. We don't get a lot of rain around here, but when we do, it pours down hard. So, if there was a leak, you'd be able to see water stains somewhere." He scanned the ceiling with the flashlight. The roof beams were visible but were painted white. Everything was painted white, it seemed—walls, the concrete floor, everything except the wall behind the desk.

"Now, these two doors on either side of the room go to the halls where the rooms are." He pointed the beam to the large wooden doors, also painted white. "That little door right there goes to a business office." He pointed to a door behind the check-in desk.

"Let's go this way," he said directing her to an arched doorway to the left of the check in desk. She followed him into a room, smaller than the lobby, painted white with a light colored lino-leum floor. A few card tables and metal chairs stood in the room, some of them covered in debris.

"This was a vending machine room. The machines were along that wall, if I remember right. And they had a TV and a micro-wave and a coffee maker in here along that counter." He pointed to a wooden shelf that ran along one wall. At the end of it was a sink with the faucets missing. "Just behind that back wall is the door we came in." He shined the beam around the room, to the floors, then to the ceiling and its painted beams, then around the walls. "They didn't have a restaurant or anything, but people could come in here and get snacks and what-not."

Tori did not say much. She nodded when Ken spoke and followed the beam of his flashlight when prompted. She wondered if a potential buyer for this property would want to restore this old hotel, or would just tear it down.

"Let's go to the rooms." Ken led the way back in to the lobby and to the right, to go down the eastern wing. He pushed open the large door and held it open, shining the light down the hall as Tori passed him. The boarded up windows Tori had seen from the outside lined the left side, and on the right were evenly spaced doorways that went into the rooms. The doors had empty holes where doorknobs would have fit. Ken noticed Tori looking at them.

"The doorknobs were made of brass, for some reason. Mighty pricey for a cheap motel, but anyway, your uncle had people come in here and buy what they wanted for a few weeks after he shut the place down. People just came in, made an offer, and drove off with what they bought. He told people to bring tools, too, in case they wanted light fixtures or anything like that. See?" He pointed to an empty hole in the ceiling with some dangling wires. "Well, somebody bought all the doorknobs."

He took a few steps toward the first room, pushed the door open with his foot and stepped in. Tori stuck her head in and followed Ken's flashlight beam.

"All the rooms are alike for the most part. Some of them have furniture left in them, some don't—it just depends." He pointed out an empty bed frame and an end table. "I guess somebody bought the mattress." He motioned for Tori to step into the room. As she did, he stepped into another little room. "All the rooms have bathrooms, but hardly any of them have any fixtures or commodes or anything left. Those were the first to go for some reason." He stepped back out into the main bedroom.

"Here's something to know." He shined the light on the back wall of the room, the wall opposite the door. "See that right there?" He held the light on a door-sized piece of paneling bolted to the back wall.

"What is that?" Tori asked.

"It's a doorway that goes out into the outside area between the two wings. I guess it used to be a courtyard or something, but the doors to it from each room are boarded over." Ken walked toward it. "It's just a big piece of wood bolted into the wall, and they're boarded up on the outside, too, if you noticed coming in." He stepped back from it and looked at Tori. "Don't ask me why they did that, cause I don't know. Maybe they had people leaving out at night without paying or something."

Tori smiled and nodded. "That makes sense."

"Or maybe this," he added with a grin. "Maybe they were bringing people in they weren't supposed to bring in."

Tori grinned back at him. "But you're not naming any names or anything, huh?"

Ken laughed. "No ma'm, not one name!" He walked back toward the room door and waited for her to step out of before following behind her and pulling the knobless door shut. He held the flashlight up over his head to illumine Tori's steps as she led the way back into the lobby, around the front desk, back into the hallway and out the back door. She stood waiting as he locked the door.

"So, do you want to see the rest of the land tomorrow?" he asked as they walked around the west wing of the building and across the front to her car. "I have all morning and most of the afternoon blocked out, if that works for you."

"Yes, I'd like that," she answered smiling. "Should I meet you back here?"

"That'd be fine. I'll bring some water and something light for lunch. It'll take several hours to see it all. How late a sleeper are you?"

"I can meet you at any time—just name it."

"Well, let's say nine o'clock. That'll give it time to start warming up a little maybe. At least get the morning chill off things."

He stood near her car as she opened the door and put one foot in.

"Ok, I'll see you in the morning." She sat in the car and looked up at him. "Thanks for showing me the building."

"No problem. See you tomorrow." He shut her car door and waved at her as she drove away. In her rearview mirror, she watched him walk toward his truck and get in. She drove slowly back toward the main highway, listening to the crunching of the gravel under her tires. She liked the sound.

❧

Tori sat up in bed, leaning back into propped up pillows, reading *Modern Hospitality*, a trade magazine for the hotel, restaurant and resort business. It was the issue from two months ago, but she had been so swamped with the new Bayside Boardwalk Project that she had gotten behind in her reading.

The magazine was opened to the feature story; in the center-fold was a picture of Tori and Vincent Macari. The caption read: "Movers and Shakers: Tori Reed and Vincent Macari, developers of the Bayside Boardwalk Entertainment Complex in Bayside, Texas." They stood there in business suits. Vincent's dark hair shined and he wore a big smile. Tori looked straight into the camera, faintly smiling, relaxed, confident. Behind them were various restaurant fronts, a small passenger train, and a large ferris wheel. Behind all that lay the gray waters of the Gulf of Mexico.

Tori took a deep breath as she finished reading the article. She set the magazine on her lap and stretched her legs out. These were her first days off in a row in weeks except for a half day here, another half there, or maybe a full Sunday every other week or so. The Bayside Boardwalk Project, or BBP, was up and running and had had three excellent quarters of business. She was exhausted but proud. Vincent had presented her and the other members of the executive staff with their bonuses at a luncheon two days ago. As the senior executive in charge of the BBP, she had overseen the entire thing from the initial idea on the back of a cocktail napkin to the first shift of valet parking attendants at the hotel and seven restaurants that made up the complex. She had made friends with the Bayside city council, a salty, windblown group of folks more interested in bait camps and fishing piers than in serious enter-tainment complexes. The council and prominent citizens had resisted when Vincent bought a thirty-acre plot in Bayside and announced his plan to turn it into a major family entertainment venue and regional tourist destination. So, he promoted Tori from the franchise division of his restaurant empire to the position of vice president of operations and development. She had been with him for nearly twenty years and he trusted her good sense and people skills. Within a month, Tori had met each council mem-ber personally, eating lunch or going fishing with them. She had convinced them that the complex would bring lots of revenue into their little town without overrunning the place so much that the locals would no longer be able to fish.

"Noise and trash," they had said. "That's what ruins the habi-tat." People had moved forty-five minutes south of Houston to the sleepy little waterfront town of Bayside to take it easy, get a little peace and quiet, get away from so much concrete and so many sirens. They ate at seafood joints surrounded by oyster shell park-ing lots and that served fried fish and shrimp po-boys, slathered thick with tartar sauce and Tabasco, off of paper plates and weath-ered unpainted picnic tables.

"We don't want a bunch of racket coming in and disturbing the peace," they had said. She agreed with them. She had spent many evenings, both alone and with friends, at the Bayside fish houses, eating fresh fried flounder and drinking beer out of long-necked bottles. She liked the sun-bleached, salt-rusted feel of the place and the people. She convinced them that the complex would be totally self–contained within the thirty acres so that not so much as one vehicle would have to park anywhere outside that thirty acre area. All of it would take place right there, on an area that at that time had nothing on it but a run-down bait shop, a closed maritime machine shop, and a few rusted boat hulls which were half submerged into the Gulf. A few old metal warehouse buildings still stood where they used to function as fish cleaning stations. Many of them were caved in and missing walls. The bulkhead was pounded away in places along the edge so that large chunks of earth were washed out. Old tires and other debris wedged themselves into these crevices. Barnacles and mud minnows made homes of them; herons and gulls used them as lookout posts into the shallows.

Tori and Vincent stayed true to the concept, and to their word. BBP was completely self-contained. Those who wanted to partake of its offerings entered under the front archway and came into a world entirely different than the rest of Bayside. Fine dining, carnival rides and games, family buffets, live music, outdoor activities, train rides with whistle stops for cotton candy—the whole thing. Outside the complex, the weathered fish houses and beer joints awaited for those who did not care for kids and stuffed animals.

The thing worked like a charm. The city council of Bayside and their blue-jeaned mayor walked around with their chests stuck out as if the whole thing had been their idea. People flocked to the area like terns, spent money like barons, and told their friends about it. Area businesses reaped the benefits of increased general traffic, property values went up, and everything looked fresher, newer, and more vigorous.

Tori was given, and accepted, much of the credit for the project. She had stepped in and done the job better than anyone expected—and people had come to expect a lot from her. She had been a star in graduate school at the Hilton School of Hospitality

Management in Houston. While attending school fulltime, she had bought, on credit, a run-down historic house in the piney woods of east Texas, had it remodeled, and turned it into one of the most successful bed-and-breakfasts in the region within one year. She then sold it for five times what she put into it.

Vincent Macari recruited hot talent from the Hilton School, so he recruited Tori. She made her way through his company doing just about anything related to the entertainment venues he created: hotels, inns, theme parks, water parks, restaurants, fast food, catering, resorts. She was a hotshot and everyone knew it. She worked harder than everyone else, was already on her second pot of coffee when everyone else dragged into the office in the mornings. She was hard on people and even harder on herself. In her view, the phrase "high quality" was a redundancy. Things were either done with quality or not. And Tori did whatever it took to get things done. She shared dinner with people she did not like. She went night fishing with people after working all day, then went straight to her office, changed into her suit and worked a twelve-hour day without anyone guessing how tired she was. She attended fundraisers for causes she cared nothing about, shook hands, kissed cheeks, smiled at the off-color jokes about homosexuals, was "one of the boys" when she needed to be and "one of the ladies" an hour later. She went from camouflage to formal wear in a heartbeat, dove hunting with the governor's staff in the afternoon, and bending their ears to her will at a black-tie dinner that evening. She did it all seamlessly, seemingly effortlessly, and with wild success. High-powered politicians wanted her to marry their sons. Their wives invited her to luncheons. People felt energized and challenged by her and could not explain why. They basked in her glow, drawing from her energy and charisma, and she used this as a tool to move them wherever she wanted them to go.

And it exhausted her. She fell nearly dead into her bed on the nights when she actually made it home. Otherwise, she faded into spent oblivion on her office couch, sleeping fitfully, dreaming the diagrams of architects' plan, seeing the line of numbers of budget reports as if on a ticker tape, mumbling in her delirium, twitching and jerking. If she managed the time for an evening out with friends, she had to force herself to stay awake and alert. Often, she went straight back to the office to sleep, simply because it was closer and she feared falling asleep at the wheel on the way home.

Over time, she lost touch with most of her friends. She did not have the energy for them, for conversation, for sustained interaction of any type really. At the beginning of BBP, she had been dating a successful woman whom she really liked. But, the relationship fizzled as Tori's work schedule increased and the woman ended up getting involved with someone else and moving away.

Stretched out on the bed now, in small Logan in the middle of gargantuan west Texas, she felt the strain of the last two years. Her neck was a permanent bundle of knots. The ache in her lower back seemed normal to her now. She took a steady stream of over-the-counter painkillers to dull the throbbing in her temples and behind her eyes. She had lost weight from forgetting to eat. Then she had gained weight from eating fast and on the run. Finally, she lost it again simply from being too tired to eat anything. Lying on the bed now, she looked down at her waist and legs. She squeezed her toes and felt the soreness in her arches from the hours and hours of wearing dress heels. She tilted her head slightly and heard her neck pop. Her eyes burned from lack of sleep even though she had slept more in the last few days than she had in months and months.

A knock on the door interrupted her.

"Yes?" She sat up in the bed and crossed her legs.

"I'm just checkin' if you need anything before I go to bed, honey." The innkeeper was a nice woman in her sixties, Tori guessed. This was her family homestead, a sprawling white clapboard house with a rock garden and cedar trees in front. She lived in it alone and turned her spare bedrooms into rooms for rent. Tori had learned of it from Ken. "Stella's Place" was the name of it; Stella was the owner.

"I'm fine, Stella, thank you." Tori sat up in bed a bit.

"Ok, I was just checkin'." Stella paused a moment. "Just come on over in the morning when you want your breakfast. It'll be ready by seven." She paused again. "Sleep well."

"Goodnight—you sleep well, too." Tori listened to Stella's steps fade away down the hall. She sat back against the pillows and sighed. She glanced at the magazine lying open on the bed beside her, but did not feel interested enough to read any more of it. With her eyes she followed the crack in the paint on the ceiling above her. It started at the light fixture and extended all the way to the right to the molding over the window. The curtain was drawn over the window, which opened out onto the backyard of the house. Next to the window was a door that led to small patio area.

She got up, slipped her feet into her moccasins, pulled her sweater over her head and opened the door. The air was cold but the wind had died down. Tori shut the door behind her and took a few steps out onto the patio. The night was clear and still. A bright half moon hung in the sky to the right. Stars blanketed the sky in cloud-like waves and bands, something Tori never saw in the city. She breathed deeply, taking in the cold clean air. She felt it rush through her nostrils and down her throat and into her chest. She closed her eyes and tilted her head to the right, then to the left and back again, stretching the muscles of her neck, releasing the tension that kept her shoulders from lowering and relaxing. She opened her eyes and took another deep breath. A touch of stillness crept into her stomach and she felt as if something were draining away down her spine.

She stood there for several minutes, taking in the quiet night. Stella had no neighbors within a half-mile, so there was nothing to hear or see outside of the immediate area of the house. Beyond the backyard, Tori thought she could make out the dark line of the horizon. No other guests were in the house, so no lights burned through any other windows. The silence was almost alarming.

Tori had relished the solitude and quiet of the long drive out here from Houston. She listened to music for some of the time, but spent many of the hours in total silence, hearing nothing but the sound of her tires on the road. She took two days to drive the nine hours between Houston and Logan. Until she spoke to Ken Honeycutt, she had spoken only a few words to waitresses at restaurants where she stopped to eat. It all added up to no more than twenty words total in the entire two days. She told her assistant where she was going, and to call her cell phone for anything urgent. But, Tori turned her phone off and left it on the seat in the car, checking it only once or twice a day for messages.

She stepped to the edge of the patio and looked over the rocky backyard. It was fenced by a knee-high row of pale, stacked rocks clearly visible in the moonlight. At its farthest point from the house the rock fence had an opening flanked on either side by tall, thin cedars. Tori always thought of cemeteries when she saw these cedars. Cemeteries always seemed to have them, at least in this part of the world. The gap in the fence opened into more land, a large openness that from Tori's vantage point on the patio seemed to have no boundaries.

She stared out through the gap and into the darkness beyond it. A dark shape on the left side of the left cedar appeared as a silhouette against the pale background of the rock fence. It moved toward the gap, lost itself from view as it passed the cedar, then appeared again against the rocks that formed the gap. It stopped and turned its head, revealing long ears. A jackrabbit. It looked in Tori's direction for a moment, and bent down to the ground, nibbling or smelling, she could not tell which. Then it hopped into the gap and disappeared into the night.

Tori smiled and without realizing it started walking slowly

toward the fence gap. She stretched her sweater sleeves over her balled hands and sucked in her breath to stave off the cold. She reached the gap and stood in it. She touched one of the cedars. Its spiny leaves were cool and brushy on her skin. She smelled their sharp fragrance on her fingers. She thought she saw the hopping shadow of the rabbit out in the field in front of her, but was not sure. She felt something stir within her, very faintly, barely perceptible. A longing, some sort of yearning, for what she did not know exactly.

She stood there a few more moments, then turned and walked back to the patio and into her room. The warmth of the room flooded over her, a stark contrast to the cold outside air. She pulled her sweater off and began to undress. The very act of undressing functioned as some sort of sedative, for by the time she stripped and slipped between the sheets of the bed she felt she had been drugged. Her heavy limbs sank into the soft bed and she barely managed to switch off the bedside lamp before falling asleep.

# Chapter Two

Tori sat in her car in front of the old hotel waiting for Ken. He was not late; she was simply early. She was always early. The sun was bright and warming, so bright that Tori's sunglasses barely cut the glare. The day was already shaping up to be warmer than yesterday. The sun had shone onto the breakfast table, illuminating the scrambled eggs, bright red and green peppers, and corn tortillas she had wolfed down like a starving woman. She had felt the sun's rays through her sweater, lighting up her arm and hands as she rolled the eggs into the tortillas, and stirred her coffee. Everything seemed fresh, clear, sharply outlined. She even seemed that way to herself. She noticed it because it was such an unusual feeling.

She leaned back in her seat and glanced over some of the paperwork from her uncle's will, items Ken had sent her. Uncle Sandy had lived in Logan most of his adult life after WWII, working as a site manager for various oil and gas companies in Texas. He traveled all over the state, going from well to well, but always came home to Logan and bought more land. The first several sections he got cheaply by taking them off the county delinquent county tax rolls. He lived frugally and funneled all his money into more acreage. It took him thirty years to buy it all. He bought out a few sheep ranchers who finally decided to call it quits in the ranching business. Finally, a dozen years ago, he bought the old hotel and its ten acres from the aging couple who owned it. He hired the son of a friend to manage it, which went well for a while, but then the son fell in love and moved away, so Uncle Sandy closed the hotel down and boarded it up. He retired, sold his house in Logan cheaply to a man in Austin, under the condition that Uncle Sandy be allowed to live in the house rent-free until he died. Which he did, eight months later, in his sleep.

Tori remembered Uncle Sandy well. He was her father's brother, and she and her parents had come out to visit him in Logan several times when she was a child. Mainly, they came out to hunt on his ever-increasing acreage. They hunted dove in the fall, quail in the winter months and javelina at various other times throughout the year. They stayed in his modest house in town, a little stucco cottage with lots of windows and light tile floors. He had a small rock garden in the back dotted with various plants and shrubs that he watered from a cistern that caught water off a metal sheet on the roof and from the steady drip of the window air conditioner. Tori remembered playing in the garden as a child, catching lizards and chasing after grasshoppers. The cistern was a good place to find lizards in the hot summer. Small trickles of water sometimes dripped from its sides and the lizards would dart forward to take a drink. Tori would sit in the cistern's shadow and wait for them.

Both of Tori's parents were avid hunters, as were the rest of the family for the most part. They had taught Tori how to shoot when she started grade school. She could hit single clay pigeons with accuracy even then. She stood waiting with the shotgun pointing downward, her hands placed properly on it. Her father would pull the cord on the throwing machine and the orange clay disk would go careening out into the field or over a gorge. She would raise the gun to her shoulder, press its glossy stock to her cheek, squint down its barrel, aim and fire. Most of the time the clay disk exploded into pieces that scattered into the canyon below.

Uncle Sandy was always affirming and enthusiastic concerning Tori's shooting skills. He had no children of his own, which partially accounted for his utter delight in Tori. He accommodated her natural curiosity about everything from oil wells to javelina eating habits to cistern building to growing aloe vera plants in a desert climate. He thrilled when she shot her first limit of dove on a hot September afternoon. He insisted that she sit in his big recliner with her feet propped up while he and her parents served her the freshly grilled dove wrapped in bacon and stuffed with hot peppers. She had, after all, brought home the bacon, so to speak. Her parents indulged Uncle Sandy as he indulged her.

She loved the times they spent in Logan and always hated to leave and go back to Houston, at least when she was young. As she got older and got involved more in school and work, she saw Logan and Uncle Sandy less and less. By the time she finished graduate school and started working for Vincent it had been over ten years since she had visited Logan.

Only one time since then had she seen Uncle Sandy, at a small family reunion in San Antonio several years ago. About twenty-five aunts, uncles, and cousins met at a big Tex-Mex restaurant one afternoon. She remembered being shocked at Uncle Sandy's appearance. He looked weathered and old. His thick sand-colored hair from which he got his nickname was thin and dull, and scraggly pieces of it hung limp into his eyes and over his ears. His face was drawn and gaunt, not at all the rosy and shining countenance she knew from her youth. His clothes were wrinkled and looked like they might not have been washed in a while. He even stank, not of alcohol, but of sweat and neglect.

Tori made it a point to talk to him that day since he seemed to retreat a bit from the other groups of family members. He was cordial and inquiring, asking about her work, how things were going and so on. She told him everything, all about Vincent's company and what she did for it. He was interested and seemed proud. He smiled and Tori thought she might have caught a glimmer of that old enthusiasm over her exploits. She had stayed close to him the rest of that afternoon as she made her way around the family. She brought him coffee, steered conversations his way, and brought a few people over to him from time to time. He had hugged her tightly when he left, said he loved her and that he was glad she was doing so well. He said it was obvious she was living right, and that she was beautiful. And then he left and she never saw him again.

Sitting in her car now, she looked at a copy of his will, and the sunlight extended across his signature at the bottom of the page: James Edward Reed. The letters were dark and sharply formed, but they veered off the signature line at several points, and they seemed disjointed from each other as if pasted together from different sources, prints and fonts. It was the signature of an old man about to die. An old man tired of signing things. Tired of things in general. A man about to fade from view.

She had no idea what had prompted him to leave everything to her. She was as surprised as everyone else in the family. She did not see much of her family anymore, especially since her parents had died. One of her cousins, however, had sent a brief email and mentioned somewhat sarcastically that Tori "must have buttered Uncle Sandy up" somehow. Tori dismissed the comment and focused on figuring out what to do with all the land now that she had it.

Her first impulse was to sell it all, as quickly as possible. That, in fact, was what she planned on discussing with Ken this afternoon after they finished the survey of the property. She guessed he knew already that she planned to sell, but she wanted to see the property for herself so she could gauge its appraisal value. Plus, she was curious to see how much of it was the same as she remembered. Ken had contacts in the area and could serve as a broker for her. He seemed knowledgeable and competent. And she liked him.

She looked in her rearview mirror and saw Ken's red truck turning in off the main road. A cloud of dust billowed behind him, rolled over her car and slammed into the building as he pulled to a stop beside her.

"Am I late?" He smiled, looked at his watch and walked toward Tori. He pushed his hat back from his face

"Not at all, I'm early," she replied, stepping out of her car. "It's a bad habit of mine." She smiled up at him as she slammed the door shut behind her.

"Sleep good?"

"Like the dead. Best night of sleep I've had in a long time." She felt herself slipping into an accent she had not used in decades. She liked it.

"Well, good," he said, genuinely glad. "Where'd you eat dinner? Stella fix you something?

"No, I ate at the little Mexican cantina there on the main road. I forget the name of it."

"Galindo's."

"Yes, that's it."

"That place has been here in Logan a long time. A family business." Ken squinted up into the sun, surveyed the canyon and looked back at Tori. "Well, you ready to go? We'll take my truck, of course. Some of the roads are pretty rough."

"I'm ready. Do I need to bring anything? It's okay to leave my car here?"

"It's fine—nobody'll bother it. And you don't need anything, really."

They climbed into his truck and started back toward the main road. Ken explained that the best entrance to the property was a little road about a mile away that fed off the main road about three miles west of Logan. Tori had seen on the map that a road of some sort wound around the perimeter of the entire property, and that roads also traversed the property at different points. Some of the roads went for a few inches on the map, and ended at a bluff or canyon. Others connected up with other small roads or trails, but then abruptly ended in the middle of nowhere. Ken said some of the roads were filled with gravel, while others were barely more than an animal trail wide enough for a vehicle to pass.

The roads were crude, uneven and deteriorating at points. The first mile or so after the initial turn-off from the main road was fine. The roadbed was made of packed gravel and was fairly even. Soon, however, Ken had to make careful turns around curves and bluffs to keep from sliding off the edge in loose gravel and sand. *It would take forever to see all this land,* Tori thought as she jostled in her seat and reached up to the handle above the window to hang on. They crossed the gorge that ran behind the hotel at a place where its sides lowered on both sides and the angle relaxed enough to allow the semblance of a road. It was actually not much more than a hog and deer crossing, which Ken pointed out as they passed.

"See those torn-up yucca plants right there?" Tori looked in the direction he pointed, but saw nothing particularly resembling a yucca. She did, however, see some foot-long spiky leaves lying bent and crooked in the sand with what was left of their roots exposed to the sun. "Javelinas rip 'em up and eat the tender roots," Ken explained. "Really makes a mess if you have 'em in your garden," he said as he eased the truck into the canyon bed.

The trees in the gorge were taller than they looked from behind the motel. They lined the creek bed on both sides and many of them stood fifteen feet tall or more. Ken pulled the truck up to the trees, stopped the truck and started to get out. Tori followed along. He walked under the trees and went down a little bank to the creek bed. All along the creek bed were little pools of water, some deeper than others, some several yards across, some not much bigger than a dinner platter.

"There's usually water in this run-off this time of year even though it may not be constant all down it." He squinted up and down the canyon, and looked back at the creek bed. "It's mainly a flagstone bottom, so the water doesn't absorb all the way. In the winter it doesn't evaporate as fast, so you'll get these little pools all up and down it." He paused for a moment. "It's good hunting in here. Quail, dove, deer—all of 'em come to little spots like this to drink." He looked up at the trees. "Doves come roost in these trees, too, especially in the fall when they're migrating down to Mexico and such." He looked up at the sky as if a few dove might fly into the trees or to one of the little pools just to make his point.

"I think I remember hunting along this creek bed, when I was little," Tori said. "Does this run all the way through much of the property?"

"Well, this little canyon plays out after a little ways, but there's lots of gorges and ravines like this all over it, and most of 'em hold water of some amount." He looked at her and smiled, somewhat surprised. "You hunt?"

"Yes," she replied simply. She looked up at the shockingly bright blue sky and then back at him, squinting at him through her sunglasses and smiling. "Uncle Sandy and my parents taught me when I was a kid, right on this land. Well, as much of it as he owned at the time. I remember hunting along a creek bed like this, late in the afternoons, waiting for the dove to come drink."

"Well, I'll be…" he said. "I didn't take you for the hunting type." He grinned at her before continuing. "That's what most people do with all the land out here now. The ranching has pretty much gone away except for a few old guys here and there who're raising angora goats, but the wool doesn't get much, hadn't for a long time, so they're not making any money at it." Ken looked across the creek bed and up the hillside on the other side, then back at Tori. "Hunting is the main thing this land is good for anymore."

There was no trace of lament in Ken's voice, just a plain statement of the facts. He gazed across the landscape as he talked, looking at Tori only for a moment before turning back to the land. It was as if he could not keep his eyes off of it. Or as if it had some magnetic pull on his vision, so that his eyes could hardly turn away from it. Tori had noticed this in herself actually. She felt it when Ken asked her a question or made a comment that required a response from her. She had to consciously turn her head to face him, tearing her eyes away from the landscape. She looked at nothing in particular. No specific hillside, or animal darting down a ravine, or hawk or eagle floating in circles far above her in the sky held fast her vision, although these things were all around her. The land itself, in general, the sheer immensity of it—its presence, weight, and givenness—seemed to command recognition. Compared to it, people were such tiny dots, but instead of making Tori feel insignificant in the face of it all, she felt invited to be a part of it, to *take* part in it somehow.

They got back in the truck and eased slowly down the creek bed for a while, then cut across it at a firm, rocky place and connected to what looked to Tori like not more than a hiking trail. "I'm taking a back way," Ken said, grinning. "Course, every way is a back way out here." Tori smiled and nodded.

They followed the trail for a half hour or more, winding around hills and small mountains, over small hollow basins and gentle ridges. Tori saw more of the trees and shrubs she had seen yesterday around the motel. Cedars, cacti of astonishing variety, other smallish trees scrubby and stiff, low scraggly bushes, bunches of grasses and trailing vines that covered the desert floor and climbed up the hillsides sometimes at odd angles. Many of the plants had sharp edges or thorns and clung to Tori's jeans when she and Ken stepped out of the truck to take in a particular view. She felt little stickers scratching her ankles as she walked. She had no idea how they had gotten down in her boots to embed themselves in her socks.

Ken explained the terrain as he drove, one elbow crooked out in the open window despite the chilly air. He spoke about various desert plants and their medicinal or dietary properties. He pointed to the roll-like bloom of the Spanish dagger, and said he and Hazel liked to eat them sautéed in butter with garlic and herbs. He alerted Tori to the various bulbs and bloom pods on plants here and there that were winter food for animals. He showed her the meandering Mormon tea plant and said he personally did not really like the taste of the tea, but that some people swore by it. Tori liked to hear Ken talk about these things. He had a calming effect on her, and she enjoyed his enthusiasm for the desert and all its characteristics and inhabitants. After a while, she started wondering what Mormon tea tasted like, and if some restaurant in Logan might serve sautéed Spanish dagger.

Things warmed up significantly as the sun climbed higher and higher, making everything appear sharp, illuminated, and clear. Tori removed her jacket and pushed up her sweater sleeves. They stopped on the edge of one of the many small canyons to eat lunch near a large juniper tree. Ken doled out the sandwiches and chips that Hazel had packed for them, and the bottles of water. They said very little as they ate, yet Tori felt comfortable in the near silence with Ken and sensed that he did, too. They simply ate, enjoying the food, the clean air, the warming sun on their backs, and enjoying each other's silent presence.

Ken finished his lunch and stretched out onto the ground on his back. "Power nap," he declared as he pulled the brim of his hat down over his eyes. "Just about ten minutes." Tori nodded at him, but said nothing. She got up and walked toward the bottom of a small but steep hill about one hundred yards from their tree. Loose gravel, rocks and small branches were strewn at the bottom of the hill. She picked her way through it all and began the climb upward along a small trail between the small bushes and rocks that jutted from the hillside. She reached the top, stepped into a small sandy clearing, turned around and looked out onto the expanse of space in front of her. She saw Ken lying under the tree, his hat over his face, his boots crossed, and thought she saw a lizard dart underneath the truck near the back tire. She saw mountains rise up from the horizon dozens of miles away. A hawk circled high and lazy over the canyon, its tiny shadow racing along the desert floor below it. A slight breeze caressed her cheeks, and the sun's warmth seeped through her auburn hair and to her scalp. She stood there, feet apart, her hands in her jeans pockets, taking it all in. Breathing deeply, letting her weight sink heavy into the ground, stabilizing herself, grounding herself. Ken sat up and looked around, then found her at the top of the hill. She waved. He waved back, and lay back down, crossing one leg over the other. Tori picked up a small rock, stretched back and threw it out across space as far as she could. The rock landed just short of the canyon's edge. She saw the puff of dust that announced its landing. She turned and began the short climb down the hill to Ken.

They made it back to the hotel in late afternoon. Ken got out of the truck to stretch his legs. Tori unlocked her car and turned back to Ken.

"So, do you have any appraisal values on this property?"

"Well, the hotel and ten acres it sits on have a different value than the rest of it. And they are deed restricted together—they can't be sold separated." He leaned back against the truck. "The hotel and its land are valued on the county tax rolls at about fifty grand. The rest of the land is at about two hundred an acre, so…that puts it at just over two million five. All combined, you're looking at around two million six, give or take."

Tori nodded. Ken waited a moment, and spoke. "There's been some interest in this land in the past. I've probably got a few names and phone numbers in my files that I can give you. Some of them might be old news, though, and no longer interested in buying."

Tori nodded and smiled. "I'd appreciate that. My first thought after you called and told me about all this was that I would sell it. I mean, my life is in Houston and I don't see that changing any time soon."

Ken nodded and smiled. "Of course."

"I actually would like to hire you to sell this for me, if you're interested. You're the only person I know out here, but besides that, I trust you." She smiled at him, and looked him in the eyes. "I've had nothing but good experiences with you." She paused a moment. "And I'll pay whatever commission you require."

"Well, that'd be fine. I'm happy to help you out with it," he replied. "And my commission is the standard rate, so…we can work that out later. Do you have any plans for supper tonight? Or are you heading back to Houston?"

"No, I was going to stay tonight and start the drive back tomorrow. I don't have to be back at the office until Monday. I took the whole week off."

"Well, would you like to come have supper with me and Hazel tonight? I could make a few phone calls this afternoon, in the next hour or so, and maybe have a few names for you by tonight."

"Sure, I'd like that. I'd like to meet Hazel."

Ken smiled broadly. "Well, good." He pulled a little notepad out of his back pocket, made a few scribbles on it, ripped the page out and handed it to Tori. "It's easy to get to our house from Stella's. We're just one street off the main road, in a little stucco cottage next to the courthouse. Here's a little map and the phone number. Call if you get lost, but you won't get lost." He stepped toward the door of his truck. "We usually eat around six thirty—is that ok with you?"

"Wonderful!" she replied, smiling as she opened her car door.

"You have any dietary restrictions?"

Tori shook her head. "No, although I'm not fond of liver."

Ken grinned. "Me neither," he said as he got in the truck.

Tori watched him drive away and waved to him as he turned onto the main road. He waved back to her in his rearview mirror. She leaned against her car and looked around. She had nowhere to go particularly, and it was only just after four o'clock. She reached into her car for a bottle of water Stella had given her this morning. She twisted off the cap and took a long drink. She noticed that she had been drinking a lot more since she had been here. She had never been one of those people who carried a bottle of water around with her all the time. She resisted the fad that had sprung around the maxim about drinking eight glasses of water a day. It annoyed her, really. People looked silly sucking out of bottles all day, at meetings, in business suits. She wondered what people did all day, sitting at their desks, to become so dehydrated. But, things were different out here in the desert.

She closed her car door and walked a few steps out away from the hotel toward the small gorge behind it. The afternoon had warmed, so she took off her sweater and threw it over her shoulder and back to hang loosely. She untucked her shirttails, and unfastened several buttons of her shirt. She fingered the smooth black silk of her undershirt. She walked to a large rock that rested a few yards from the edge of the gorge. She laid her sweater out on the ground beside it, and sat down facing the gorge, her back against the rock.

She just stared out into space for a while, not thinking about anything in particular. This, in itself, was unusual and she noticed it after a few moments. She did not remember the last time she did not have streams and piles of ideas racing through her mind. She often had to forcibly make herself stop thinking about things in order to even go to sleep. She would locate a sound in the room, the hum of the air conditioning, or the distant din of traffic on the freeway near her loft townhome, and focus her mind on that sound so that eventually it would lull her to sleep. She noticed now, however, that she had not had to use that technique ever since she had arrived in Logan. Maybe it was because she had very little to do out here. She knew no one, really, other than Ken, so she had little interaction with anyone. She had finished the BBP and the new project was being handled by her staff for now, so she had no unfinished business to plague her on these days off.

She scooted out from the rock and laid flat on her back on her sweater. She stared into the clear sky above her and stretched her arms out beside her, her hands turned palm down. She pressed her fingers into the sandy soil, feeling it jam itself under her fingernails. She grasped the dirt in her fingers and raised her hands, letting the sand slip between her fingers. She brought one hand to her nose and smelled the dirt, dry and clean. She licked her finger and tasted the grainy mineral earth.

She dropped her arms, crossed her hands over her stomach, closed her eyes and took a deep breath. She thought about her work back in Houston, her office downtown on the twelfth floor. From her desk she could see across the city for miles. She did not realize how many trees Houston had until she first saw the city from her office. Most single-story buildings were not visible from that height, simply because they were hidden under trees. Most of the city existed under the shade of trees, big lush dark green trees of myriad variety. Palms, pines, cedars, oaks, birches of different sorts, elms, ornamental trees of dozens of fruits, imported trees, like the quickly growing tallow trees that invade an area within a decade. Houston's tropical climate encouraged the profusion of plant growth. Indeed, the mild climate insured that everything grew—mold, mildew, all manner of allergy-producing agents as well as insects of seemingly endless species. Nothing ever died, in fact. At least it never got killed off by cold winters. It simply reproduced or rejuvenated itself on the moist warmth of the coastal atmosphere.

Tori had always liked the lushness of southeast Texas, despite the annual risk of hurricanes. She liked the mild winters and did not mind the deadly humid heat of the summers. She had never minded the lack of brilliant color from dropping leaves in the fall, or the mostly unremarkable temperature changes between the seasons. She liked wearing shorts at Thanksgiving, and setting out in February the one tomato plant she grew every year on her patio. She liked not having to carry around heavy coats and parkas except for just a few days out of the year. Usually, silk long johns with a wool business suit, a scarf, and a nice pair of gloves were enough. The trees and tall buildings served as big windbreakers in the winter and sunshades in the summer. She had grown up in it, was comfortable in it, and never really longed for or thought about anything else.

Now, though, lying here on the ground in the Chihuahuan desert of West Texas, she felt for the first time a slight affinity for something different. Maybe because she had spent time here as a child, something about the desert hearkened back to fond memories. Maybe she associated the desert with her parents and her uncle, who were gone from her life, and to be out here on this land brought them back to her in some subtle way. She did not know. But she thought about it, lying there with the sun beating down on her head, highlighting the lightened streaks in her short auburn hair. There was something about the harsh cleanness of the desert, the sparseness of the landscape, the clear sharpness of nearly everything, whether from the endless days of bright sunshine or the literal thorns and blades that protruded from them. Something about all of it spoke to her and she felt deeply comfortable despite never having lived here.

She stayed there by the rock, flat on her back, her eyes closed until she drifted off to sleep. The silence enveloped her like a grave. Several times, she awakened for a moment at the shrill cry of a hawk, or when the breeze grew into a quick gust that blew tiny pieces of sand into her cheeks. But she fell immediately back into a drowse, her body pressing into the stolid earth, heavy with fatigue. With relaxation and much needed solitude. With relief.

She awakened after a time, feeling the chill begin as the sun sank in the west. She looked at her watch, and saw that she had about a half-hour until time for dinner. She stood, picked up her sweater, and started for her car to drive to Stella's to change clothes. She rolled down her window as she drove out, listening again to the gravel under her tires. She smiled faintly and sped off down the main road to Logan.

❧

Ken was sitting in the swing on his porch when Tori drove up. The front porch had a concrete floor, and its wood railing was painted a pale blue that nicely matched the beige stucco of the main part of the house. Near the swing, on the edge of the porch sat a smoking chiminea, terra cotta in color.

"Come on up here," he called happily as she stepped out of the car. He waved her up onto the front steps.

"Hi, Ken," she reached out to shake his hand.

"How're you doing? You get some rest this afternoon? You looked a little peak-ed when we got done." Ken sat back down on the swing and motioned for her to sit in a metal chair close to the fire.

"A little bit. I did feel a little tired, you're right." She sat and immediately felt the warmth radiating from the chiminea. She instinctively stretched her open palms out to it.

"Hazel'll be out here in a minute. She just went in to refill our coffee cups. You want something to drink? We've got fresh coffee, some iced tea, and a beer or two, I think." He stood up waiting for her order.

"Coffee's fine, thank you. Black."

He stepped into the front doorway, called to Hazel to bring an extra cup of black coffee, and sat back down on the swing.

"Is something special burning in that fire? It smells different."

"It's pinion pine," he answered. "It does have a distinct smell. I get it from off the ranches I hunt on. It burns well." He stared at the fire. "I never really thought about it having a peculiar smell before."

The front door opened and a smallish woman in blue slacks and a cream sweater stepped onto the porch carrying a small tray with coffee cups. Her dark hair was streaked with gray and was blunt cut, jaw length. She came toward Tori with the tray. "You must be Tori. I'm Hazel, it's nice to meet you." Tori took the first cup on the near edge of the tray, and smiled up at Hazel.

"I'm glad to finally meet you, too." She smiled into Hazel's sparkling gray eyes. "I wanted to meet the creator of those wonderful avocado sandwiches from earlier today."

Hazel laughed and moved toward Ken with the coffee tray. He took both their cups, and she sat the tray down on the ground, and planted herself on the swing next to him. She looked up plainly at Tori.

"So, you all had a big day out on the property today, huh?" She took a sip from her cup. "Was it what you remembered?"

Tori nodded and took a sip, too, realizing that Ken must have told her some of her background. "Yes, in many ways it was. But I don't think my uncle owned all of it at the time when I was here as a child." She paused a moment. "But, yes, it was a lot like I remember it—lots of space, lots of scrubby bushes, and lots of sandy soil. And lots of stickers and things."

They all laughed softly. Tori wrapped her fingers around the warm coffee cup and looked into the fire. Then she looked back to Hazel. "Ken tells me you run a crafts store. Do you sell your own crafts or those of other people?"

"Well, I'm not a very crafty person, to tell the truth. But, I know a few good things when I see them. So, I sell pottery, wind chimes, stoneware, small garden ware – stuff like that—mostly from people in Texas. We know people in Austin and in the Hill Country who make things and ship them down to me. Then, there's a few people in Alpine about three hours away who let me sell their stuff. It's all on consignment." She took a sip of coffee. "It's not much, but I enjoy it. It's something to do, at least."

"Is there a big market for crafts out here?" Tori could not imagine there would be, but thought she would ask anyway. Hazel laughed, and Ken chuckled.

"Well, from a Houston perspective, no, there's not much of a market. But, this is a main road between the bigger cities in central Texas and the big national park a few hundred miles away. Also, lots of people in the state use this road to get to El Paso. And there's not a lot of towns with anything in them to speak of on this particular stretch except for Logan. So, I get drive-by traffic, people traveling on the way to somewhere, and they stop, refill with gas, maybe get something to eat. And my little shop is right next to the major gas station and the only real restaurant in town."

"Would that be Galindos?" Tori asked.

"Yes, you know it, I guess. Ken said you ate there last night. It's a good place, most of the time." Hazel made a small frown into her coffee as she took a sip, but her face seemed not to hold frowns very well. Within a second, what seemed like a subtle, permanent smile reappeared.

"What do you mean?" Tori grinned inquisitively.

Ken cleared his throat and turned away from the fire, where he had been staring for several minutes. "What she means is that it depends on who's cooking whether it's good or not." He looked at Hazel for verification of his claim. She nodded. Ken continued. "I think I mentioned to you that it's a family business. Been here a long time, but the woman who started it is really old. She and her husband started it nearly forty years ago, but she's too old to cook and, really, too old to even remember her recipes, I guess."

Hazel listened and nodded, looking into the fire. "She's so old…I don't even know how old she must be."

"One of her daughters cooks sometimes, then some of her granddaughters take turns in there sometimes. It just depends on what day you go in." Ken looked back at the fire, then at Tori. "I've always thought it could do real good if they'd put some money into it. It's always made a modest little living, but they get mainly drive-by traffic, too, because hardly anybody around here eats there. We don't go there, do we Hazel?"

She shook her head, and made another small frown that quickly vanished. "I don't remember the last time we went there." She paused a moment, trying to remember. "Maybe once last month when I wasn't feeling well that one night. Didn't you go eat there then?"

"Yeah, I did." Ken took a long drag from his coffee cup. "It wasn't very good that time." He shook his head, as if dismissing the topic from his head. "They're not business people, so they make just enough to get by. If somebody owned it that really worked with it, they could draw people in that live out here, get some regulars, do a little advertising, whatever. But…" He sat up on the edge of the swing and looked at Hazel. "Speaking of things good to eat, I'm about ready for 'em, aren't you Tori?" Ken and Hazel stood up from the swing.

"Sure, I'm ready when you are. It's getting chilly out here even with the fire." Tori followed them into the house. The living room was dimly lit and warm, and smelled of rosemary and cinnamon. A large overstuffed leather couch, eggplant in color, took up most of the space along one wall. A matching chair sat at an angle near it. A small table with a lamp on it stood between them and they shared a coffee table. The lamp was bright enough to illumine several large rugs that covered most of the hardwood floors. None of them matched each other, but they were pleasingly arranged and gave the room a warm feeling. On the wall opposite the couch and chair stood a large armoire entertainment center, its doors opened wide. Tori followed Ken and Hazel to the bright light coming through a doorway at the far end of the room.

They entered the kitchen and Ken motioned for Tori to take a seat at a small dining table. Hazel went immediately to the stove. Ken walked to a cabinet above the bar that separated the cooking area from the dining area and pulled down plates and glasses. He laid them out in their places on the table, and returned for napkins and silverware. When he came back, Tori reached out for them. He gave them to her, then reached for two trivets on the bar, and put them on the table. He went back to Hazel at the stove while Tori put out the forks, spoons and napkins for each place. She looked around the room. The walls were painted cranberry, which contrasted nicely with the sand-colored tiles of the floor and counters. Cranberry-colored accent tiles meandered in an understated vegetal pattern across the countertops to the stove. A rack of copper pots hung above a butcher-block island in the kitchen area. A baker's rack of cranberry wrought iron stood along the one wall not lined with counters. Glass Mason jars of dried spices and beans, preserves, pickles, and syrup stood gleaming on its shelves. The lower shelf was stuffed with cookbooks.

Ken stood at the stove with a potholder in each hand, waiting for Hazel to finish stirring in one of the two pots on the stove. She stepped back. "Okay, go ahead." He carefully picked up the large pot and followed her to the table, setting the pot on the table. He returned for the second pot, a smaller one. They both sat down and smiled at Tori.

"Oh! I forgot the tea." Hazel jumped up and went to the refrigerator. "Is tea okay?" she asked as she brought it to the table.

"Of course," Tori answered, suddenly hungry now that Ken had taken the lid off the large pot in front of her. A rich, meaty stew bubbled within it. Tori could make out red and green pepper slices, onions, carrots, jalapenos, celery, potatoes, and beans of several varieties. Ken uncovered the other pot, full of rice. "Wow, this really looks and smells wonderful." She closed her eyes and took in a deep breath, savoring the spicy aroma. "I didn't realize how hungry I was." She smiled and looked at Ken and Hazel. "Thank you for having me tonight."

"Oh, the pleasure is ours," Ken said as passed the rice pot. "We're just glad to have some company for a change. I think the last people we had down here was at the holidays, wasn't it Hazel?" She nodded as she stirred sweetener into her tea. "Here, pass me your plate when you get the rice in it," he said. He filled both their plates with steaming stew and then filled his own. "You ever had *cabrito*?"

"Yes, I have. It's wonderful, but I get the feeling this will be the best I've had." She held a spoonful to her lips, blowing it softly, then put it in her mouth. She savored the rich flavor of the meat, and the explosion of spices and peppers that immediately consumed her taste buds. Her eyes began to water from both heat and pepper. She reached for her tea glass. "This is really good, Hazel." She swallowed and smiled. They were grinning at her. "It's really hot, but really good." They all laughed, and proceeded to eat.

"So, tell us about your work in Houston," Hazel said. "Ken hadn't told me much about it, he says because you haven't told *him* much about it." She took in a big spoonful of stew, chewed for a moment, and continued. "I read in *Texas Monthly* about that big thing outside of Houston. You worked on that, didn't you?"

Tori swallowed her food, took another long drink and nodded. "You saw that, huh? Yes, I was the senior project developer for that.

I've spent most of the last three years on it." She took another bite. "I'm glad it's finished."

"The pictures looked like it was a pretty big project—big rides, lots of restaurants, different things…where'd you learn to do all that?" Ken grinned at her.

"Well, I got my graduate degree in hospitality management, and I went to work for Vincent Macari right out of graduate school, which was nearly twenty years ago. I've been with the company a long time and I've worked in most of the departments all over it. So…that's how I learned how to do all that." Tori grinned back at Ken.

"I expect it's a good market over there for that kind of things, being on the water and having so many people in the Houston area," Hazel commented. "I was there last year visiting a friend in the medical center area and was shocked at how big it is. The city is just huge, so many people and cars. And it just goes on for miles."

Tori nodded. "Yes, we designed the project not just for out of town tourists, but also for regional tourists, people in the area who want to come for the day or for a weekend. Or just for an afternoon and dinner." Ken and Hazel listened intently as she spoke. "People are used to driving in Houston, since it's so big and wide, so to drive down to Bayside is very feasible to them. It's worked out well so far. Business has been very good, for both regional and out-of-town customers."

"Vincent Macari, is he good to work for?" Ken asked. "I've heard about him for years, from real estate people and what not, because he buys up lots of commercial property for all his stuff. One of my broker friends did a big deal with him up in Dallas once, several prime spots in the city where he put his restaurants. Said he was pretty driven. Said it wouldn't hurt him to drink a little decaf." Ken raised his eyebrows and Hazel laughed.

Tori smiled. "Well, that's true. He's got a fire under him most of the time, and when he gets an idea in his head, he doesn't let it go until it's done." She paused for a moment. "I like him. I've always liked him. I even consider him a friend, and we've spent a lot of time together over the years. But, he can be hard to work with. And for. He sets the bar fairly high." She paused again and took another bite. "Of course, I'm sure people have said that about me, too. But I'm no Vincent Macari."

Tori felt at ease with them both as they listened with genuine interest and shared their own lives easily. She learned much about them as the conversation continued through the meal. That they had been very successful in commercial real estate in Austin. That Hazel had been editor for several regional magazines in Texas and had worked in county government. That they had two grown sons who lived in the northeast. One was a doctor, the other was a stock broker who was gay and never seemed to have a steady boyfriend. She learned that Ken loved western novels, and that Hazel loved ruby red Depression glass. That Ken was almost as good a cook as Hazel, even she said so. Tori listened to them, taking it all in, making comments here and there, interjecting relevant details from her life. That she knew people in the publishing business, too. That she had no siblings, and her parents were deceased. That she had hobbies, but had forgotten what they were since she had been consumed with work in recent years. That she was single.

"Do you like your work?" Hazel asked after a while, looking at Tori directly and simply. She had finished her dinner and sat with her elbows on the table, her hands folded beneath her chin.

"Yes, I do," she replied, nodding. "Without seeming arrogant, I hope, I can say that I'm good at it, and I like that I'm good at it. I enjoy being good at it. It gives me satisfaction."

"Well, that's good," Ken said. "I always tell people they need to do what they like and what they're good at because we spend a lot of our lives at work, so you need to do what you like. Otherwise, you'll be miserable." Hazel nodded in agreement, still looking intently at Tori.

"But," Hazel added, "what you like can change. What you're good at can change." She looked at him. "That was true for you, wasn't it honey? You were always good at your work when we lived in Austin, but you grew away from it. You were still good at it, but you no longer liked it in the way you always had. So we came down here." Ken nodded. "You're doing the same things, but you like it a lot better down here." She paused. "And you're happier and I'm happier, right?" She looked at Ken, but then turned back to Tori without blinking.

Ken nodded in agreement and looked at Tori. "You like living in the big city?"

"Yes, for the most part. I enjoy all the restaurants, and there's always a lot to do. Plus, I grew up in it, so I'm comfortable with it. I don't mind the things that everyone else gripes about, like the traffic and the construction and the smog. To me, it's all just normal. It's part of the package. You get used to it."

"I don't think I'd be happy in a big city anymore," Hazel said, breaking her gaze. She took her napkin from her lap and placed it in her empty bowl. "I liked it in Austin, although that's not near as big as Houston. But, I went to college in Dallas, which is pretty big. It was fun and all, but…I don't know. It got to me after a while, the same way it got to Ken. He noticed it first, though, I think. Or at least he suggested changing our lives because of it before I did." She got up and started to clear the dishes. Ken immediately got up to help. So did Tori.

After a few minutes, Ken motioned Tori into the livingroom. Hazel said she was making more coffee and would bring it in to them. Ken relaxed into the big chair and Tori sank into the nearby couch. Ken leaned back and looked at Tori.

"Well, I made a few calls and talked to two people. One guy expressed interest in your land about a year ago, before Sandy died. 'Course, Sandy brushed him off, but I kept his name just in case. His name is Williams, he's over in El Paso. Says he's not as interested now as he was, but that'd he'd think some more about it and get back with me within a week or so. I gave him a ballpark price range—nothing firm before I cleared it with you." He leaned up and peered into an open manila file folder on the coffee table.

"The other guy runs a hunting outfit out of San Angelo. His name is Haskins…wait, sorry…Hastings." Ken ran his index finger along a line of handwritten notes. "Ronald Hastings. And the name of his club is Mesa Adventures. He buys and leases lots of land all within a two or three hour drive of San Angelo and runs hunting excursions on it for deer, hogs and quail. And he raises some exotics, too, various antelope and whatnot." Ken leaned back in the chair. "He's never inquired about your land, but I called him because he came to mind as someone who might be interested. I talked to him for a few minutes, gave him the run-down on it. He said he'd get with his accountant and see what kind of financial state they were in and get back with me." Ken paused for a moment. "I left voice mail messages with two other people, one in San Antonio and another in Alpine, a little town a few hours away. These are people I've brokered land for before and I know what their interests are. They might bite at this." He looked past Tori at Hazel coming in with a small plate of coffeecake.

"Coffee's almost ready. You want another cup?" She looked at Tori. "We're basically addicted to it, so don't feel like you have to drink it to keep up with us."

"Sure, I'd love a cup. And this coffee cake looks marvelous." She smiled up at Hazel and then looked back at Ken as Hazel disappeared into the kitchen. "Thanks, Ken. That's fast work." She crossed her legs and sank deeper into the couch. It seemed to be sucking her into itself, wrapping its smooth leather around her thighs and lower back, warming her deeply and softly. She took in a deep breath, and exhaled slowly.

"Tired?" Ken asked.

"Not really," she smiled. "Just relaxed. I admit—it's a strange feeling."

"You oughta do something about that," he said, looking away briefly. They sat in silence.

"This trip out here's been a nice break." As she spoke, she immediately heard the noise of her tires on the long road out here, saw the desert hills and spreading cacti, smelled the clean air made sharp by the cold. More than anything, she felt what these things seemed to bring to her and what they drew her into. She felt herself being seduced by a lover she had never known, but somehow recognized. "I had forgotten about all this out here." She smiled at Ken simply.

"Well, you look different." Ken's eyes were bright as he looked directly into hers. "I don't know you very well at all, but just in the short while you've been here and we've spent time together, you look different than you did the first time I saw you yesterday morning."

"Really?"

He nodded.

"How?"

"Your face is less clenched, seems like. Doesn't seem to be so much crowding up just behind here." He balled his fingers together and tapped them to his forehead between his eyes. He had leaned up to the edge of the couch, but now sat back. "I know the look. I had it myself for a long time." He took a cup of coffee from a tray Hazel now handed down to him. "I left it behind in Austin when I came out here." He sipped from the cup carefully, swallowed, and balanced the cup on his leg. "I haven't missed it at all."

"God knows, I haven't missed it either—yours or mine," Hazel said. They all laughed and Tori sipped her coffee.

"Don't let him preach to you, Tori. I know what he's up to, and he's only known you for two days." Hazel stirred her coffee as she talked. She smiled at Ken and looked back at Tori. "He wants everybody to move out here, but then he doesn't stop to think that if they did, it wouldn't be the same kind of place anymore. He sells all this land for people and wonders why they don't just come out here and live instead of selling it all. And they sell it to hunters and other people who don't come out here but maybe once or twice a year." Ken grinned and nodded as she spoke, agreeing and disagreeing with her at the same time.

"I don't want *all* of them to move out here. Just the ones I like," he corrected.

Tori stood in the shower at Stella's, letting the hot water pound the back of her neck and back. She crossed her arms and cupped her shoulders so that some of it ran across her chest and pooled in her breasts before running down her stomach and legs. She breathed in the steam, taking it in through both her nose and mouth, feeling it invade her throat and lungs.

She thought about Ken and Hazel. She had enjoyed the evening with them, their banter with each other, their warmth and their easy friendliness. She felt immediately comfortable with them, like they were family or old friends. They seemed to like her, too, especially Ken. She wondered if they reminded her of her parents, but that was not it exactly. They were at least a decade younger than her parents; they did not treat her as a daughter, at least not exclusively. More like a friend or colleague.

She propped herself in bed and began reading through the land folder again. She had read it through several times already, of course, ever since the estate lawyer had send it to her. But, she read through it all again, reviewing the maps, the parcel numbers, the longitude and latitude descriptions, the county designations of acreage, valuation, deed recordings and so on. She stared at the two photographs that were part of the file, one of the deteriorating hotel and the other a wide angle shot of the acreage with dim mountains in the distance and a small hill and line of scrubby trees in the foreground. *Must be along a creek bed*, she thought, wondering if she recognized the exact location of that shot from the trip that morning.

She stared at the photos for a long time. She remembered Ken's words about the hunting ranch operations in the area. *That's probably what this land will end up being*, she thought. A hunting ranch of some sort.

She put everything back in the folder, turned out the light and sank deep into the soft bed. After a minute, her eyes adjusted to the darkness of the room. She could pick out a small crack in the curtains and saw through it to the dark night beyond. Myriad stars crowded into the small slice of blackness between the curtains. The moon was not visible but its light silhouetted one arm of a cactus that Tori could see through the crack.

She got up, grabbed the sweater that was tossed over the chair and wrapped it around her like a shawl. She opened the back door and stood looking over the yard. The still, cold air rushed into her nostrils and chilled her cheeks and ears. The stars exploded into view, along with the moon off to the right. She stared into the twinkling sky, listening to the silence so quiet it almost felt heavy, as if it were a physical weight pressing down on her shoulders and chest from above, and pulling at her thighs and hips from the ground. It was as if something wanted to plant her there in the desert sand of the yard, to socket her down into it like one would screw in a light bulb or sink a fencepost.

She stood there until she felt her jaws begin to tremble from the cold. She returned inside and slid back into the bed, pulling the comforter up to her ears and allowing its weight to press her into the plush mattress. She looked back at the crack in the curtains, picking out the individual stars visible through it.

*I don't really want to go home tomorrow*, she thought.

# Chapter Three

Tori sat in her chair and looked out the floor-to-ceiling window that comprised the whole back wall of her office. She could see the first round edge of the sun as it appeared on the horizon, past the mid-size buildings and tall oaks of the city. She watched the glowing curve grow until its deep orange changed to golden and then into a yellow so bright she could no longer look at it directly.

She had come to the office early after having driven nearly all day yesterday to return home from Logan. The drive back was not nearly as uneventful as the drive away had been. Her phone buzzed with emails, text messages and phone calls from mid-morning until she shut it off before going to bed at home that night. She took several phone calls on the drive, which distracted her from a vague sense of sadness that crept into her chest as the desert terrain faded into the distance behind her and the signs of urban life appeared larger and ever nearer in front of her.

By the morning, she had several hours of work to do merely to answer all her emails, in addition to the work to be done for the new Green Lake development project she had been assigned to lead. She had gotten up early and come to the office before dawn just to get started on it all. Now she stopped working for a while, hands cupped around her coffee mug, looking out her window at the sunrise.

She thought about Logan and the people she knew there. *Ken is probably drinking coffee with Hazel now. Stella is preparing for her next guest who'll drive in later today. The sun is probably not quite up yet over the mesas out on the property. The air is probably chilly and gray, and a few bright stars linger in the slowly brightening sky.*

She still felt the sadness from the drive back to Houston. She attributed it to the normal sadness many people feel when vacation is over and the time comes to get back to normal life. Some sadness was to be expected, she told herself. In a few days she would snap back into step with things in her real life. She turned to her desk and began going over financials for the Green Lake project.

By lunchtime, she had attended three meetings and led two more. She had calls in to all the major contracting firms of engineers, architects, lawyers, accountants and suppliers who were principals on the project. Contracts were being finalized, signed and filed. Permits, fees, notices, and clearances from myriad federal, state, county, and municipal entities were in process. Dozens of office suites, each containing dozens of people, had sprung into action, and Tori was in the middle of it all, orchestrating, managing, directing, leading, correcting, troubleshooting, and getting it all done.

At 7:30pm she answered her desk phone without looking to see who was calling. Her receptionist had gone home nearly two hours before and only Tori remained in the office suite, other than the cleaning crew.

"Hello, this is Tori Reed,"

"Hello, stranger. I figured I'd find you there."

Tori took a second, and recognized the familiar voice. She smiled into the phone. "Hey, Sharon. How are you?"

"I'm fine now that I'm downtown at Samba's with a Bloody Mary and a big plate of calamari in front of me. Why don't you join me? I haven't seen you in forever." Tori heard Sharon pop a piece of the fried goodness into her mouth. "I want to hear about your trip to the wild west," she said while chewing. "Were there any people out there?"

"Yes, there were people out there, silly." Tori dropped a file on her desk and turned to stare out her window into the darkened city. Sharon was a high-powered divorce attorney who worked long hours and was very successful. She always managed, however, to find time for fun, friends, and cocktails. Tori had met her years ago at a dinner party and they had become easy friends. They even dated each other for a few weeks, enjoying a long weekend together at The Four Seasons in Houston where they had gotten the top floor penthouse and stayed in the bed or the jacuzzi, eating room service or each other most of the time. It did not last, though, and neither of them wanted or expected it to. Since then, they were best friends with occasional benefits.

"I can't join you tonight," Tori said. "I've got too much stuff to do here to catch up for being gone. Later this week, though."

"Oh, you are so boring," Sharon said with mock exasperation. "How about Thursday night? That steak place across from the ballpark downtown. I've got a late deposition an hour away but can be there by seven. Will that work?"

"Sure. I'll be glad to see you."

"Me, too, sweetie." Sharon took another bite. "I just ordered another plate of this for you. I guess I'll have to eat it all myself. Lucky me! See you on Thursday. Don't work too hard. It's not good for you."

"Okay, have fun. See you Thursday." Tori hung up the phone

and smiled as she sat down to her computer. Sharon was fun and easy to talk to. She was one of the few friends Tori had kept over the span of several years in the midst of her heavy work and travel schedule. She and Sharon could go weeks without seeing or speaking to each other, each busy with work and life and other things. But then, one would call the other, or they would run into each other at a civic event or meeting, and it would be like no time had passed at all.

They were very different in most ways. Tori was introverted, quiet, focused, driven. Sharon was extroverted, loud, and seemingly too scattered to even get herself dressed in the mornings, but she loved her work and was intuitively gifted at it. Even on her worst days—tired and hung over from partying with friends or staying up all night with a sexy new girlfriend—she still was better than most other Texas lawyers in her field. Tori respected her and enjoyed spending time with her when they got around to it.

By 9pm, Tori turned off her computer screen, packed her briefcases and walked across the mostly empty parking garage to her car. She slid into the leather seats and drove out onto the landscaped streets of midtown. The air was crisp and the night clear, and the streetlights bathed the pavement and the sidewalks in a pale golden light. She drove along down Banks Avenue toward her townhome a few miles away. The sidewalks were alive with people, sitting outside at cafes, listening to music, or visiting with friends. Along the bayou, people walked holding hands with lovers, or with dogs on leashes. Soon everyone would retreat into their homes for the night, but for now people were outside enjoying the mild weather of the Gulf Coast winter. Tori took it all in as she drove home. This was her city and she loved every bit of it, even the parts that were not so lovable.

She pulled into her parking space in her building, hauled her two briefcases to the elevator, and made her way down the hall to her door. Once inside, she stopped to pick up the mail that had been dropped through the slot in the front door. She dumped her briefcases on a barstool and started undressing as she made her way to the refrigerator, kicking off her heels, taking off her suit jacket and throwing it across a dining chair, untucking her blouse, unhooking her bra and snaking if off underneath her blouse, and tossing it onto the chair with the suit coat.

She was glad she had remembered to place a grocery delivery order at The Epicure earlier that morning. She reached for one of several pre-made salads and a bottle of sparkling water. She scrolled through emails on her phone as she shoveled mouthfulls of spinach, sprouts and grilled shrimp. She was still reading them and typing responses to them as she gathered her cast-off clothes and padded to the bedroom to finish undressing. She switched on the television, listening to the evening news as she stepped into the hot shower and scrubbed the make-up off her face. She answered a last email as she finished toweling off and fell into bed naked and warm from the water.

She turned off the lamp and lay there in the darkness. It had been a good day. She had gotten a lot done, and things were progressing well with the Green Lake deal. She was glad to be in her own bed. And she would get to see Sharon later in the week. She took a deep breath in and breathed it out.

She wondered if Ken and Hazel were asleep yet, and if that rabbit had emerged yet from under the cedars in Stella's yard.

"Come over for a little while," Sharon had said as they left the restaurant and walked across the parking lot to their cars. "Tomorrow is Friday. You can go in late or leave early or something." She threaded her fingers through Tori's and squeezed. "I miss you."

Tori squeezed Sharon's hand in return and looked at her. "Okay, just for a little while."

Theirs was not the passion of lovers, but the love of friends who deeply understand each other and whose understanding can sometimes be expressed best through sexual intimacy. They felt not only aroused, but also soothed by each other's bodies—the smells, tastes and textures, the curves and angles. Tori wrapped herself around Sharon's rounded body, burying herself in her smooth breasts. They tangled and rolled, gasping for air between hard kisses. Each relished the struggle and the desperation, the teasing and painful longing, until finally they both dissolved into shudders that left them shaking and worn.

Tori nestled on Sharon's arm, her leg draped over Sharon's thighs. Sharon turned her head to kiss Tori's hair, took a deep breath, and exhaled.

"I miss this with you sometimes," she said.

Tori was quiet for a moment, still recovering, still coasting the waves of her own electrified body. "Me, too, " she said into the crook of Sharon's neck and shoulder.

They stayed still for a while, resting, breathing, enjoying each other and the quiet. Finally, one of them jerked in the middle of drowsing and broke the spell for both of them. They unfolded from each other, legs and arms numb and tingling, and got up.

"Want some water?" Sharon asked as she disappeared through the bedroom door and down the hallway into the kitchen.

"Yes, please. And I'm using some of your mouthwash." Tori stepped into the bathroom, filled her mouth with blue liquid and swished it around as she retrieved her clothes from around the bedroom and started getting dressed.

Sharon returned with the water, plunked it down on the nightstand beside Tori, and sat back against the headboard, her long legs stretched out on the bed in front of her. She took a long drag from her own water bottle, watching Tori dress as she drank and swallowed.

"So, you're going to sell the land. Is it a good time to sell? I don't even know what the market's like for land out there. I haven't had any cases with assets or property in West Texas lately."

"Yeah, I'm selling," she answered, after spitting out the mouthwash. "Ken Honeycutt, the realtor I told you about who showed me the property—the one who's the executor of my uncle's will—he's taking care of it for me." She pulled her blouse up over her arms, leaving it unbuttoned as she pulled on her pants, and then sat on the bed beside Sharon to put on her shoes. "I can get a good price for it. I mean, it's in the middle of nowhere and most of it is considered trash land, but still…It's land. They're not making any more of it. And this is a big chunk of it."

Sharon looked at her intently and took another drink from her water bottle. "Do you have any emotional attachment to it from when you were a kid?" she asked.

Tori started buttoning her blouse. "Not really, I don't think." She looked at Sharon and thought for a moment. "Do I seem like I do?"

"No, not really," she said. "I just wondered." Sharon watched Tori get up and walk to the dresser where she had managed to place her earrings, wristwatch and a delicate necklace in the midst of their blind stumbling earlier.

"I have memories of the land, or at least parts of it. And it's really pretty to me. I like the desert a lot. More than I remember liking it as a kid." She pushed the studs into her ears and looked at Sharon, who looked back at her with a faint smile and slightly squinted eyes. "What?" Tori asked. "Why are you looking at me like that?"

"Well," Sharon said "I don't know…There seems to be something about that place out there, the way you talk about it, or the way you seem to feel about it…something. I can't quite put my finger on it."

Tori sat down on the edge of the bed, fastening the cuffs of her sleeves. "I don't know," she said. "Maybe there is something."

She stood up, bent over to quickly kiss the top of Sharon's bare thigh, then gathered her suit jacket and folded it over her arm. She stood looking at Sharon who was still sitting naked on the bed. In a flash, she imagined Sharon in the bed at Stella's, in the exact same position, except the door was open onto the rocky yard allowing in the strong smell of the cedars.

"I do really like it out there, " Tori said. "I guess I could keep it, but what would be the point really? I work so much. I'd probably never go out there. I'd have to put money into it to make it livable at all, and even then there's nothing out there to do really." She grabbed her water bottle and took a step toward the hallway. "It's best that I sell it. Ken'll find somebody fast probably, and then it'll be done."

Sharon got up, walked over to Tori, and put her arms around her neck. "You're probably right." She bit Tori's lip playfully. "Thanks for coming over. I really enjoyed the evening with you."

Tori hugged Sharon to her, pulling her bare hip into her own clothed one. "I enjoyed it, too." She kissed her lightly. "Call me next week or something. I may have some time."

Sharon walked Tori to the door. "Let me know if anything happens with the land," she said, her arm linked through Tori's. "Let me know if you need a lawyer—I can hook you up, you know. I know a few of 'em." She grinned.

"Thanks, I will." Tori grabbed Sharon's hand and kissed the tips of her fingers. "See you later."

She got to her car and began the twenty-minute drive home. It was past midnight and the night was clear and bright with lights from the city. She put her fingers to her lips and nose, and breathed in the remnants of Sharon's body, her distinct scent. She was lucky to have Sharon as a friend. Sharon was smart. She knew people. She intuited things about them. Was Sharon right? Was there something about the land? About selling it?

Tori drove along, enjoying the feel of her car on the parkway, resting her fingers on her lips, mulling over Sharon's comments. After a few minutes, she reached over into her purse to grab her phone. She had not looked at it in hours, which was unusual. It was blinking, which meant she had a message. She pressed the button and saw the name on the message: Ken Honeycutt. He had called at 9pm.

She pulled into the garage and turned off her car. She stared at the phone message alert and almost started to listen to the message. Instead, she put the phone back in her purse, grabbed her briefcase, and went into the house.

"Tori, this is Ken out in Logan. I've got a good bite on your land out here, especially the parcel with the old hotel. He really wants that more than anything, but I told him I wasn't sure you'd sell it apart from the other land. So, call me when you get a chance. We can talk about it. Bye."

Tori put the phone in the cup holder of her car and sat there for a minute. She watched a few people walk past her toward the elevator bank that went from the parking garage to the first floor lobby. She took a sip of coffee.

She picked up the phone and dialed Ken.

"Hello," he answered.

"Hi, Ken—this is Tori Reed. Good morning."

"Tori, hey! Good morning, how're you doin'?" Tori heard some shuffling in the background. "Hang on a minute, let me pull my other boot on—just a second…" She heard more shuffling and then what sounded like footsteps. "Okay, I'm back—I've been sitting here on my computer in front of the fireplace and hadn't even put my boots on yet. Sorry."

"No problem," she said. "I hope I didn't call too early." She did not think so, though, because it was already past 8am and she figured Ken for an early riser.

"No, no, not at all. I've been up working for a while, checking email, setting up webpages and stuff. I was about to set up a page for your land but since I got that call from this one guy who's really interested, I was thinking to wait to see if we even need to advertise. This guy seems ready to make a deal."

"Yeah, I got that impression from your message. Tell me about him."

"Well, he's from San Angelo, so he's not a local, but he leases a lot of land out here and runs hunts on it. He's out here several months of the year the last few years. He leases a wing of that little motel—the Desert Sage, I don' t know if you remember it, it's on the opposite side of town from Stella's. Anyway, he rents out several rooms there for the whole winter season, one for himself and a few others for groups of hunters who come down to pay to hunt on his land. Deer, quail, hog—the usual. He does a nice little business, I think." Ken stopped and Tori heard him blowing on something, and take a sip. He continued "Anyway, I think he's got a mind to refurbish that old hotel and use it for his hunting business instead of leasing from the Desert Sage. That's the part of your land he's most interested in. I told him you might not sell it to him apart from the other acreage. He said he wasn't sure he could swing all of it, but was open to the idea. So…"

Tori took this all in. "So, he has the money? Or can get financing?"

"He seemed confident about the hotel parcel—I got the sense that he's got nearly immediate financing for that. I don't know about the rest. We can find out easy enough, though."

Tori thought for a few seconds.

"Well, let's see what he has in mind. Can we do that? I'd like to try to sell it all at once, if possible—it just seems simpler all the way around."

"Sure, I'll talk to him again. I think it makes good sense to push for all of it going together. Then, if he resists, we can reconsider, see if he's willing to pay more for just the hotel parcel." Tori heard Ken's truck start up in the background.

"Okay, well, I'll let you go—I know you must be busy." Tori said.

"I'm doing Hazel a favor and driving up to the Hill Country to pick up some furniture for her shop. It's too big to fit in her car, and I need to see a sick friend up there anyway, so...I'm not sure exactly why Hazel thinks furniture is going to sell in her crafts store, but, you never know..." he trailed off. "I'll get ahold of this guy and get back to you as soon as I get some information. It might be a few days—he said something about being out of town."

"That's fine, Ken. I really appreciate it. It's only been a few days since I was there, so this is fast work as far as I'm concerned." She got out of her car and started walking to the elevator. "I'm about to get in the elevator and I'll lose you on the cellphone, so I'll talk to you later. Be careful driving."

"Okay, thanks. I'll call when I know something. Take care."

A barrage of work hit her as soon as she walked into the office suite. People, messages, emails, deadlines, phone calls, meetings, conference calls. She thought of nothing but Green Lake until later that night as she drove home. Gliding down Banks Avenue toward home, she saw movement off to the side in the shadows of the streetlights. She turned and caught a glimpse of a raccoon, making its way toward the bank of the bayou that ran through the heart of the city. It has crossed the road safely and was now ambling down the slope toward rows of bushes that lined the walkway that ran alongside the water. Tori slowed to watch it, struggling to pick out its round form in the darkness. She saw it go under a bush and emerge on the other side, an even darker shadow now against the black of the water in the background. It disappeared from Tori's view. She sped up and continued down the avenue toward home.

She remembered the rabbit at Stella's, making its way through the night, going about its business, feeding on leaves and prickly pear in the darkness. The raccoon, too, in the middle of the big city, would spend its night on the bayou's bank, eating crawfish and minnows, washing them with its childlike hands, eating them live. Tori would spend her night, if she were lucky, in deep sleep so she could get up the next day and spend nearly every waking moment of it in an office, at a desk, staring into a computer screen, reading spreadsheets, making phone calls, listening to people in meetings, and going through check-lists.

She felt a hollowness seep into her chest.

She pushed it away as she rode the elevator and went into her loft. Again she undressed as she made her way through the living room and kitchen. She opened a bottle of wine, poured herself a glass, grabbed a salad from the refrigerator, and plopped down on the sofa. She switched on the television. She ate and listened to a news report about real estate markets being down in suburban and rural parts of the country. Her mind wandered out to the land. Her land. In her mind, she felt the sand between her fingers, the smell of the cedar on her hands, the bright sun warming her through the leather of her jacket.

She grabbed her phone to look at the messages. Nothing from Ken. All work stuff.

She turned back to the television. She finished her salad and sat sipping her wine. After a few more minutes, she turned off the television and sat there in the silence. She swished the last swallow of wine in her glass. Finally, she finished it off and went to the shower, leaving her phone, the empty glass and the salad plate on the coffee table.

Tori decided not to spend the entire next day in the office. Instead, she pulled up just before 7am to the circle driveway in front of the office building, called for her assistant to come down, and the two of them drove two hours north to the Green Lake development site. The sky was clear blue and the day was breezy, and they rode with the moon roof open, the air chilly on their ears and fingers. They kept the heat on full blast to stay warm, unwilling to deny themselves the fresh air from the open roof.

The urban landscape of one-way streets and tall buildings gave way to the suburban landscape of wide avenues, large upscale shopping areas and strip centers. Finally, even that faded into the rearview mirror about an hour after leaving downtown. Tori exited the main freeway and veered onto a rural, single lane highway. Her car ran smooth and sleek along the black asphalt, hugging the curves that wound through cattle pastures and fallow fields. She could have stayed on the freeway almost all the way to Green Lake but this was a better route—less traffic and more scenery.

They passed farmhouses surrounded by outbuildings and old tractors, grain silos towering above small communities, isolated clusters of mobile homes with clothes lines in the yard, tiny churches with graveyards, liquor stores, and grimy gas stations that flashed signs for tire repair right alongside those for cracked pecans, farm eggs, and fresh shrimp from the Gulf. Tori sped past it all, noticing buildings that seemed empty, seeing a "For Sale" sign here and there. That was how she had found her first business, the bed and breakfast she had owned during graduate school. She had been driving through the country, off the main highway, and seen a gorgeous old house in significant disrepair. It sat on what looked like several acres covered in old growth oaks and pecan trees. A few miles down the road was a state park with a small lake and a beautiful creek that gurgled through hundreds of acres of adjacent national forest. The little town nearby had a few little shops and a picturesque courthouse square. So, she had inquired about the old house, found out about the out-of-state owner who had inherited it from his great aunt. He had no plans for the place and figured it would eventually just rot down and he would be left with the land. Tori made an offer, he accepted, and within one year she had turned it into a bed and breakfast that was booked solid for months out. After four years, she sold it for five times what she had put into it.

Her eyes instinctively looked for opportunities on roads that were not so popular, in areas that were not trendy. "Trendy" was created, not inborn. Those with vision and know-how could create "trendy" from virtually anything. She had known that intuitively but had learned how to really live it and work it from Vincent. He had shown her how to assess things for profitability without running numbers or calling focus groups. She learned to see and judge intangible things: the sensibility of a place, the look on the faces of the locals, the feeling that emerged from the buildings, both empty and abandoned. The feeling evoked by the geography, whether it was flat pasture, rolling meadows, hilly streets full of track houses, a shoreline lined with bait shops or, in her case with that first venture, an overgrown lot with big trees and an old house that, with work, could be turned into something special.

She had mentioned the Green Lake area to Vincent a few years before, and they had gone together to drive around the area and see if it offered anything worth pursuing. The lake's water was clear and green, true to its name. The lake was dotted with jungly islands in its middle, and rimmed with knobby moss-laden cypress trees around its banks. A few small communities had sprung up around it at different points. Nothing extravagant or planned, just a few small houses clustered at the northeast end, and a few streets of mobile homes about five miles down the shoreline on the lake's east side. A boat marina, a few more houses, a store and a gas station took up the south end near a small state park that contained a swimming area, a dozen camping spots, and an event pavilion.

The entire west side of the lake, several hundred acres, was vacant of any development, mainly because it had been bought years before by an energy exploration company that had planned to put natural gas wells on it. Nearby residents had complained to their representatives and the plan had been stopped for environmental reasons. The company had moved on to other ventures, but had kept the land without doing anything with it.

Vincent and Tori saw an opportunity after their second tour of the area, inquired about the land, and made a move. The Green Lake development comprised three hundred acres of land that would become a wooded, master-planned community made up of one to three acre home sites as well as a small retail and entertainment district. Everyone in the industry already predicted it would be a success. They had a list of over two hundred people who had already pre-registered with deposits to get first crack at the lots. Retailers had pre-registered as well.

Tori thought of all this as she turned into the main entrance of the development. A newly asphalted road meandered through wooded areas of pine, oak, elm and dogwood that alternated with cleared meadows covered in browned winter grass. She rounded a curve and slowed to avoid surveyors standing on the shoulder of the road, their bright orange vests beaming in the sun. Bulldozers were parked in some of the meadows. Work had already begun on the canals and that would snake through the development, all of them connecting back to the main body of the lake.

Finally, the road ended in a large circle about a hundred yards from the lake's edge. Tori turned off the engine and got out of the car, leaving her assistant Stephen inside on the cell phone with an engineer. The sun had warmed the day considerably since they had left downtown. Tori felt its warmth on her face and through the wool of her suit jacket. She stepped off the asphalt of the road, walking carefully in her nice heels across the rough ground toward the water. A small, variable breeze rippled the lake's surface in crisscrossed patterns. The wavelets reflected the light in a solid column that stretched across the lake from east to west, and seemed to lead almost up to Tori's feet. She inhaled a deep breath and let it out slowly as she gazed out over the expanse of the lake, and the woods and meadows that flanked it.

*This will do well,* she thought. *People will like this.*

Stephen came to stand beside her, his black loafers already dusty from the short walk off the pavement. "Ray says there should be no problem. It turns out they were looking at an older version of the contract. He'll go down to the courthouse and fix it with the county. The revised permits should come in just a few days."

"He's fixing it today, I presume."

"Yes, I told him we needed it done immediately, so he was already in the tunnel on the way over there when I hung up with him.

"Good. Thanks, Stephen."

They both stood silently and looked out over the lake. A flock of ducks careened in from the north, circled a small grassy island about five hundred yards offshore, and settled into the still water near its edge. Tori could see a few of them raising their breasts in the water, fluffing their wings, then settling back down to float with the rest.

"Are you hungry? Did you eat breakfast?" she asked Stephen.

"I left it in the microwave to come down to the car when you called," he said without taking his eyes off the lake.

"Well, take the car and go to that little gas station we passed about five miles back. They have a café in there with pretty good breakfast burritos. Get us a few of them. Get some money out of my purse. It's in the car." Stephen looked at her, smiled and started back toward the car.

"Get me a large coffee, too," she called after him. "Get yourself whatever you want."

"I want bacon," he called back without turning around.

"Answer my phone if it rings!" she called louder. He raised his hand in acknowledgment, again without looking back.

Tori smiled and returned her gaze to the lake. She found a grassy spot not covered with with clods of dirt, took off her suit coat and spread it out on the ground. She sat down, leaned back on her elbows and stretched her legs in front of her. The wool of her black turtleneck blouse captured the sun's heat and warmed her stomach, chest and shoulders.

In a way, all this felt done to her. The whole project seemed finished even though the ground literally had hardly been broken on it. She had done this enough times to know that, at this point, it was just a matter of execution. Her job was to manage all the major moving parts of the process until, piece by piece, it all came together and was ready for move-in. Nothing would go wrong, at least not anything that could not be managed. If anything were going to go irrevocably wrong, it would have already happened by now. Things would progress more or less just as they planned—including the planned overruns and the planned work stoppages for weather, re-permitting, equipment failures, the occasional strike and whatnot—and then it would be done, a dazzling success. Vincent's company would make yet another boatload of money. Tori would get a fat bonus. And then she would move on to the next project, whatever that was, and do it all over again.

She felt the hollowness from last night again in her chest.

"What's wrong with me," she said aloud to herself. "Am I sick?" She pressed her hand to her forehead to detect a fever, but she knew she was not sick. It was something else. Something had shifted inside her. She felt she had reached the end of something, something more than just the end of a project. She felt "done" in a way, although not in the sense of wanting to give up or quit life or anything. More than anything, she felt exhausted and bored. The exhaustion was not physical, or even mental or emotional. It was an exhaustion of meaning. None of this—these projects, the company, finding the next big deal for Vincent—none of it meant anything to her anymore. She had exhausted it all and, on a deep level, she was finished.

Soon, Stephen returned with a paper bag of breakfast burritos and two large coffees. An extra bag held wads of napkins and packets of hot sauce. He took off his jacket and laid it out beside Tori's and they ate, enjoying the clear morning and the crisp air. Tori listened to Stephen's updates from various members of the project team, asking questions and giving instructions when necessary. Stephen retrieved his laptop from the car, and they worked for a while, he on his computer and Tori on her smartphone.

Tori took the scenic way to the freeway again on their way back into town. Cows gathered in groups around large, round bales of hay. Every other pasture seemed to have a weathered barn with a rusty metal roof. Farmhouses stood far off the main road, plain and stolid against the elements. She wondered how many of these places would still be here in ten or twenty years, with so much development happening around the area, including that which she was leading. Many of these old farms and ranches would be bought up from heirs who no longer cared to work the land or even live in the region. Subdivisions would come in, along with shopping areas, manufacturing and other commercial development. It would slowly evolve into being a further outpost of the suburbs instead of being "the country" outside the city.

As she turned her car onto the freeway and headed for downtown, she felt a moment of sadness at leaving the rural peacefulness of the morning. She remembered the same feeling from a week before, driving back from Logan with the desert sparseness and silence fading into the background as she came nearer and nearer to the suburban and urban areas close to home.

Later that night, she stood staring out over the city from her third floor balcony window, eating a banana and drinking a Perrier. She picked out cars along the parkway a few blocks away. She peered past the treetops to the skyscrapers in the distance, their lights glittering in long columns against the night sky. She watched a helicopter land on the rooftop of one of the medical buildings.

She wondered if Logan had an airstrip of any kind. She had not thought to ask. As soon as she thought this, she noticed it yet again. That she was thinking about Logan and the land. Thoughts of the land, the town, the old hotel, and Ken and Hazel had come to her randomly but consistently in the last week. She had heard nothing from Ken about the potential buyer for the land, but she had not expected to until next week. Part of her wished for his call, though, just to talk and to have some kind of connection to the life out there.

She did have a connection, though. The land. She owned it and could do with it what she wanted. And, at that moment, the thought of selling it and cutting her connection to it seemed exactly the wrong thing to do. Maybe she should just keep it and hold it as an investment. She could go out there from time to time to check on things. She could have the old hotel razed so that any danger or liability from that was removed, and just leave that land undeveloped. Thousands of acres of it, stretching almost as far as you could see.

She thought of that for a moment and liked the idea of it.

# Chapter Four

The Cessna's engines changed from a purr to a roar as the plane gained speed down the runway and nosed itself into the air headed west. Tori sat relaxed in her seat and looked out the window as the ground slipped further and further away. As the plane lifted, the blinking lights of the coastal areas around Galveston became remotely visible to the south. Tori turned to glance across the aisle through the windows on the other side. The skyscrapers of downtown clustered tall and gray in the distance, barely visible other than their lights in the darkness before dawn.

She sat back, switched on the overhead reading light, opened her leather portfolio, and started reviewing her notes for the meeting in El Paso later than morning. The Green Lake project was well underway and a new entertainment district in El Paso was in the concept stages. Tori had meetings scheduled with various government and community representatives over the next few weeks. Most of those meetings could be done via teleconference, but Tori preferred to attend a few of them in person. She could engage the principals in a project personally, using the various "soft skills" that these kinds of deals often required. Also, she could get a better sense of things—the people involved, the concerns of the stakeholders, the nuts and bolts of the politics, even just the overall "feel" of a deal—if she appeared in person from time to time.

Several weeks had passed since the trip to Logan. The man who had shown initial interest in the hotel and the land had not come back with an offer. Ken felt he might still be interested and could be talked into something if pursued with enticements, like a reduced price for the hotel parcel or a reduced package price for the whole thing. Tori had held off, though. She found herself not that eager to sell. If the right offer came along, then that was one thing. But, to go out and beat the bushes for a buyer seemed more than she was willing to do. If Ken wondered about this, he did not let on to Tori. He just kept the listing on his website and promoted it like he did any other piece of real estate.

Tori had called Ken the night before and asked if he would be around for lunch today, since her meeting would be done in El Paso by late morning. He had said he would be happy to see her and that he could meet her at the tiny landing strip about five miles outside of Logan. The strip was rarely used, and Ken was one of the few people in the area certified to manage air traffic from the control tower there, which was no more than a metal building with a tall antenna on the top. Logan was almost directly on the flight path and was only about 45 minutes from El Paso. Ken would meet Tori and the pilot at the Logan airstrip at just about noon, in time for lunch.

The plane landed at a small airport in an El Paso suburb about two and a half hours after leaving Houston. A small group of men who represented various interests in the city greeted Tori as she stepped from the plane. She joined them in a black Suburban parked on the tarmac, and they drove to the breakfast meeting in the downtown business district. On the drive and on the elevator up to the conference room, she did what she always did. She asked questions about the city—its history, any recent challenges, any odd weather events, and so on. She expressed interest in the personal histories of the individual representatives—what they did in the city, what they loved about it, what brought them to the city in the first place. She remarked positively on anything she could think of about the city, comparing it favorably to Houston, which was Texas' largest and most cosmopolitan city. Her job was to get the deal done, and part of doing that was giving a good impression of the principal dealmakers—in this case, her and Vincent. Prices, tax allotments, receipts, percentages, land, boundary lines, capital investments and improvements—all these things and many more could and would be negotiated. What was not negotiable was respect, and the idea that the dealmakers respected the people and the city of El Paso. Sure, the entertainment district would bring jobs and money to the city, but it would also disrupt some things along the way, and even change them permanently. Some small businesses would not make it through the transition. Some neighborhoods would be altered in quality of life. Some tax districts would be left out of the direct benefits in ways that could be challenging for commissioners and others who signed onto the deal. Tori had to show knowledge of and sympathy toward all these things—and myriad more that would become visible to her as the process of the project went forward—and she would have to find ways to compensate, convince and reassure the stakeholders that she and Vincent were "good people" whom they could trust. If that meant flying out there to eat gargantuan plates of scrambled eggs and chicken fried steak, and to offer some personal attention and back-slapping, that is what it meant.

Of course, it helped that Tori was attractive. She was at her best in these situations, immaculately dressed and perfectly poised, as well as articulate, efficient and expertly knowledgeable about the business at hand. Her short, auburn hair brushed back in layers from her face, which revealed an open and accessible countenance. Her blue-green eyes exuded both warmth and brilliance, and her facial expressions transitioned easily from somber seriousness to casual laughter. She sat, stood or walked comfortably in her clothes, the tailored fabrics hanging elegantly from her squared shoulders and trim hips. She was a person of natural beauty, intelligence, and charisma. When she switched those buttons to the "on" position—every day at work, especially during meetings like this—she was hard to resist.

She called Vincent to brief him after the meeting as she sat in her seat on the jet, waiting for the pilot to go through final aircraft checks. Things had gone well, with only a few unexpected concerns and requests. By the time her hosts had dropped her back on the tarmac in front of the jet, she had created enough comfort with them to hug and cheek-kiss them goodbye. Probably within a month, all the primary contracts would be signed, the major paperwork completed, and she or Vincent, or both, would be back out there doing a photo-op with the Mayor, announcing the deal.

She looked at her watch. It was just after 11am. In less than an hour, she would be on the ground in Logan. She put her portfolio away in her briefcase and snapped her seatbelt together, ready for take-off. She surprised herself with how excited she was to see Ken and to be back in that dusty little town. She had nothing in particular to do there, at least in terms of business or her land. When she learned of the day trip to El Paso, though, she immediately thought to make a stop in Logan. Meeting with Ken seemed the only obvious thing to do.

She watched the streets and buildings of El Paso fade into the distance as the plane ascended, and the multi-colored brown of the West Texas desert emerge to take its place in rectangle of the jet's window at her seat. The plane flew at only about 15,000 feet so she could see a highway here, a cluster of small mountains or mesas there, a winding strip of green along what must be a creek or riverbed. Large swaths of dirt alternated with those of yellow grasses and brush. From the air, some property lines were clearly marked and visible, their 640-acre sections and combinations of sections distinguished from others by the distinct coloring of the sand or stone, or by a series of roads and fences. Other large areas were not divided at all—they simply stretched on for hundreds, even thousands of acres at a time, across sandy hills, mesas, bluffs, flat grasslands, and small mountains that jutted from the desert floor at sharp angles on one side but which merged on the other back into the hardened sand in a gentle, descending slope. Occasionally, the terrain would be interrupted by a cluster of small buildings, or by a lone structure in the middle of it all. Tori could pick out a single road, or a crisscross of roads in these areas, but not much more. Everything was too easily swallowed up in the sheer size and scope of the landscape, which appeared immense even from the air. The little jet could go down in the middle of that desert and, quite possibly, no one would hear or see it.

*There aren't too many places like this left in this part of the world,* Tori thought.

She remembered at that moment the overwhelming silence of the place, as she had experienced it that day Ken took her out onto her land. The only sound had been the rustling of the wind in the brush and low trees, or the cry of a hawk or a crow overhead. The silence felt almost tangible, and like it had weight and heft to it. She could feel it on her chest, pressing into her shoulders, abdomen and thighs, pressing them gently into the sand as she lay there that day with her legs, arms and fingers splayed open to the warmth of the sun. It had been a pleasant, seductive sensation.

"We're descending, Tori," announced the pilot, Jack, from the cockpit. His voice sounded distant and small over the intercom despite him being only a few feet away. "About five minutes to land." The plane turned a bit to the right and Tori felt it begin its steady descent. Within a minute, she saw the landing strip and what must be Logan beyond it. She had not seen it before from the air, and was struck with how small and insignificant it was. The jet flew directly over the little town for another minute, and turned sharply to retrace its path, crossing over the town toward the landing strip. Three minutes later the jet touched down and Tori saw Ken's truck parked next to the metal building "tower" as they raced past it toward the end of the runway. The plane slowed enough to make the turnaround at the runway's end, and began the slow taxi back to the building. Ken stood outside waving as they pulled up and stopped next to the orange cones he had stationed on the pitted tarmac. Tori caught his eye, smiled and waved back.

"Welcome back!" he said as she stepped off the plane. He held his arms wide for a hug. She circled her arms around his neck and kissed his cheek. He squeezed her tight, as if they had known each other for years.

"I'm so glad to see you," she said, pulling back. "Thanks for meeting us here on short notice." She turned toward Jack, who had killed the engine and was stepping out of the pilot's door onto the ground. "Ken, this is Jack, our best company pilot. Jack, this is my friend Ken. He's a realtor and he's helping me with some land out here."

Ken and Jack shook hands. "Here, ya'll wait here for a minute. Let's get a few things done before we leave," Ken said as he turned to go into the door of the building. He returned with a flight log and Tori stood back as he and Jack completed the forms. "That'll do it!" Ken snapped the book shut, put the pen in his jacket pocket. "Let me lock up and we can go to lunch."

Jack stood with Tori as they waited for Ken. The sky was overcast and the air was cold and dry. "Not much out here," Jack said, squinting into the wind as he surveyed the flat, arid land that stretched out for several acres beyond the landing strip.

"No, not much," she replied. "That's mostly why I like it," she added, not consciously thinking about it until she heard herself say it. It was true—something about the sparse emptiness of it all appealed to her. It was an emptiness that also seemed full at the same time. She did not quite understand it.

Ken opened the truck and they climbed in, Tori in the front passenger seat and Jack in the back. "You are in luck coming to Logan today for lunch," he told them as he pulled out onto the main road. "Galindo's has a new chef in from the West Coast." He smiled mischievously at Tori. "Her name is Elena and she's from here in Logan, but she moved away a long time ago to go to culinary school and whatnot. Ended up working in fancy restaurants in the San Francisco and Oakland area. Did really well, from what I hear. Ended up on television on those cooking channels and everything." He rolled down his window a bit despite the chill. Tori gladly took in the clean desert air.

"Anyway, she moved back to Logan not long ago to take care of her mother. Gloria's getting old and I think she's pretty sick, although I'm not sure exactly what's wrong with her." He paused for a minute. "Tori, you remember Galindo's? That little Mexican place?" Tori nodded. "Well, they talked Elena into coming there to manage the place and to cook the lunch special most days. It's about the only days the lunch is any good there anymore. So, we'll go there if it's alright with you."

"That sounds great to me," Tori said. "That okay with you Jack?" She turned toward the back seat.

"Sounds fantastic," he said. "If you'll excuse me, though, I just got a text message from my daughter in Boston. She's home with a new baby and says she can Skype with me if I can get coverage out here. Would you two mind eating just yourselves while I sneak off to a corner booth or something and chat with my daughter?"

Ken smiled and looked at Jack in the rearview mirror. "That's fantastic! Congratulations! Is this your first grandbaby?" Tori looked back as Jack responded.

"Yes, it is—a little girl. Cutest thing in the world." Jack grinned and looked out his window, then back at Ken and Tori. "I'm not biased or anything, though."

"That's just great, " Ken said. "It's not loud in the restaurant, even if there's a crowd, so you should be fine to do a call in there."

They drove on and Tori felt herself doing what she often did in towns like this, noticing empty buildings and "For Sale" signs and vacant lots. She tried to remember if anything had changed from when she was here several weeks ago. She did not actually remember "scouting" the town during her last visit at all. Now, she felt more interested and engaged.

They pulled in to Galindo's and parked alongside a half a dozen other vehicles, mostly dusty trucks or low-slung early model sedans with mismatched hoods and fenders. One SUV had kayaks on a rack on its roof. The cinder block facade of the building was painted gray with red trim around the window frames. White letters in a curly, cursive font spelled out the restaurant's name across the door. Inside, a few wait staff tended to several tables of people, carrying trays of iced tea, cold beer, chips, salsa, guacamole, pico de gallo and sizzling fajitas. Tori inhaled the unmistakable smell of fried tortilla chips and grilled meat. Ken picked a table for the two of them and pointed Jack toward a booth in the back corner.

A young waitress came with glasses of water and menus. Tori looked around at the other patrons. A mix of people, white and Hispanic, most in jeans or work clothes. One table of three who looked to be in their early twenties had maps spread out on their table between plates of food. *Probably the tourists with the kayaks,* Tori thought.

She glanced at the menu. "We'll ask what the special is when she comes back," Ken said. "That's gonna be the thing to order. Let me go tell that to Jack." He got up walked over to Jack's table, relayed the message, and came back. Tori watched him as he went, his loping gait and relaxed body. His jeans were worn and his shirt had a few faded stains on the chest. He typified what many people think of when they think "Texan"—rugged, capable, honest, forthright. He was also friendly, thoughtful, and nice to be around, at least in Tori's experience.

"What's the special today. Is Elena cooking?" Ken asked the waitress when she returned for their order.

"Grilled quail served over jalapeño rice with a side of grilled seasonal vegetables. Your choice of soup: tortilla or bean. Comes with a drink of your choice. No refills on alcohol." She ticked off this information as if she had been saying it all her life. Tori and Ken smiled at each other and looked back at her.

"We'll have two of the specials then, " Ken said. "I want iced tea with mine and the bean soup."

"I'll have the same," Tori said. The waitress scribbled it all on a pad, gathered their menus, and hurried away. She returned a moment later with chips and salsa. Tori grabbed a chip and dunked it in the red salsa.

"These chips are Elena's too, " Ken said, after eating a few of them. "She makes them here. Notice how thick they are—not thin like those ones that come in bulk in most restaurants." He grabbed another one, loading it carefully with red salsa before putting the whole thing in his mouth.

"They're really good, " Tori said, and she was not kidding. She had eaten her fair share of chips and salsa, and these were distinctive. Thick, as Ken said, substantial, crunchy, and very flavorful. "Does Elena make the salsa too?" It was chunky with a pleasant burn of spice and a faint smoky flavor.

"I don't know, maybe. We'll ask her before we leave," he said. He ate another chip, crossed his arms and leaned forward. "So! What's going on with you? This is a business trip today, right?"

Tori filled him in on the details of the El Paso venture, as well as the Green Lake project. He took it all in, asking questions about many of the details and nuances. Tori could tell from his questions that, despite his "down home" appearance in worn jeans and a stained shirt, he was an experienced person who knew about business and how things got done. She felt good talking to him about it, explaining her role and job in everything. She felt that he understood not only the work, but also her and what she brought to the work.

The entree was as good as Ken said it would be. They both stopped talking for a few minutes when the food arrived, naturally suspending their conversation as they each took their first bites of tender quail. The meat was rich and light at the same time, perfectly grilled and balanced nicely with the grilled vegetables of squash, carrots, and onions seasoned with an herb Tori did not recognize. When they resumed their conversation, Ken changed the topic.

"So, what are you thinking about your land?" he asked.

Tori hesitated a moment. "Well, I guess I'm thinking the same as I have all along, to sell it all in one piece if I'm going to sell it." She took another bite of rice and looked at him.

"Really? Okay, well, we can certainly do that." he said. He looked at her for a moment. "I just wanted to make sure that was still the plan." He took a long drink from his glass. "I haven't pressed too much since the first buyer didn't work out because I kinda got the feeling you weren't up for pushing too hard." He paused. "Like maybe you weren't dead set on selling it."

She nodded slightly and finished chewing before speaking. "I understand. It's true—I haven't felt any urgency about it, even though I thought I would at first. Certainly, when I first drove out here I was thinking to get it done as quickly as possible. But…" she trailed off, and swallowed. She laid her fork down on her plate and sat back in her chair. She looked at Ken. "The truth is I'm not too eager to sell it."

She listened to herself say those words. As she felt herself saying them, she knew she was telling the truth to herself and to Ken for perhaps the first time in several weeks. The truth was that she did not want to sell the land, not at all. The truth was that she, for reasons she could not quite articulate, felt a connection to that land, and that it pulled her a little more every day, every week that passed that it still belonged to her. The truth was that she thought about it—the fact of its existence, the details of its plants and colors and smells and curvature—every day, often several times a day. The truth was that she felt happy, giddy even, every time she thought about it, which is why she immediately jumped at the chance to stop by today on her way back from El Paso. She planned to ask Ken to drop by the old hotel before going back to the airport just so she could stand on her land and breathe the air and gain yet another memory of it to take back with her to the city. The truth was that before the jet landed her back home, she would begin thinking of the next time she would arrange to come out here again.

Ken nodded slightly. "Well, do you want to pull down the listing?" He looked at her plainly and waited for her answer.

"I think I do, yes, " Tori said. She took her last bite of quail and pushed her plate aside. "We can always put it back up if I change my mind, right?"

"Certainly, " Ken said. "No problem at all." He folded his napkin and laid it across his empty plate. "I'll take care of it this afternoon. You just let me know if and when you want to try again to sell it."

"Thanks," she said. "I appreciate it." She sensed that Ken had more to say about it. She thought she detected a slight smile on his face that was more than a simple expression of pleasantness, but she was not sure. She was about to ask him about it when he suddenly looked past her, over her shoulder, and his face broke into a wide grin.

"Elena, hey!" He called the chef over. "Another fine meal today. That quail was fantastic!" Tori turned. Elena walked across the room toward them, reaching her hand out to Ken's as she got to their table. He partially stood up and she leaned down to kiss his cheek.

"How are you, Ken? Thanks for coming in," she said. She stood back, looked at Tori, and extended her hand. "Hello, welcome to Galindo's. I hope you enjoyed your lunch."

Tori shook her hand and smiled up at Elena, looking directly into her dark eyes. "I enjoyed it very much, thank you. The quail was quite nice."

"I told Tori that there was a new chef in town here and that we needed to come over," Ken said. "This is Tori Reed from Houston. She's a client of mine and, well . . " he stopped and glanced at Tori. "Well, she's *been* a client of mine in some real estate and she happened to be in the neighborhood today." Ken continued with the introduction. "Tori, Elena is a local who's recently come back, like I told you, from the West Coast. She was a big fancy chef out there. We're sure glad to have her back here in Logan."

Tori watched Elena as Ken said those few words of introduction. She stood up straight but looked down, her hands on her hips, smiling faintly and waiting for Ken to finish speaking. Her straight black hair was pulled back into a tight ponytail. She wore a stiff, unbuttoned white chef's coat over a black v-neck t-shirt and jeans. Her sleeves were pushed up and two pens were clipped onto the coat between two breast buttons.

"It's nice to meet you," she said to Tori.

"Likewise," Tori replied. "How long have you been back in Logan?" She took a drink from her glass.

"Just a month or so," Elena said. "It's good to be home." She smiled at Tori, holding her gaze for a moment before turning back to Ken. "What are you up to today? Running more errands for Hazel?"

Tori listened as Elena and Ken chatted about things around town. Elena seemed relaxed and comfortable in the midst of all the activity around her. Once she glanced at the kitchen and made a motion to one of the waitstaff to give attention to one of the tables. As Elena continued to chat with Ken, Tori's napkin slid onto the floor. Before Tori noticed it, Elena bent down, retrieved it, stuffed it into her coat pocket, leaned over to grab a clean one off the adjacent table and laid it gently in front of Tori—all without taking her eyes off Ken as he was speaking, and without creating a break in the conversation.

After a few moments, Elena turned to Tori. "Will you be staying in Logan for long?"

"No, I'm just here for lunch. I go back to Houston in a little while." Tori stopped, but then added. "But, I'll be back soon probably. I own land out here and plan to come out from time to time." She felt an unexpected joy in hearing herself say those words aloud. She looked at Ken and he grinned at her.

"Oh, really? Where is your land?" Elena asked.

"It's a few miles out of town, where that old hotel is on the main road," Tori answered. "It used to belong to my uncle, who recently passed away."

"Sandy? Was he your uncle?" she asked.

"Yes. You knew him?

"Yes, I did." Elena put her hand on the back of Tori's chair and leaned toward her a bit. "Well, I grew up knowing who he was. I was a kid, a teenager mostly, when I was around him the most." Elena stopped, as if bringing something to remembrance. "He used to help out at school during the basketball games, keeping the score and buzzing the timeouts and things like that." She paused for a moment, pushing a stray strand of hair off her face, curling it onto her ear. "I heard he died recently. I'm sorry for your loss."

"Everyone knew Sandy around here," Ken said. "And everyone liked him. He was a good man."

"Thank you both." Tori replied, not really wanting to talk too much about it since it seemed that they knew more about Uncle Sandy than she did, especially in his later years. "He was a special person to me when I was young. That's when I came out here the most. I lost touch with him in his later years."

Elena glanced toward the kitchen and looked back at Tori. "If you'll excuse me, I need to get back inside." She stretched her hand to Tori again, and Tori shook it, noticing the smooth warm skin of her palm. "I hope you'll come by again the next time you're in Logan."

"I will, thank you." Tori said.

"As for you, old man, will I get to see you tomorrow?" Elena punched Ken lightly on the shoulder with her fist and began to walk away.

"Sure, I'll be here. I'll bring Hazel in tomorrow. What's the special going to be?"

Elena turned with her back to the swinging kitchen door, and stopped for a moment. "Hmmmm...I haven't decided." She closed her eyes in concentration, her brow furrowed, then opened her eyes and relaxed her face into a wide smile. "Rabbit." She said it with confidence and certainty. "That's it. Rabbit." She waved, and disappeared behind the swinging door.

Jack joined them as they were putting on their jackets to leave. He face beamed as he showed Ken and Tori a new picture of his granddaughter on his phone. He and Ken chatted about grandchildren and other such things as they paid, walked out and got in the truck. Tori listened only partially to the conversation. She was still thinking about what she had told Ken about her land and not wanting to sell it. She felt a sense of relief welling up within her, one that answered an anxiety and discomfort that she had not fully recognized was there until now. She remembered the hollowness she had felt on a few occasions recently. In the last half-hour, since she had told Ken not to sell the land, she had felt a new excitement—about what, she could not say—that seemed to push away that hollowness from the last few weeks. Something seemed possible now that had not been before.

Ken did as Tori asked and pulled in to the crumbling and dusty parking lot of the old hotel. All three of them got out of the truck and stood in front of the building.

"So, you own this?" Jack asked.

"Yep, I do," Tori replied simply, smiling. "Ain't it grand?"

Jack laughed. "Well, it certainly could have been once upon a time."

Ken chimed in "It was a nice enough place when it was up and running. I mean, it was nothing fancy, but it was as nice a place as you'll find out here in this part of the state." He kicked the toe of his boot against a large boulder that marked one corner of the concrete entrance that was mostly crumbled into small rocks and dust. The two men followed Tori as she traced her way around the back of the hotel and out toward the gorge beyond it. She followed what looked like a small animal trail, a simple but visible indention in the sand that formed a thin strip of pathway cleared of thorny ground cactus or other plants.

They stood on the edge of the gorge and looked across it to the far side and beyond that to the mesas in the foreground. The colors were not as vibrant in the overcast sky as they had been on the blindingly bright day Tori had been there last. The variations of brown, golden, dark green, beige, and gray were muted, yet seemed to stretch on infinitely until they gradually dissolved into the slate gray of the distant mountains on the far horizon, which themselves were only a shade or two darker than the sky itself.

"Most all of this is mine, too," Tori said, continuing her answer to Jack's question from earlier. "Almost as far as you can see." She felt the vague, but clearly identifiable excitement well up inside her again, in her chest and throat, and felt herself begin to smile at the sensation of it.

"Nice," he nodded. He stuffed his hands into his jacket pocket.

"You can have a lot of fun with land like this. I've done some camping and hunting on land that's very much like this a few hours from here. I've always liked this particular terrain—the desert, the roughness—lots of people don't like it, but I do. I think it's really beautiful and distinct. I like that you can see a long way." He scanned the horizon slowly with his eyes as he spoke, taking it all in as much as he could.

"I do, too," she said, turning to meet Jack's eyes. "I really like it, far more than I remembered as a kid when I used to come hunting out here with my family." She turned back to the land, following the jagged edge of the gorge with her eyes. "It's really beautiful to me, too."

Ken smiled, glanced at Tori, and did not say anything. She kept her eyes fixed outward toward the view across the gorge.

They stood a few more moments before turning to walk back to the truck. At the airstrip, Ken hugged Tori tightly.

"Do you think you'll be back any time soon?" he asked.

"I think so," she replied. "I've probably got a few more trips to El Paso coming up in the coming weeks and months, so I might be able to stop in again like today. Thanks again for meeting us for lunch."

Jack extended his hand to Ken. "It was a pleasure. Hope to see you again soon."

"The pleasure was all mine. You both be safe and, Tori, keep in touch. I'm nearly always here, so let me know when you think you'll be back. I'll be glad to see you."

Jack began his checks of the plane and Ken went inside the building to take care of the flight log and other details. Tori leaned against the side of the building, waiting for Jack to motion to her that she was cleared to board. She took a look at her phone, scrolled through the caller ID of voice messages, and put it away. All of them could wait.

As the jet raced down the runway, she waved to Ken sitting

at the control desk in the big window of the building. The jet careened upward and she saw again, as she had a few hours before when arriving, the tiny town surrounded by hundreds of miles of desert. She was sad to be leaving. She felt that sadness clearly now and let herself feel it and acknowledge it. But she also felt relieved that it—the town, the desert, the land, *her* land, the gorge, the mesas, even the old hotel—was not going anywhere, that it would all be there waiting for her when she came back again in a few days or weeks or months.

She settled back into her seat and closed her eyes, opening her palms on her thighs and relaxing her shoulders down. She stretched her neck gently to one side then to the other, feeling the tension release. She felt good. Calm, stilled, and even happy. She thought of Ken and how grateful she was for his friendship, new as it was. She thought of her uncle and how he loved her and how she hoped he had felt he had a good life. She thought of the little animal trail that she had walked and how she had not noticed it when she was there before. She thought of the grilled quail and the delicate flavor of the white, tender meat. And she thought of Elena, standing there in front of the swinging kitchen door, waving goodbye to them with her slender, brown arm.

# Chapter Five

Elena Rios had not intended to come back to her hometown in the West Texas desert, at least not so soon. She had left just a few months out of high school and had come back to visit in those twenty-five years only a handful of times, mainly to see her mother. Her father had left them when she was just starting grade school, so she and her mother were each other's only family from then on. Eventually, though, Logan became too small, too suffocating, too ingrown for Elena. She arranged for a late-night ride to El Paso, and caught a plane to the West Coast with $500 and what would fit inside a military surplus duffel bag.

She had landed in San Diego early in the morning and by the end of the day had rented a room in a youth hostel. A week later, she had gotten her bar tending license and went to work at an upscale men's club. Her shiny dark hair, gleaming smile and brown skin earned her as many tips as her bar tending skills, which were enough to earn her a promotion within six months to food and beverage manager for that club as well as three others owned by the same company. So, she spent her days going from club to club, inspecting their inventories, systems, equipment and procedures, and her evenings standing back watching the whole thing work until she was satisfied that they would make it to closing time that night without screwing everything up. She had offices in every club that, although small and stinking of vomit half the time, she treated like her own personal kingdoms. She did her work efficiently, without many words, and tolerated no drama or interruptions. The dancers knew not to come to her with their requests for advances or better costumes or dance tracks. They did, however, know to come to her, and her alone, when they got slapped around too much by a drunk boyfriend and needed a ticket out of the city for good, or if they needed to see a doctor. She respected the women, but she did not pity them. They made their choices in life. She made hers. Each had to make their way.

Nightclub work took its toll after a few years. She grew tired of the culture, of the long days and the seemingly endless nights filled with drunk, desperate people. She had lived frugally and the company paid her well, despite her being female in a male-dominated business. So one day she simply quit, announcing her resignation immediately at the end of a managers meeting with the owners. She felt free as she walked out the front doors and through the parking lot to her car. As she loaded a box of things from her club office into the back seat, one of the longtime dancers—a beautiful, increasingly worn woman with deep gray eyes and a kind smile—came over to hug her goodbye. They stood in each other's arms for a few minutes, kissed briefly, and stepped away from each other. Elena got in her car and drove away, leaving San Diego for good that day.

She talked to her mother, Gloria, regularly during those years. Gloria even came to visit her several times when she moved to San Francisco to go to culinary school after leaving the nightclub business. She started working in kitchens before she started school, moving from restaurant to restaurant every year or so, learning new skills at each one. She had a knack for cooking, for knowing what flavors blend together well, and which ones comfort people. Only the rare palette can truly appreciate—much less desire in the first place—the exotic or the bizarre in the food world. Mostly, people who come to restaurants want to eat things that are in the category of the familiar, but have been embellished into something extra special or surprising. Elena knew how to give people that. Basic cuts of beef, pork and poultry she enlivened with marinades and spice rubs, and then injected an extra pulse of flavor with a special grilling or roasting technique. Ordinary sides like carrots, squash, potatoes, even pasta she would douse with infused oils, citrus salts, expose them to a high, fast heat, or nearly frozen ice baths, bringing out subtle tones and textures. Desserts seemed whimsical and complicated, because of the styling or presentation, but dissolved on the tongue as a flavor loved for a lifetime even if it were new to that particular palate. All of it was recognizable, none of it was intimidating, and every bite of it was highly delicious.

By the time she finished culinary school, she had a reputation in the area for her food, and also for her beauty and her elusiveness. She was a private person who rarely hung with the after-hours restaurant crowd, the chefs and their staff who met regularly after closing for all night parties laced with cocaine, heroin and sexual exploits. She lost co-workers and employees to that culture. She watched them go from job to job, glazed over and stoned or frenetic and edgy, barely making it through their shifts, coasting on raw talent, caffeine and diet pills. She found one of her sous chefs dead in the bathroom one night, drowned with his head submerged in a toilet filled with his own vomit, a bloody syringe on the floor beside him. He had hid his addiction well. She would have fired him if she had known, or paid for rehab for him if he had asked.

Her big break came when a famous television chef visited a

restaurant in Yountville where she worked as the executive chef. He had spent all day in the wine country and his friends had gone for dinner up the road at a famous restaurant with a three-month reservation waiting list. He, however, had decided to go off alone to something more inconspicuous, so he walked in unannounced and the nervous hostess seated him at the chef's table, which offered an open view of the kitchen and its staff. Elena did not realize he was there until the meal was nearly done. He watched her make her way through the busy kitchen, overseeing and instructing, tasting and inspecting, jumping in to help a struggling pastry chef and even the prep cook when things got behind. She moved with precision and elegance, almost without effort, in a completely casual way. She wore jeans, a t-shirt and a chef coat, her plank straight hair pulled back in a ponytail. It was her uniform. On days off, she shed the chef coat and replaced it with a jacket or sweater. Everything else stayed the same, including the open, somewhat blank, but slightly bemused look that most often inhabited her face. When she laughed, her whole face seemed to break open, but she laughed only rarely, especially at work.

The famous television chef happened to catch her on one of those rare occasions. A regular customer brought his little girl back to the kitchen door to see the chef. Elena came out, greeted the patron and bent down to greet the little girl, who planted a sticky kiss on Elena's cheek. They both dissolved into giggles as Elena picked up the little girl and took her on a quick tour of the kitchen, stopping long enough for the child to pick a fresh strawberry out of the colander, before Elena handed her back to her father and they went away. Within a week, Elena got a phone call from the chef's producers, and within another month she was cooking on camera for millions.

The television appearances bolstered her brand, and she did stints at many of the best restaurants in San Francisco, Los Angeles, Hollywood, and even went to New York for a few months to advise on the opening of a Latin American restaurant. She always came back to the West Coast, though. The climate suited her as well as the pace of things and the culture—open, liberal, indulgent of alternative lifestyles. She did not see herself as particularly alternative, but she appreciated the freedom nonetheless. She liked having space, both the physical space of the long Pacific coastline and the seemingly endless ocean, and the personal space to do what she wanted without being questioned or pressured too much. She had had lots of the former in Logan, but not so much of the latter.

She had dated several women, and a few men, but she worked too much to be part of the "scene" of lifestyles that paraded up and down the streets in some parts of the Bay Area. She had lived with a woman—Alison—for a while, first as a roommate but then as a lover. Alison had shared her workstation the first day of culinary school and, as a team, they had succeeded in a pastry challenge their teacher had sprung on the class. Alison had just arrived from Toledo, Ohio the week before and had yet to find a place to live, so Elena invited her to rent the spare bedroom in her apartment. Somewhere between walking to class, teaming up on desserts or at the plating station, and working late training shifts in the Mission District, they ended up in bed together. They became a couple, of sorts, known as "love birds" to their classmates who teased them for making out in the walk-in cooler and for holding hands during class sessions. But, Alison was not as talented as Elena and eventually the competition between them took its toll. Alison moved out of their apartment and took a job as a line cook in a small, anonymous cafe in the wine country. Elena saw her again only a few times before she heard she had moved back to Ohio.

Occasionally, she thought about returning to Logan, but she never held the thought in mind for very long, although her memory of the place softened over the years. Her mother had gradually conceded this to Elena. Gloria had expected Elena to do what most other Hispanic girls did in Logan: finish high school, get married, have children, and stay close to family. Elena had dated a boy from a well-known family in Logan, Luis Palacios, and everyone had expected them to stay together and get married after they finished school. But, Elena had not even told Luis she was leaving when she caught that midnight ride to El Paso—she knew he would try to talk her out of it, or want to come with her, neither of which she wanted. He was as surprised as Gloria was when she left, and almost as sad, maybe even sadder.

He was equally as glad when he learned that Elena was coming back to Logan. He had known that Gloria was sick, although very few in Logan knew exactly what was wrong with her. Everyone suspected cancer of some sort, and indeed it was—pancreatic cancer that was too far progressed to treat in any meaningful way. Gloria opted to go without treatment and to spend the remaining months or years of her life—the doctors had said she had anywhere from six months to two years—without suffering the effects of the treatment as well as the disease, both of which were deadly. Elena had tried to get her to come live with her in California, saying she would sell her place in the Bay Area and buy a cottage for them in the wine country overlooking the vineyards. Gloria had loved the Napa area when she had visited Elena several years before. But, Gloria refused, saying she wanted to die where she had lived all her adult life.

Gloria did not directly ask Elena to come back to Logan, and Elena never really talked with her about it. She just did it, as simply and definitively as she had left Logan that night twenty-five years ago. She sold her place in the Bay Area within two weeks of putting it on the market, put most of her stuff in storage, and drove back to Logan in her silver Tahoe. Luis happened to be standing in the gas station parking lot on the main road, pumping gas into his truck, when she drove back into town. He watched absent-mindedly as the vehicle glided past, noticing the attractive, dark-haired woman driving. Not until she passed and he saw the California license plate on the back and the vehicle turn off the main road into Gloria's neighborhood did he realize he had just seen Elena.

In the month she had been back, she had made the rounds of most of the friends and family still there from when she was young. They all welcomed her back, happy that she had returned to care for her mother, proud of her for her accomplishments, and proud that their little town had produced someone who had been on television. Elena, in many ways, was still the same person they remembered, or thought they remembered. She was still polite and thoughtful with people, still even-tempered and calm in personality, still smart and industrious. And she was still beautiful. The tiny lines around her eyes and mouth served only to accentuate it. She still had smooth brown skin, a dazzling smile made all the more so because it was rare, and an attractive figure slightly voluptuous at the hips and breasts.

Luis noticed this about her immediately upon meeting her again for the first time after her return. Gloria had called him to come check her propane tank in the side yard beside the house. She had not told Elena he was coming, and was not certain that Elena would be there when he arrived. Not until she heard his truck pull into the gravel driveway while Elena was clearing away the breakfast dishes did Gloria know that things would work out the way she hoped. Elena answered the door and welcomed Luis into the house. Gloria beamed as Elena hugged him like she had hugged all the other old friends and relatives the last few weeks, smiling and asking after his family. Elena had stayed in the kitchen while he and Gloria went to check the propane tank. She stood over the sink washing winter greens, and occasionally glanced up to see him in the side yard. He looked much the way she remembered as well—not too tall, but strong and trim. His black hair was now flecked with gray, and his neck was creased from the sun and age. But his eyes were still kind, and his square jaw and longish nose gave him an appearance of authority, as if he were in command of things no matter the situation, even without saying a word.

Indeed, Luis took care of things around Logan. He managed cattle for some of the non-resident landowners in the area, he was the captain of the volunteer fire department, and he was a fire-arms instructor for the Border Control academy fifty miles south. People in Logan appointed him to meet with county officials about their property taxes, or to set up a petition for a water treatment plant outside town, or to spearhead the drive to pay for hotel, meals, and travel for the six-man football team when they went to the state championship. And he did things for people, like Gloria. Although his plans to marry Elena years ago had failed, he loved Gloria and still treated her as if she were a relative.

He still loved Elena, too.

Elena had been in the kitchen since 6am on the day Ken and Tori first ate lunch together at Galindo's. The rest of the staff did not usually arrive until 8am but she liked to get there early to have time to herself and to get things done without distractions. Urleen Galindo, the café owner, was in her seventies and had not actively managed the place for several years. One of her daughters, Sofia, had done the work for a while, but her third grandchild had just been born and she did not want to spend so much time in the café anymore. When Urleen sat down with several other older women for *tres leches* and Nescafe at Gloria's house one afternoon after Elena had returned, she had mentioned to Elena about cooking at the café. Elena had not immediately agreed, but had walked in to the café one morning a few days later wearing her chef coat and asked what needed to be done. She had been working as the chef and manager for the three weeks since then. The salary was barely more than a token, but it was only a few hours a day and it gave her something to do. Gloria did not need her at home all the time anyway, at least not yet.

That morning, she had been going through an old walk-in cooler tucked away in a hallway in the back of the restaurant. The cooler had not worked in decades and had been used as a storage room for things that mostly should have been thrown away, but which Urleen or Sofia or someone else had simply stacked and forgotten about. By the time the kitchen staff straggled in at 8am, she had retrieved an old set of terracotta bowls and plates, several dozen of them each, and had placed them on the sink rack to be washed for use in the lunch service that day. Three broken cane-backed chairs, several boxes of rotting linens, and a thoroughly decomposed sack of what looked like cracked pecans she had tossed outside on the back steps to go into the trash for the landfill.

She put the staff to work at their various tasks, taking one of them aside to teach him how to use the portable grill setup on top of the gas stove burners. She brought over a large mixing bowl of dressed quail, their pink bodies bobbing in the caramel colored marinade. Luis had brought them to her house last night after an afternoon hunt with his cousins. They had killed thirty-eight birds, nice plump ones. She decided they would become the lunch special today. The young cook watched her as she skewered three birds and positioned the metal ends of the skewer in the slots on either side of the portable grill so that the birds hung suspended just right over the flames of the gas burner. She supervised him as he impaled a second batch onto another skewer and placed it in matching groove a few inches away. She instructed him on basting and turning techniques.

The quail were a big hit. In fact, Tori and Ken were the last two patrons to get to eat them before she ran out. She could have sold another dozen or more specials. People liked quail out here and knew about them, unlike in the West Coast cities where people often did not order them for fear of them tasting gamey. Quail very nearly constituted comfort food in this part of the country, so she did with it what she had done her entire culinary career; she embellished the familiar to make it special and made it taste like the best version of the thing customers had eaten their entire lives.

She was glad to see Ken in the café dining room when he called her over. It was his fourth or fifth time to eat at Galindo's since she had started working there. Usually he came with Hazel. He had not lived there when she as a kid, so she had no history with him. Everyone considered him a native, however, even though he had only been in Logan for ten years. She liked him a lot. She got a good feeling from him, and from Hazel as well. She wondered who the woman was with him as she walked toward their table. She seemed quite over-dressed for a place like Galindo's. For any place in Logan, really.

She reached her hand out to Ken's as she got to their table, but she naturally leaned down to kiss his cheek when he partially stood up. He was an easy person to feel comfortable with.

"How are you, Ken? Thanks for coming in," she said. She turned to face Ken's female guest and extended her hand. "Hello, welcome to Galindo's. I hope you enjoyed your lunch."

The woman shook her hand and smiled up at Elena, looking directly into her dark eyes. "I enjoyed it very much, thank you. The quail was quite nice," she said.

Elena smiled back at her, noticing her firm handshake and her confident look. She reminded Elena of patrons in her restaurants on the West Coast: polished, professional, urban, probably wealthy, and attractive.

She felt the woman watching her as Ken introduced her as the fancy chef who had come back home to live in Logan. She stood still, waiting patiently, and was glad when the introduction shifted to the woman. "It's nice to meet you, Tori," she said to her.

"Likewise," Tori replied. "How long have you been back in Logan?" She took a drink from her glass.

"Just a month or so," Elena said. "It's good to be home." She smiled at Tori, holding her gaze for a moment before turning back to Ken. "What are you up to today? Running more errands for Hazel?"

"No, not today," Ken said. "I think I'm off the hook for a few weeks on that. I've got some road work to do out on a piece of property I'm trying to sell for this guy in Amarillo, so I'm taking my tractor out there. Luis let me borrow his trailer to haul it."

Everyone in town knew Luis, so it did not surprise her really that Ken did. However, she wondered if he mentioned this detail about Luis to her for any particular reason. Perhaps he knew through the town grapevine that the two of them had a history together. That her mother had a not-so-secret hope for them to get back together. That Luis himself probably wanted that, too. She did not comment about it.

"How is the real estate business out here these days?" she asked instead. "Has the recession hurt the market any?" She wanted to move the conversation along.

As Ken answered her, she noticed a group of patrons in the corner who had been seated several minutes ago, but who still had no drinks or place settings. She motioned to one of the staff to take care of them, glancing at Tori as she turned back to Ken. Tori sat back in her chair, arms folded in her lap, smiling at Elena and Ken as they chatted. She did not notice that her napkin had just fallen off her lap. Elena saw it out of her side vision, scooped it up and replaced it with a clean one from the next table, stuffing the old one into her pocket.

After a few moments, she turned to Tori. "Will you be staying in Logan for long?"

"No, I'm just here for lunch. I go back to Houston in a little while." Tori stopped, but then added. "But, I'll be back soon probably. I own land out here and plan to come out from time to time."

"Oh, really? Where is your land?" Elena asked, wondering if there were a secret or inside joke, since Tori and Ken grinned at each other when Tori said she owned land.

"It's a few miles out of town, where that old hotel is on the main road," Tori answered. "It used to belong to my uncle, who recently passed away."

"Sandy? Was he your uncle?" she asked.

"Yes. You knew him?

"Yes, I did." Elena put her hand on the back of Tori's chair and leaned toward her a bit. "Well, I grew up knowing who he was. I was a kid, a teenager mostly, when I was around him the most." She remembered him well in that moment—a kind man, always helpful and interested in things around the school. He always seemed tired, though, or sad or lonely. "He used to help out at school during the basketball games, keeping the score and buzzing the timeouts and things like that." She paused for a moment, pushing a stray strand of hair back off her face. "I heard he died recently. I'm sorry for your loss."

"Everyone knew Sandy around here," Ken said. "And everyone liked him. He was a good man." He was right, as Elena remembered it. Sandy was a longtime and well-respected resident. People looked up to him for how hard he worked.

"Thank you both." Tori replied. "He was a special person to me when I was young. That's when I came out here the most. I lost touch with him in his later years."

Elena glanced toward the kitchen and looked back at Tori. "If you'll excuse me, I need to get back inside." She shook Tori's hand, again noticing the firmness of her grip, but also the softness of her skin. "I hope you'll come by again the next time you're in Logan."

"I will, thank you." Tori said.

She waved goodbye to them as she returned to the kitchen. She reached for a pen from her lapel and fished in her pocket for a pad of paper. She wanted to make a note about the rabbit she had just told Ken would be the special tomorrow. She had several whole ones in the freezer, but did not remember how many servings each rabbit would yield. She needed to look it up. She pulled Tori's old napkin out of her pocket and laid it on the counter as she wrote. When she reached up to push back that stubborn strand of hair, she detected a faint scent of perfume wafting in the air. She noticed it because she had not put any perfume on that day, and no one had walked past her in that moment. Instinctively, she sniffed her hands, and there it was—the smell of perfume. Confused, she breathed in the mixture of citrus, flowers and herbs that emanated from her palm and the underside of her fingers. Then she looked back at the napkin on the counter. She picked it up and brought it to her nose. The smell was even stronger. It was Tori's perfume.

*Nice*, Elena thought, smiling a bit. *Really nice*. She returned the napkin to her pocket and continued writing her note about rabbit servings.

Gloria was taking a nap when Elena got home from the restaurant in mid-afternoon. She stood in the doorway of her mother's bedroom and watched the old woman sleeping on the bed. She lay on her side, her knees curled up with a pillow between them, one end of the pink chenille bedspread pulled over them. Elena could see the corner of a wadded up tissue peeking through the balled fingers of one hand. Gloria's face was still, although not exactly peaceful. She had lost a good bit of weight in the last few months, so her face was not as fleshy and vibrant as it had been well into her late sixties. Now, her cheeks were hollow and Elena could make out the contours of her eye sockets and her jawbone. Her hair was still mostly black, with very little gray, but it had become thin and dull.

Elena eased down the hall away from the bedroom, trying to walk so as to not make the wooden floors creak. She stepped into the kitchen and started some hot water for tea. Wide swaths of afternoon sun streaked across the linoleum floors. Rico, her mother's orange tabby, lounged in one of the bright beams, drowsing and squinting his eyes into the sun and barely turning to acknowledge Elena when she entered. Only the very end of his tail moved at the sight of her, curling up and down, up and down, two times only.

She sorted through a small stack of mail she had brought in with her from the mailbox on the road. Mostly her mother's bills, some health insurance and Medicare statements, various pieces of junk mail, a sweepstakes entry, and an issue of *Modern Hospitality* magazine. She was glad to see the post office finally forward her subscription to Logan. She opened the magazine and began thumbing through the first few pages. She had missed a few months' issues with the move. She scanned the table of contents, and the letters to the editor. Her eyes stopped at the section which featured the cover of the issue from a few months ago. Two people were featured on the cover, a woman and a man, and the woman looked vaguely familiar to her. She read the text next to the cover image: *Go online to see the latest brainchild of Vincent Macari and Tori Reed - a master development designed with upscale hospitality in mind.* Elena brought the magazine closer to better see the image. Sure enough, it was the woman who had been with Ken in the café for lunch earlier. Tori Reed.

*How interesting,* she thought. *And Sandy was her uncle.* She got up to take the kettle off the burner and pour her tea. She reached over to her purse to retrieve her phone. It was the only Internet she had in her mother's house. She wanted to go to the magazine's link and read more. Just as she was typing the web address into the keypad, she heard tires turn on to the gravel driveway outside. She looked up and saw Luis' navy truck. She put her phone and the magazine aside on the table with the mail, got up and went outside.

She stood on the porch and watched Luis step out of his truck and walk the pathway of concrete steps along the front of the house that led to the porch. She brought her shirt-sleeves down over her balled hands and folded her arms, protecting herself from the chilly air. She smiled at him. He stopped in front of her and stood on the concrete step at the bottom of the porch, his hands in his jeans pockets, his canvas jacket zipped up.

"Hey," he said, smiling up at her. "How are you?"

"Quite well," she answered. She knew that there was a chance her mother had asked him to come over to fix something, but the way he was standing there, with a tense smile on his face told her that was not the case. He had come to see her. She wondered how long she would be back in Logan before this encounter happened. She waited for him to speak.

"I figured you were home from the café by now. I thought I would stop by, see how you were doing. Just visit for a while." He squeezed the back of his neck with one hand, then stuffed it back in his pocket and looked at her, his face plain and direct.

"I just put on some tea. Would you like some?"

He smiled. "Sure, that sounds nice." He followed her inside.

"Mama is asleep, so try to be quiet," she instructed as he unzipped his jacket and began walking across the wood floors to the kitchen. He sat down at the table and watched her as she poured the hot water over the bag into the cup. She brought his tea to the table and sat down across from him, curling her hands around her warm cup. She looked up at him and waited for him to speak.

He stirred the hot liquid and looked up at her. "How are things going at the café? I bet it's different from what you were used to in San Francisco." He slid the sugar bowl across the table, heaped a spoonful of it into his cup and continued to stir.

"It's fine," she said. "It's small and uncomplicated, so…it's different than what I'm used to, but it's challenging in its own way. To cook in a way that appeals to a small community like this, but is still interesting." She took a tentative sip from her tea, frowning over the liquid that was still too hot.

"People have been raving about it. Even a few guys I know at the Border Control have come up to eat and they loved it." He took a sip of his tea. "You could make a name for yourself in all these little towns scattered out here," he said, half joking at the suggestion.

"Mama said you teach at the Border Control Academy," she said, wanting to change the conversation away from herself.

"Yeah, I teach the basic fire arms course." He explained the curriculum and the guns they used. They began with pistols—first revolvers, then semi-automatics, and then progressed to shotguns and rifles. Most of the cadets were familiar with guns from growing up on ranches and hunting. They were nice guys mostly—and mostly guys. Elena listened to him and could easily imagine him being a good teacher. He was nice, competent, and patient. He had been that way when they were young and he seemed not to have changed.

"How's your mom?" he asked, his face growing serious but not somber.

"She's okay, I think." Elena nodded as she said it. "She has good days and bad days. Some days she feels good, other days she has no energy and no appetite. I think she got tired early today. She was asleep when I came home."

"She's lost a good bit of weight, it seems like." He fingered the handle of his cup.

Elena nodded again. "Yes, she has, even just since I've been back, I think." She took a sip of tea. "Again, she has good days and bad days—on good days, she eats more, on bad days…" she shrugged and looked at him. "I don't press her."

"It's good you came back," he said after a moment. "She needs you."

Elena looked at him and smiled slightly. She understood the ethos of the Hispanic community in that area, in which girls rarely moved away from their families unless they did so with a husband. And she had known that she was breaking that ethos when she left years ago. It helped that she came back to visit her mother every now and then and, after she became successful, her mother would come back to Logan after visiting Elena in California and brag about how well she was doing, how beautiful her home was, how successful she was, and how everyone loved her. Gloria never took issue with Elena leaving Logan, at least not once she knew she was safe in her new city. She had known instinctively that Elena would leave, for a time at least. She had not expected her to stay away as long as she had, however. Elena herself had not expected to stay in California for over two decades either, but the years simply passed by and before she knew it, she had lived there longer than she had lived anywhere else in her life.

Coming back to Logan had been an easy decision, for the most part. Sure, she would have preferred her mother to come stay with her in California—for her mother to spend her last months and years in the cottage in Napa that Elena proposed she buy for them. When Gloria refused, she knew she had to come home. It was the only way. She was her mother's only daughter, her only child. Her mother had no one else, no one who was family at least, family enough to live with her and take care of her as she was dying.

"I love her very much," Elena said simply.

Luis nodded, sipped his tea, and asked more about Gloria's condition. Elena told him the basic facts—that she was no longer doing any treatment, that the only drugs she consented to take down the stretch would be for pain, and that she could have months or even a year or more to live, it was hard to know.

"You're planning to stay, I guess," Luis asked.

"You mean while she's sick?" Before he could answer she continued. "Yes, I'll stay until it's over." Elena looked down at her tea and back at him. "I won't leave her alone. If I were going to do that, I would have simply stayed in California."

"Well, I meant more than that…" he said. "I meant are you planning to stay indefinitely?" He paused. "Do you think you'll go back to California, or will you stay here at home?"

She knew that was what he wanted to know. Her mother wanted to know, too, even though Gloria knew that she herself would not be alive to experience it one way or the other. Elena was not entirely sure. Would she go back to California? Maybe. Probably. But maybe not. Maybe she would go somewhere else. She was not likely to stay in Logan, though. She had no reason to stay, really, especially if her mother were no longer alive.

"It's hard to know, Luis," she replied. "I'll make that decision when I need to." She took a sip of her tea. "Right now, I'm here, the café gives me something to do, and I'm just down the road if Mama needs me."

They both turned toward the hallway as they heard footsteps coming toward the kitchen. Gloria rounded the corner into the room and stopped, blinking at the two of them. Rico got up, stretched a long, luxurious stretch, and walked over to rub against her calves.

"Well, hello," she said. "What a surprise to see you both sitting there. You were so quiet." She smiled at both of them. Her eyes were still puffy with sleep, and a faint crease ran the length of her face from her nose to her mouth where she had slept with her cheek buried in the pillow.

Elena pulled a chair from the table and got up. "Here, Mama, sit here. I'll get you some tea." She held it as her mother eased over and sat down, stifling a yawn as she let her full weight rest on the chair. Elena went to the stove and turned the kettle on again.

"How are you, Luis?" Gloria looked at him. "The propane is working now. Thanks for fixing the connector on the tank."

"You're welcome, Ms. Rios, " he said. "I just came by to check on things and to see Elena, see how things were going at the café." He smiled over at Elena then looked back at Gloria. "She cooked those quail my cousins and I got hunting yesterday—it was the lunch special today. I heard it sold out."

"Is that true, *mija?*" Gloria turned back toward Elena standing at the stove. "That's a lot of people, and a lot of food. I hope you didn't work too hard."

"It was fine, Mama. I enjoyed it. And I don't cook everything myself, you know. I show the staff how to do it. It's not that tiring." She watched Rico sitting at her mother's feet, wanting her lap. After a moment, he tentatively reared up to put his front paws on Gloria's lap. She opened her arms and he leaped up. Elena watched her mother's fingers work through the orange fur up and down his back. She wore one ring, her grandmother's wedding ring, and it seemed to swallow the thin finger it surrounded. Her knuckles were swollen and her fingers did not seem to straighten. But, her nails were filed and shaped perfectly, and were painted a deep mauve color. The skin of her hands looked paper thin, and Elena could see most of her veins through it, but her hands were steady. Gloria looked down at Rico as she stroked him. He closed his eyes in ecstasy, purring loudly, and began kneading her legs through her old purple sweatpants.

Elena came to the table with her mother's tea and sat back down. Luis slid the sugar bowl toward her. Gloria petted the cat with one hand and stirred sugar into her tea with the other. After a moment, she turned to Luis.

"You should stay and eat supper with us." She said it as a matter of fact, not as a request. "Elena will cook something nice for us, won't you *mija*? " She turned to her daughter and smiled. She turned back to Luis. "And you can put some wood in the chiminea outside. We can drink a glass of wine in front of the fire."

Luis looked a bit surprised and glanced at Elena. Elena had her head on her hand and was looking out the window across the road toward the mountains in the distance. She did not move when Gloria made her suggestion. She listened to Luis' response.

"Well, I have some steaks thawing at home I'd planned to cook, so I should probably go on home, " he said, somewhat tentatively.

"Go home and get them, and bring them back. You can grill them here, " Gloria said. She turned to her daughter. "*Mija*, is that okay? What did you have planned for supper?"

Elena turned back to them. "Actually, I have one filet thawed that I'd planned to do something with, but…" She looked at her mother then back at Luis. "Why don't you go get your steaks, and bring some skewers if you have them. We've got some random vegetables and other stuff. I'll put it all on the fire outside." She waited for a moment. "How does that sound?"

Gloria smiled broadly. Elena was happy to see her mother happy. She knew her mother loved Luis like a son; she had loved him since they were kids. The least she could do was to help her mother make some nice memories with people she loved in the time she had left.

"That sounds wonderful, Elena. Thank you. Thank you both." He got up, grabbed his jacket off the back of the chair and started toward the door, fishing his truck keys out of the pocket. "Do you need anything other than the meat and skewers? Any more wood or anything?"

"Bring more wood if you have it, but I think we have enough," Elena answered, standing up as he walked toward the door.

"Okay, be back in a little bit," he said and waved as he shut the door behind him.

Elena walked to the refrigerator, took out the filet and set it in a dish on the counter, to allow it to get to room temperature. She walked to the pantry and took some onions and peppers out of a hanging wire basket in the corner. She piled them all on the counter next to the filet. She sat back down with her mother and took a big swallow of her tea.

"He's a good man, Elena," Gloria said and looked at her. "He's helped me a lot over the years." There was no condemnation or harshness in her voice. She had said nothing about Elena *not* being there over the years. She was simply making a statement of fact.

"I know, Mama. He is a good man. He always has been." She put her hand on her mother's and smiled at her. "It's just been a long time."

"I know, *mija.*" Gloria sighed and looked at her daughter. Elena was so familiar, and yet so hidden. She had been that way ever since she was a little girl. Always kind, gentle, even thoughtful. Seemingly open, but not really so. She could make you feel that you were her closest friend, and would treat you with the care and concern of such. But, at some point you realized that you did not really know what was deepest in her heart. That she kept tucked away, sharing it rarely, and then only with a look, a phrase, or an unexpected laugh that indicated a deep chord had been struck somewhere within her. She would share that laugh with you, her eyes watering from the joy of it, but then return again to her own inner depths, looking out at the world and everyone in it through clear eyes and a mostly placid, but pleasant face.

"I think he never got over you leaving," Gloria said. She knew she risked upsetting her daughter, but she was an old, dying woman and she had no time to worry about such things any longer. "Lots of girls around here tried to get him after you left. He wouldn't have anything to do with them, not really. He could have had any of them. He moved into his grandmother's house after she died and he's lived there ever since, all alone." She took a sip of her tea. "Everyone loves Luis."

Elena watched her mother as she spoke. She knew that although her mother would be thrilled if she and Luis resumed their high school romance from twenty-five years ago and got married, she would probably never say as much. She had stopped pressing Elena to do things years ago, knowing that it would only drive her daughter deeper into her own recesses. Elena had followed her own mind and heart in most matters for all her adult life, regardless of other people's hopes and dreams.

She had not thought about Luis too much over the years. She had seen him a few times—at a basketball game, at someone's house—during the times she had come back to Logan for short visits. But, they had never spent significant time together or even had prolonged conversations. She had not told him she was leaving that night she got a ride with a schoolmate's brother to El Paso with her duffel bag to move to California. And they never talked about it afterward. She wondered if it hurt him, figuring it probably did. But he was always cordial and seemed happy to see her during her short visits. Soon, he became just another person in Logan who was friends with her mother, who helped her keep her yard up, who looked in on her when she had a cold, who changed the oil in her car for her.

She had thought about him, though, if only a few times. Once, she thought she saw him on Fisherman's Wharf one bright afternoon, walking along the pier and holding the hand of a small child. She realized almost immediately that it was not him, but it made her wonder about him—if he wanted children, how he would look and be as a father, and how her life would have been different if she had stayed in Logan and done what everyone thought she would do, which was marry Luis and have a family with him.

Another time, many years ago, a man had come into one of her restaurants, and he looked like Luis. He did not have the same features exactly, but he had the same feel and presence. He inhabited his own skin like Luis, relaxed and calm, and he wore his clothes like Luis, neat and crisp even when wearing something casual like jeans and boots. The man had become a regular patron of the restaurant and finally he had asked Elena to go out with him to dinner one night when her restaurant was closed. They had driven up the coastline in his convertible to a tiny, cliffside bistro overlooking the ocean. She thought she imagined Luis' scent later that night as they embraced on the beach near her house.

"It's been a long time, Mama," Elena repeated. She patted her mother's hand and pulled it back to her teacup. She turned to look out the window again, finding the rim of the Santa Elena mountain in the far distance to the south, near the Rio Grande. As a little girl, she believed it was named after her. Or that she had been named after it. Neither was true, but she felt connected to that mountain regardless, even after having been away for so long.

Before long, Luis' navy truck pulled back into the gravel driveway. He carried a bundle of pinion pine around to the back and set it beside the large, terracotta chiminea. Elena met him out there with lighter fluid and a fire starter. Gloria had arranged the metal lawn chairs in a semicircle in front of the chiminea and watched as Luis started a blazing flame in it. The old woman smiled into the fire, its light reflecting on her cheeks and into her dark eyes. Elena went back into the house and returned with a bottle of wine and three glasses. She poured each person a glass and set the wine bottle on the edge of the porch.

"Salud!" Gloria said, lifting her wine glass toward the fire. "Salud" said Elena and Luis together, touching their glasses to Gloria's. They all took a sip, looking at each other and at the fire, smiling into the dusky sky and the moon that was just beginning to rise from the other side of the house.

Elena got the skewers ready while Luis and her mother sat

outside by the fire. She left the back door open to smell the sharp, pleasant aroma of the burning pinion pine. She listened to them talking as she cut the meat into cubes and threaded it, along with pieces of onion and pepper, onto the metal skewers. They talked about things around town, various bits of news and information about people and happenings. They talked easily with each other, and it was immediately clear to Elena that Luis and her mother were friends, quite apart from any past she and Luis had from years ago. She watched them sitting there together, holding their wine glasses and looking into the fire, their forms in dark outline against the glow of the fire. She smiled at them. She was glad her mother had Luis. He was a good friend.

Luis had brought enough wood to last for a few hours. Once enough wood had burned to form a bed of hot coals in the chiminea's bottom, Elena placed a metal grate inside it over the coals and carefully laid the skewers on top of it. The meat sizzled as it grilled, and she basted herbed butter over the vegetables with a long brush. The smell was heavenly, as only food cooked over open flames in the outdoors can be.

They ate outside in front of the fire. Elena listened to stories of the latest grassfire incident involving the volunteer fire department. She heard news of Mr. Molina's mohair goats, how they had gotten out of their rocky pasture through a hole in the fence and were feeding in the sweet grass that grew in the run-off near the gate. The llamas he had bought to guard them from coyotes had jumped the fence after them and stood over them, half in the road, half in the ditch, almost daring any cars to hit them. The llamas were large and black, and the biggest one stood nearly seven feet tall at his eyebrows. By the time Mr. Molina came on his tractor with a round of bailing wire to fix the fence, fours cars of people had stopped on the side of the road just down from the flock and their woolly guards, and were standing outside watching them simply out of curiosity. Luis had come, too, after Mr. Molina called him, to help him get the flock back into the pasture.

Gloria grew tired just as the flames were starting to die down in the chiminea. Her wineglass was empty and her cheeks and hands were warm from the heat radiating from the terracotta. Luis gathered the dishes while Elena helped her mother to her room, got her into her nightgown and into bed. She threw an extra quilt over her and tucked her tightly into bed.

"Sleep well, Mama," she said as she kissed her forehead and smelled the woodsmoke in her hair. Rico jumped onto the bed and curled into a little ball in the crook of Gloria's knees.

"Thank you, *mija*." Her mother said wearily. "I love you. It was a good night." She smiled and closed her eyes.

Elena patted her mother's shoulder and walked out of the room. The kitchen was empty. She looked through the screen door out into the yard and saw Luis sitting in his chair in front of the waning coals. She walked out and stood behind him, looking up into the band of glittering stars across the dark sky.

"Sit for just a minute?" he asked and motioned toward the chair beside him. "I just have a little more wine in my glass to finish, then I'll go."

She sat down and stretched her feet out toward the terracotta fireplace, feeling the heat coming through the soles of her shoes after just a moment.

'This was nice, Elena. I think your mother enjoyed it," he said.

Elena nodded. "Yes, she did. Thank you for staying and for bringing the steaks." She stared into the coals and he took another sip of his wine. They sat there silently together, enjoying the stillness of the night and the smell of the fire, captives to the glow of the embers and the warmth of the wine. It felt easy, uncomplicated and simple, especially against such an expanse of landscape and the infinite canopy of stars.

She walked with Luis around the house to his truck after he finished his wine. He opened the door and turned to her.

"Thanks for inviting me. I enjoyed the evening," he said. He reached out to touch her shoulder.

She smiled up at him, leaned over and hugged him lightly. "You're welcome anytime, Luis." She stepped back. "Maybe I'll see you later this week at the café."

Luis smiled. "Sure." He got in the truck, closed the door, started it and began to back out. He waved as he pulled away down the driveway and into the road. She watched his brake lights for a moment as he drove away, then turned and went back around the side of the house to turn the water hose on the fire.

Back in the house, she suddenly felt sleepy. She had been up since 5am and would get up early again in the morning to be at the cafe by at least 7am, if not earlier. She locked the doors, stacked everything in the kitchen sink, and turned off all the lights except for a small nightlight near the kitchen table. She grabbed her phone and magazine from where she had set them earlier in the afternoon and went to her room.

She brought her phone and the magazine into bed with her, thinking she would check email and maybe read a bit, although she did not get many emails anymore and did not think she could read for very long before falling asleep. She touched the screen on her phone and it lighted up, revealing the keypad screen and the half typed-in address of the article about Tori Reed, Vincent Macari and their new project. She thought for a second about putting it aside until tomorrow. Instead, she opened the magazine to the page with the address and finished copying it into the text box.

When the article opened, the first thing she saw was Vincent Macari's highly magnified throat. She adjusted the picture to fit the screen and there was Tori, the woman she had met earlier that day. She stood there next to Vincent in a black suit with a pearl silk blouse. A delicate turquoise scarf circled her neck. Her auburn hair was short, but its layers brushed back from her face in gentle waves. Her face was open and smiling, her blue-green eyes staring straight into the camera. She and Vincent stood in front of a lake with greenish water, which matched the color of Tori's eyes and seemed to amplify their intensity and intelligence.

Elena scanned the article, picking out the relevant details and the parts that focused on Tori, that explained her role in the leadership of the project and quoted her as she explained her vision for it. She finished the article and scrolled back several pages on her phone to the Tori's picture. After a moment, she put the phone and the magazine on the nightstand, and turned out the light. The room was immediately blanketed in thick darkness as Elena slid down between the sheets and covered all but her head with a heavy down comforter.

She feel asleep wondering if perhaps she had met Tori before somehow. She doubted it. In fact, she was almost positive they had never met. She surely would have remembered if they had.

# Chapter Six

After three months back in Logan, Elena settled into a comfortable rhythm. Her weekdays were filled with Galindo's, at least during the early part of the day. The café had extended its service to include breakfast as well as lunch. Urleen Galindo, the owner, was thrilled to see so much energy in the café, which had nearly gone out of business before Elena came. Before, they had been lucky to get forty customers a week. Now, they had that many every day, sometimes close to twice that many.

Elena was not surprised at this. There was no mystery to it. Put a restaurant on a main road in a small town with little or no competition, serve good food at a reasonable price, and you will do well. She took it all in stride, pleased at her success, and happy that people enjoyed coming to the café.

She also, somewhat to her surprise, liked being at what felt like the center of the town. Nearly everyone who lived in Logan now came to eat at Galindo's at least once a week, so she got to know people who had moved there after she left, like Ken and Hazel and dozens of others. She also got reacquainted with people she knew from before. And they got reacquainted with her, updating their visions of the pretty high school girl with the nice smile and stunning eyes with the full-grown woman who was beautiful in ways the high school girl never could have been. Beauty like Elena's—which included the features of silky hair, bright smile, sparkling eyes and smooth skin—derived not so much from these things in themselves, but from the energy of self that seemed to permeate just underneath the surface of them. It was a beauty born of experience, knowledge, self-confidence, and quiet, high-level competency. It flowed naturally from her as it does from anyone who does what they love and what they are good at.

So, when Luis came to the café nearly every day for a meal or just for coffee, he watched this beauty in action, learning newly the particular arch of her lower back as she stood over receipts or a plate of *migas*. Or the slight and somewhat permanent lines at the corners of her eyes when she smiled at a customer or sent a tired delivery driver off with a free take-out box for the road. Or the strength in her arms as she helped her mother slide into the booth with friends on the one day every week or two when they came to the café for lunch. To Luis and to many others who came to know her, or to know her again, Elena seemed as native to Logan as someone who had never left.

She herself had transitioned during those months to the slower pace and lifestyle of Logan. Even though Galindo's was busier than it had ever been, it still did not rival even a slow night at any one of the places she had cooked in San Francisco or Oakland. And the customers were not as demanding in Logan. Mostly they were local people, retirees, blue collar workers, and ranch hands. Non-locals were travelers and tourists making their way across Texas who stumbled in glazed over from hours in the car, numbed by the nearly fifteen hour drive from the eastern to the western borders of the state. She liked the regularity of seeing customers wipe their plate clean with a soft tortilla or a piece of bread, leaving nothing behind but a wadded up napkin. Customers never did that on the West Coast, no matter how good the food was.

She walked to and from the restaurant many days. Sometimes she crossed through vacant lots and followed a trail worn clean by school kids, loose neighborhood dogs and wild nocturnal animals. Other times, she stayed in the sidewalk until it fed onto the road shoulder and followed it to her mother's neighborhood street. Elena was walking home one afternoon, about to turn the corner off the main road when a red pickup truck honked lightly, slowed down and stopped in the intersection. The driver side window rolled down and Ken leaned out.

"Elena, hello!" he smiled and waved.

She smiled and walked up to the truck, her head barely level with the rear view mirrors. "Hey! I'm well. Just walking home." She put her hand on the window and looked past Ken into the passenger seat. Tori Reed sat there smiling and looking at her through her sunglasses.

"Hello," she said to Elena. "My name is Tori—we met a few months ago at the café when I was in town for lunch with Ken. It's good to see you again."

"Yes, I remember. Welcome back, " she smiled and looked back at Ken. "What are you two up to this afternoon?"

"Well, Tori had a few days, so she decided to drive out here so I could show her more of her land. She hasn't really seen all of it, so we've been out driving around and are just coming back to town for some coffee at my house." His face was flushed from the wind and the sun of the day. His gray hair stuck out in tufts from under his cowboy hat.

"That sounds nice, "Elena said. "It's been a beautiful day, a nice day to drive around and be outside—as long as you have a jacket."

Tori nodded in agreement. "Yes, I really enjoyed it. I can't really navigate the terrain in my car. Ken is nice to take the time to drive us around in the big truck." She patted the dashboard as she spoke and smiled at Ken.

"Why don't you come have coffee with us?" Ken asked.

"Yes, please do," Tori added. "I'd like to hear more about what you're doing at the café. Ken tells me you've become quite a sensation these last few months."

Elena had no particular plans for that afternoon or evening. Her mother was spending the afternoon with a few of her old friends on the other side of town and would not be dropped off until well after dinner. Luis had invited her to come to his house for dinner, but she had declined.

She looked at Ken and Tori. "Sure, that sounds good."

"Great," Ken said. He watched her in his rear view mirror as she opened the back door and climbed up into the back seat of the truck. He turned out onto the road.

Tori turned sideways in her seat so she could face both Ken and Elena. The sleeves of her green turtleneck sweater were pushed up on her arms. She had draped her leather jacket over the back of her seat. She wore jeans and her discarded scarf lay piled up in her lap.

"Do you walk a lot around town?" she asked Elena. Between her own and Tori's sunglasses, Elena could not see her eyes very well.

"I walk back and forth to the café about half the time. Just for the exercise, when the weather is nice. There's not much traffic on the road usually, so it's okay to walk. It seems silly to drive when it's less than a mile between the house and the café."

"Elena's mother's house is the one right there on the corner where we stopped," Ken added, looking at her again in the rearview mirror. "I'm glad we caught you before you disappeared into the house." He paused for a moment. "How is your mother?"

"She's doing well. Thanks for asking." Elena looked out to find the Santa Elena mountain along the horizon, and looked back to Tori once she found it. "My mother is dying of cancer, so I've come back here to live with her." She said this frankly, as a simple matter of fact. "She's doing very well, though. She is getting around okay and has felt pretty good this week. She's been seeing her friends a lot lately, which is good."

"I'm glad to hear it," Ken said. "I'm sure she enjoys being with them—feeling good enough to visit. They've been a tight group over the years. Hazel plays dominos with them every now and then." Elena nodded as he spoke.

"I'm sorry to hear about your mother," Tori said. "It must be very hard." She took her sunglasses off and looked at Elena in a way that was sympathetic, but not sentimentally so.

Elena nodded slightly. "Thank you." She noticed Ken watching her in the rear view mirror. "It hasn't been too hard yet. Hopefully, the pain medications will work as things progress. Right now, she is tired a lot, but she feels okay. She sleeps and eats well enough."

"That's good," Ken said definitively. "Let's hope it stays that way for a good, long while." He said it with the confidence of a declaration, almost willing it to come true.

They reached Ken's house and Hazel met them at the door as they walked up onto the porch. "What a nice surprise! Hello, Elena. Come in everyone. I've got the coffee making right now."

"Thanks, honey." Ken leaned over and kissed his wife's cheek. He had texted her earlier to say that he and Tori were leaving the property and coming to the house for coffee.

They made their way into the kitchen and arranged themselves in chairs around the table. Ken took off his jacket and hat, and hung them both on pegs just inside the kitchen doorway. Hazel sat a tray of cookies, nuts and coffeecake onto the table in front of them.

"How wonderful!" Tori said. "Thank you." She reached for a few nuts and popped them into her mouth. She wiped her hands on her jeans, then slid the tray of cookies over to Elena and got up to help Hazel with the coffee cups. Elena thought Tori seemed different from when she saw her in the café a few months ago. She was in jeans, a sweater and boots today, not in a suit and heels. Her hair today was loose across her forehead and down the side of her neck instead of carefully combed and styled. She had on very little makeup, and her sunglasses were perched in the tousled hair on top of her head. She seemed very comfortable with Ken and Hazel, almost at home.

"So, how was it today?" Hazel asked. "Anything notable out there on the land? I was afraid you all wouldn't get very far because of a road being washed out. We had some fairly heavy rains here not long ago. They're not much compared to Houston rains, but when they come, they come hard and those run-off areas can flood in a hurry."

Tori shook her head but did not speak because of the coffee-cake in her mouth. She listened as Ken filled Hazel in on the details of their land-scouting trip that day. She had come back to the table with coffee cups and had sat down beside Elena, who had slid the tray back toward her.

Tori swallowed. "I hadn't seen any of the area we saw today. It was more up and down than the other parts I've seen. Lots of small hills and curves and little cliffs. And more brush, too. It seemed to have more plants than the other parts I've seen, which were more spare and mostly sand." She took another handful of nuts from the tray. "I think it's all really beautiful." Elena noticed a change in the inflection of her voice as she described the land. She spoke with almost childlike excitement about it, as if she were discovering it all for the first time, which was literally true, as it turned out. Elena felt the emotion in Tori's voice—an attachment or reverence toward the land. She felt a moment of pride listening to Tori describe the landscape that she herself had grown up in and which seemed so common and normal, especially when she was young and only wanted to get away from the emptiness of the desert and the smallness of the town. She noticed how Tori's face lit up and her hands and arms became more animated when she described the plants, cliffs and gorges. And the deer and quail and doves they had seen, too.

Elena drank her coffee and listened to the conversation between Ken, Hazel and Tori, nodding and smiling at them, taking it all in, not agreeing or disagreeing, but interested in their fascination and apparent love for the landscape surrounding their little town. Of the four of them, she was the only native, and the one who had lived in Logan the longest overall. Listening to them, she imagined that they were speaking about another place altogether—some spare, exacting, beautiful landscape filled with thorns and bladed plants, stinging and biting insects, and resilient animals who can withstand the brutal heat that turns everything into various shades of brown—a place that demands respect because it can kill you as easily as nurture you, which is part of its appeal. A dangerous landscape that seems almost a living entity in its ability to churn out death, violence, and harshness at the same time that it nourishes tender desert flowers so delicate their petals can hardly be felt on the tip of a finger, so dear their stalks cannot bear the weight of the blooms so they creep along the desert floor, shimmering in the radiations of heat, trembling under the steps of scorpions and spiders, not to mention panther and deer and wild hog. A living landscape that takes even the *idea* of water and turns seemingly dead, burned plants into full bloom—purple sage, Spanish dagger, prickly pear. Elena listened to descriptions of this exotic location as if it were a distant land, but then made herself remember that it was Logan, her little town, the town she had left as a girl but to which she had returned a middle-aged woman. She had changed, no doubt. Perhaps Logan changed, too, at least in her seeing and hearing of it in that moment through the eyes of others.

After a little while, Tori turned to Elena quite suddenly, as if noticing her sitting next to her for the first time. "I bet coming back here was a huge shift for you." She said it as a statement, not as a question. She looked at Elena with a look of curiosity and interest, smiling just a bit and narrowing her eyes. Elena looked directly back at her and took a sip of her coffee, swallowed it, and nodded, speaking after a short pause.

"I had forgotten how beautiful this place can be," she said simply. She looked at Ken, then back at Tori. "It has been an adjustment. The culture here is very different than on the West Coast. But, I'm from here, so it comes back to me fairly easily. At least it has so far." Tori looked intently into Elena's eyes and seemed highly interested in every word she said.

Tori turned her gaze to Ken and Hazel, looking at them with almost as much focus as she had directd to Elena. "Something about this place got to you two, as well, didn't it?" She looked at them both. "You left your lives in Austin and moved down here and started over, so to speak." She turned back to Elena. "And you, you're from here, but you've been gone a long time, I gather. Of course, a sad circumstance brought you back here, but…here you are. And you left a significant life and career behind to do so." It was as if she were solving a mathematical problem or quandary in her mind as she spoke.

Ken and Hazel talked a bit about their experience of leaving their lives in Austin to move to Logan. They had left most of their friends behind and saw only the few who ever came to visit. Why did they do it? Because they loved the easy and simple way of life, the sense of quiet, the landscape, and grandness and enormity of it all. To live in Logan, Texas, surrounded by hundreds of thousands of acres of Chihuahuan desert was to live knowing that you are not the most important thing in the world, that processes and realities exist that will kill or heal you with equal disinterestedness, and that there is a terrible beauty in all of it that is rare to find and see in a contemporary world that lives its life mostly on the screens of computers and smartphones. Ken and Hazel did not say this exactly, but it was between the lines of what they said. At least, that is how both Tori and Elena heard it.

The conversation changed to more mundane things, like the goings on of the county school board and the high school sports teams and the spring rains that seemed to not be coming. Elena proffered whatever bits of news she gleaned from the tables at the café, as did Hazel from her crafts store and Ken from his client dealings. Tori took it all in, imagining the people and asking questions. Tori caught Elena's eye often and Elena caught herself glancing at Tori when she thought she was not looking. For a moment, she felt herself almost back in middle school when kids wonder if another person likes them as much as they like the other person. But, Elena pushed that thought away and allowed herself to be the grown woman she was. She liked this woman and she could tell that this woman liked her. And she was completely okay with the flirting that was going on between them.

Ken looked at his watch and then at Hazel. "We gotta leave soon, honey." He turned to Tori and Elena. "We are meeting some friends up in Stockdale for dinner. They are traveling through the central part of the state and wanted to see us, so Stockdale is the midway point. Elena, I can take you back home now or we can drop you off on the way out of town, whichever you'd like."

Elena was about to answer when Tori spoke up.

"Ken, my car's here," She looked at Elena. "I can take you home no problem. It's just a few blocks down from Stella's. Is that okay?"

"Sure—whatever is easiest for everyone." Elena stood up and began to put on her jacket. She turned to Hazel. "Thank you for the coffee and snacks. I really like the cardamom in the coffeecake."

"You noticed!" Hazel rejoiced. "So many people like it when they taste it but can't name it or have never heard of it. It's one of my favorite flavors."

Ken and Hazel walked them to the door and waved as they got into the car and began to back out of the driveway. Elena waved back and smiled.

"They are nice people," she said, as Tori pulled her car out onto the main road.

"Yes, they are. They've been a godsend to me these last few months with the land and all."

They drove in silence for a moment, looking out over the darkening land on either side of the road.

"So, you stay at Stella's when you come out here?" Elena turned to face her instead of facing out the window.

"Yes, so far. It's perfectly fine and she's a nice woman." Tori turned to smile at Elena, then looked back at the road. "She serves breakfast, then usually leaves me a plate in the refrigerator of whatever she had for dinner. It's very sweet."

Elena looked down the road and could make out in the distance the street sign on the corner where her mother's house stood.

"Why don't you call her and tell her not to trouble herself tonight, and have dinner with me instead at my house?"

Tori turned to her and then looked back at the road. She said nothing but kept driving, slowing as she came Elena's street. She turned into the street then immediately into the gravel driveway of the house. She put the car in park, turned off the engine, turned, and looked at Elena.

"Well, that sounds wonderful," Tori said.

Elena listened to Tori's story as she cooked a dinner of oven-broiled pork chops, wilted kale and quinoa. She had asked Tori general questions about her life, but then admitted having seen the article in *Modern Hospitality* about her.

"You saw that?" Tori asked, seeming surprised.

"I've been a faithful subscriber for many years." Elena replied.

"It was an interesting piece." She refilled Tori's wine glass. "The picture of you was very good."

Tori grinned up at her. "Thanks. For the wine and the compliment." She held her glass up in a cheer. Elena, back at the stove, raised her glass and tipped it slightly, returning the gesture.

"So, the El Paso thing—is that next?" Elena asked.

"No, it's mostly done, at least for me. The bulk of my job with that is over. I'll still go out there a few more times probably, but…Vincent has another project lined up—another master planned community that features our chain of restaurants and other brands." She took a deep breath. "That's what will be next for them."

Elena heard something in that last sentence. She turned to Tori.

"For *them*?" she asked. "Not for you?"

Tori looked at her, her face relaxed but intense. "I think I'm going to take a leave of absence for a while." She started to say something else but stopped and just looked at Elena.

Elena raised her eyebrows in a questioning way. "A long while?" She didn't want to pry, but she was curious.

"Yeah. I think I want to start something of my own again." She took a sip of her wine. "And I think I'm going to do it out here in Logan on my land." She paused for a moment, looking at Elena. "You know, your success with Galindo's was part of what helped me come to the decision."

Elena stopped what she was doing at the counter. "What do you mean?"

"Well, obviously, I haven't talked with you much at all until tonight, but I've heard from Ken about your success these last few months and, of course, he being how he is, he told me some of your background and your work on the West Coast. And, me being who I am, I Googled you and learned that basically you are a rock star in your field." She grinned as she said this last sentence, but then her face focused into seriousness. "And what your success here shows me is that there is a market for quality hospitality products out here: dining, entertainment, lodging, etc. And in the hands of someone capable, like you or me—we're both in this industry, right?—that market can be tapped and something special can be created. Like what you've done with Galindo's." She stopped and sat back in her chair, as if she had just laid out the premise of an argument that was unassailable in its conclusion.

Elena felt Tori's intensity and excitement as she listened. She was poised and polished, even in jeans and a turtleneck sweater, but as she described her idea in just a few sentences, her whole body seemed to come alive with energy even though she remained mostly still. She leaned forward in her chair, laying her hands out flatly on the table in front of her, as if laying out an invisible plan or a map of her ideas. Her voice became not louder, but slightly deeper and more impassioned as she spoke. And then, when she sat back in her chair after speaking, she relaxed as if the spirit of the idea had released her from its grasp for a moment.

"So, what's your plan?" Elena asked.

"A hunting resort on my land." She grinned as she took another sip of her wine. Elena wondered if Tori might actually squeal, it seemed she was so excited about the idea.

"That's what my land is good for. That's what most people use land for out here, other than the isolated areas that can support some kind of ranching. I didn't have my land on the market for very long, but the one interested buyer that Ken found for me is a guy that leases a lot of land out here for hunting and then sells access to it to individual hunters for a day or two. He boards them at that junky little Desert Sage motel down the road. Now, of course, thanks to you, they have a nice place to eat breakfast and lunch most days. But, in terms of a full-blown hospitality experience, there's nothing out here. So, that's what I plan to create: a full-service hunting resort that offers a total experience. Great hunting and fine dining in a resort setting, all against the backdrop of the great American west—or at least the sizable piece of it we have here in Logan." She paused for a moment, and sat back in her chair again since during speaking she had leaned forward as the spirit of the idea took hold of her again. "Okay—you're a pro in this field—so…what do you think?"

Elena sat plates of food down on the table and Tori refilled their wine glasses. Elena unfolded her napkin and placed it in her lap. She looked up at Tori, smiling directly into her eyes. "I think it's brilliant, and it will do well." She paused as Tori's face slid into a pleased grin. "I don't know why someone's not thought of it sooner." She held up her glass to toast Tori's idea. Tori clinked her glass to Elena's and they watched each other as they drank. Elena noticed how the dark wine colored Tori's lips, and the gentle move of her throat as she swallowed.

"So, tell me more—what other details have you worked out?" Elena asked as she cut into her meat and began eating. Tori explained how she planned to demolish most of the old hotel, but retain its basic layout and a few key structural pieces. She described the ambiance she wanted to create inside the building and on the grounds that surrounded it—sort of like a desert oasis with pretty flowers, greenery, running water, cooling trees and shrubs and walking paths that would contrast with the starkness of the natural desert that began just a few hundred yards away. She described the amenities she envisioned, including fine dining in the evenings in the lodge as well as gourmet meals out in the field during hunts, basic spa features, maybe skeet shooting or a driving range, and meeting rooms with business services. Elena listened intently, envisioning it all as Tori spoke, already liking the rugged, but luxurious feel of the place. Indeed, it was a great concept and could be done fairly easily. With the right marketing and publicity plan, it could take off.

Elena was impressed and, as she watched and listened to Tori explain her thinking behind every facet of the resort idea, Elena saw for herself why Tori ended up on that magazine cover and why she was so successful. She was magnetic, brilliant, convincing and thorough—and she treated this resort idea like it was already a living, breathing thing that existed out there on her land in some sort of hidden, occulted way but was waiting to be brought forth out of the ether and into the material realities of wood and stone. Tori treated all her projects this way—as real and deserving of minute care and nurturing, even from as early as the concept stage, because real human beings would eventually inhabit those spaces, spending their hard earned money there, choosing to spend their precious few vacation days there, and even living their lives, raising their kids, taking care of their parents, and working out their marriages in the houses built on the lots that she sketched out on a yellow legal pad in her office or living room late at night. These were not just money-making projects, although they certainly made money and had made Tori wealthy; they were also human development projects—development that would reach its fullest and truest potential only through the people who lived, worked or played within them. The people were the point. The point was to create an experience for them they could get nowhere else, which meant plugging into the deepest feelings of the landscape, the local flavor and the native benefits of any area. Tori was a master at this and Elena saw this mastery in her mother's kitchen over plates of broiled pork and kale. She admired it and was a little bit in awe of it.

Elena made a French press of coffee and they sat outside in the cool, spring evening drinking it and watching the stars. Elena always felt stilled by the nighttime sky in the desert, and usually if she were with someone, she could easily block the person out and enjoy the experience as if alone, not registering the interference of another person's consciousness. She had done this with Luis several times when he had come over and stayed up late with her. She enjoyed him, and they had a long history that she found surprisingly comforting as she integrated herself back into Logan. So, as she allowed him to hold her in his arms as they stood and watched the arcs of stars and meteors across the sky, she would let the sky itself envelop her into its solitude and silence, separating herself from Luis in a fundamental way in order to be stilled and calmed, to remain centered and focused on who she was apart from anyone else's arms.

She sat in a lawn chair alongside Tori. They both slumped in their chairs, their necks braced against the chair backs, their faces turned upward to the sky, balancing their coffee cups on their legs. Elena immediately got her bearing by picking out her favorite constellations, which were nearly lost in the starry band above them. She breathed deeply and relaxed even further into her chair. She heard Tori take a deep breath and, like usual, felt the urge to retreat into the inky recesses of the sky above.

Instead of separating, however, she stayed there, in the moment, enjoying the silence and the night air and the sharing of it with this new person.

After several minutes, Elena rolled her head to the side and faced Tori. She put her hand lightly on Tori's forearm. "Thank you for telling me all about your plans. I think it's fantastic and am really excited to see it all come about." She left her hand on Tori's arm for an extended moment, feeling the soft lambskin of her jacket, then slid her hand off.

Tori turned to her and smiled at her in the darkness. "Thank you for listening. You are the first person I've told out here. I knew when we picked you up on the road today that I would tell you if I had a chance. I knew somehow that you would get it." She turned back to the sky.

"And, I must tell you something else," Tori said after another minute.

"Yes?" Elena said.

Tori rolled her head to face Elena. "I want you to partner with me and be the executive chef at the resort."

Elena smiled and did not look at Tori. She felt her heart quicken in her chest. She rubbed her hands along her thighs, splaying her long fingers across the denim. Again, she felt Tori's eyes on her as she had so many times throughout the evening. Finally, she turned to face Tori.

"I'd be honored. When do we start?" she said simply.

Tori reached over and grabbed Elena's hand and squeezed it, holding it still on Elena's leg. She laughed aloud, closing her eyes and opening them again to take in the infinite sky. She looked back at Elena, her face beaming even in the darkness.

"Soon. Very soon." She squeezed Elena's hand again. "Thank you, thank you!"

# Chapter Seven

Y ou're really going to do this, aren't you?" Sharon said after swallowing a mouthful of salad. She looked across the table at Tori, who sat back in the booth drinking a glass of wine, waiting for her entree to arrive.

"I'm already doing it," she replied. "The old hotel demolition began this week and I've already signed off on the architectural plans for the new building and the grounds. Sharon, it's going to be *really* beautiful!" The pitch of her voice raised in glee as she said those last words.

Sharon put her fork down and leaned back, studying Tori and smiling. "You know, I had a feeling about this. I told you after you came back from that first time being out there. Remember?"

Tori nodded. "You were right. Something about the place gets to me. I don't know if it has to do with my childhood or not—it doesn't really matter. What matters is that I'm happy when I'm out there, I like the people I've met out there, and I'm really excited about this plan." She took a sip of her wine. "It's been a long time since I've done something creative that was mine, really mine. Not Vincent's. " She paused for a moment. "I'm not complaining—I've been very happy working with Vincent and am grateful for the opportunities I've had in his company. And I may come back to it after the twelve-month leave is finished. We'll see…"

Sharon leaned forward and returned to her salad. Tori's fish came and she began to eat.

"So, there's Ken, the realtor, his wife Hazel, Stella who owns the B&B where you stay, Elena the chef you've talked into working with you—and who else? Who else do you know out there?"

"None as well as those. But that'll change, I'm sure, once I'm out there fulltime. I've met via phone the contractor who's handling most of the demolition and rebuilding—Eugene Brooks. Ken recommended him and the architect out there knew him too and spoke highly of him. I'll meet him personally next week when I go out there."

"Tell me about the chef—what's she like? How do you know she'll be good to work with on this? Didn't you just meet her?"

Tori swallowed her bite of food and smiled at Sharon. "Don't we have a lot of questions!" She took another bite, still grinning at Sharon.

"Tori, this is a big deal! You're my friend and I love you. I just want to know the situation. I mean, you're a grown woman and you always do well, so I'm not worried about that. " She pushed her salad away, wiped her mouth and looked at Tori. "I just want to have an idea of the people and the place, so that I can envision you out there. Especially during the times that I'll miss you." She smiled sheepishly and turned away as her eyes began to fill, but then turned back to face Tori.

Tori reached over and grabbed her hand. She looked into Sharon's eyes, so alive with energy and intelligence. She loved those eyes and would miss Sharon.

"I'm not moving to Mars, sweetie. Just to the western part of our state." She squeezed her hand playfully. "There's a nice road straight from here to there—and once you get past Del Rio, you can drive really fast without getting a ticket. You'll like that, won't you? You can drive out and visit me anytime. In fact, that's not an option—you are *required* to come see me."

Sharon squeezed Tori's hand and let it go. "Well, it's a good thing you're building a resort out there because I don't think Stella's will work for me," she said with a wry smile. "Your place sounds more my style, if you know what I mean." She raised her wine glass and tipped it slightly to Tori before taking a long sip.

"So…Elena the chef. She's good, huh?" she asked.

Tori nodded and told her the basics of Elena's story, and the terms of their partnership agreement.

"Is she cute?" Sharon asked after a listening for a while.

"What?!" Tori exclaimed in mock surprise.

"Oh don't even act surprised…" Sharon said, rolling her eyes. "Come on, is she cute? I hope so, since you're going to be working together a lot."

Tori laughed and nodded. "That's true…so, yes, she's cute. But that's not why I asked her to partner with me. She's a total badass in the business who happens to be right there in tiny little Logan, so I'd be a fool not to take advantage of her."

"Uh-huh…" Sharon chewed her food, smiling and nodding. She swallowed and continued. "I bet you end up taking advantage of her, one way or the other."

"You are terrible!" Tori cried with mock exasperation. "Terrible!" She finished her last bite of fish and pushed her plate aside. "Anyway…to return to more *serious* matters, I can't wait to see what she comes up with for both the restaurant and the field service."

"What's does that mean—field service?"

"It means the meals served out in the field while people are hunting. It's one of the concepts I have for the experience that I think most places like this don't do too much—it will make us distinct." Tori spoke with unbridled confidence. Sharon looked confused.

"Okay, remember the movie *Out of Africa*?" Tori asked. Sharon nodded. "Well, remember when they are on safari and they ate all their meals in camp? They sat at tables with tablecloths and china and wine glasses and nice flatware. And the camp cooks made this fantastic food in the camp, sometimes from what they killed on the safari. Remember that?" Tori was leaning forward in excitement now—again seized by the spirit of her resort idea.

"Yeah, I vaguely remember that. Mostly, I remember that young woman who went on safari with Robert Redford—I don't remember the actress' name, but she was hot," Sharon said.

"Yes, she was, although her physical beauty pales against the overall excellence of Meryl Streep, but…." Tori grinned and Sharon snorted in mock exasperation at the absurdity of her comment. "Okay—that's not my point," Tori continued. "What I'm saying is that the experience of the safari in that movie is what I want our guests to experience when they hunt with us. Coming back to camp, after being in the field, to a relaxing, elegant set-up and meal that doesn't remove them from the land at all, but keeps them in it and extends their encounter with it and all that it involves."

Sharon smiled at her friend and looked at her in a knowing way. "I'm really happy for you. You're so totally into this…I'm glad to see it. It's been a while, you're right."

Tori sighed a deep breath. "Thank you, Sharon. I really appreciate you saying that. I feel really good about this and I'm so excited to be doing it. Who knows—it may be a bust, but even if it turns out not to work, I'm still really excited to try it. I mean, what's the worst thing that can happen? It doesn't work, I lose a bunch of money, and come back home to Houston and go to work for Vincent again and make it all back. The end. Right?"

Sharon looked deeply at Tori. "I don't think you'll work for

Vincent again." She thought for a few moments. "You may not stay out there—I don't know—but I don't think you'll go back to Vincent. This is the end of the line for that for you, I think."

Tori shrugged and then nodded. "Maybe you're right. I don't know. For now, it's a possibility and a back-up option if this thing in Logan blows up. We'll see."

"It's not going to blow up and be a bust. You know that."

Tori shrugged. "We'll see." She took the last sip of her wine. "I intend for it to be a success."

"Of course you do, " Sharon said. "So, cheers to your new endeavor and the new life that comes with it." She raised her wine glass and Tori reached for hers. They clinked the glasses together and smiled at each other across the rims as they drank.

"What's the name of your new place?" Sharon asked.

Tori put her glass down and swallowed. "Sandy Creek Ranch. After my Uncle Sandy." As she said those words, she felt a pang of sadness that her uncle would never see the resort named after him, and that she could never personally thank him for the incredible gift of his land. She missed him, far more than she ever expected, yet she could not identify exactly what she missed about him. His absence simply felt like a small hole in things that never got filled. Not a big hole, not one that let all the air out of life, but a hole nevertheless. The hole felt a bit filled, at least temporarily, whenever she said or saw the name of her ranch. More than anything, that helped her settle on the name.

"Sandy Creek Ranch. That sounds nice. Like a nice place." Sharon said.

"It is. It will be," Tori said. "Wait and see."

Eugene Brooks liked the idea of Sandy Creek Ranch from the
minute he heard about it. He had grown up hunting dove and
quail in West Texas and he loved to eat the rich meat of the wild
birds. He also enjoyed the terrain of the desert and the scrub brush,
and being out in it, seemingly surrounded by an infinite expanse
of desert plains, mesas and gorges. When he saw the architectural
plans for the ranch, he understood the guiding design concepts
almost intuitively and knew exactly how to execute the plan. He
had talked with Tori about it all over the phone a few times, and
liked her a lot. She was like him—focused on business, getting
things done, not wasting time, and not cutting corners. His mind
raced constantly with myriad details and to-do lists that accompanied any job, especially one like this with an owner who knew
exactly what they were doing and what they wanted.

His body seemed to mirror his mind—wiry, tight, compact and
much stronger than one would expect looking at him. He combed
his thin, brown hair back and flat against his skull and, amazingly,
it stayed that way nearly all day, even when he wore a hardhat. His
blue eyes twinkled from behind wire-rimmed glasses perched atop
a thin, hooked nose. His voice was slightly nasal, but firm—firm
enough to garner attention when he barked out orders to his crew
in English or Spanish. And he wore the same thing every day to
a job: work jeans with loops for tools, a collared shirt tucked in
with an undershirt, steel-toed work boots, and, in the wintertime,
a quilted brown denim work jacket with pencils, a calculator, a
measuring tape and peppermints in the pockets.

It was his thin frame that Tori picked out of the crew when
she pulled up to the hotel site after construction had begun. She
had seen the progress of things daily when Eugene would do a
walk-through of that day's completions on videophone nearly every
night before leaving the site. She would peer into her computer or
phone screen, examining what Eugene was showing her through
the lens of his phone camera, listening to his narration, asking

questions, requesting details and ordering do-overs. Overall, she was pleased with the pace of things and she thrilled at what she saw each night and each week as the building and grounds came together. Now, driving up to it all, she felt the excitement in her stomach as she took her first glances of the place in its entirety in person, as opposed to seeing only small frames of it pieced together across distance.

The rutted and potholed parking lot in front of the hotel had been replaced with smooth, black asphalt. Tori drove into it from the main road and pulled up to the façade of the building, sitting in her car to take in the view for a moment in the air conditioning. The light of the sun reflected off the new, smooth stucco in a way that made the building seem like a white block of pure light in the middle of the desert plain. Extending from the terracotta roof tiles on the front was a large porch with exposed, dark wood crossbeams. The porch rested on smooth wood support posts and was surrounded by railing of the same wood. An expansive set of stone masonry steps led up to the porch and to the large, dark set of heavy doors flanked by windows that comprised the front entrance. Along the building on both sides of the porch were large windows of tinted glass—enough to block the heat of the sun but not to block all the natural light.

Tori turned off the ignition and stepped out of her car, the dry desert heat hitting her face like a blast furnace. She stepped up onto the porch, feeling the immediate coolness under its shade. She looked down at the stone tiles, liking the way they felt and sounded under her boots. She ran her hands along the wood railing and the support posts, enjoying their smoothness on her palms and fingers. She turned to look out over the parking lot and the six or so acres between it and the main road. *Cedars*, she thought. *That's what needs to flank the road entrance on both sides.*

The front doors were unlocked, so she went in, pushed her sunglasses onto her head and waited a few moments for her eyes to adjust. The lobby walls were of the same stucco as the exterior, and the dark beams in the ceiling and along the walls were exposed just as on the porch outside. The large check-in desk from the old hotel remained in place, but had been repaired and refurbished into a lustrous, chocolate shine. Instead of tiles, the floor was concrete, stained and polished into the color of black walnut with swirls of caramel and gold. On either side of the check-in desk were glass doors that led to the outside. Tori went through the left side door that opened out onto the covered walkway that stretched the entire length of the left wing of the building. She took a few steps and stopped, observing all the activity. As she had pulled up, she had seen Eugene only briefly before he had disappeared from her view behind the far end of this wing of the building. Now, she saw him again, standing in the open doorway of one of the twelve rooms that lined the entire left wing. She heard hammering, sawing and sanding coming from seemingly all directions, including from the individual rooms. Eugene stood observing a crewman cutting pieces of drywall and another man preparing a set of bathroom cabinets for installation. He turned and saw Tori, turned back to the men and made a few comments, then started down the walkway toward her. He smiled as he neared her.

"Tori, it's nice to meet you in person finally!" He shook her hand vigorously. "I hope the drive wasn't too bad."

"The drive was fine, Eugene. I'm glad to meet you in person, too." She gestured toward all the work going on and on the scene as a whole. "This looks fantastic! I'm so pleased with the front entrance and how it's all coming together. The stucco is so fresh and bright in the sun! It's beautiful."

"Yes, I'm pleased with it all, too. I'm glad you like it." He turned to look back down the walkway toward the crew he had just left, and turned back to Tori. "Here, let me take you over to the west wing to see the layout over there." He pointed her to the patio area that butted up against the outside of the wall whose interior was the check-in desk. They made their way across the patio, stepping over two men on their knees smoothing the concrete with electric hand sanders. They wore masks over their nose and mouth, and bright yellow kneepads. One of them nodded in greeting as she passed. They came to the covered walkway that stretched the entire length of the west wing, matching the one on the east wing. They turned toward their right, re-entering the entrance lobby through the glass door opposite the one Tori had come from. They made an immediate left turn and walked into and through three large rooms with big windows. The floors were raw concrete that had yet to be stained. Capped electric wires hung from the ceiling where light fixtures and ceiling fans would go. Eugene stood in the middle of the third room and turned to Tori.

"These are meeting rooms or common rooms—we've obviously still got to do the floors and I'll probably put another coat of sealer on the stucco, just like I did in the lobby." He turned and walked through a large open doorway on the opposite end of the room. Tori followed him and realized she had walked into the kitchen.

"Here's where I need your chef's help. We have the basic layout of the kitchen from the plans, but I want specifics from her in terms of the appliances and counters so I can position the outlets at the right height, put the vent hoods in the right places, etc." He scanned the ceiling and the walls as he spoke. "We're putting industrial stone tile in here instead of leaving the concrete. Believe it or not, it's easier on the kitchen people's feet and knees than straight concrete."

"Elena should be here any minute," Tori said as she surveyed the room. "Those are for the walk-ins, right?" She pointed to two large blocks of space, facing each other along the back wall, bricked off from the rest of the room.

Eugene nodded. "Yes, they'll fit right into those spaces. I've already cleared that with the manufacturer, to make sure the space is adequate. And by bricking in the space, you'll save on the electric bill to cool them—it helps insulate them better. The wiring's already in. One will be a cooler, the other a freezer. It's big enough to hang a few deer in it at once, plus store others on racks if you need to. You can load in through that metal door on the wall between them—it takes you straight outside. That way you aren't tracking supplies through the front lobby or the courtyard. Do you want me to pour a service entrance driveway around this side of the building that turns off from the main parking lot or the entrance drive?" He paused for a moment before adding "I think it'd be a good idea. A nice touch that keeps operations out of view of the guests."

"I think that's a great idea. That's not in the architect's plans?" Tori asked.

"No, it's not…well, I think it is, but the intention was for it to be a gravel road, so it's technically not part of the build-out. But, I think it'd look better and would be more useful if it were an asphalt road just like the entrance drive and the parking lot."

Tori nodded. "You're right, Eugene. Thanks for thinking about it. Will you draw up a simple plan for it with a budget amendment and reliable measurements and send it to the architect? I want them to add it to the master plan, just to be thorough."

"Sure thing." He turned to continue down the wing, going across the large kitchen and through a large door into the final room of the wing. "The dining room," he said simply.

Tori stepped into the center of the room and looked around her. The three walls that comprised the end of the wing were mostly windows, which gave the entire room an expansive view of the courtyard in between the wings as well as the desert area beyond which extended south to the edge of the gorge and then to the mesas and mountains behind it. Large glass double doors opened from the southernmost back wall onto a small patio area for outside dining. A large stone fireplace took up the southwest corner of the room. In another corner, a crewman worked on installing a bar cabinet of dark wood. Dark wood shelves with slots for wine bottles and other bar accessories had already been installed, the plastic still covering them to keep out the construction dust.

Tori looked through the large floor-to-ceiling windows into the courtyard. A few workmen were installing a large fountain in the center of the courtyard between the two wings, and others were laying the thick metal meshing for meandering sidewalks that would wind from the building through the courtyard, around the fountain and other decorative elements, and out to the pool area and other sitting areas south of the wings. She smiled and nodded slowly as she took in everything she saw, both in the room and outside in the courtyard and beyond. She turned to Eugene.

"This is fantastic, Eugene. I'm really happy. Thank you." She reached out to shake his hand, to formally acknowledge her endorsement of his work and her gratitude for it. She felt his callous, firm hand in her own.

"You're welcome, Tori," he replied, patting her arm after shaking her hand. "It's a pleasure to do this job for you. I really like your vision for it and am happy to be a part of it." They both stood for a moment watching the men struggle to position the large concrete fountain into the proper position.

"Hello," a voice called from behind them in the kitchen or living area. "Tori? Eugene?" They both turned and glimpsed the dark ponytail of someone in the kitchen area who disappeared from their view in the direction of the bricked areas for the coolers.

"Hi—we're here!" Tori called and began walking back toward the kitchen. Eugene followed her. As they entered, Elena turned, met Tori's eyes first, smiled and took a few steps toward her. Tori smiled broadly and met her in the middle of the kitchen and, without thinking, reached out to hug her. She felt Elena's cheek against hers as well as one of Elena's arms as it encircled her waist. She felt Elena's fingers slip under the hem of her shirt and splay across the skin of her lower back. Elena kissed her cheek beside her ear lightly as she pulled away, but did not meet Tori's eyes. Instead she turned directly to Eugene to greet him.

"Hi, I'm Elena Rios—you must be Eugene," she said, extending her hand and drawing close to him in a familiar and friendly way.

"Nice to meet you, Elena. Thanks for coming out here." He smiled warmly at her, then at Tori. "I was just showing Tori around and I mentioned to her that I needed your help in this kitchen to be sure to finish it out in a way that would work for your preferences." Tori listened to Eugene but looked at Elena. Her black ponytail was pulled high and tight, revealing the smooth, brown skin of her forehead and cheeks. Dangly beaded earrings swung against her neck. Her sunglasses hung folded in the V of the neck of her shirt, pulling it down into a sharp point. Her usual black t-shirt had been replaced with a white one that fit snuggly around her breasts and draped loosely over the top of her jeans. She wore black leather sandals that displayed her metallic green painted toenails. Tori was gazing at Elena's legs when she realized the conversation had stopped. She looked up to see Elena and Eugene looking at her expectantly. Elena grinned and then glanced away toward the cooler area.

"I'm going to walk down toward the gorge. Why don't the two of you just take care of whatever you need to take care of," she said and stepped away from them toward the big door space that led to the dining room.

"Okay, I'll come get you if we have questions or anything." Eugene said. Elena was still grinning and Tori felt her eyes on her as she moved out of the room. She glanced back to catch Elena's eyes for a second before Elena turned her attention to Eugene and the issue of the appliances.

Tori put on her sunglasses and walked through one of the double doors at the end of the wing that was propped open to allow a breeze to ventilate the building. She stepped out from the shade of the overhang and felt the heat of the sun on her face, which helped to mask the slight flush she had felt in Elena's presence. Without consciously thinking to do it, she reached her hand back under her shirttail to touch the skin of her back that Elena's fingers had caressed. She smiled as she remembered the feeling, picking her way through the construction piles surrounding the building until she found the small animal trail that led to the gorge.

Tori had sensed a connection between them the first time they had spent significant time together, which was the night she had had gone to Elena's for dinner after coffee with Ken and Hazel. Tori found Elena attractive from the minute she had first met her that day months ago with Ken in the restaurant at lunch. By the time she went to Elena's for dinner that night weeks later, she had already become drawn to Elena as a professional who could help her with Sandy Creek. She had been a bit surprised when Elena seemed to be drawn to her as well. Tori could sense it in the way she looked at her as she refilled her wine glass, or the way she complimented Tori's picture in the magazine. They talked only a bit about their personal backgrounds that night, though, at least not more than the basics. Tori did not know if Elena had had relationships with women before or if she were even open to such a thing. But, she had detected interest from her nonetheless. She was not sure what to do about it, if anything.

She usually did not mix business with pleasure. Not once had she dated anyone she worked with, not even someone who was a peer and who worked for a different company. She had always been so focused on work projects that relationships of any kind suffered under the strain. Also, while plenty of men who were her business peers expressed interest in her, not many women had done so, mainly because there weren't many women at her level. When Vincent's company worked with other companies that were headed or managed by women, usually the women were married or straight. So, it had never been an issue for Tori and she was not quite sure how to proceed now with Elena. She figured it was probably best to set it aside for the sake of working together. Plus, she remembered something Ken had mentioned about Elena having a longtime connection with a man, Luis, which stretched back to high school. *Probably best to set it aside*, she thought.

She reached the edge of the gorge and looked out across it. Movement on her right caught her eye and she turned in time to see the white tails of several deer as they bounded through the brush away from her. They disappeared down the incline of the gorge and into the shadow formed where the top edge of the gorge cut off the sun shining from the west. Tori took off her sunglasses and squinted into the shadow, to see if she could still pick them out, but they were gone or invisible. She put her sunglasses back on and turned to face the southeastern mesas across the gorge that gleamed and shimmered in the rays of heat from the sun. She imagined the wild game that lived in them and beyond—the doves, quail, and deer that made the desert their home. People had lived in this area for thousands of years. Ken had pointed out petroglyphs under a cliff on the side of a high rock wall as they had stood in a creek bed a few hundred yards off the gravel road. She had looked at them through binoculars, picking out the crude shapes of animals and other symbols. Those people had lived in this desert and hunted the animals that lived there with them. She looked down at the stones and sand between her feet. She shifted her boots, sinking them further down into the sand. She looked back across the mesas and took in a deep breath of the clean, hot air. She and everything she was building on this land would be only the latest of numerous, even ancient human habitations that had been erected here. She vowed to remember that fact as she continued her work, welcomed her guests, and hunted the animals that lived and thrived there, as had their animal ancestors.

She noticed that the thin animal trail that led from the hotel to the gorge did not end at the lip of the gorge. It continued over the rim between rocks and around clumps of shrubs for about twenty-five yards down the gorge at a place where the incline was relatively shallow compared to the drop of the rest of it. Tori took a few steps down the trail, spreading her legs and holding her arms for balance on the angle. She picked her way around rocks and brush, following the thin trail until it stopped on a flat, sunken rock about four feet wide. The trail continued downward from under the rock but it was too steep for Tori. She stood on the flat rock and turned back. Her head was just below the level of the top edge of the gorge. In an hour or so, the gorge's wall would block the sun and her whole body would be in the shade. At the moment, only her legs from the thighs down were shaded. She stooped to sit down on the rock, swinging her legs off its edge and facing out into the gorge. She immediately felt the coolness on her back and head and they dipped into the shade. She took off her sunglasses and wiped her eyes and forehead with her sleeved shoulder. She sat still for a moment, resting in the silence and coolness. The gorge wall had blocked any remaining sounds from the construction site. She could hear nothing, really, not even any wind in the brush. The silence was almost palpable.

Suddenly, a pebble bounded down the incline of the gorge a few yards to her right. She turned to see if an animal had dislodged it or if perhaps she was in the path of rocks that were beginning a slide down the slope. She saw the silhouette of a slight figure standing at the rim of the gorge. She squinted and then put on her glasses. It was Elena, who waved and began to step slowly down the path toward Tori.

Tori watched her as she picked her way through the rocks and then put her sandaled feet onto the flat rock on which Tori sat. Without thinking, Tori rested her hand on Elena's foot beside her and looked up at her, still squinting since the top part of Elena's body was silhouetted against the sun.

"Scoot over," Elena said. Tori moved to the left to make room on the rock. Elena bent down, placed one hand on Tori's right shoulder for balance and her other hand on the rock's flat surface, and lowered herself onto the rock beside Tori. Tori watched her as she looked out across the gorge. "Nice view," she said and turned to Tori, taking off her sunglasses and putting them in the V of her shirt. "And nice that it's in the shade."

Tori nodded and looked out over the gorge. "Yeah, I just found this spot today. I followed the animal trail that leads from the hotel to here." She pointed behind her. "It goes all the way down, I guess, but this is as far as I got." She peered down below her feet and legs to the sharp incline that led to the bottom of the creek bed. "I saw deer over there when I first walked up to the edge. Several of them." She looked past Elena and pointed to the right where she had seen the herd disappear into the shadow. Elena looked in the direction where she pointed then turned back to Tori.

"Did you and Eugene get squared away?" Tori asked, trying not to be distracted by the sway of the earring against the brown skin of Elena's neck.

Elena nodded and swung her legs hanging off the cliff of the rock. "Yes, we did. He already had it pretty much figured out—there weren't any corrections I needed to make really. Just a few outlet placements and some drainage. He's going to put in an extra drain hole between those two walk-ins. It'll make it easier to mop and keep clean, since that'll be a loading area of sorts." She looked at Tori. "It's really coming together nicely, don't you think? The whole place, I mean, not just the kitchen."

"Yeah, I'm really happy with it all. I really like the stucco. It's so bright and shining on the outside, but also on the inside. I think people will really like the feel of the place when it's all finished." She paused for a moment. "Eugene's doing a great job."

"Luis said he was good," Elena said. "He knows him from some of the guys he hunts with. Some of them have worked on crews for Eugene and they spoke really highly of him."

Tori waited for her to say something else about Luis, but Elena said nothing. Ken had spoken to her a few times about Luis, mainly as someone who could manage the hunting component of Sandy Creek. He was an avid hunter himself but, more importantly, he knew the desert landscape and how to hunt it in a way that preserved the overall ecosystem. He had hired himself out as a guide to various hunting ranches in the area several times over the years. Guiding was simply one of the various jobs he strung together throughout the year to make a living. Guiding, along with his work with the Border Patrol and his work with the county volunteer fire department, provided for him and for his mother when she had been alive, and kept him busy and at the center of things. He knew nearly everyone, and nearly everyone knew him and liked him. Ken had suggested to Tori that Luis would be a good overall manager of what Tori was calling Outdoor Operations, which included hunting, camping, and hiking. Plus, he had said, Luis has a good relationship, as he put it, with Elena, so the two of them would work well together.

"What are you doing for dinner tonight?" Elena asked.

"Probably eating leftovers or something at Stella's," Tori answered. She had made an arrangement with Stella that involved a long term lease of one of her bedrooms—the one Tori liked that had a door out onto the rocky yard with the cedar and the rabbit—and the addition to the room of some items that Tori bought and had delivered to Stella's door: a small refrigerator, a baker's rack, and a microwave, toaster oven and a coffee pot. That way, Tori could come and go as she pleased through her own door, and she could manage meals for herself without troubling Stella. Stella liked Tori and had been thrilled to have Tori as a long-term tenant.

"Why don't you come over and eat with us?" Elena asked. "Luis is bringing antelope steaks over for Mama and me. I'm cooking them in the outdoor fireplace. I'll tell him to bring an extra one."

Tori's stomach jumped a bit at the sound of Luis' name, and she immediately was surprised at her visceral reaction. *Calm down,* she told herself silently. *Set it aside. Especially if you plan to hire Luis.*

"It sounds like I would be intruding," she said. "I have stuff to eat at home." She heard herself call Stella's bedroom "home" and smiled. It was true. Already this place—Logan, Stella's, what was becoming Sandy Creek Ranch, this gorge, all of it—was starting to feel like home to her. She could hardly believe it, and figured it would fade when she returned to her highrise home in Houston in a few days.

"Don't be silly. I wouldn't invite you if you were intruding. Just come." Elena leaned over and bumped her shoulder playfully against Tori's. She smiled and looked into Tori's eyes, then at her lips, then back to her eyes. Tori felt her stomach jump again and willed it to stop.

"Okay, that sounds great. I've wanted to meet Luis anyway. I've heard a lot of good things about him," she said. "Shall I bring some wine? I have some at home."

"Sure, that would be great." Elena paused for a moment, looking directly at Tori as if wanting to say something, but then suddenly turned, braced her hand again on Tori's shoulder and got up. She extended her hand to Tori and helped her up, and they both turned to make their way back up the trail. They walked silently back to the hotel, watching the crew men finishing up their various jobs as they got closer to the building site. The fountain was set firmly in its place. The sidewalks that meandered through the courtyard were framed and lined with metal meshing, ready for the concrete that would come in the morning. They walked around the west wing, past where the kitchen's loading door would be installed and the service entrance paved, and on to the front where Elena's silver Tahoe was parked next to Tori's car.

Tori stopped in the parking lot and turned to face the hotel entrance again. She scanned the façade of the building, taking in all the details again, smiling and nodding faintly. Elena stood beside her and looked it all over as well.

"It's really nice, Tori," she said.

Tori looked at her and grinned, then looked back at the building. "Yeah, I think so too. I'm really happy with it." She suddenly turned to Elena. "Okay, so what time? I've got some emails to do back at Stella's then I'll come."

"Whenever you get done with your emails. Just come. Or, we have wireless at the house now. Come now and bring your laptop."

"Okay, then. See you in a bit."

❧

Elena answered the door with a magazine in her hand and a pencil over her ear. Tori stepped over Rico, who was lounging on the rug inside the front door, and stepped into the living room.

"Come in," she said. "I'm just doing some research on game meats. Would you like some tea or coffee?" She rubbed her bare foot across Rico's exposed furry stomach, and headed toward the kitchen.

"Sure, whatever you're having," she followed Elena to the kitchen table and sat the wine bottle down. "What are you learning about game meats?"

"Well, I'm learning that people don't think they like them. So you have to pair them with things they do like in order to get them to eat it." She put on a kettle of water and handed the magazine to Tori, pointing to an article about venison. "Also, most people haven't eaten them very much, so they really have no idea about them. In short, people don't really know anything about game meats, yet they have strong feelings about them. It's a wonderful challenge." She smiled brightly.

"When I was a kid, we ate most everything fried, except maybe for the dove meat, which we sometimes grilled," Tori said. "There are plenty of other ways to cook it all, I'm sure."

"Yeah, although fried is good. People like fried. Grilled is also good. I think the key will be complimentary flavors through marinades, seasonings, side dishes, and other such things. Don't worry—I'll figure something out."

"I'm not worried. I have complete faith in you, or else I wouldn't have asked you to partner with me on this." Tori smiled back at her.

Elena turned and looked through the living room window to see Luis' truck pull into the gravel driveway behind Tori's car. She walked toward the front door, slid the rug off to the side with Rico still on it, and opened the front door. Tori watched as Luis came up the stairs and, as Elena held the screen door open for him, leaned down to kiss her cheek. "Hey," he said quietly to her as he pulled back. "Hey yourself," she replied, smiling slightly and then stepping aside so Luis could pass through the doorway. He walked through the living room toward the kitchen, Elena following behind in bare feet.

"You must be Tori," he said and put out his hand. "I'm glad to finally meet you after hearing so much about you from Elena and Ken." He laid a package wrapped in butcher paper on the counter and turned to Elena.

"We were just going over some menu ideas, and I was making water for tea. Would you like some?" Elena moved toward the stove.

"Sure," he said. He pulled out a chair at the kitchen table and sat down. "Where's Gloria?"

"She's soaking in the bath. Her back was hurting. She'll be out in a little while." Luis' smile disappeared for a moment and he looked at Elena.

"Is she ok?" he asked.

"Yeah, she's fine. Don't worry." She sat cups with tea bags down in front of both Luis and Tori. "She just feels achy in her lower back sometimes now. A hot soaking bath usually helps." She returned to the counter and began unrolling the butcher paper.

She peeled away the last layer to reveal several thick cuts of burgundy colored meat. She spread them out on the paper. "These are really pretty, Luis. Very lean." She turned and smiled at him.

"Yeah, they're from an antelope Ricardo got this past season. I've eaten some of the steaks already. It's really good."

Elena got a bowl, filled it with cold water and dropped the steaks into it to soak some of the blood out of the meat. "This is a key concept in cooking red game meats," she said to Tori, pointing at the bowl. "Rinsing some of the blood out removes any gamey taste—or what people typically think of as a gamey taste. There's still plenty of flavor left in the meat, especially when it's lean like this. It's very rich."

Tori nodded and raised her eyebrows. "Good to know. So how will you cook it?"

"I think grilled. Open flame is so good on cuts like this." She put her hand into the bowl and stirred the meat, squeezing it a bit.

"You want me to start a fire in the chiminea outside?" Luis asked.

"No, it's too hot, now that I think about it. There's a little propane grill outside on the porch. I'll use that." The water began to boil, so she removed the kettle and poured water into their cups as well as into a cup of her own. She sat down at the table with them.

"So, how are things going out at your building site? It seems like the work is really coming along out there." Luis looked at Tori and smiled. He slid his chair toward Elena's and sat back in it, crossing one leg over the other, resting his arm casually across the back of Elena's chair and cupping his hand around Elena's shoulder. Elena leaned forward to pull her ponytail out from under his arm, and sat back.

Tori looked at her tea bag, bounced it up and down in the cup and then let it sit. "Yes, things are coming along well," she said, looking back at Luis. "Eugene Brooks is really good at keeping things on schedule, and we don't have many weather delays out here in this part of the state like we do in Houston."

Luis listened intently as Tori told him all about the construction. He asked questions which indicated to her that he knew his way around a construction site and also that he respected her as someone who knew her business. She liked his easy, conversational manner and the way in which he seemed comfortable in his own skin. His eyes were clear and his smile was disarming. She saw quickly why everyone in town not only knew him but also liked him, including Elena. Elena seemed relaxed and comfortable sitting next to him with his arm around her shoulder. She smiled when he made a joke or said something funny, and seemed very interested in his comments and questions about things. At one point, while Luis was commenting about the different colors of stucco, Elena reached out and, with her thumbnail, scraped some dried dirt off the exposed heel of the boot on his crossed leg. She cupped her other hand below it to catch the falling dirt, then leaned over toward the stove to drop it into the trashcan.

After a while, Gloria joined them in the kitchen, smelling of lavender from her bath. She smiled and extended a thin arm to Tori to shake her hand.

"I'm happy to see you Ms. Rios," Tori said, taking the soft, frail hand into her own. "I hope you feel better after your bath."

Luis pulled out another chair and held it as Gloria eased herself down into it. She smiled up at Luis as he sat back down in his chair beside Elena. She turned back to Tori. "I feel okay. My back was a little sore today, that's all."

"Mama, would you like some tea?" Elena stood.

"Yes, *mija*, that would be nice." She fanned her hands out on the table, as if steadying herself even as she sat in her chair. She smiled at them all, passing her gaze from one to the other. Tori thought she looked as if she were either committing their faces to memory, or trying hard to remember who they were. Her smile seemed genuine, but also slightly vacant and frozen. Tori wondered if perhaps she were on painkillers that created such a look on her face.

Elena sat a cup down in front of her mother and poured the water over the tea bag inside it. Gloria stared down at the steaming water, still smiling, and circled her thin brown fingers around the cup as if to warm herself, despite the heat outside. "Mama, Tori was just telling Luis all about the new ranch. We were also talking about the menus I'm planning for the restaurant out there."

Gloria looked back up at them. "That's so nice, *mija*. You are such a good cook." She turned to Tori. "What is the name of the ranch?"

"Sandy Creek Ranch. It's named after my uncle who lived out here and owned the land before he died."

"Ah, yes. I remember Elena telling me about your uncle. I knew him from the school. He always helped out with the kids and sports and all." Gloria's face was still frozen into a smile, but her words made perfect sense. She listened closely as Tori told the story of Uncle Sandy, the times she had spent in Logan visiting him with her parents as a child, and how she thought he would be happy with her plans for his land that he entrusted with her.

"I'm sure he would be very proud of you, " Gloria said when Tori paused in her story. "He must have loved you a lot."

"I think he did. I loved him a lot." Tori looked into Gloria's watery brown eyes and immediately felt how hard it must be for Elena to see her mother slowly slide toward death. Tori had lost both her parents suddenly in a car accident, which had been devastating for its unexpectedness and violence. But after she had gotten over the initial waves of shock and anger, and worked her way through much of the grief, she managed to feel thankful that her parents had not suffered the humiliations of old age—the gradual decline into decrepitude and sickness. They had been spared the seemingly endless doctor visits, procedures, pill regimens and the slow, but definitive march toward dependency and confusion. She, of course, would pay any amount of money in the world to have just one afternoon with them again—alive and vibrant as she remembered them the last time she saw them, just a few days before they were killed, when she drove away from their beach house in Galveston on her way back to Houston. They stood in the driveway in their shorts and t-shirts, wearing their big matching sunglasses, waving to her as she pulled away. They loved her and had given her the best of everything they had, and they were proud of her for all she had accomplished. She loved them and was glad to see them finally enjoying themselves in retirement after years of hard work. She missed them so much some days. She had lost them early—far earlier than anyone expected or wanted—and she felt that loss regularly and deeply. But she was glad they had been spared the indignities of old age. She was glad she would never see her parents as she now saw Gloria across the table from her—still holding on for now to some semblance of herself, but losing the battle slowly and inexorably.

"Your uncle was a good man," Luis said. "Everyone liked him. I hunted with him a few times out on his land. Out on your land. When I was a kid and after I got older."

"Thank you for saying that. I've heard good things from several people out here about him." She took a sip from her tea. "Speaking of hunting…I want to talk with you about something, Luis." Elena got up to drain the bloody water from the meat bowl and fill it with fresh water.

"I am lucky to have come to Logan at a time when a first class executive chef happened to be living here." She grinned and they all turned to look at Elena, who smiled faintly but kept her eyes focused on squeezing blood from the antelope meat.

"What I need now is to find someone with equal talent in the hunting, outfitting and game management area. Basically, I need someone to manage the outdoor operations part of Sandy Creek Ranch. Are you up for it, or do you know anyone out here who is?" She looked directly into Luis' eyes in the way she always did when she discussed business.

Luis raised his eyebrows in surprise. He uncrossed his leg and leaned forward in his chair. "Well, I'm flattered that you ask. What does the job entail?"

She explained the job in a nutshell—managing and guiding all the hunts, outfitting the guests with the equipment they needed both for the hunt and for the semi-camping situations during the day-long hunts, making sure all state and federal laws were obeyed, establishing hiking trails near the lodge that would not be in conflict with hunters, managing the game populations on the ranch, setting up photography stations in active wildlife areas for people who shot with a camera instead of a gun, working with state experts to make sure the habitat was properly cared for so that the animals continued to thrive, and so on. Much of the work would happen before the first guest even arrived. In fact, Tori said, she wanted the outdoor operations manager to begin as soon as possible to work on trails, campsites, photography stations and wildlife management.

Luis sat back and took it all in. He listened intently to Tori, thoughtfully nodding as she went through the list of all the duties. Elena stood at the counter, squeezing and stirring the antelope meat, looking down into the water.

"That sounds like a good job for you," Gloria said, looking at Luis. "You and Elena could work together."

In that statement, Gloria said aloud what both Elena and Luis had been thinking—that this was working out exactly according to plan, at least according to Luis' and Gloria's plan. Elena did not share their plan, but she knew that Luis would do a good job and Tori was smart to ask him to do it.

"I imagine that it's somewhat seasonal, but not completely— given that hunting seasons run only certain times of the year. Of course there's work to be done in the off-season," Luis said.

"True, there's a seasonal component to it. Although, my plan is to develop a menu of outdoor activities, in addition to hunting—like hiking and photography—that can operate year-round. I don't want the resort to have to close down during the off-season, certainly not the restaurant. " She turned to Elena. "I'd like the restaurant to be a regional, year-round attraction for fine dining in the evenings, at least on a Thursday, Friday Saturday schedule—if not more."

Elena looked up from the bowl. "That makes sense. If we're going to invest as much as you are in the kitchen, we might as well make it work for a larger clientele than simply those who come to the resort. People are used to driving long distances out here. People would drive forty-five minutes to an hour for a nice dinner. Also, lots of people travel through here—we could pull the more high-end tourist traffic into one or two-night stays, especially in the off-season when rooms aren't taken up with hunters paying premium prices."

"Exactly," Tori said, loving that Elena so naturally saw the market possibilities for the ranch and, even more, enjoying in that moment the act of brainstorming with her. She felt herself enlivened by the idea of it all again, as she did on a regular basis. "Exactly! That's the regional tourism angle on it all." She turned back to Luis.

Luis smiled and looked back and forth between her and Elena. "Well, I'm certainly interested. Can I think about it a few days and get back to you?"

"Of course," Tori said. "In fact, why don't I draw up a more formal offer and job description and give it to you. That way, you can really consider it."

Gloria looked between them, then back at Luis. "You don't need a job description, Luis. You know that this is good for you." She smiled serenely at him, speaking to him as a friend but also as if she were his mother. Luis looked down at the floor and back up at Gloria.

"You're probably right," he said simply. He turned to Tori, then to Elena, then back to Tori. "Why don't we just agree that I'll do it starting the first of next month. In the meantime, I'll send you a resume and you write up the offer and description. We can talk again if anything seems problematic either way. I doubt it will, though."

Tori held up her teacup toward Luis. "That sounds fine with me. To the deal…" she said as Luis held up his cup and clinked it against Tori's. They both smiled and drank a sip from their cups, looking at each other over the rim.

Elena watched them, and then reached for the bottle of wine that Tori brought. "How about something a little more official?" she asked, holding up the bottle and reaching for a wineglass from the cabinet. "It's past five o'clock."

# Chapter Eight

Tori sat on a low rock in the brush about forty yards from the edge of the water. It was an hour or more before sunset. The water hole was no more than a shallow flat of water about eight feet wide, fifty feet long, and a few inches deep but it was the only water for a mile or more and was surrounded by clear sandy banks a dozen yards away from the nearest bush or shrub. It was the perfect place for doves and quail to water in the mornings and evenings, which is exactly what Luis and Ricardo had in mind when they built it. The Texas Parks and Wildlife people had told them to focus on water. Everything in the desert needs water—if you provide that, the animals will stay in the area. They will be able to thrive and raise their young.

A tall windmill stood a hundred yards away from the pond, pumping water from deep in the earth with every turn of the blades. The water ran from the windmill to the pond through a long, thin pipe that ran a few inches from the ground, braced by rocks and stones, covered in brush, and painted the color of the sand. The water dripped from the pipe into the pond in a thin, sporadic stream, creating small ripples across the pond's surface. Tori watched a few thin clouds move as reflections across the water. The sky began its turn from bright blue to yellow and pink and orange as the sun made its way down to meet the horizon.

One by one, they began coming. Whitewing doves and mourning doves. An entire covey of quail. A herd of four mule deer, their large donkey-like ears erect to detect the slightest noise. A javelina, short and squat, the thick bristles on its face grimy with dirt. They all came to the water to drink, to step their hooves or feet into the dampness. The low-slung doves eased their way to the very edge, seemingly staring at their own reflections in the water, turning their heads from side to side before curving their necks to drink like dogs. The quail, deer and javelina came on foot, but the doves came through the air. First as singles or pairs, then as threes and fours. Then as a cascade of wings and feathers, the bright white bands on their wings shining in the late sun as they fluttered and landed, and fluffed and arranged before waddling to the water. Hundreds of birds came in the last minutes before sunset. Tori stopped counting at a dozen flocks, each with a hundred birds or more.

*This will do well*, she thought. *Quite well.*

The first guests would arrive at Sandy Creek Ranch on Friday for the opening weekend of dove season. All the guest rooms were booked. Tori smiled at the thought of them seeing the huge flock of birds and going back to the lodge, tired and hungry from the heat, with their limits of fresh meat.

Eugene Brooks had been true to his word. All the construction was completed and ready for business by the middle of September, just a week ago. The furniture had arrived in large trucks—beds, dressers, couches, chairs, mirrors, tables, vases. The kitchen appliances were installed. Linens, tableware, glassware for the dining room as well as the bar—all of it had arrived and was ready for use. Everyone was jumping in and doing what needed to be done, including Tori, who for the time being was taking the role of general manager in addition to owner. Elena and Letty, the young waitress who had waited on Ken and Tori at Galindo's and who was a quick study in the kitchen, were busy writing out menus and procedures, and organizing inventory which was already arriving. Betty Terrell moved among all the guest rooms, setting them up with linens, toiletries, alarm clocks and coffee pots. She had already arranged the living room area, the courtyard and the pool area. Betty was a friend of Hazel's in Austin. Her husband had died just a few years before retirement and Betty had struggled with sadness, so Hazel had talked her into moving to Logan indefinitely just for a change of pace and to spend time with her old friend. She was the first person Hazel thought of when Tori asked her if she knew anyone who could be a front desk person and general "take care of things or find the one who can" person for the ranch. Luis and his assistant, his young cousin Ricardo, spent their days out on the land clearing roads and trails, building water containment areas, and repairing the few old windmills that had collapsed years ago, their wooden beams long since turned to desert dust. Luis had been ecstatic the day he had come to tell Tori that he and Ricardo had found not only two old windmills, but also two wellheads to which they were attached. A week later, the wellheads were primed and ready to pump water again.

Water is life in the desert, and Tori made sure that Sandy Creek Ranch made ample use of it in terms of establishing not only a thriving habitat for the animals, but also in creating a soothing, cooling space for the human guests. The courtyard fountain was a shallow pool of water out of which rose a concrete pillar that stood seven feet tall comprised of three layers of bird baths, each smaller than the one below it. A small spout of water shot from the very top of the spindle and cascaded down into the shallow dishes beneath them, overflowing their edges and falling further until all the water landed in the pool below, which was lined with brightly colored and mirrored tile pieces. The sound of the fountain permeated the entire courtyard, ricocheting off the glass and stucco of both facing wings, and extending even out to the sitting area and the pool and jacuzzi patio to the south. Betty could hear the fountain while she worked at the front desk. Elena could hear it in the kitchen, especially if the glass doors to the dining room or living room were open. Guests could hear it from their rooms if they left their doors or windows open. In a way, the entire hotel seemed to be oriented around the fountain, instead of the fountain being ornamentation for the hotel. All the sidewalks meandered back to the fountain, as well as all the landscaped beds that lined them. Mist from the fountain drifted onto the cactus, prickly pear, sage and desert rose plants that now grew in the beds, swelling their stems and leaves as they absorbed every molecule of the moisture.

From the courtyard, a landscaped sidewalk led to the swimming pool and jacuzzi patio. The pool was designed like a lagoon or a *cenote*. Its water was dark blue, giving the illusion of great depth even though it was only five feet deep. Its perimeter was lined in natural rocks from the desert—long, flat rocks in multicolors of beige, brown, rust, and gray. Sage and yucca plants rose from the rock clusters, especially at the dominant end of the pool where large boulders formed a structure of more than fifteen feet from which a waterfall descended into the pool, rushing its way through the crevices and cracks in the rocks as it fell. The jacuzzi sat across the patio from the pool and was designed in the same theme except without the large boulders and the waterfall. The jacuzzi's external walls were made of natural rock, and raised beds of desert sand that held various plants and flowers circled its rim. Both the pool and the jacuzzi were excellent vantage points from which to view the desert, either from the cold water of the pool on a hot day, or from the hot water of the jacuzzi on a cold night when the sky nearly vibrated with bands of stars.

In every way, the ranch reflected both its owners: the desert and Tori. Its colors and hues, its materials of stucco and stone and wood were all derived from the desert floor on which it stood. Its amenities of water, beautiful landscaping and, yes, even the food—the meat of animals who lived and thrived in the sand, gorges, draws and grassy plains within ten miles of the building—were reflections of the desert biosphere. And as every day passed that the new wood became slightly more faded from the sun, and the fresh stucco became harder from the heat, the desert climate reflected the fact that, sooner or later, all things return to the dust from which they came. Tori felt this deep within herself—this deep connection to the sand and the mesas and the rocks—that somehow she had come from it and had now returned to it. She felt it the first time she visited, but had not been able to identify it. Now, after months spent in the desert's embrace, she understood. She acknowledged its supremacy, its sharp power and its sparse elegance. These lands were not southern gardens draped in azalea and kudzu, reeking of sweetness from jasmine and magnolia, and bedded in soft grasses so green the blades seemed black. They were not high plains mountains crested in aspen and birch and pine, inhabited by odd-eyed birds and tufted mammals that crawled among firs, building their nests amidst snowdrifts and thickets. This was the desert, where everything was sand, rock or thorn—or a variation of such. Plants' leaves were shaped like blades, and could cut like them. Rock edges could sever a boot shank or a vein. Flowers with petals as delicate as foam powered themselves up through the hard dirt and rock, defied the scorching and maiming heat, and soaked up through their roots even the memory of moisture. Animals with soft underbellies as tender as those of their counterparts who walked on carpeted forests, scraped and scrabbled about on the hot sand and sharp rocks, picking their way through thorns and sharp leaves, finding food and moisture in a landscape that seemed bereft of both.

The ranch reflected these realities and, in this, the ranch reflected its other owner, the woman who had overseen the choice of every detail of its construction. Its rustic simplicity was a reflection of her own unvarnished elegance which was as much on display when she wore the jeans and boots of a ranch owner as when she wore the silk and heels of an urban executive. Everything about the place felt luxurious yet supremely simple. After all, nothing is more simple than good food after a day of hunting for meat, a cold pool after a hot walk in the desert, or a soft bed with the sound of running water wafting through an open window after a day of exertion in the field. Tori combined years of experience in hospitality with her deep, newfound kinship to the desert into a place she felt contained her deepest aspirations and beliefs, not only as a professional but as human being. She believed in the human capacity to enjoy the earth and its bounty. She believed in the endeavor to create islands of civilization within the larger wilds of the planet. She believed in living in a way that was mindful of the source of human life—the earth and the sun. She believed in knowing where meat came from, so that from the first bite into succulent flesh, one felt gratitude and blessing from the animal whose sacrifice allowed it. And she believed that life needed little embellishment to be good. What mattered and gave life its sweetness was connection and relationship—with the natural world and with other people. Every place she had ever built contained these principles to some extent or the other, but none to the degree to which Sandy Creek Ranch did. This ranch was Tori Reed in stucco, wood, concrete and water. She designed it that way and felt its life-breath as if it were her own.

Sitting there watching the whitewing doves drink, she felt her breathing quicken with every new flock. She felt waves of gratitude wash over her—gratitude for her uncle who had left her his land, for Ken and Hazel who had welcomed her to Logan and who felt almost like parents to her, for all the others who had helped in the building, for the guests who would come, and for the animals who would live and die within the purview of the ranch and its activities.

And for Elena. She had worked with all sorts of executive chefs and foodies over the years; most of them were highly talented and worked hard, and she appreciated their contributions to the projects for which she was responsible. None of them, however, had seemed to "get it" like Elena. From the beginning, Elena had seemed to grasp the entire vision of Sandy Creek Ranch even before Tori herself had hashed out all the details. Sometimes, as she would share a new idea or inspiration for some part of the ranch with Elena, Elena would listen, smile and nod, as if she already knew it or had been shown it in a dream or vision, and was simply waiting for Tori to see it and put it into words. Maybe it was because she was from Logan and, despite having left for a long time, she had the desert and its rhythms and textures in her blood. Maybe it was because she was spooky good at her work, the way Tori was. Whatever the reason, Tori had come to rely on Elena as a tuning fork who confirmed the perfect pitch of the ranch and, in doing so, helped and guided Tori in keeping it all in tune.

It helped that they were beginning to love one another. It had begun in the afternoons at Elena's house after she finished at Galindo's, when they would sit together working on menus, drawing sketches of kitchens and dining spaces. And in the mornings on weekends when they would accompany Luis and Ricardo out into the field where, while they cleared roads and trails and built sun shelters and outdoor shower stalls, she and Elena tested out the field dining service. They tried out recipes, table configurations, and created semi-permanent campsites at certain accessible spots in the desert, in the shade of a rock wall or a line of willow trees along a dry creek bed. Some menus and dish ideas worked fantastically well. Other times, things did not work out as planned, like the day Elena scorched nearly everything she tried to cook on a camp stove with a broken temperature regulator. Or when someone forgot the cooking oil and they had to eat saltines and raw vegetables that day out in the field. Or when Tori accidentally poked the end of a knife sharpener into the side of the container that held the only drinking water they had, draining it all out before anyone noticed, so that they had to drive out of the ranch and go back to town before they all got dizzy from the heat. Their love began in the evenings when Tori would sit in the kitchen while Elena helped her mother bathe and get into bed, returning to the kitchen afterward with sadness in her eyes and around the corners of her mouth. It started even when Luis was by Elena's side, his arm around her waist or shoulders, his decades-long love for her spilling out of his eyes. Tori watched Elena with him, and saw the way she cared for him even though it was clear to Tori that Elena did not return his love, at least not in the same measure.

To all who saw them as they worked in a corner booth at Galindo's, or walked together to Elena's house, or stood in the unfinished wings of the hotel discussing layouts, or anywhere at all in the little town, they appeared to be colleagues who had become good friends. As often as not, Luis was with them or joined them at some point, and the three of them appeared comfortable and happy together. Tori and Elena, however, knew that there was something else underneath the friendly surface. A force field of attraction existed between them that they kept under control, not acting on it or even acknowledging it. Sometimes Tori would go for days without feeling the pull of her attraction to Elena, and would think that the flirtations of their early meetings were far behind them. Then, without warning, Elena would enter a room, or turn to speak to her, or rip the band from her ponytail so that her hair sprawled over her shoulders until she gathered it all back up into a neat, thick chord and banded it again—and Tori would feel the deep warmth in her abdomen again and the tightness in her throat.

As for Elena, she cloaked her attraction to Tori under the guise of her general affection. She could be aloof and distant to strangers, but to friends she was often warm and affectionate, touching their arms to make a point, punching their shoulders playfully to ask a question, or hugging them and kissing their cheeks to say hello or goodbye. She hugged and kissed Tori almost every time she saw her first in the day or said goodbye to her at night, and with each hug there was the slight brushing of fingers against bare skin, and with every kiss there was the extra second spent lingering with her lips on Tori's cheek, her nose and breath near Tori's ear. She breathed in Tori's perfume the way she breathed it off the napkin that day at Galindo's, growing familiar with it, coming to expect it, and even to crave it. Tori knew this, or felt it on some level, and she figured Elena did too. But, they did not talk about it. They simply did their work together, enjoying each other's talents, knowledge, and attention, and occasionally each other's long look or caress. All of it added up to love, and it was the beginning of what would eventually overtake them and alter their lives forever.

Sitting in the brush, however, watching whitewings over a shallow pond, Tori felt mainly appreciation for Elena. She felt fortunate that her life journey had brought her into contact with such a person, and that she herself was awake enough in her own life to not only respond—to be expanded and challenged by the person—but also to be thankful for them in the moment, and not only after they had passed from her life, or from life itself.

When the sun disappeared behind a mesa, Tori emerged from the brush slowly and began to back away from the water, trying hard not to scare the remaining birds drinking from the bank. After a dozen or so steps backward, she turned and walked toward the path that led from the pond back to the ranch road. She stood up straight, stretching her arms over her head, flexing her back and thigh muscles, which were tight from sitting still in the brush for so long. The sky was dark blue and purple, fading toward black.

Stars had already begun to dot its purplish expanse, and the moon had arisen over one of the far mountains. She reached the truck, one of the four she had bought for the ranch, and climbed in. She rolled down the windows on both sides to feel the breeze, the smell the desert, and to hear the crunch of gravel under the tires. Just before coming to the ranch gate at the main county road, two deer crossed the road in front of her, their white rumps shining in the headlights. Tori touched the brakes and watched them disappear into the brush, then began to ease forward again toward the gate. She unlocked and locked the heavy chain on the gate as quietly as she could, not wanting to disturb the deep stillness that had settled into her and, seemingly, into everything around her with the night.

She parked the truck in the parking lot in front of the hotel and began the walk to her cabin about four hundred yards away. She had been living in it for only a week. She had thought to stay on at Stella's, but she was so involved in the daily operations of the ranch, she really wanted to be on-site. Eugene had suggested a pre-fabricated cabin on the eastern edge of the property, as far off the road as the hotel, and within walking distance of the hotel. He knew the designer of such a cabin and had it delivered and assembled within a week. He even put a layer of stucco on the outside of it so it would match the hotel, and instead of asphalt shingles, he put terracotta tiles on the roof. Inside, it was nothing special, but it was efficiently designed and felt spacious despite its small square footage. Eugene had a covered porch affixed to the front of the cabin, which faced the main road. The door opened onto the living area that was separated by a small bar from a kitchenette and a breakfast nook. A staircase ran diagonally up the right wall to a sleeping loft. In the wall cavity of the stairwell was a small storage closet and a bathroom with a small corner shower. The floors were concrete, stained the same dark walnut color as the hotel floors. Between the kitchen and the dining nook was a back door, which opened into a half door that led to a back patio area Eugene had constructed with sandstone and crushed granite. Tori could walk from her back door to the rim of the gorge, and then west for four hundred yards along the rim, and then up the path onto the hotel's back patio in less than fifteen minutes.

Tori stepped into her livingroom and laid her purse, keys, phone, a pile of her mail from the hotel, and her sunglasses on the bar. She held on to the bar for balance as she removed each of her boots, prying them off at the heel with the other foot. She peeled off her socks, dropped them on top of the boots and rounded the bar corner to the small refrigerator. She retrieved a large bottle of carbonated water, grabbed the mail pile and her phone, and flopped on the leather couch, her feet out in front of her on the coffee table. She inhaled deeply, enjoying the smell of the new leather, took a long drag from the water bottle, and began to sort through the mail. As soon as she got settled the phone rang. She saw that it was Elena.

"Hi, what's up?" Tori said.

"Hey, did you see a lot of doves? Luis wants to know." Elena said.

"Lots and lots. It was fantastic." Tori listened as Elena repeated those words to Luis.

"He wants to know if there were any quail."

"Yes, I saw a large covey—maybe thirty or forty birds. They came right down to the water." Elena relayed this to Luis.

"What are you doing now? Where are you?" Elena asked.

"Sitting on the couch at home. Going through mail."

"Do you want to come over to eat with us? I'm making pork chops."

"No, I don't think so." Tori took a deep breath. "I just sat down and I'm tired. I think I'll just eat a salad and go to bed soon. Maybe do some reading." She slid farther down onto the couch and ran the finger of one hand back through her hair.

"Well…suit yourself." Elena was quiet on the phone. "Are you okay?"

"Yeah, I'm fine. I'm just a little tired and sapped from the heat, that's all."

"Okay, well, if you change your mind, just come over."

"Thanks. I'll probably just see you tomorrow. You'll be at Galindo's in the morning, right?"

"Yeah, for a while. I'll come to the ranch after I go home and check on Mama."

"Okay, well, tell her hello for me. I'll see you tomorrow."

"Love you."

"Love you, too. Bye."

Elena ended the call and stared at her phone a second before setting it down on the kitchen table. She looked out the dark window and saw the beam of Luis' flashlight as he checked the levels on the propane tank in the side yard of the house. She was disappointed that Tori would not be coming over for dinner. She had not seen her much that day. When Elena had arrived at the ranch from Galindo's, Tori was busy with some men from the county who had come to solve some issues with the water pressure. Tori had stuck her head in the kitchen after she was done with them to say she was heading out to the field to scout doves coming in to one of the water holes. Elena wanted to go with her, but Tori seemed in a hurry and Elena had about thirty minutes worth of inventory work left to do. So, Tori left without Elena seeing very much of her.

Elena liked seeing Tori every day as the days and weeks had passed over the summer, and this surprised her. She had been attracted to Tori nearly from the beginning of their relationship and figured Tori had picked up on subtle signals. She liked Tori's energy, her mind, her vision, and her appreciation of the desert that Elena herself had not appreciated despite being born and raised in Logan. She wanted to know what Tori thought about everything and, really, anything—from the trivial to the serious. Elena noticed this about herself when Tori went back to Houston for a long weekend to take care of some loose ends with her townhome lease and with a project at Vincent's company. Elena did not see or talk to Tori for over three days and she felt somewhat at a loss for what to do with herself. She had her mother, of course, who needed her a bit more every day. She had her work at Galindo's and at the ranch, although the work at Galindo's was mostly routine by this point. The staff was trained enough in all the recipes and procedures that Elena went there every day more to interact with the customers than for anything else. As for the ranch work, she was in her kitchen office most days, hammering out menus, procedures, and recipes. Or she accompanied Luis, Ricardo and Tori out to the field to build semi-permanent campsites and to experiment with field menus. She and Tori did the campsite work while the guys cut roads and trails, moved rocks and built sun shades.

During those days when Tori left town for a weekend, however, Elena had felt a sudden tinge of emptiness. She shook it off at first, feeling like a silly teenager mooning after a crush. But, the feeling returned and lingered until Tori returned that Monday afternoon. Elena was standing at the check-in desk in the lobby talking to Betty about how to record dinner reservations on the computer when she saw Tori's car pull into the parking lot. Her heart jumped and she felt the muscles in her face move into an involuntary smile. When Tori walked in with her sunglasses, jeans, boots, a tight t-shirt and a sixty-four-ounce Diet Coke from the road, Elena felt like wrestling her to the ground in a bear hug. Instead, she smiled, held out one arm and gave her a casual side hug, asking her how the drive had been. Still, however, she could not resist sliding her fingers along Tori's naked arm in a seemingly mindless caress before returning her hand to her jeans pocket.

She felt a hint of that same emptiness now, glancing at the blank screen on her phone, even though she had seen Tori yesterday, and again felt a bit silly about it. She watched a bouncing flashlight beam move across the yard and around to the back door. She heard Luis' boots on the back porch and the clatter of the blinds on the door as he opened it and came inside.

"There's plenty of gas in the tank," he said, switching the flashlight off and placing it in a drawer with batteries, tape, rubber bands, and small screwdrivers. "She won't need a refill for a few months probably."

"Good," Elena nodded and smiled. "Thanks for checking on it. She gets so paranoid about it. I think it's one of the few things in her life she still can manage, so…"

"No problem." He smiled and gave her an understanding look. He walked toward her and put his arms around her waist, drawing her close to him. He leaned down and kissed her lightly on the cheek, and then held her, looking into her eyes.

Luis was a kind, thoughtful and good man. And Elena enjoyed his company, as did most everyone who ever spent any time with him. He was easygoing, smart, interested in things, willing to talk about all sorts of topics, and knowledgeable about most. He was handsome, and had only grown more so as he had aged in the years since Elena had been gone. His dark hair had flecks of gray around the temples, and the laugh lines on his face were deep enough to give character and depth, but not to detract from his youthful energy and overall appearance. He was competent, hardworking, and knew how to get things done, and Elena appreciated and respected him for it.

She even loved him. When he had drawn her close the first time after her return to Logan, she almost turned him away. She had no desire to return to the past, or pick up a loose thread, or complete a circle, or finish a high school love story. Too much time had passed. She was a different person and had been for many years. She was a different person than he knew even then, way back in high school, else he would not have been so surprised when she left Logan. But, she had not turned away from his affection. Frankly, she missed being touched and wanted, and Luis was more than eager to love and hold her as much as she would allow. She had not slept with him, although he hinted at staying the night with her once when her mother stayed with friends after a late night playing cards. She thought about it, and thought that she might even enjoy it, were he anyone else. She cared for him too much to go through with it, though. It would hurt him too much in the end.

"I love you, you know," he said, still looking into her eyes and rocking her back and forth at the waist. "I have loved you for a long time."

Elena looked at him and then moved her gaze down his face to his neck and to his open collar. She touched her fingers to the button at his collar and ran them down the placket of his shirt, following her fingers with her eyes. She looked back at him and smiled, not saying anything.

"You don't have to say anything back to me, " he said. "I know you need some time. And you have your mama to think about right now. She's the most important thing." He swayed her back and forth, his hips leaned into hers. "I can wait, Elena. I can wait as long as you need. I've waited this long already."

Elena felt her stomach jump and her throat tighten. She knew that she would never love Luis in the way that he loved her, and that no amount of time would ever change that. She was careful in her words to him, and hoped that she was not leading him on too badly. He must know that she did not return his feelings exactly. She held her hand still on his chest for a moment, and pulled away from him, squeezing his hand lightly as she backed away.

"Are you hungry?" she asked, moving toward the stove.

Luis watched her and then deliberately shifted the look on his face and his body posture, to reflect Elena's shift in conversation and mood. "Yes, I've been hungry for hours. I didn't eat lunch."

"I'm doing these pork chops, " Elena said, bending down into the refrigerator to retrieve the wrapped package of meat. "I want to try out a sauce I just learned about."

"Sounds great," he said. He moved to sit down at the kitchen table, but stopped himself. "Do you need me to help you with anything?"

"No, not at all," she said, motioning with her hand for him to sit down. "I'm doing them in the pan here on the stove. Do you want a glass of wine?"

"Sure. I'll get it." He got up and went to the pantry, returning with a bottle that had been opened already. He poured them a glass apiece, sat Elena's glass on the counter beside the stove, and sat back down at the kitchen table.

He watched her while she cooked, and she felt his eyes on her even as she steered the conversation to mundane issues going on in town: with the ranch, at Galindo's and with various people that they knew in common. He told her about events that the mayor was planning for the holidays, sort of a citywide celebration of Logan's twenty-fifth year as the county seat. Mainly, it was an excuse to clean the city up and lure state and county officials to town in order to court them for favors and kudos during the legislative session in Austin. Luis said the mayor had asked him if Sandy Creek Ranch restaurant would be open to the public or only to resident guests during that time.

"I think he wants Logan to make a good impression and I think he thinks the ranch will be the nicest place in town." He took a sip of his wine. "He's right about that. Tori has not cut corners on that place, that's for sure."

At the mention of Tori's name, she put the meat tongs aside

and turned to Luis. "Will you come watch these while I go check on Mama?"

"Of course," he said, jumping up from his chair.

"Just don't let them burn. Pick them up with the tongs and move them around in the pan, making sure they stay coated with oil on the bottom. Whatever you do, don't stick them with a fork—use the tongs. I'll be back in a minute."

"Sure thing, boss," he said, grinning at her and making a salute with his right hand. He watched her as she disappeared down the hall.

Her mother's door was pulled closed with only a tiny crack of opening. Elena eased open the door and peered in to see if her mother was awake or asleep. Gloria lay on her back, the covers pulled up to her chest and her arms laid out neatly at her sides. When Elena pushed the door open, Gloria opened her eyes and turned her head in the direction of the door. She saw Elena and smiled weakly. Elena came over and sat on the edge of the bed.

"How are you, Mama? Aren't you hot under all these covers?"

"No, honey. I'm fine." She took a deep breath and let it out, stretching one arm and resting it on top of the covers. "What are you cooking? Do I smell something cooking?"

"Pork chops. They are on the stove. Luis is watching them." She brushed her mother's hair back from her forehead. "Are you hungry? Do you feel like eating anything?"

"I'm not sure, *mija*. Give me a little time to see if I'm up to it. Help me sit up and get my feet on the floor." She began to raise herself from the bed. Elena stood and helped her mother sit up and remove enough of the cover to swing her legs out over the side of the bed. Elena reached under the edge of the bed to pull out her mother's slippers. Gloria slipped her feet into them and grabbed Elena's shoulder with one hand. Elena braced Gloria's elbow and back as she lifted herself up on her feet and got her balance. Gloria took a big breath.

"Okay, well…I think I can walk a bit now." She took a few steps, still holding on to Elena's shoulder.

"I'll walk with you." Elena walked alongside her mother as she made her way toward the bathroom. She looked down at her mother's thin legs and knuckly toes. Gloria was losing a few pounds every week and most of her clothes were now too big for her to wear. She spent most of the day in a gown or housedress. She still managed to eat, go to the bathroom, and give herself a shower as she sat on a chair in the stall. Elena was nearby, though, to help her most of the time.

Elena stood outside the bathroom door and waited for her mother to finish. "Let me know if you need me to come in there," she said. After a few minutes, Elena heard the toilet flush and the water running in the sink. She gently opened the bathroom door just as Gloria was turning to come out. Elena stood aside as her mother passed by her and walked toward the bedroom door. She pulled her housecoat off a hook and Elena reached to help her put it on.

"I'll come say hello to Luis and sit with you all for a while," she said. "Luis needs to check the propane tank."

"He checked it, Mama. He says it's got plenty of gas in it, enough to last for a few more months." She followed her mother through the bedroom door into the hallway.

"He did? Is he sure?" Gloria motored down the hallway faster now, as if gaining her wind and strength. Elena followed her and they rounded the corner into the kitchen together.

"Hello, beautiful," Luis said to Gloria. He put down the tongs and moved over to pull a chair out for her at the kitchen table. She smiled at him and eased herself down into the chair.

"Are you cooking?" she asked Luis, somewhat incredulously. "What are you cooking?"

"I'm watching the pork chops that Elena is cooking," he said grinning. "They smell really good. Are you hungry? Do you want something to drink? Some wine?"

Gloria shrugged. "I don't know. I need to sit here a little bit to see how I feel." She looked around the kitchen as if it had been a while since she had been there. Gradually her gaze went up and down Luis' body then over to Elena's.

"How are things at the new ranch?" she asked when her eyes met Elena's. "Doesn't it open soon?"

Luis looked at Elena first then to Gloria. "Yes, it opens in a few days. The first group of hunters comes on Friday to begin the dove season on Saturday. Tori was out in the field this afternoon at one of the water holes we built and said there were hundreds and hundreds of doves." He stepped to the side as Elena took the tongs from his hands and began shifting the pork chops around in the pan. "So, it looks like we'll have a good opening weekend." He stepped to the kitchen table and sat down next to Gloria.

Gloria looked at Elena standing at the stove. Elena looked down into the pan, not really paying attention to the conversation. "Are you ready for them, *mija*?" she asked.

Elena turned when she heard her mother say "*mija*" and looked at her. "Ready for what?"

"The first hunters, the ranch guests."

Elena turned back to the pan. "Oh, yes. I'm ready. It's not too complicated really. We have a full house for the weekend, which in this case I think is only about twenty people. But, Tori wanted to go ahead and open the dining room to the public for reservations on Friday and Saturday nights. After opening weekend, we'll add Thursday nights as well maybe. We'll see…"

Gloria listened to this as if in thought. After a moment she spoke, to no one in particular. "Tori's a smart person, isn't she. A real business person." She looked at her daughter at the stove. "She's a lot like you, *mija*. You both know how to create things that people like and will spend money on."

Elena smiled a bit shyly and turned to Gloria. "Thank you, Mama." She turned back to the stove and began taking the chops out onto a warming plate for the oven. "Yes, Tori's a smart woman. She's done very well in her career, and I expect that this new ranch will be no different."

Luis nodded and took a sip of wine. "I think it's going to be a success. I mean, look—it's brand new and already it's booked to capacity for the first weekend in business. And Betty says the reservations are coming in steady every day all the way through the end of quail season in February." He sat his glass down and leaned back in his seat. "That's a lot of money being spent on hunting and food and lodging, let me tell you. And that doesn't count the extra dining customers from the community, Elena." He paused for a moment then continued. "This could be a big thing for Logan, if it's successful and the game is managed well so it can keep going. A big thing for a small town like this that would bring in money, people, growth…" He trailed off, looking at Gloria.

Gloria nodded. "Yes, it's good for small towns like this to have new energy come in. It's easy to get stuck doing things a certain way." She looked at her daughter again. "It's not just Tori—it's you too, *mija*. You coming back to Logan has brought new energy. People meet at Galindo's all the time now and visit and spend time together, all because you made it a nice place to eat. It wasn't like that before. It'll be the same way at the ranch, you'll see. People will eat your food at all meals of the day between the both of them!" She laughed and her face opened and relaxed.

Elena smiled and laughed a bit. "We'll see, Mama. Maybe so." She knew, though, that her mother was right. Elena knew her way around a sound hospitality concept as well as Tori, and she knew this would be a success. Tori had done everything right, including asking Elena to partner with her as executive chef. She could feel it and she was excited about it. She felt proud of Tori and of herself.

Gloria decided she could eat and drink a little. Luis poured her a few sips of wine in a juice glass and, when the food was ready, Elena gave her a small plate of sauteed spinach, lemon rice and a small pork chop covered in a honey mustard and herb cream sauce. The sauce is what most interested Elena—she had added some uncommon herbs to the common honey and mustard flavors. Luis went to the stove for seconds, ladling large spoonfuls of the sauce over his meat and his rice. His and Gloria's plates lay empty in the sink a half-hour later. There were no leftovers to speak of. Elena decided the sauce was a hit.

Luis cleaned up the kitchen while Elena helped her mother get ready for bed. When Elena emerged from the hallway into the kitchen, Luis was sitting in the livingroom watching television with the volume down low enough to keep from waking Gloria. Elena grabbed a glass from the dish drainer, filled it with tap water and went to the living room.

"Come sit," he said, as she stood behind him staring at the television. She rounded the couch and sat beside him. He opened his arm out along the back of the couch so that as she sat down, she slid into his side and his arm fell softly around her shoulders. He pulled her close and she felt his lips as he kissed her hair on the side of her head near her temples. He let his lips linger as he breathed in her scent and caressed her naked arm with his free hand. She turned her arm upward and grasped his hand as he ran it down the length of her arm toward her wrist. She held his hand still in hers, resting on her thigh, as he continued to kiss her tenderly, now moving closer to her cheek, in an attempt to lure her to turn her lips to him.

He stopped for a moment. "What's the matter?" he asked. "Are you okay?"

She turned to him then turned back to the television. "Yeah, I'm fine." She lifted his hand in hers and brought it back down onto his leg. "I'm sorry Luis. I guess I'm just tired and…I don't know…thinking about Mama." It was true, but it was not the entire truth. She stared at the television, which was running a commercial about a pill for erectile dysfunction. *Perfect*, she thought wryly.

Luis pulled back and sighed softly. "It's okay, honey. I understand." He took her hand in both his hands, squeezing it and bringing her fingertips to his lips. She felt his warm skin on her fingers as he slid them slowly across his lips, kissing them and caressing them with his mouth. She leaned over and kissed him lightly on the lips, and pulled her hand away from his.

"Thank you, Luis," she said simply. She looked into his eyes and smiled. Then she stood up, which he took as a sign that the evening was over, which was true.

She walked him to his truck and hugged him through the open window once he had stepped up into the seat. She leaned her chin on the window frame. "Thanks for checking on the propane again."

"You're quite welcome," he said, smiling as he put the truck in gear and began to ease out of the driveway. "See you tomorrow."

"Yeah, sleep well," she said as she stepped back into the yard, watched him back out, and waved as he turned out onto the main road.

She crawled into bed a little while later with a magazine and her phone. She scrolled to her recent calls and saw Tori's name and number on her screen. She wanted to call her, to talk to her before she went to sleep. For no reason, really, except just to hear her voice. But she figured Tori was already asleep since she had said she was tired earlier.

*Are you still awake?* she texted to Tori's number. She put her phone on the bed beside her and began thumbing through the magazine. Several minutes passed and she got no response. She got up, went to the kitchen for another sip of water, and returned to the bed. Still no response from Tori.

*No big deal. Just wanted to say goodnight. Love you* she texted to Tori. She turned her phone face down on the nightstand and switched off the lamp. As she lay there in the darkness, she thought about Luis. Eventually she would need to be more clear and explicit to him about her feelings, or lack of them. When she first returned to Logan, she had wondered if the years of distance and change had shifted anything so that, with time, she would come to feel drawn to Luis, enough to fall in love with him. Certainly, that was the narrative plan that apparently everyone in town had for the two of them, including her mother.

But, she knew that was not going to happen. Sure, if she were another kind of person, she could gradually come to embrace Luis as a life partner, someone who was faithful, kind, thoughtful, and would create a good life for them both. She was not that kind of person, though, especially now.

The truth, Elena was coming to realize, was that she was falling in love with Tori Reed. And she was not quite sure what to do about it.

# Chapter Nine

Tori stood in the dark September morning outside the hotel and watched the two ranch trucks drive out of the parking lot and onto the main road. It would take them about thirty minutes to get to the first watering hole, where Ricardo and several hunters would station themselves. Luis and another group of hunters would continue on the ranch road for another fifteen minutes to a second watering hole a few miles away. After the morning flight of doves, they would meet Elena and Tori at a campsite in between the two ponds to have a big brunch in the field. Everyone would return to the hotel, or those who had not filled their limit could stay in the field for a while longer. Others would go into town to prowl around at Hazel's craft store, eat a late lunch at Galindo's, or lounge by the pool and jacuzzi, take a nap or have cocktails. In the evening, everyone would meet back at the hotel for a sit-down dinner.

Tori walked back into the hotel lobby and around to the dining room to pour herself a cup of coffee and grab an apple. It was an hour or more before dawn. Elena would arrive soon to load up the field unit to take out to the campsite for breakfast. Tori planned to go with her to help out in the field so that Letty could stay in the kitchen doing prep for the minimalist lunch service and the dinner service for that night. In addition to the hunters, they had another few dozen reservations from Logan and the surrounding community. It would be a big first night.

She stepped out onto the courtyard and followed the path out to the pool patio. She pulled up a chaise lounge and positioned it so that it faced southward toward the gorge and the mountains beyond it. She stretched out in the chaise, curling her fingers around the coffee cup, enjoying the sound of the fountain and the still quiet of the desert underneath it. She turned her head to the left and saw what she thought might be the first indications of brightening in the east. She straightened her head and laid it back against the chaise, looking up into the bands of stars above her. Nine months had passed since she first came out to meet Ken, and the sheer number of all those stars visible on any clear night still overwhelmed and thrilled her. She wondered how she lived in Houston all those years without seeing stars like this on a regular basis.

She saw movement to her right in her peripheral vision, out from the jacuzzi, where the stone patio ended. She held still and tried to discern in the spare light what had moved. It moved again, a short jolt, and she recognized it. A rabbit, not unlike the one she had seen months ago in Stella's yard on that first visit. She could barely pick out its shape in the darkness as long as it stood still. She held herself still and quiet, hoping it would move again. In a moment, it did—hopping a few steps in her direction angled toward the patio. She wondered if it were drawn to the water in the pool or to the tender plants in the landscaped beds. Or maybe it was just passing through for the night. Slowly she eased the apple to her lips and bit a piece from it very quietly. She held the piece in her teeth as she slowly put the apple in her lap. She took the piece from her teeth and flicked it toward the rabbit with as little motion as possible, using her wrist and fingers more than her arms. When the apple piece landed, the rabbit turned and took a few hops in the opposite direction, but then held still. Tori held herself as still as the rabbit. It turned its head toward the apple piece, and then its body. Tori dared not breathe, because to eat the apple piece, the rabbit would have to come perhaps five or six yards closer to her. After a few more moments, the rabbit took a step, halted, and took a few more steps. Finally, it stood over the apple piece. The rabbit picked it up and dropped it several times. Tori could not see if the rabbit was eating or not. Finally, it grabbed the apple piece in its teeth, turned, ran off the patio, and disappeared into the darkness.

Tori relaxed into the chaise lounge again, breathing normally after holding her breath and tensing her body. She could no longer see the rabbit in the darkness and did not know if he still stood out there even. She imagined it there, though, chewing in its mouth the apple piece that had been in her own. She smiled at the thought of that, and stared off into the slightly lightening east.

She must have dozed off briefly, because she awoke to a hand caressing her shoulder. She turned her cheek to it and felt the soft skin. She knew it was Elena. She reached up to clasp the fingers of the hand, holding it still against her face before looking up and behind her to see Elena standing over her, silhouetted against the light from the courtyard. A dull gray light enveloped them now, as the sun was a few minutes from peeping over the eastern rim of mesas.

"Good morning," Tori said, still holding Elena's hand. "I must have dozed off. Have you been here long?"

"No, just a few minutes." Elena looked down on her with a steady gaze, smiling slightly. She wiggled her thumb from Tori's grasp and brushed Tori's cheek with it, back and forth. "Was that a bad apple?"

Tori was confused for a second, and then looked down to see her cold coffee cup wedged in her crotch and the apple in her lap with its one bite of yellowing flesh exposed. She remembered the rabbit and shook her head. "No, the rabbit liked it." She looked back up at Elena behind her. Elena furrowed her brow in confusion.

Tori dropped Elena's hand, leaned forward, swung her legs to the side of the chaise and got up. She turned to face Elena. "There was a rabbit that came up right over there," she said, pointing to the patio near the jacuzzi. "I bit off a piece of apple and threw it to him. He picked it up and ran off with it." She looked at Elena with a smile of satisfaction and accomplishment.

Elena nodded and smiled at her the way people smile when they are indulging people who are a little bit crazy. "I didn't know rabbits ate apples." She grabbed the apple from the chaise where Tori had left it. She looked at it, and took a bite of it.

"Well, apparently they do." Tori looked up and around at the sky and the mesas and the mountains. She stretched her arms over her head, arching her back and standing up on her tiptoes. She looked back at Elena. "It's a good day for the opening of dove season. And the opening of Sandy Creek Ranch. Right, partner?"

Elena stepped forward and circled her arms around Tori's neck in a hug. "That's right, partner," she said in her ear. She pulled back. "You're coming with me to the field for brunch, right? We can take my truck out there."

Tori followed Elena through the courtyard and back into the kitchen. They worked efficiently for the next hour getting everything packed and loaded to take to the field. Tori packed and loaded several footlockers of cooking and serving gear into the back of Elena's Tahoe. Elena loaded ice chests and cambros of prepared food and drinks, boxes of sundries, and pallets of bottled water. They piled it all into the truck and headed out for the campsite in the southeast sector of the ranch as soon as Betty arrived to handle the front desk.

The ranch road was rough but passable in Elena's truck as long as they picked their way slowly through the areas where flash floods had washed the dirt from around the rocks so that their sharp points and edges jutted up into the paths of the tires. Tori sat in the passenger seat with her elbow leaned out of the open window. She took in the scenery from behind her sunglasses.

"You should have worn your darker sunglasses today. You'll get a headache before we're done," Elena said. "Look in the glove compartment—I think there are some in there."

"Yeah, I broke the dark ones yesterday and these are the only other ones I have." Tori opened the glove compartment and searched around in the all the papers, pencils, tire pressure gauges, little flashlights, handi-wipes and other stuff that was in there. "Jeez, what all do you have in here?" Deep in the back crevice of the compartment she found the glasses. She took hers off, put on the darker ones and turned to Elena. They were larger and more round than Tori's usual glasses, which were either a classic ray ban or an aviator style.

Elena looked at her briefly, snorted, and looked back at the road. "You look like you have compound eyes. Can you see behind you and in front of you at the same time?"

Tori pulled the sun visor down and looked into the mirror. "Wow," she said and folded the mirror and visor back up. "Well, you bought them, not me." She rested her elbow on the window and adjusted the glasses on her face.

"They look good on *me*," Elena said, non-plussed.

"I bet they do, " Tori said with a playful smirk.

They thought they heard shooting over the din of the truck engine when they passed the area near where Luis' group was hunting at the first watering hole. They drove on toward the area where Ricardo's group was, veering southward about a mile before getting there. They arrived to their campsite within another mile, pulling up to a small storage building that stood on one side of a stand of small trees. The campsite was near a dry creek that channeled enough rainwater every year for trees to thrive near it. The trees provided a nice area of shade and coolness in the midst of a quickly warming morning. From the shaded campsite, a few animal trails ran down the craggy sides of the bank until they ended on the soft sand of the creek bed. Tori walked to the shade and followed the animal trail to the edge of the bank. Willow trees curved out from the rocky sides of the creek bank, seemingly growing straight out of the rocks themselves, and made moving shadows on the sand of the bed below. Tori liked the sound of the breeze in the willows.

They unpacked all the gear and placed it on the ground between two long picnic tables at the edge of the stand of trees opposite the storage shed. Tori pulled wooden folding chairs and tables from the storage shed, as well as folding chaise lounges and a few freestanding hammocks. Elena unpacked the footlockers and the boxes they had brought from the hotel, setting up one picnic table as the preparation table and the other as the serving table. She handed Tori a plastic sack of white linens to go over the five sets of dining tables and chairs that she had set up in the shade of the trees. Tori arranged the chaise lounges and the hammocks under the trees along the creek. She returned to get a pair of scissors from the supplies and went in search of flowering sage or other blooming plants in the area to use for table bouquets.

Their practice runs over the summer served them well. They knew the drill even though this was the first time they were performing it for paying customers. Each of them knew what needed to be done and knew what the other one was doing at all times. They could almost read each other's minds, so that just as one felt a need for a box of flatware or a cylinder of propane, the other one was placing it into her hand, having known already that it was needed. They worked with calm, relaxed efficiency—not harried, rushed, or confused. They worked steadily, creating in that campsite in their piece of the desert the best approximation they could manage of the ideal vision that drove the whole concept of Sandy Creek Ranch—an experience of elegance and luxury in the midst of a sparse, ruggedly beautiful landscape with little in the way of ornamentation.

They had been there one hour when Luis called Elena's cellphone to say they were on their way to the campsite. He had called Ricardo and his group was on its way as well. Tori put the final touches on the serving table: brushing a long dried leaf off the white linen cover, arranging the glassware and coffee mugs just so, making sure the coffee and juice carafes were aligned and had spill plates beneath their spouts, sinking the champagne bottle and the vodka bottle deeper into their ice buckets, lining up the trays of cheese, crackers, and meat cuts. A large vase of blooming purple sage decorated the table, which matched the smaller vases of it that adorned each individual table. Elena stood near the stove, watching the pots of potatoes and black beans that were simmering on the burners as she chopped onions, cilantro and peppers and put them in little dishes beside the stove near several pallets of eggs. She stopped, wiped her hands on the towel over her shoulder, and walked to the serving table.

"They're on their way?" Tori asked. Elena nodded, grabbed one of the champagne bottles, and wrapped her towel around its neck. The top twisted off in a muted pop. She poured two glasses, sat the bottle back in the ice bucket, handed Tori a glass and held up her own.

"To good food, to paying customers, to the desert and the animals who will feed us this morning." She clinked Tori's glass and they both drank. Tori held up her glass again and added, "And to us!" Elena clinked her glass against Tori's and they both drank again, hearing the trucks approaching just as they swallowed.

Tori knew the hunt had gone well the minute she saw Luis' face as he stepped out of his truck. His eyes were hidden behind dark sunglasses, but his white teeth shone in a broad smile and he bounded out of the truck in an explosion of talking and laughing with the other hunters. Ricardo's truck filed in right behind and within minutes the campsite was teeming with excited and hungry men.

"Welcome gentlemen," Tori called as she stood with Elena greeting them as they came into the camp. She had met many of them the day before, but now she shook hands with them again and ushered them to the service table. The hunters were giddy and talked over each other as they related their stories and experiences of the morning hunt. Doves had come in by the hundreds, in huge flocks, swooping and swerving over the watering holes just as Tori had seen them earlier in the week. Other animals had appeared as well in the early dawn before all the shooting had begun, as Tori expected: deer, javalina, quail, even a bobcat. Most of the men were experienced hunters, especially the older men who were retired. Some of the younger men, however, had had few or no experiences like the one they had enjoyed that morning and were beaming with the thrill of it all.

And they all were wowed by the camp. Once they greeted Tori and Elena, they began to look around at the campsite with its upscale appointments—the glassware, linen tablecloths, sterling flatware and flowers—appreciating its elegance out in the middle of nowhere. They filled their small plates with cheese, fruit, and meat cuts. They poured and drank their glasses of mimosas or bloody Marys. They chugged whole bottles of water at once, the heat already beginning to tire them as much as the early wake-up time.

As they sat and began to eat, Luis retrieved a dozen fat doves from his game bag and began plucking the feathers from their warm bodies. Elena took them from him one at a time, rinsing them in a cold ice bath, and threading them onto metal skewers that fit in small brackets over the open flames of the stove. Within twenty minutes, the doves were grilled, so she removed them from the skewers and took the meat off the bone, chopping it into small pieces that would be scrambled in with the eggs, peppers and onions. The hunters breathed in the delectable aromas of grilling meat as they ate their first course. Tori watched them and remembered the old maxim that all food tastes and smells better when cooked outside over an open flame.

Soon, Elena called them all to brunch. While they made their way down the line filling large plates with eggs, pan-fried herb potatoes, black beans and tortillas, Tori cleared their tables to make room for them. Later, Luis and Ricardo went from table to table refilling glasses, good-naturedly teasing the hunters who had missed easy shots and praising those who had shot like expert marksmen. Tori felt energized by all of it even though she was knee deep in operations now more than she had been in years. As an executive, she had not arranged flowers on a table or set up a line of beverage carafes in nearly fifteen years. But here she was doing it all, serving people, making sure they had everything they needed, supporting Elena as she dished out the food at just the right time to maximize the flavors. She remembered why she loved the hospitality business in the first place—for the hospitality itself, the gift of serving people, of creating wonderful food and experiences for them to enjoy, and tending to their process of enjoyment step by step. The benefits came in many forms, including the financial. But just as often they came in watching people line up the perfect shot on their camera as they snapped photos, or from the excitement in their voices as they described the place into their cellphones and narrated their experiences to people back home. Tori and Elena caught each other's eyes several times during the morning, after nearly all the guests came back for seconds, after several of them piled their crumpled napkins on their empty plates and ambled their way down to a nearby chaise lounge or hammock to nap. Eventually, all of them—except for a kindly, gray-haired gentlemen who hunted in an expensive pair of brush pants and a neatly pressed shooting shirt who sat at a table off to the side reading from a Kindle—ended up asleep under the willows, their boots on the sand beside them, their shirts untucked, their hats over their faces or lying still on their chests.

As stillness and quiet returned to the camp, Tori and Elena looked at each other and smiled. It had worked. And it would work dozens more times nearly every day in the weeks and months ahead.

Tori sat in the hotel dining room with a cup of coffee watching the guests in the courtyard and pool area. Luis had taken a few of the hunters from the morning back out into the field to get their limits of dove, but most of them had decided to call it a day by the time they roused themselves from their creek side naps and made it back to the hotel. Most of them were either in the pool, napping again in chaise lounges beside it, or hitting golf balls at the driving range on the west side of the hotel before it got too dark. Three or four of them had gone into town to have a drink at Galindo's and walk around at the craft stores. Letty had rolled the mobile bar out to the pool area, so a few guests sat at tables drinking and playing cards and backgammon in their swimsuits. Luis would return soon with the afternoon hunters and dinner guests would start arriving not long afterward.

The whole scene felt right to Tori. It looked and sounded like people enjoying themselves, which was the whole point of the ranch. It would continue tonight during the dinner service, which was completely full with guests and outside reservations. The marketing for the ranch had been successful in terms of bringing in hunters. Local people, however, knew of Elena through the food at Galindo's, so steady reservations came in at the ranch for dinner for those who wished to try out the local celebrity chef's new stuff. Elena had decided to offer three fixed menu options as a matter of routine for the dinner service. Every night would include a fish option, a beef or poultry option, and a seasonal wild game option. The wild game would come from that day's hunts—mostly from Luis and Ricardo, or any of the guests who wished to offer their game meat for the dinner service. Tori had not thought of this but Elena insisted upon it in order to give extra meaning to the meal. In Elena's view, meat tasted best when it was fresh, never having been frozen, and meat was meaningful to people when they themselves had killed the animal from which it came. Elena thought, and Tori came to agree with her, the meals at the ranch should contribute to the overall guest experience not only by tasting good, but also by bringing meaning to the act of eating by deriving the food from the ranch's land and from the efforts of the hunting guests themselves.

Tori had seen Elena's theory in action that morning at the brunch when the hunters had marveled at the scrambled egg dish that included the fresh grilled dove meat from that morning's hunt. None of them had eaten dove meat in this way before, and very few of them had eaten it in the field literally minutes after having shot the doves. Tori and Elena had watched the guests as they ate, and listened to them tell grand stories of that morning's hunt as if it had taken place years ago, as if all of them had not been there themselves just an hour or so before. Within the space of one hour, the hunt had taken on a status far beyond what it had been in actuality. It was clear, at least to Elena and later to Tori, that a key ingredient in the hunt's expansion in the hunters' minds was the simple fact of eating, while still in the field, the meat they had killed just a short time before. That expansion of meaning and its entire ethos would be continued in the evening at dinner, and at all the evening dinners to follow at the ranch.

As she sat drinking her coffee, she could hear Elena and her team in the kitchen preparing for the evening. She really wanted to join them in there, if for no other reason than to watch Elena work. But, she did not want to hover over them and get on their nerves, especially Elena's. Tori knew her way around a professional kitchen well enough to know if a chef or team were doing a good job or not. She could analyze systems, procedures, inventories, and menu costing sheets to know if things were being run efficiently. But, that is why she had partnered with Elena in the first place—to not have to do those things herself, and to have someone who was a peer, but also an expert in that area to do it instead. Tori was a business person who recognized artistry when she saw it and could generate it from the right people; Elena was an artist who understood business and how to seduce people into paying top dollar for edible creations. Together, they made a great match for Sandy Creek Ranch as long as they respected each other and stayed out of each other's way.

Now, though, Tori wondered why she had not designed a viewing window between the dining room and the kitchen. Surely some of the guests would enjoy watching the activity of the kitchen staff as they prepared the food. The "chef's table" could be a special reservation near the window with a full view. And with such a window in place, she could watch her friend and partner execute her art from a distance and without disturbing her. She was struck by her own voyeuristic desire as these thoughts ran through her mind. She had caught herself watching Elena in the field earlier, enchanted by the singular focus and ease with which she did her work, which inevitably exceeded people's expectations both in presentation and flavor. Elena, while working, juggled many things at once, keeping all the balls in the air of a busy upscale kitchen, but never seemed harried or rushed or overwhelmed. She moved deliberately, with confidence and quiet speed, her face relaxed, her eyes intense, and with hands that could adapt in a moment from the iron grip needed to bone a pork shank to the delicate touch necessary for the perfect point on a dollop of mousse. Tori was entranced watching her and, in those moments, found herself attracted to Elena even more than usual. She felt a twang of self-consciousness flush in her chest and neck, and she shifted in her chair to drain it away and try to think of something else. Still, the viewing window onto the kitchen was a good idea, she thought. She might talk to Elena about it and have it installed on a slow weekday when it would not be too disruptive.

As if on cue, Elena emerged from the kitchen through the swinging door, drinking from a big bottle of water and brushing her hair back. She saw Tori and made her way to the table.

"Hey, I didn't know you were out here. Why didn't you come in to the kitchen?" she said, pulling a chair out beside Tori and sitting down.

"I didn't want to get in the way," she said. "You all sound busy in there."

Elena nodded. "It's coming together. Letty is doing well and she's helping the others, especially the wait staff." She sat back in her chair and took another long drag from the bottle, looking out onto the courtyard and past it to the pool patio. "They look like they're having fun," she said after she swallowed.

Tori turned to watch the guests again. "Yeah, I think they are. A few of them are around at the driving range, too. That was a good idea, I think. Better than a skeet range, which is what most hunting ranches have. Don't you think?" She turned to Elena.

Elena nodded again, not moving her eyes from the people in the pool. "Yeah, definitely. It's easier to pick up golf balls than those little pieces of bright orange clay from the clay pigeons. Who wants a field full of *that*? Plus, it's quieter."

Tori smiled. "My thinking exactly. Great minds…"

Elena looked at her and grinned. "Okay, well, fellow great mind, come help me decide if this cream sauce is too heavy for the blackened redfish."

She followed Elena into the kitchen and immediately found herself immersed in the distinctly decadent sights, smells and sounds of a working upscale restaurant. Rich aromas of baking bread and simmering sauces filled the room. Filets of fish and meat sizzled on open flames and in broiler plates in the oven. Bunches of fresh herbs and flowers stood on tables, ready to be used in a pinch for flavoring in a dish, or for garnish on a plate. Crates of colorful, raw vegetables sat ready for the cutting board and the sauté pan. Letty stood at the end of one of the long preparation tables with three waiters, their young faces serious with concentration as they listened to her explanation of the dishes. They wrote down her exact words on little notebooks, pronouncing aloud for her approval the names of the entree, the toppings, the sides, the desserts and all the unique components that created the flavors for each fixed menu. At her instruction, they each took bites of the items on each menu, tasting for themselves what the guests would taste, learning personally the exact flavors of each item so that they could speak about them knowingly and convincingly to the guests. Other staff members stacked plates near each plating station, or cut single servings from large chunks of meat, or stirred with their hands several dozen dove breasts marinating for the grill, or loaded things in and out of the walk-in coolers.

Elena stopped in front of a set of burners installed in the middle of a large cooking surface that ran half the length of the kitchen. She stirred a simmering saucepan, then reached for a small plate on which she placed a few bites she took from a redfish filet that lay sizzling in a grill pan beside the pot. She stretched to the other side of the plating station for a fork, laid it on the plate and handed it to Tori. She took a ladle and spooned a bit of the sauce onto the redfish bites, drizzling it in thin lines across the pieces. She stood back, waiting for Tori to taste it.

Tori took a bite, letting the delicate meat melt onto her tongue and the sauce expand throughout her mouth. The sauce was creamy with a touch of citrus and a flavor she could not identify. It complemented the redfish perfectly, especially the parts of the fish that were charred a bit from the grill pan.

She nodded her head slowly to Elena and swallowed. "That's really nice. I don't think it's too heavy at all. The flavor is very rich, but the texture is light so it doesn't feel heavy in my mouth."

"Okay, good. That's how Letty and I taste it, too, but I wanted someone else who hasn't been testing it for days to try it." She looked at the sauce again and stirred it.

"What's that herb in it? I taste the citrus, but there's something else." Tori ate the second bite of fish from her plate.

Elena smiled and watched Tori's mouth as she chewed. "You like it, huh?" she asked with a slight tease in her voice.

"What is it?" she asked again.

"It's a secret ingredient. I could tell you but then I'd have to kill you," she said simply and walked away, taking the saucepan to Letty and the waiters for them to try.

"What is it?!" Tori demanded, with mock impatience.

Elena shook her head and pretended to ignore her demand. "Sorry. I like you too much to have to kill you, especially on our first night in business." She stood in the middle of her kitchen with her hands on her hips. Her chef coat was open, revealing the black t-shirt with the Sandy Creek logo on the front. Tori had ordered them in khaki and black, in both t-shirt and collared styles, so that there would be options for the staff but also so that Elena would not have to alter her normal work attire of jeans and a black t-shirt. Her t-shirt was a v-neck, and Tori forced herself to not look at the smooth skin of Elena's chest as she stood there in cool, mock defiance. It took all the strength she could muster.

Tori smiled wryly and started toward the kitchen door, sensing that her presence there was no longer needed. "Fine. I'll get it out of you sooner or later." She turned to face Elena once more as she backed through the swinging door into the dining room. "I'll be back. I'm going home to change." Elena waved her off and then turned toward Letty and the waiters.

The dining room stayed nearly filled with guests all evening, and Elena ran out of the grilled dove kabob for the wild game menu option that night. Tori had spent much of her time going from table to table, greeting customers and visiting with them. She carried a glass of red wine around with her that a waiter refilled for her every so often. She did not really stop to eat until Ken and Hazel arrived. Ken beamed at her from across the room before they even took their seats, waving for her to come over. She was excited to see them both and gave them big hugs. Elena came out shortly afterward to bring them a special appetizer plate that she had prepared for them when she saw their names on the reservation list. Tori asked one of the waiters to bring her a soup and salad, and she sat to eat with Ken and Hazel for a while. It was Ken who pointed out the town mayor when he entered with his wife and son. Elena had seen the mayor enter through the kitchen door window. Tori watched her as she stood at their table, talking with them both, instructing the waiters to bring them a few on-the-house items.

Nothing really went wrong, even when they ran out of the wild game course. People took it in stride, as indication that it was exceptionally good and promised to themselves and each other that they would arrive earlier next time. Tori overheard comments of appreciation about the interior of the dining room, the beauty of the courtyard, the nice ambiance punctuated by the sound of the outdoor fountain and, of course, the food. Elena and her staff were in fine form and it was clear by the end of the evening that something special had occurred that night over grilled meats, rich sauces and sautéed vegetables garnished with fresh flowers and herbs. They both could sense it—it felt like the energies of the town had come together in that one place to revel in their own vitality. The old and the new, the local and the guests, the natives and the transplants. Some of the waiters' parents, aunts, and uncles came to see their son or daughter at work in the new place, but also to partake of the new place themselves, having heard about it for a few weeks. Some of the regulars at Galindo's came, their jeans starched and pressed, their collared shirts buttoned up and tucked in nicely, to check out the beautiful chef's new place, to see if her dinners were as good as her breakfasts and lunches. Ken and Hazel, and people like them—people who had moved to Logan and ended up starting new lives with new businesses or projects—came to see Tori, to welcome the newest major addition to the community. The hotel guests—some from as far away as Minnesota—came to eat the meat they had killed and to continue their experience of a West Texas desert ranch.

It was after 11pm when Tori waved goodbye to the last guests and turned to survey the empty dining room. A few staff members were stripping linens from the tables and wiping down the bar area. She walked to the kitchen door and peeped through the small window. Staff members were loading dirty dishes and unloading clean ones, rolling carts and boxes into the coolers, wiping down surfaces, and mopping floors. In the far left corner, Elena sat in her kitchen office, secluded in the quiet behind glass windows and a door. She was bent over her desk, reading through the order tickets and receipts, adding items on a calculator. Tori backed away from the door and stepped out into the courtyard and into the lobby to enter the kitchen from the other direction, near the door to Elena's office. She tapped on the metal door and heard "Yes" from inside. She opened it. Elena did not look up from her tickets. "Yes?" she said.

"How'd we do?" Tori asked.

Elena turned around suddenly. "Hey! I didn't realize it was you. Come in—sit down." She grabbed a stack of books and files from a chair and moved them to sit atop another pile in the corner of her desk. She sat back down and handed Tori the printout from the cash register. "The number on the left is cash in. The number on the right is costs, including labor and raw goods." Tori looked at the numbers, then looked at Elena.

"These are the totals for the dinner alone?" she asked.

"Yes."

The total receipt amounts over cost was more than both of them had expected.

"Elena, this is great. I mean, really great." Tori was astonished.

"Yes, it is." Elena sat back in her chair, her arms crossed over her chest. "I don't think we can count on this as a norm—only one night is opening night—but even half to two thirds of that on a regular basis is healthy."

Tori looked at the ticket again and then slowly smiled at Elena. "Well done, partner. Well done!" She leaned over to give Elena a high five. Elena smiled and brought her hand up but threaded her fingers through Tori's fingers instead of slapping her hand. She grasped Tori's hand and brought it to rest on the top of the desk, holding it still for a moment before releasing it.

Tori leaned back in her chair and took a deep breath, suddenly feeling the tiredness from the long day, which had begun before dawn with the first groups of hunters. She looked at Elena and felt a rush of joyfulness.

"Thank you, Elena. For everything—for all this." She motioned with her arm around the office and toward the rest of the kitchen. "This has your stamp all over it and that's why it worked today and tonight, and will keep on working, I just know it." She looked directly into Elena's eyes. "I really mean it. Thank you for saying yes to me when I asked you to come in on this."

Elena smiled and looked at her quietly for a moment. "You are quite welcome, Tori," she said simply. "Thank you for asking me."

"We make a good team," Tori said.

Elena nodded. "Yes, we do. We certainly do."

# Chapter Ten

Elena knew that Gloria would eventually require more care than she and her mother's closest friends could give her there in her own house. She refused to go anywhere else, and no one suggested it. There was no place else to go, at least not in Logan, and Gloria wanted to die in her own bed. Elena had stopped by the offices of a hospice agency, weeks ago, when she had been in Stockdale buying inventory for the ranch. The agency had served several clients in Logan over the years, and was happy to send staff out to her mother whenever they were needed, up to twenty-four hours a day, for as long as she needed them. Fortunately, her mother had taken out a long-term care policy that paid for most of it. Elena had been shocked to learn of the policy, it not being common in the families she knew of in Logan. Perhaps her mother did not count on her only daughter coming home to take care of her. Or maybe she did, but she did not want the financial burden to fall on her. Either way, Elena was grateful for her mother's foresight and made sure everything was ready for the day when Gloria needed it.

That day came just after a busy Thanksgiving weekend at the
ranch. Elena was at Galindo's going over receipts at the end of
the lunch service. She had left her mother late that morning and
had waited until one of her mother's closest friends, a kindly, no-
nonsense woman everyone called Tita Maria, arrived to sit with
her. Elena watched her mother sleep while she waited. Her breathing had become somewhat ragged, its smoothness interrupted by
wheezing and occasional coughing fits that sent her into a fitful
exhaustion. Her frame was smaller than Elena had ever imagined
possible. She seemed literally to have shrunk to half the person she
had been for all of her adult life. Her arms and legs looked ready to
break at the pressure of any weight, and her ribs had already been
cracked when a home health worker squeezed her too hard around
the waist getting her up and down from the shower seat. Her hair
had thinned, exposing her pale scalp. Her face was drawn and
gaunt, the plump cheeks and full lips long gone, and gone forever.

Tita Maria had eased into the kitchen from the back door and
had slipped down the hall quietly. She entered Gloria's bedroom
and put her hand on Elena's shoulder. Elena jumped with surprise, and smiled weakly up at her. She kissed her mother's cheek
and tiptoed out of the room, leaving Tita Maria to sit in her chair.
She had been at Galindo's only about two hours when her phone
rang. It was Tita Maria saying that she had called the hospice
emergency number because Gloria was having trouble breathing
and was crying out in panic and pain. She had also called Luis so
that the Volunteer Fire Department's first responder team could
help her with breathing until the hospice people got there.

She raced home, arriving just after one of Luis' colleagues. She
ran down the hall to her mother's room. Tita Maria met her in
the doorway and ushered her in. "She's better," she said as Elena
went past her. The man was leaning over Gloria's bed, holding
an oxygen mask to her face, instructing her to take deep, regular
breaths. Gloria turned her head slightly when she saw Elena, her

eyes darting with fear. Elena crossed to the other side of the bed from the man and leaned over to rest her elbows on the bed next to her mother. She took her hand and brushed a few thin wisps of hair back from her face.

"You're doing good, Mama. Just do what he says. The hospice people will be here soon." Elena smiled into her mother's scared eyes. She kissed her hand and turned to the man. He looked at her, nodded curtly, and looked back at Gloria.

"That's right, Mrs. Rios. Just deep breaths. Take deep breaths." His voice was deep and calming, and his hands were steady as he held the mask to Gloria's face. He looked at Elena.

"Do you have the cell number of the hospice people? I can call them and ask if there's anything I have that I can give her for pain until they get here. You'll need to hold this mask, though." He looked at Gloria. "Is that okay with you?"

Gloria nodded and looked at Elena. Elena put her hands on the mask and the man raised up, taking a piece of paper from Tita Maria. "Just keep it sealed against her face. Not hard, just sealed." He stepped out of the room and Elena heard his steps disappear down the hallway. She looked into her mother's eyes, which seemed slightly less scared than a few moments ago.

"Is this helping?" she asked her mother. Gloria nodded, but did not speak.

In a few minutes, the man returned to the room. He leaned over the bed, speaking both to Gloria and to Elena. "They are about fifteen minutes away. They have all your records and doctor's orders with them, Mrs. Rios, and they will take good care of you as soon as they get here. You'll be fine." He looked at Elena and back to Gloria. "They said, if you wanted me to, I could give you an injection of a medicine we use to calm people down after they've had accidents or when they're restless from pain. I have some of it with me now. Would you like me to do that for you?" He paused for a moment. "All it will do is relax you, maybe make you drowsy and take away some of your pain."

Gloria looked at Elena, then back at him and nodded. "Okay, then." He turned to his bag, removed a few items and laid them carefully on the bedside table. He snapped on a pair of latex gloves, prepped Gloria's arm, and inserted a small IV. He injected a dose into the IV, waited a moment, and removed the IV from Gloria's vein.

Elena looked into her mother's eyes during the whole process, willing her mother's fear and pain to subside. It seemed to work, or at least the medicine did. Within just a few moments, Gloria's body stilled and her eyelids drooped. Her face relaxed and her fingers came unclenched from the tight balls of fist they had been for over an hour.

When the hospice team arrived, Elena walked the man down the hallway and out to the porch.

"Thank you so much," she said. "I can't tell you how much I appreciate you being here so fast and helping her. My name's Elena, by the way." She put out her hand.

"My name's Gerald. I've been a friend of Luis' for a long time." He shook her hand and smiled at her. "I've known your mother for a while, too. I knew she was sick. I'm glad I was able to help her." He stepped off the porch. "Don't hesitate to call for us anytime. Luis knows how to get in touch with all of us."

"Thank you. Thank you so much." She waved to him as he walked to his truck parked on the street.

By the afternoon, the hospice team had taken full responsibility for Gloria's care. They had ordered equipment and supplies from Stockdale, some of which were already being delivered that day. Someone from the team would be with her around the clock for the remainder of her illness. Elena stood in the doorway, watching them do their work—rearranging furniture to make room for various monitors and machines, setting up a small laptop station for records and charts, logging drugs in and out of a small refrigerator they had set up in the room. Watching all this, she felt immense relief and gratitude for their compassion, and for the fact that her mother would be cared for in the best way possible. She felt a wave of new sadness also, though, because this meant the beginning of the end.

Gloria rested peacefully through the afternoon. Elena sat at the kitchen table drinking tea and reading over all the materials the hospice team had given her. Luis and Tori had both left messages on her phone, but she had not returned their calls and wanted to wait until things settled down a bit in the house before talking to them. Actually, she did not want to talk to anyone really, except maybe to Tori. And she did not really want to talk to Tori; she just wanted to be with her.

Luis was out with hunters on a quail hunt, and only a few of them were staying the night at the ranch and would be eating dinner. Letty managed the dinner service on the nights when it was closed to the public and was served only to the hotel guests. She knew Luis would want to come straight over as soon as he finished up at the ranch. She texted him: *All is ok here. Mama is sleeping. I'm tired. Going to bed early. Call when you get done.* Right after she hit "send", she texted Tori: *All is ok here. Mama is sleeping. Come over later? Around 9?* Tori would have finished eating or visiting with the hunters at dinner by then.

Within a few minutes, she got return messages from both of them.

From Luis: *I will call you soon. I love you. Need me to come stay?*
From Tori: *Of course. See you at 9. Love you.*

Elena prepared herself something to eat and sat in her mother's room flipping mindlessly through magazines. The hospice nurse sat at the computer station, typing and doing other work, getting up to check Gloria's monitors or to adjust the oxygen mask. Gloria had awakened for a little while and had asked for Elena. Elena had stretched beside her on the bed for a little while, talking to her about how the hospice people were there to take care of her, that she need not worry about anything, and that she should tell her or any one of them if she needed or wanted anything. Gloria had worried that Elena would have to quit her work at the ranch and at Galindo's in order to take care of her. Elena had reminded her that taking care of her was why she moved back to Logan in the first place, and that she was working in order to be able to buy her mother the best care possible. Lying beside her now, resting her cheek on her mother's shoulder like she did when she was a girl, she reassured her that everything was alright. She did not say it in exact words, of course, but she tried to communicate to her mother in as calming and comforting a way as possible that she, Gloria Rios, had done everything she needed to do. She did not need to worry about one more thing, see to any other detail, or give one more instruction about anything at all. Her labor was complete. She owed no one anything, not another second of thought or concern. The only labor left to do was that which would happen on its own in her body whether she intended it or not. That was the labor of dying.

Gloria dozed off, breathing evenly and peacefully. Her body was relaxed and soft, which Elena interpreted as meaning she was in no pain. Elena eased herself off the bead, smiled at the hospice nurse and went into the kitchen. Luis called.

"Hi, Luis."

"Hey sweetheart. Are you okay? How's Gloria?"

"She's good. She's asleep now. They got her breathing back to normal and adjusted her pain meds up." She sat down on the couch in the living room and stared at the television even though it was not turned on.

"What happened, honey? Did she fall or something? Gerald texted me after he left your house saying she was okay, but he didn't give any details."

Elena told him the whole story in as brief as way as possible. She could hear the concern and anxiety in his voice, and felt bad that she really did not want to see him or even talk to him that much.

"So, hospice is there all the time now?"

"Yes, all the time. Day and night." She took a deep breath and blew it out.

"Why don't I come over. You sound like you shouldn't to be alone."

"No, Luis. I'm fine. Really. And I'm not alone—the nurse is here. These hospice people are really nice."

"I know you aren't technically alone. You know what I mean, Elena."

"I do. Really, though. I'm going to bed soon—I'm tired." She paused for a moment. He did not say anything. "It was scary today, but it's okay now. I'll need you more later…there'll be other days harder than this, I'm sure."

She heard him sigh a deep breath. "Okay, well…if you say so. But call me immediately if anything changes."

"I will, I promise." She thought she heard his truck door slam. "Where are you?"

"I just pulled up at home."

"Was the hunt good this afternoon?"

"Yeah, it was. All but one guy got their limit. They had a good time. It wasn't too cold. The wind wasn't blowing as hard as it was yesterday."

"That's good." She waited a second. "Okay, well, I'll talk to you tomorrow. Thanks for sending Gerald over so quickly. He really made a difference."

"He's a nice guy. A good EMT, too."

"Yeah."

"Okay, honey. Call me if you need me. I'm right here. I love you."

"Thanks. Goodnight."

She ended the call and laid the phone down beside her on the couch. She knew she had to break away from Luis at some point. But, she also knew that the coming weeks during which her mother would slip away more and more would be weeks in which he would be more present in her daily personal life than in any other time since she had been back. She could not think about it or deal with it now. It would have to wait. He would have to wait.

She sat in the darkness and let herself feel the sadness that had been in her stomach all day since she had walked in and seen her mother gasping for breath. Slowly, her eyes filled and she began to weep silently, the grief welling up inside her and tightening inside her throat and flushing her face. She had no unfinished business with her mother. She loved her. They loved each other. They had enjoyed each other in the time since Elena had returned. Any old wounds or misunderstandings or confusions had long since healed over. Now, there was only love between them. Not the clinging, dependant love between a mother and a child, but a deep, abiding love between two adults who know and respect each other as such. One just happened to be the other one's mother. Elena would accept her mother's death. She already had, as a concept. The reality of the process, however, the daily and even hourly nature of it, was devastating.

She heard gravel under tires outside. She wiped her eyes and looked outside. It was Tori. She felt her heart quicken and her mind begin to race as put on her jacket. She stepped outside onto the porch without turning on the porch light. She closed the door behind her quietly and stepped down off the porch. Tori opened her car door and got out, and Elena approached her in the darkness lit only by bands of stars overhead. Tori shut the door behind her and stood with her arms outstretched.

Elena walked to her and buried her face in Tori's neck. She let her full weight press into Tori's body, and soaked in its warmth, breathing in its scent at once so familiar but also strangely new for its closeness. Her mind reeled with sadness, grief and desire. She pulled back and looked into Tori's face.

"I want to feel something besides sadness," she said simply, her voice shaking. "And I want to feel it with you."

She took Tori's face in her hands and covered her lips with her own, seized by a great urgency. The deeper she probed into Tori's willing mouth, the more the sadness in her throat crept away and relaxed its chokehold on her. She felt her body soften and harden alternately as she gave it over to Tori and took Tori's in return, enveloping her in the darkness, grasping for every part of her, pushing the ache of grief aside for that of longing and lust. Elena's head lolled with heavy desire and she found Tori's eyes in the darkness, gazing deeply into them as if intoxicated.

"I've wanted you for so long…" one of them said, it mattered not which, the voice low and shaken.

Elena felt herself begin to quicken and she yielded to the surge, willing it to blot out everything but itself. She leaned her whole weight into Tori's hip, pushing the pressure to its maximum. She cried out in a crash of heat and vibration as Tori's body stiffened and arched them both backward against the car.

They held each other in that position for a moment, shaking from desire and surprise. Finally, Tori eased up from the side of the car, straightening herself and loosening her grip on Elena. Elena pushed a strand of her hair back, one hand still gripping Tori's shoulder, now for balance to keep from collapsing in a heap on the gravel driveway.

They said nothing for a few moments. They simply looked into each other's faces, taking each other in despite the darkness, basking in their new closeness, regaining their equilibrium.

"I love you," Elena finally said.

"I love you, too," Tori replied.

"No, I mean I'm *in love with you*, Tori." Elena said emphatically, stepping back and putting her hands on her hips. She took in a deep breath and let it out. She continued before Tori could say anything. "I've fallen completely in love with you. But I can't do anything about it right now. Other than this…what just happened. I can't talk about it really—to you, to Luis, to anyone. Not yet." She paused for a moment, and then her face broke and melted into sobs. She covered her face with her hands and buried herself again into Tori's chest.

"Shhhh…" She heard Tori's voice, and felt her smoothing her hair and rubbing her back. Elena rested there on Tori's chest for a moment, took another deep breath in and out, and pulled back. She wiped her face with her hand, the other hand still grasping Tori's.

"Thank you" she said through tears. She wiped her eyes again and looked at Tori. She looked up at the sky, then over at the house, then back at Tori.

"I have to go to sleep now. I'm sorry." She took one step back as if to turn away, but then lunged forward to grasp Tori's face in her hands again and kissed her hard. She pulled back, nearly crying again, and looked into Tori's eyes and face, almost incredulous.

"I…I'm sorry if this is a mess. I really can't do anything about it right now," she said in a desperate whisper. She turned in a flurry, skipped the steps up onto the porch, flung the door open and disappeared inside the house, clicking the door shut behind her. She stood there leaned against the door for a moment, waiting for her heart to calm and her tears to dry before going any further into the house. She stilled herself, her arms folded around across her chest, grasping herself as tightly as she could. She felt her breathing return to normal, and the heat seep out of her abdomen into the air around her. She began to relax. She lowered her arms.

She heard the engine start outside and the crunching of the gravel under the tires as Tori backed out into the street and drove away.

Tori rolled her car windows down for the short drive home from Elena's, mainly to get some air and to cool off. Her face was flushed, and she felt swollen and tender all over. She stared straight ahead, keeping her eyes on the road illuminated in her headlights, trying to focus. Her mind buzzed with a barrage of sensory details—hair, skin, taste, scent, soft flesh. She instinctively put her fingers to her mouth, touching her tongue with them.

She pulled into the entrance of the hotel, veering onto the gravel driveway that led to her cabin. She stopped her car, opened the roof, turned off the engine and sat still in the cool silence. The wind blew through the open windows of her car, chilling her cheeks and ears. She leaned her head back and looked through the open roof into the inky sky dotted with millions of stars. It all had been so sudden, although not shocking. The two of them had been surfing the sexual tension between them for months. Something would have happened eventually, she knew. Now that it had happened, she felt like she had been dealt a blow: the intensity and attraction that had exploded between them felt overwhelming, like it had a presence and power all its own, independent of them, and far stronger than Tori had expected.

She had not expected Elena to say that she was in love with her, either. No one had said these words to her since she was in college, nor had she said them to anyone since then. Her first and only love had been Elisabeth, the graduate student assistant in her freshman English class who had just realized she was a lesbian. Together, they began learning the ins and outs of being in a relationship—figuring out who you are both with and apart from the other person, learning which battles are worth fighting and which ones are a waste of your life, negotiating the demands of work, school and family, pushing beyond merely having sex with someone to also making love to them, learning that you cannot fix things for other people and that, ultimately, people can only make themselves happy at the deepest levels. The two of them stayed together for several years, and they loved each other—were in love with each other—deeply during those years. It ended when Elisabeth finished her graduate degree and took a university job in England. Tori had her own life plan; moving to England was not part of it. So, they split up and went on with their lives without each other.

The handful of other relationships she had had seemed never to reach the level of what she considered being "in love with" someone. Something deeper had been missing from all of them, something fundamental—a sense that the relationship was inevitable in some sense, or a piece of fate, and resistance was futile.

The futility of denying Elena any longer felt like a blow to Tori's stomach as she sat in her car in the dark stillness. She knew intuitively that she could not resist Elena now, after what had happened just a few moments ago. All the mechanisms of self-denial, control, and professionalism that she had used to keep things within the realm of being colleagues and friends were useless now. There was no point in even dragging them back up as barriers. They would simply be bowled over with the first unguarded glance or touch between them. Tori knew this deep inside, and felt the sharp mixture of joy as well as dread in the pit of her stomach. Joy because no thought or person provoked an involuntary shudder of desire throughout most of her body the way Elena did, especially after tonight. Just the mere memory of Elena massaging herself on her hip was enough to make Tori's stomach drop and her eyes lose their focus momentarily. She had not had this kind of bodily reaction to another person since Elisabeth, and perhaps not ever. And the joy that emerged from this was inexpressible to her in language. Perhaps, the body itself was its only mode of expression.

The joy mingled with dread, however. Dread because Elena was in the throes of grief, which is imperious and mercurial in its nature. It drives people to feel things at sharper angles than they would normally, or that are justified by the situation. In the clarity of its rarified air, people are moved to make rash choices and issue wild declarations. Tori knew grief. She had been maniacal after the death of her parents. She had felt the wild edges of despair and anger and sadness as they wrenched her from place to place, decision to decision, all in the supposedly "clear" light of the now intimate realities of life and death which bring what matters, or should matter, into sharper relief. She had lashed out at people, even at Vincent. She had slept with people she barely knew. She had almost sold everything she owned to buy a private island off the coast of Nicaragua. Only Sharon had been able to stay with her, to ride their friendship like a bucking horse that finally grows tired and resigned to its new role.

Tori knew something of what Elena was already beginning to experience and what would only become stronger, more poignant, more devastating and more altering in the weeks and months to come, as long as Gloria kept herself in this life. In the light of this, what was she to make of what had happened tonight? And of Elena's statement that she had fallen in love with her? Was it real? Was it true? Or was this the grief talking? Tori knew what she herself felt. And she knew that Elena *believed* herself to be speaking what was true for her as well. But, was it?

What if were not true and Elena ended up marrying Luis? Or leaving Logan and everyone in it forever after her mother died?

As these thoughts came, Tori dropped her head, squeezed her eyes shut and wrapped her arms tightly around her stomach as if to protect herself from a body blow. The dread roiled in her abdomen and she felt a flush of pain rise in her neck. She took a deep breath in, held it, and breathed it out slowly. After a few more breaths, she unclenched her eyes and arms, allowing herself to relax a bit, enough to regain some equilibrium. She sat for a moment longer, staring ahead at her cabin, and leaned her head back again to gaze through the roof at the stars.

She would figure it out, one way or the other. She trusted

herself to do that. She loved Elena. Yes, she was *in love* with Elena. She would take it all as it came, whatever came, and deal with it in the way that made the most sense in the moment. That is all anyone ever does anyway. That is all anyone *can* do no matter what they might hope or plan. That is what she would do.

She got out of her car and went inside. Within moments, she had stripped off her clothes, climbed naked into the bed, and lay on her back under deep layers of cotton down. She trailed her fingers lightly over her belly and her breasts, remembering.

# Chapter Eleven

The next morning, Tori joined Letty in the field for the brunch service for a group of quail hunters Luis had taken out. The air was cold but the sky was clear and by the time the hunters made it into camp, things had warmed up and Tori did not feel the shaking in her stomach quite as badly. Elena had arranged for Letty to cover the field service that day prior the events of last night, but Tori could not help but feel that it was a prescient decision on her part. Things still felt too raw and combustible, at least to Tori. She would see Elena later in the day for their regular meeting to go over ranch costs. She would be less shaky then perhaps.

Tori helped Letty set up the camp, again taking charge of the tables, chairs, linens, decorations and the service table. Unlike the other campsites, this one was positioned near a rocky gorge, the same one that ran behind the hotel, except here it was several miles away. No trees stood anywhere near to offer shade, which made this campsite best on cold, bright days like this one when sunlight was a friend. She set up chaise lounges and hammocks alongside the edge of the gorge, facing the southwest. The sun would warm the hunters' backs and shoulders and the landscape in front of them would dazzle in the light. She found interesting, colorful rocks to place in decorative piles as table centerpieces.

Letty focused on the food and making sure everything was timed perfectly. When Luis came in with the jubilant hunters, she quickly gathered several quail from Luis' game bag, dressed them in a flash and had them sizzling on the grill before all the hunters had even seated themselves with their first course. Tori visited with the hunters, helping Luis fetch coffee and cocktails for them, but kept an eye on Letty as well. She watched how Letty managed the meal, noticing practices and techniques she had learned from Elena both at the ranch and at Galindo's. She moved from task to task efficiently and quickly, not quite as calmly and with the elegant ease that Elena did, but with every bit as much focus and confidence. She had learned a lot in the year that she had worked and studied with Elena, first at Galindo's and now at the ranch, and Elena relied on her more and more to keep things going, especially as Gloria declined and Elena needed flexibility in her schedule.

The hunters immersed themselves in the food and setting in the way that was now common among nearly all the groups that came to Sandy Creek Ranch. Soon, they were sluggish from the rich food, the early wake-up time, and the morning spent walking among the brush in the rocky desert. They made their way from the tables of empty plates to the hammocks and chaise lounges along the gorge. Soon they were dozing in the bright sun, its heat warming them in the cool air through their longjohns.

Letty, Tori, and Luis fell into what by now were established routines. They each fixed themselves a plate of food and sat down together to eat at one of the tables the furthest away from the hunters. There, they talked generally about the goings on at the ranch.

Luis described details of the hunt that morning. Letty updated them on the public dinner reservations coming in for the week. Tori shared feedback she had received from guests during her visits with them. It all felt routine and regular to Tori, which helped to settle the faint shaking in her stomach and to ease her nervousness about meeting with Elena later in the day. After they ate, they began the process of packing up, quietly so not to disturb the napping hunters too much. Luis went to his truck to clean and arrange some of his equipment and to peek in on the tired bird dog that lay curled up and sleeping in his crate. Tori helped Letty with a few things, but then left her to do the rest of it the way she preferred, the way Elena had trained her to pack the field kit.

Tori walked to the edge of the gorge, a few dozen yards down from where the hunters lay stretched on their chairs. She found a flat rock near the edge and sat down on it, feeling the warmth of the sun warming her back. She looked out across the gorge and down its sharp sides to the bottom. Bushes, sand and loose rocks covered the bottom strip of flat ground that ran like a sandy ribbon along the bottom of the gorge. She followed the ribbon with her eye as far as she could see in one direction from her position on the rock, then traced it back and followed it as far as she could see in the other direction. She wondered if a hiking trail along the bottom of the gorge could be created. It could begin behind the hotel, perhaps near the animal trail she always followed to the gorge's lip. People might like that, especially in the summer when the high walls of the gorge would provide shade from the scorching heat. She told herself to remember to bring that up in the next staff meeting.

She heard steps behind her and turned around just as Luis' long shadow blocked her from the sun. She smiled up at him, seeing only his silhouette in the glare.

"Mind if I join you?" he asked.

"Of course not," she replied. "Pull up a rock." He found a small flat stone a few yards away from her and eased himself down onto it, his legs curving over its edge to a smaller rock a foot further down the gorge's descending lip. Tori watched him and smiled, feeling a tinge of the shaking in her stomach resume. She looked back out over the gorge and the distance beyond it, waiting for him to speak.

Luis looked out across the gorge, scanning the distance along the horizon. After a moment, he spoke.

"Tori, I've wanted to talk to you for a while." He turned to look at her. Tori felt a jump in her stomach as she heard his words. She turned to him.

"Sure, Luis. About what?" she asked.

"Well, I've wanted to thank you." He stopped and looked back out over the landscape, turning his head away from Tori then slowly turning back to her. He rubbed his hands along the tops of his tight thighs.

"I want to thank you for what you've done here in Logan with this ranch." He stopped and smiled. "And what you've done for me."

Tori smiled back at him.

"Luis, I should be the one thanking you. So much of our success has come because of you and the work you do on the hunts." She felt a pang of guilt as she said this. She really meant what she said. He was a godsend to her. And, yet, last night she had her mouth on the breasts of the woman he clearly loved. She forced the muscles of her face to stay in the shape of a smile.

"I appreciate you saying that, but…really…I just want to thank you because this ranch concept couldn't have come at a better time for me." He stopped himself for a moment, as if considering how much more to speak. He inhaled and let out a big breath, looking up into Tori's face.

"As I'm sure you know, Elena and I have a long history. We were together in high school and if she hadn't left I think we would have gotten married." He stopped, looked down at his legs and back up again. "I didn't expect her to come back really, but she did. I think working with you has been really good for her. The two of you are a lot alike…" Tori listened to these words and felt her throat tighten.

"…You both are old hands in this business of hotels and restaurants and such, and she respects you so much. I wondered if there was enough for her to stay in Logan after her mother passes." He looked at Tori directly. "I wondered if I was enough." Tori looked down at the dirt beside her, touching her fingers to the tiny rocks embedded in it. Her throat tightened even more.

"But, I think this ranch is enough for her here. She loves working with you, which I'm sure you can see. I know things can't just pick up from where they left off twenty-five years ago, and this is a difficult time with Gloria's illness and all, but…I feel good about things now in a way I haven't in a long time. And I want to thank you for coming out here and starting this place." He motioned to the air around him with his arm. "You've helped me and Elena a lot. And other people too—Letty, Ricardo, the others." He stopped for a moment and smiled a bit sheepishly. "So, I just wanted to say that."

Tori listened to him, staring down at the lines she drew in the dirt with her fingernail. The guilty pang from a few moments ago turned into a dull stab. She wanted to get up from the rock, run to the truck and drive away, but that was impossible. She had to say something. She had to respond in kind to Luis' generous and gracious words. She raised her face to look at him.

"I appreciate you saying that, Luis. I really do." She looked at him directly and tried to speak truthfully despite feeling that she was betraying him and everything he had just shared with her. "I have come to love this place—Logan and the people in it. I feel blessed by my uncle and I…I'm just glad everything has worked out so well." She paused for a moment. "Really, thank you, Luis."

He smiled, nodded and they both turned away from each other

to look out over the gorge. They sat in silence for a little while. Luis seemed lost in his own thoughts. Tori did not want to get up too quickly, so she sat still except for her fingers between which she rolled a piece of thorn. Finally, they heard the sound of voices coming from the direction of the hunters. They turned back and saw a couple of them swinging around to sit sideways on their chaise lounges to put on their boots.

"I guess it's about that time, huh?" Luis said, smiling brightly at Tori.

"I guess so," she replied.

They got up and joined the group. Letty had packed everything in the truck she and Tori had driven out. Luis helped Tori gather the furniture and she began returning things to the storage shed as he loaded up the hunters. By the time she finished and stepped up into the truck to join Letty, he was several minutes ahead of her on the way back to the ranch.

❦

Tori sat at the bar in her cabin that afternoon going through ranch mail. She had pulled into the hotel entrance with Letty and had veered around to the service entrance door on the west side of the building. She glanced at Elena's silver Tahoe as they passed it in the parking lot. She had parked the truck, left the keys with Letty and walked around the back of the hotel, across the pool patio and across the desert field to her cabin. She had an hour or two to kill before her meeting with Elena.

The message light on her phone was blinking when she walked into the cabin. As soon as she got settled at the bar, she checked the voicemail list and saw the caller's identity: Sharon. She listened to the message.

"Hey, gorgeous, it's me. Just calling to say hey and to see if you're still alive out there in the desert with all those hunters and guns and all. I've got a few days free coming up soon and wondered if it was a good time to come out and see the place and, shall we say, *spend some quality time*. Let me know when you get a chance. I miss you. Bye."

Tori put the phone down and stared out the back window onto her patio. This time yesterday, things had been clear and simple and uncomplicated. Now, not even twenty-four hours later, the knots in her stomach were increasing at regular intervals. First, she and Elena crash into each other in a sudden explosion of desire. Then, Luis bares his soul to her about his dreams for a life with Elena. Now, Sharon wants to come out for a visit. She wanted to see Sharon, and had thought about her many times in the last several months. She had missed her wit, the sense of fun that she always brought to things, and the ease that Tori felt talking to her about her life. And she had missed her body and the connection between them. Certainly, now was a great time to have someone to talk to about things. She felt unsure now, though, about Sharon's "quality time" comment. She would have to think about that now, after what happened last night.

An hour passed and it was time to go over to the hotel to meet with Elena. She stepped out onto her patio and adjusted the thermostat on the jacuzzi. She had installed it earlier in the fall because she felt weird sharing the one at the hotel with the guests. As fall was turning to winter, she enjoyed sitting in it on chilly nights, the warm water up to her neck, the jets on full blast. Often she would dry off and crawl straight into bed, warming the sheets with her heated body. It was a great way to end the day.

She lifted the lid of the jacuzzi a bit, stuck her fingers down into the water and brought them back out. She wiped them on her jeans, took a deep breath, and started across the desert field toward the hotel. She rounded the east wing into the pool area and smiled at two people in the hotel jacuzzi, their heads and necks barely visible through the blades of yucca plants that grew from the raised beds surrounding it. She walked past the fountain and into the dining room. One of the young waiters, Jared, was putting new linens on the tables and smiled at her when she walked in.

"How are you, Jared?" she asked, smiling back at him.

"I'm fine Ms. Reed, thank you." He watched her as she walked toward the kitchen door and peered in through the small rectangular window. She saw Letty working at the center table and another staff person sitting at the end of the table working with the pile of freshly dressed quail in front of him. Tori looked past them to the corner kitchen office and saw Elena sitting inside her glassed-in room, looking down at her desk.

Tori walked through the door and into the kitchen. Letty looked up when she heard the door open.

"You're not doing the dinner service, too, are you?" Tori asked her. Normally, Elena and Letty traded off the field and dinner services. Since Letty had done the morning field service, Elena would normally do the dinner service alone.

"No, I'm going home in a little bit. I'm just getting stuff ready." She smiled as Tori walked past her toward Elena's office.

Tori did not know if Elena had seen her come in or not. She knocked on the door lightly and opened the door to peek in.

"May I come in?" she asked.

Elena looked up from her laptop and spreadsheets. Her face brightened into a wide smile. Her dark eyes gleamed.

"Of course!" She got up and reached one arm out to encircle Tori's neck as she hugged her and kissed her cheek. "I'm glad to see you," she said as she pulled back and looked into Tori's eyes, her face beaming.

Tori felt the skin on her chest and neck begin to flush. Seeing Elena in the broad daylight after last night's encounter was like seeing her for the first time. She looked at her face now knowing the texture of Elena's skin against her lips, the feel of the bend in her jawbone, and the taste of her neck.

"I'm glad to see you, too," she said, smiling at Elena even though her face felt a bit hot and her stomach buzzed. "Is this still a good time to meet?"

"Yes, sit down," Elena pulled the extra chair up to her desk and motioned for Tori to sit. She plopped down in her own office chair, curling one leg under her and leaning one elbow on the desk, the other hand resting on her thigh. She gazed at Tori, still smiling, not seeming to be in a hurry to do anything but look at her.

Tori smiled back at her, feeling a bit self-conscious at being looked at so intently and so casually at the same time. Within seconds, however, the self-consciousness waned somewhat and she felt herself beginning to swim in the depth of Elena's eyes.

"How are you?" Tori asked. "I hope you were able to sleep." She sat back in her chair and crossed her legs.

Elena's face did not change at the question. She simply held her smiling gaze directed at Tori for a few more seconds before answering. Finally, after what seemed like ten minutes to Tori, she spoke.

"I fell asleep almost immediately," she said. Her eyes never left Tori's. She paused for a moment. "I had nice dreams," she added, grinning slightly.

Tori had not expected this. Elena seemed calm and happy, even giddy. Not sad or sorrowful or awash in a bundle of emotions as she had been last night when Tori left her. She wondered if there was a catch, if this was a temporary mood and Elena would collapse into sobs or some other emotional state in a moment, or in an hour.

"How is your mother? How did the night go for her?" Tori asked.

"She slept all night and woke up this morning hungry. I cooked her eggs and beans for breakfast, and when I left for Galindo's she was propped up in bed watching Spanish TV game shows with

Tita Maria. They both were laughing so hard I wondered if the hospice person could get any work done." She took a deep breath and blew it out, her mouth wide in a smile. She resumed her gaze.

"Oh, Elena, that's wonderful," Tori said, genuinely relieved to hear that Gloria was doing so well. "I'm so glad to hear this. I guess the medicines really make a difference, huh?"

Elena nodded and leaned back more in her chair. "Yeah, they do. I'm so glad." Something in the kitchen caught her eye and she turned to look out. Tori turned to see Letty holding up a large bowl of pink quail carcasses, ready for grilling. Elena looked at them, smiled and gave Letty a thumbs-up through the window glass. She turned back to Tori.

"Thank you for last night," she said, again looking directly into Tori's eyes. She splayed her fingers slightly on her thigh as she spoke.

Tori looked at her for a moment, returning her gaze with more confidence now, the self-consciousness fading. "I was glad to be there for you," she said. "And with you." She smiled slightly and swallowed, feeling her throat tighten faintly with desire.

Elena sat still for a moment, then leaned forward in her chair, reached over and grasped Tori's hand. She brought Tori's hand to her face, turned it over and kissed her palm. Tori felt her stomach drop. Elena sat back in her chair, still smiling and sitting there with the ease she would have if they were talking about braising carrots for the dinner service.

"I meant every word of what I said to you," Elena said frankly. "I don't want to talk about it really, but you need to know that I meant every word." She waited a moment, looking deeply into Tori's eyes. "I have limits right now, with Mama and everything…but I'm in love with you, Tori, and there's really nothing to be done about it. At least, that's how I see it."

Tori felt walloped. She had not expected this either—this frankness and simplicity and clarity. But as soon as Elena said it, she felt something give way inside her, like a strained rope being cut and relaxed. As soon as she heard Elena's words, even though her insides were still roiling from the palm kiss, she knew that Elena was right. She had thought it herself last night sitting in the car. They were in love with each other. It was a simple, undeniable fact—as real as the stucco hotel in the middle of the desert in which they sat. And it was a gift. No matter what ended up happening, even if their love lasted only today or a week, it had been a gift for which she was grateful. She felt herself shift inside with Elena's words, as if what she said had prompted an inner calibration of perspective, feeling and knowing. Here again, Elena was playing her role as the tuning fork, the human instrument that detects and determines perfect pitch and tone in multiple circumstances.

Tori looked into Elena's eyes and smiled, narrowing her own eyes in concentration and focus.

"Who knew that when I moved out here I would meet someone like you?" she said. She raised her hand to her mouth and brushed her fingers across her lips. She moved them back and forth, in slow repetition, as if doing so helped her to frame her thoughts and words. Finally, she dropped her palm onto her jeaned thigh, still looking directly into Elena's eyes.

"I'm in love with you, too, Elena Rios," she said simply. She quivered deep inside as she said these words, but knew them to be true, as true as anything she had ever said. "I have lots of questions about things…but I will follow your lead on this…however you want to proceed."

Elena's faced cracked slightly, and she raised her hand to her mouth and turned away from Tori to look out into the kitchen. She held herself still, pinching her fingers over her mouth, then turned back to Tori. Her eyes glistened with tears, but she lowered her hand and her face broke into a wide smile. She nodded quickly and took a short breath in. "Okay…" she said, still nodding and seeming to try to catch her breath. "Okay…thank you." She swallowed hard and took a deeper breath.

Tori beamed back at her, feeling waves of relief and a swell of emotion in her chest. Had there been no one in the kitchen, she would have leaned over to grab the arm of Elena's rolling chair to pull her toward her. Instead, she simply took a deep breath, smiled into Elena's eyes, and then looked at the pile of spreadsheets on Elena's desk.

"Shall we go over this month's financials then?" she asked brightly, rounding and widening her eyes in a look that affirmed what an odd transition that was.

Elena laughed, throwing her had back and grabbing the pony-tail behind her head. She uncurled her leg from underneath her and rolled her chair closer to her desk.

"Absolutely!" she said. "Let's take a look."

❧

Tori stood on her patio and unbuttoned her shirt. The only light came either from the moon and the bands of stars surrounding it, or from the lights illuminating the water inside the jacuzzi. She stared into the blinking expanse above her as she slipped the shirt off her shoulders and began unbuttoning her jeans. When those were off, she stripped off her undergarments and stepped up and over the edge of the jacuzzi and into the bubbling water.

She took a deep breath and settled into the middle of the pool, squatting so that she was submerged up to her earlobes. She looked at her arms stretched out in front of her in the water. Tiny bubbles clung to the soft hairs on her arm, visible now because of the chill bumps that covered nearly all her skin. She waved her arms around her, closed her eyes and stretched her neck from side to side, feeling the warmth penetrate her shoulders and back. After a few moments she moved off to the side, to the deepest chair built in to the jacuzzi wall. She settled in, positioning herself for the jets to massage her lower back and neck. She reached behind her for the wine glass she had filled and placed on the edge. She took a sip, returned the glass to its place on the edge, and eased herself down in the chair so she could view the moon and stars overhead.

She thought about the events of the day. Luis' sharing with her on the morning hunt. Her meeting with Elena, at which she told someone she was in love with them for only the second time in her life. Elena's profession of love for her for the second time in less than twenty-four hours. Her and Elena's confirmation of what both of them had suspected based on prior calculations and data about the ranch—that it was doing remarkably well. Sandy Creek Ranch was quickly becoming a success, in both its hunting operations aimed mostly at out-of-towners as well as in its local business, which centered around the restaurant. As her mind buzzed with these thoughts, Tori closed her eyes and smiled up at the moon and the sky. She felt an overwhelming sense of joy and accomplishment, as well as a sense of fulfillment she did not think she had ever felt in her life. It was as if all the pieces were finally in place all at the same time, both personally and professionally.

Luis, however, was a difficult piece of the puzzle. Tori liked him so much, and she knew that Elena loved him, even if she did not love him the way he loved her. She wondered how Elena would handle the situation. And *when* she would handle it. And how would it affect the workings at the ranch. She knew that Elena had no plans to talk with her about these things, at least not yet. Elena was clear on that—she had limitations now on what she would or could pay attention to during these last weeks and months of her mother's life, and limits on what she would discuss about it with others, even with Tori. Everyone would have to wait, apparently, including Luis and Tori, for Elena's decisions about the future.

A movement in the darkness beyond her patio caught her eye.

She squinted her eyes to dim the glare coming up from the jacuzzi lights and stared out into the darkness. She saw the outline of a figure walking toward her and within a few steps she knew who it was.

She smiled as Elena stepped across the rock barrier that separated the patio from the desert floor. She walked the few steps toward the jacuzzi, her hands in her jacket pockets, and stood at its side opposite where Tori sat. Elena's eyes moved to capture the shimmering image of Tori's body in the bubbling water. Tori watched her take it all in.

"How did dinner go?" she asked when Elena's eyes came back to meet hers.

"It went well. Uneventful. Everyone seemed pleased with everything," she replied with a shrug and smile. She took a few steps around the edge of the jacuzzi toward Tori. Tori leaned her head back on the ledge to keep Elena in her sight as she circled around behind her. Elena took the glass of wine, smelled it, took a long drink, and lowered it back to its place on the ledge. She swallowed and smiled down at Tori as she bent to kiss her. Tori tasted the wine on her tongue.

"That's nice wine, isn't it," she said to Elena who held her face directly above Tori's upside down.

Elena nodded, smiling faintly. "Turn around," she said softly. "I only have a few minutes. I have to go home to Mama."

Tori raised herself and found Elena's willing mouth, feeding deeply from it as she encircled her arms around Elena's back under her shirt, relishing the feel of her soft, bare skin. Elena reached back at some point and loosened her ponytail, toppling her hair in long sprays over her shoulders. Tori ran her fingers through it, gathering it in bunches between her fingers and squeezing it in her hands until she could feel the slight pull from Elena's scalp.

"I want you so much…" Elena said with a ragged breath. "I just needed to see you for a minute…" She lowered her head to Tori's breasts.

"Please come in with me, " Tori begged. "Or I'll come out there to you."

"I can't. I have to go," Elena said, pulling up. "I've already been here too long." She paused for a moment, both of them catching their breath. "I'm sorry. I hope it's okay that I came. I just wanted to see you before I went home to Mama."

"Oh God, Elena! I'm so glad you did," Tori said as she pulled her close and buried her face in Elena's neck.

They held each other still for a few more moments, their heart rates and breathing still quickened. Soon, Elena loosened herself from Tori's embrace and took another long drink from Tori's wine glass. She sat it down, swallowed hard, and smiled broadly.

"Thank you," she said.

Tori reached for her again, but Elena took a step back, shaking her head, and laughed aloud.

"No, I can't. Get back in that water." She ran her fingers through her hair, fastening it back into its ponytail, and took a few deep breaths. "I'm serious. I'll lose myself…"

Tori watched her as she walked to the edge of the patio, stepped over the rock boundary and turned around. She stood still while Tori sank down into the warm water. As soon as Tori settled back into her seat, Elena blew her a kiss, turned and disappeared into the darkness.

Tori reached for the wine glass on the ledge, brought it to her lips and drained it.

# Chapter Twelve

Elena held Rico in her lap while the hospice nurses moved her mother onto a stretcher so they could change the sheets on her bed. Gloria had drifted back to sleep almost as soon as they had settled her on the stretcher. Elena ran her fingers through Rico's orange fur, scratching and massaging the skin around his neck. He purred and twitched his tail, but Elena knew he would leave the minute she let go of him to return to the soft hollow on the bed between Gloria's legs. Sometimes she stood by her mother's bed and spoke to her, but got no response even though Gloria's fingers were curled around Rico's neck, working his fur ever so slightly. She wondered how the cat would be once her mother was gone. She wondered how *she* would be.

When the nurses finished and both Gloria and Rico were resting comfortably on the fresh bed, Elena kissed her mother's forehead and left for the ranch. The restaurant was completely booked that night with hunters and with local customers even though it was only a week before Christmas. Betty had taken several calls from people who wanted to come to the ranch for evening meals on Christmas Eve or Christmas night, but Tori and Elena had decided to close the ranch for those days to give everyone on the staff a much needed break. The ranch was booked solid until Christmas Eve.

She pulled into the hotel driveway and parked next to Luis' navy truck. He and Ricardo were out with quail hunters and would return in a couple of hours. She stepped out of her Tahoe and glanced toward Tori's cabin as she swung the door shut. She saw Tori's car and Sharon's car, a red Mercedes convertible, parked right next to it in front of the cabin. Sharon had arrived yesterday afternoon, but Elena had not met her yet. Tori had taken her out with Luis and Letty on the morning hunt to see part of the ranch and have brunch out in the desert. Elena was not sure if they were in the cabin now or not. Perhaps they were somewhere in one of the ranch trucks. The two of them were joining Ken and Hazel for dinner at the ranch that night. Tori asked Elena to manage the kitchen so Sharon would have the best possible meal, and she had agreed to do it. She swung her bag over her shoulder, skipped the steps up onto the porch and went inside to begin work.

Letty was elbow deep in a large wash pan of marinating quail when Elena entered the kitchen. She looked up at her and smiled, blowing a wispy strand of hair out of her eyes.

"Hey," she said to Elena.

"Hey, I figured you'd be gone by now," she said, coming up to stand beside Letty and look down into the wash pan. Pink quail bodies soaked in the murky brown marinade that smelled of smoke, honey and peppers. "Why don't you take off? I'll do all this."

"It's almost done now," she said, lifting her arms from the wash pan and walking toward the sink to rinse them under the faucet. The marinade clung to her forearms and dripped down to her elbows. "Jared is the only one here yet—he's doing linens and table settings in the dining room. Luis and Ricardo brought in forty-five quail from the morning hunt—that's what those are. They'll bring more in a little while hopefully. Everyone else should be here any minute to finish getting everything prepped. We're full tonight." She did not look at Elena as she spoke. Elena stood with one hand in the quail marinade, swishing the birds around a bit and listening to Letty's report. She looked up at her when she finished speaking.

"Sounds great," she smiled at her. "Thanks for staying. How did it go this morning?" She wondered about Sharon, what she was like, if Letty had any impressions of her. She did not want to be too obvious about asking, though.

Letty shrugged. "Normal," she said, drying her hands and arms. "The hunters got a lot of birds and they ate a lot. The sun was out so it wasn't too cold by the time they got there. The wind wasn't blowing, which helped me with the grill." She spread the towel on the rack behind her. "I still think we should have a brick oven or chiminea out there for grilling instead of that portable one that goes on the camp stove." She looked at Elena and shook her head. "The portable thing is so frail and when the wind blows it takes twice as long to get a nice char on anything, but..." She leaned down to brush a dash of flour off her jeans, then looked back up at Elena. "That's just my opinion. You're the pro."

Elena grinned at her young protégé, still stirring the quail in the marinade. She was growing to love Letty. She had not had an assistant chef as naturally gifted as Letty in several years, and it had been even longer since she had had one as hardworking.

Letty immediately understood nearly everything Elena taught her—various cooking techniques, myriad flavor pairings, dozens of different ways to prepare the same handful of basic foods, ways to tease out distinct flavors with minimal ingredients and effort, the artistry of plating and presentation—and when she did not understand something, she pestered Elena about it until she did.

She arrived early, stayed late and consciously imitated Elena in nearly everything—holding a whisk, putting her hair in a ponytail for work, instructing the waiters, and more. She was beginning to develop her own opinions, though, and the issue of the outdoor grill had come up a few times. Elena agreed with her, and so did Tori. They planned to build semi-permanent rock grills at all the campsites during the off-season and show them to Letty as a surprise.

"I think you may be right," she said, nodding. "We'll see about it after we get through this first season." She took her hand from the marinade and walked to the sink. She rinsed her hand, her back turned to Letty. "Tori was out with you this morning, right?" she asked without turning around.

"Yeah, she met me here and helped me load up," Letty said, focusing on a small knife cut on her thumb. "She and her friend drove out in another truck."

Elena turned around and reached for the towel Letty had put on the rack. "How was her friend? What's her name—Sharon?" She very well knew her name, and immediately felt silly for pretending otherwise. *Be a grownup*, she thought, scolding herself.

Letty nodded and put her thumb to her mouth to bite off a piece of cut skin. She pulled her thumb back, looked at it intently, and wiped it on her jeans. "Sharon, yeah. She seems nice enough. She tried to help out. She's definitely from the city, though." Letty grinned a little.

"Yeah?" Elena asked.

Letty nodded. "You know, the clothes, the sunglasses, lots of questions about things. I mean, Tori's from the city, too, but she's more natural out here. I guess 'cause she was out here a lot when she was a kid—that's what she told me once."

Elena reached to return the wet towel to its rack. "What about her clothes?" she asked, confused at Letty's comment.

"She had some fancy hunting pants and one of those wool

coats with the patches on the sleeves and those tall leather boots that go over your pants." Letty furrowed her brow a bit as she described Sharon's upscale hunting outfit, clearly having not seen Luis, Ricardo or anyone wearing such clothes.

Elena smiled in recognition. "It sounds like a classic European hunting outfit. Not exactly what we do out here, but still…"

Letty raised her eyebrows in appreciation. "She looked good…very *city*, like I said. Tori was explaining everything to her, about how we do the field brunch and about eating the game meat and everything. I think she got it. She seemed to be impressed with it all." Letty looked at her thumb again, and put her hand in her pocket. "She ate a lot, so I guess she liked the food."

"She ate a lot?" Elena asked.

"Two helpings—she kept saying how everything tastes better when it's cooked outside." Letty pulled her cell phone out of her back pocket and looked at it. "Ok, I gotta go. My brother just texted me he's almost here. Remind me never to loan him my car again."

"Why? He didn't wreck it or anything, did he?"

"No, he just *takes his time* with it." She rolled her eyes and shook her head in exasperation. She walked over to the door by Elena's office and grabbed her coat off one of several hooks bolted onto the wall. "Call me if you need me tonight. I can be here fast—I'm not doing anything. I'll just be at home hanging with the fam."

"Thanks sweetie. I'll call you if I need you." Elena smiled at her as she disappeared through the swinging door. She heard voices in the living area and within seconds several staff members came in, smiling and greeting Elena as they took off their coats and put on their aprons. Within minutes the kitchen sprang into a jumble of activity as everyone took up specific tasks for the evening. Luis and Ricardo returned with more quail, which Elena quickly dressed alongside a staff person who then sank them all into a marinade. Elena moved in and among all the staff people, helping when necessary, teaching and demonstrating if things were not coming easily, and keeping a constant eye on the clock. Things had to be done efficiently and on time for everything to work on the menus. Plus, she was eager for the dinner service to begin so she could see Tori and meet this Sharon for herself.

The dinner service was well underway when Ken and Hazel arrived and were seated at their reserved table. Elena saw them through the kitchen window and went to greet them.

"Hi!" she said brightly.

"Hey yourself! How're you doin'?" Ken boomed, smiling broadly and standing to hug Elena. She put her arms around his waist and squeezed him. When she pulled back, Hazel was standing and smiling, waiting her turn for a hug. Elena kissed her cheek and hugged her around the neck.

"Sit with us for a second, can you?" Ken pulled out a chair for her. She sat down on the edge of the chair, careful to not touch the place setting that would be for either Tori or Sharon. "How are things going out here? I hear nothing but good things from everyone."

She smiled and nodded. "Yeah, things are going really well. We're booked solid through the holidays and beyond. We're totally booked tonight and for the rest of the weekend here in the restaurant."

"That's fantastic!" Hazel said. "I'm so proud of you girls for doing this! This ranch and all is exactly what this town needed." She looked at Ken and and back at Elena, beaming as if the two women were her own daughters.

"We're having a lot of fun with it," Elena said. "Thank you for saying that, Hazel. That means a lot to me and I know it would to Tori, too."

At that moment, Ken turned toward the courtyard and held out his arm. "Speak of the devil!" he said, rising from his chair. Elena turned to see Tori coming into the dining room from the courtyard. A tall, striking blonde woman wearing black trousers and a black blouse, accented with a long, red scarf and red stilettos followed behind her. Ken, Hazel, and Elena stood up from the table.

Ken wrapped Tori in a bear hug, squeezing her until her feet came up off the floor a little bit. When he put her down, she pulled back and introduced the woman who came in with her.

"Ken, this is my dear friend Sharon Lee, visiting from Houston. She arrived last night." Tori put her arm around Sharon and brought her forward to Ken.

"I've heard so many wonderful things about you, Ken," Sharon said, smiling brightly and looking at Ken directly in the eyes. She held out her hand. "It's a pleasure to finally meet you in person."

Ken grinned and grasped her hand. "Well, I'm glad to meet you, too. Welcome to West Texas. Any friend of Tori's is a friend of mine, I tell ya." He stepped back and opened his arm to bring Hazel into the circle. "And this is my better half, Hazel—we both love Tori and this ranch, and everything she and Elena have done with it."

Hazel and Sharon greeted each other and Tori explained that Hazel had a crafts store in town. Tori caught Elena's eye while Sharon and Hazel exchanged pleasantries. Elena looked at her and smiled faintly. Tori stepped forward quickly, kissed her on the cheek and winked at her as she pulled back, her light eyes sparkling even in the dim candle-lit dining room. She looked back at Sharon and held her arm out to bring her toward Elena.

"Sharon, this is Elena—my partner, my friend, my...well...nearly my everything out here." She laughed as she said this. Elena felt her stomach drop. "None of this would be as successful as it is without her," Tori continued.

Elena smiled, looking directly in Sharon's hazel eyes as she reached for her hand. "Happy to meet you. I'm glad you made it out here. Tori's been really excited for you to come." She squeezed Sharon's hand, noticing its dry warmth.

Sharon met Elena's gaze, smiling broadly as she grasped Elena's hand. Elena felt Sharon squeeze her hand and hold it for a few moments, all the while looking into Elena's eyes. She immediately sensed a kind of magnetism in Sharon, and felt drawn to her despite not wanting to be. She swallowed and waited for Sharon to speak. "I'm so glad my friend found you," she said finally, pulling Elena close to her and raising her free arm to hug her. Elena raised her chin to rest on Sharon's shoulder as she embraced her and felt a strand of her soft, blonde hair against her cheek. She looked at Tori across Sharon's shoulder. Tori was beaming.

"These two, I tell you, they are shaking it up around here with this place," Ken boomed. "They are a business match made in heaven and I'm glad to say I had a role in it. Right, Tori? Remember that day you flew in here and we ate at Galindo's and I introduced the two of you?" He and Hazel moved back toward the table as he spoke. Tori followed them, as did Sharon as soon as she pulled back from Elena, smiling at her and holding her hand for a few seconds more before dropping it.

"I remember it well, Ken. Very well." Tori said, laughing. She liked the way he treated her and Elena, like a proud father or uncle. She glanced at Elena, who was smiling and nodding at the memory of that day not quite a year ago. So much had changed since then.

"I've got to get back inside for a bit." Elena said, moving to stand between Tori and Ken seated at the table. She put her hand on the back of both chairs, her fingertips resting lightly on Tori's back. "I'll send Jared over with the wine list. We've got lots of fresh quail on the menu from today's hunts, which I always recommend. We also have Dungeness crab flown in fresh from San Francisco—never frozen. It's seasonal, very good and they're huge. Just tell Jared what you want—he's our best waiter and he'll take very good care of you."

"You'll come sit with us if you can, yes?" Tori asked, looking up at her and speaking more softly as if just to her and not to the rest of the table. Elena looked down at her and moved her fingers in a circle on Tori's shoulder blade.

"I will in a little while. Especially if the two of you can hang out toward closing." She looked back across the table, smiled at all of them and moved away toward the kitchen door.

She stopped at a few tables on her way back. She greeted a young couple that lived on a small ranch between Stockdale and Logan who visited the restaurant nearly every week, instructing one of the waiters to bring them a special appetizer. They each ran successful internet businesses and, from what Elena had learned about them on their several visits, had moved out west from Georgia because the dry climate helped with the husband's allergies and the woman's arthritis. She also stopped at a table full of hunters, chatting with them about their day out in the field. A few of them had donated all their birds to the restaurant that night, so she thanked them by announcing their gift to the entire restaurant and leading all the guests in a round of applause.

As she visited with these guests, she felt eyes upon her coming from Tori's table. She assumed it was Tori and looked back toward her, but Tori was in a conversation with Ken and was facing him. It was Sharon's eyes she felt. Sharon sat relaxed in her chair with her hands folded in her lap and her legs crossed, which presented her red Jimmy Choo for review as it held her arched foot. Her scarf was draped loosely around her shoulders and over her forearms. Diamonds glittered against her neck and wrists. She gazed at Elena deeply and calmly. Elena met her gaze and held it for a moment. Then, as she turned to disappear behind the swinging door of the kitchen, she winked at Sharon, as Tori had winked at her. She saw Sharon's face break into a wide smile.

Elena split the next two hours of her time between the kitchen, the dining room and the patio area near the pool. Dustin, one of the other experienced waiters whom she liked as much as Jared, had set up portable column heaters and had started a large fire in the outdoor fireplace which was open on all sides. The flames leaped into the night sky, sending sparks in a long spiraling column to join the glittering stars in the inky darkness above. Many guests had finished their dinner, vacated their table for new reservations, and had moved to the patio to continue their evening. Other guests had come simply for desert and drinks on the patio, and they clustered with the others around the heaters or the fireplace. Finally, some of the hotel guests had finished their dinner, gone back to their rooms to change, and were now enjoying the warm jets of the jacuzzi at the patio's far edge. Elena enjoyed the sounds and smells of the courtyard—the gentle flowing of the fountain, the sounds of laughter and conversation, and the smell of the crackling pinion pine as it burned in the fireplace. She liked the contrast in feeling between the cozy, elegant dining room and the open, chilly patio. And from either of these spaces, returning to the kitchen was like entering again into a sensual vortex of smell, taste and texture.

Eventually, the dinner service ended and the only remaining guests were the hotel guests. A few of them lingered in the jacuzzi and some huddled in small groups around the fireplace. Gradually, they returned to their rooms and the only people stirring were the staff stripping tables, breaking down equipment and cleaning floors. Ken and Hazel had stayed longer than usual, visiting with Tori and Sharon. Elena had stopped by their table a few times throughout the evening, but saved her visiting until now. Sharon and Tori had walked Ken and Hazel out to their truck, said their goodbyes and were now sitting at a table on the far edge of the patio near a column heater by the pool waiting for Elena to join them. Elena put Jared in charge for the rest of the shift, grabbed three glasses and a bottle of sparkling shiraz she had chilled earlier, and walked out to them.

Both Tori and Sharon stood up to hug and kiss her in greeting as she came to the table. She leaned into both of them, her hands full with the glasses and the wine bottle, and received their kisses on her cheeks. She sat the wine and glasses down, and then plopped herself down in a chair, her legs spread out in front of her and her arms resting on the arms of the chair. She leaned her head back, peered into the sky, took a deep breath, and then looked back at both of them.

"That was a busy night," she said with a wide smile. She turned to Tori. "That's the most customers I think we've had in one night since opening night. In fact, I think we had a few more than opening night. I'll know for sure when Jared closes the batch on the register."

"Are you serious? That's fantastic!" Tori exclaimed, leaning toward Elena to grab her hand. "It seemed really busy, but I was visiting and talking, I didn't really see the extent of it. Elena, that's great!" Elena felt Tori squeeze her hand and she squeezed it back, and loosened her grip to thread her fingers through Tori's, holding it there in mid-air between their two chairs.

Sharon watched them both and grinned, and then reached for the bottle of sparkling wine. Elena reached for a folded cloth napkin in her chef coat pocket and handed it across the table to her. Sharon took it, wrapped it around the cork and popped it, spilling the foamy red contents into the three tall glasses. When the glasses were filled, she sat the bottle down and looked at the two of them.

"Well, I have to say: I am so totally impressed. I had an idea of what to expect based on what you have told me about things as they've developed out here." She looked at Tori with a look of love and admiration. "I know you, and I know that everything you do is excellent and is successful." Then she turned to Elena. "And you, my beautiful dear, I knew that if Tori said you were a food star, then you were a true star. But this exceeded even my already high expectations." She smiled warmly, her eyes shining and bright. She motioned around her, looking at the hotel, the courtyard, the sky, the fountain, then back at Tori and Elena. "All this is simply fantastic. I could not be happier for both of you."

Tori and Elena looked at each other and smiled, their fingers still threaded together.

"So, let us raise our glasses," Sharon instructed in an official sounding voice. "A toast to two of the most talented, most beautiful, most superfantastic women I know. To the success of their endeavors, both in business…and in life." She paused before saying those last three words, and grinned over her glass rim as she clinked it against the other two. They drank and drank again, laughing and giggling with happiness, relief and even joy.

Elena felt herself relax with every minute she sat there holding Tori's hand, celebrating success with her new love and her love's best friend who was funny, gracious and who seemed to know about the new relationship between them. For the next hour she forgot about her dying mother and the ache she felt in her heart every morning when she saw her emaciated body in the bed. She forgot about Luis and the dread she felt at knowing that no matter what she did, short of marrying him, she would end up hurting him.

And she knew exactly what she would do, once her mother was safely on the other side of this life. She would end it with him and live the rest of her life with Tori, if Tori would have her. It could be here in Logan, or in Houston, or back on the West Coast. She cared not, as long as she was with Tori.

For now, though, she could wait, and so could everyone else. She felt an almost irrational need to keep things as recognizable as possible to her mother until she died, even though Gloria faded in and out of awareness most days now. Things just needed to stay together as they were for a little while longer. When Gloria was ready to let go of her end of the thread, Elena would let go of hers, and it would be done. New lives could be started after that. For now, the old one was still holding on and deserved respect. Elena knew her mother's hope for her to marry Luis. She was not going to do it, but she could keep that hope in place until her mother was no longer there to hold it. It was the least she could do. Luis was a grown man. He had waited for twenty-five years without Elena asking or wanting him to, or promising anything at all to him. He could wait a little while longer, and then they all could move on from there.

"Ms. Rios, everything is done. We're ready to close," Jared said from behind Elena and a few feet away from their table. They had been talking and laughing, and had not noticed him approach them from across the patio. Elena turned around to him and smiled.

"Thank you, Jared," she said. As she spoke, she noticed his eyes move to her hand, which still clasped Tori's in mid-air between their two chairs. He looked back up at her face, glanced at Tori, and then looked back at her. He smiled faintly. She held his gaze, not wanting to suddenly drop Tori's hand as if she were doing something wrong. The fact, however, was that she had lost herself in the moment with Tori and Sharon, and had not thought about the possibility of someone seeing her holding Tori's hand out on the dark edge of the patio.

"And, Jared…please call me Elena. You don't have to be formal with me. Save *Ms. Rios* for my mother." She grinned at him. She had liked him from the first week he had come to the ranch. Letty knew both him and Dustin, another of the ranch's main staff and Jared's seemingly constant companion, from a few years ago when they were in high school. Jared had been a star on the six-man football team and still had the lean, muscular look of an athlete. His dark hair was trimmed short, and his smooth olive complexion contrasted nicely with the stiff white collar of his shirt. He had loosened his tie and rolled up his sleeves, and was still wearing an apron to protect his nice clothes from getting stained during clean-up. Elena depended on him more and more. He was getting a business degree online and clearly had a knack for customer service and management. Between him and Letty, she felt she had good leadership around her. And she liked him as a person.

"And I'm not *Ms. Reed*, at least to you," Tori added, turning away from Sharon to face him. Elena felt Tori squeeze her hand and hold it still.

Jared grinned a bit sheepishly at both of them. "Okay. Thank you." He looked at their clasped hands again, then back up at their faces. "May I bring you anything else while I'm here?"

"I think we're fine, Jared. Go ahead and take off. It's been a long, busy night." Elena said.

Jared stepped closer and reached past them to grab the empty wine bottle to take with him as he left. He looked at Elena and Tori again before turning away. "Goodnight, then," he said, smiling at them. He glanced at Sharon, nodded, and walked away.

"He's cute," Sharon said. She leaned back in her chair, her scarf wrapped around her shoulders and upper arms, and watched him as he walked across the patio and into the dining room. "Does he have a boyfriend?"

"What?" Tori said, crinkling her brow at Sharon. Elena looked behind her to see Jared through the glass dining room wall just as he flipped the lights off and disappeared through the swinging door into the kitchen. She turned back to Sharon.

"Does he have a boyfriend? Can they do that out here in the wild west, or will they get beat up?" Sharon spoke with what Elena deemed equal doses of seriousness and humor.

"Is Jared gay?" Tori asked, looking at Elena.

"How would I know?" she replied. Now that Sharon had mentioned it, though, maybe that was what she found so dear about him.

"He's too beautiful not to be gay," Sharon said definitively, mocking her own sweeping certainty in saying such a thing. Tori and Elena chuckled.

Elena nodded. "He's definitely cute. And sweet and smart. I like him a lot."

After a little while longer, they were the only three people left on the patio. The temperature dropped and they found themselves huddling ever closer to the column heater. Elena looked at her watch and knew it was past time she should go home. She stood up and reached for the dial on the heater to turn it off.

"Shall we call it a night? I need to go home," she said.

Tori and Sharon got up and walked with Elena to the courtyard.

"Why don't you let me drive you around to the cabin instead of walking that trail across the field," Elena said. She looked down at Sharon's shoes, then back up at her. "Those may not make the trek intact, especially in the dark."

"No kidding," Sharon said. "I told Tori I was going to wear my new fancy hunting boots the entire time from now on. God knows I paid enough for them. They look fabulous, though, I have to say." She grinned and put her arms through Elena's and Tori's, standing between them.

Elena passed through the kitchen, turning off lights and locking her office door while Tori and Sharon waited for her in the lobby. They walked out together, locking the front door behind them. Sharon took the front passenger seat of Elena's Tahoe. She reached over to touch her hand to Elena's forearm as they drove the short distance to the cabin.

"I'm sorry about your mother's illness," she said, caressing Elena's arm lightly. "It must be so difficult." She squeezed her arm and then returned her hand to her lap.

Elena sighed, nodded, and looked at Sharon. "Thank you," she said. "It's hard losing her this way, gradually bit by bit every day. But, the main thing is that she is comfortable and not in any pain really."

"Yeah…that's good," Sharon said quietly.

Elena pulled up to the cabin. Sharon opened her arms, leaned over and hugged her around the neck. "Thank you for a fantastic evening! I am so impressed with you and everything you have done out here." She pulled back and paused for a moment. "And thank you for being who you are for my dear one here." She kept her eyes on Elena's as she reached out to put her hand on Tori's knee.

"You're welcome. Your opinion means a lot to me," Elena said, looking at Tori and then back at Sharon. "And I love Tori." She smiled into Sharon's beautiful face and hazel eyes.

Sharon got out of the truck and Tori leaned forward from the back seat. She touched Elena's cheek, and Elena turned her face to Tori's to kiss her lightly.

"I'll see you tomorrow, right?" Tori asked softly, smiling into Elena's lips.

"Sure. I'll be home all day with Mama until the dinner service," She kissed Tori again, tasting a remnant of wine. "Come find me—here or at home."

Tori joined Sharon on the porch. Elena kept her headlights on them so Tori could see to insert the key into the front door. They both waved to her when they opened it and disappeared into the cabin. A pang of jealousy shot through her stomach at the thought of Sharon, instead of her, sleeping in bed with Tori that night. She took a deep breath, exhaled and the feeling slowly dulled. She knew Tori loved Sharon and was really glad to spend time with her. Whatever erotic connections they had had in the past, or still had even today, seemed separate from her and what had erupted between her and Tori in the last few weeks. It was none of her business, really, at least not at this point in things. Besides, Sharon clearly loved Tori and had loved her for a long time. Everyone should be loved and cared for deeply by another human being, preferably by more than one. There could never be *too much* love in the world.

❧

Tori dumped her keys and purse on the bar while Sharon stripped her feet from her shoes and unwrapped the scarf from around her neck and shoulders. Sharon plopped down on the sofa and Tori followed her, settling in to the opposite end. She grabbed Sharon's legs and swung them up, bringing her feet into her lap. She began massaging Sharon's high arches and the places where her shoes had pinched.

"Well…" Sharon began. "She's amazing." She looked directly and intently at Tori. "She's simply amazing." She brought her hand down hard on the back of the couch as if to emphasize the point.

Tori grinned at her. "I'm so glad you think so." She squeezed Sharon's toes and felt her own heart swell. She knew Sharon would like Elena, and vice versa, but she had not expected Sharon to embrace Elena so fully so quickly, as if she had been in Tori's life for years, or were a family member. Then again, she knew she should not be surprised. Sharon was one of the most generous people she had ever known. She appeared shallow and ditsy to many people, of course, because of the blonde hair, her vanity, the clothes, the partying, the lifestyle—the whole "package" of what she seemed on the outside. But, beyond that exterior, Sharon was deeply grounded and had a capacity for love and understanding that surpassed most people. Sharon had few emotional boundaries, mainly because she found them mostly a function of small-mindedness and convention. As such, she thought they served to limit people in their expressions of themselves. Tori learned this about Sharon early in their relationship, when at times it seemed that Sharon had an erotic connection to almost everyone she met. Not because she had slept with them or even wanted to do so, but because she did not guard her interest, appreciation or fascination with them. This applied to close friends as well as to virtual strangers. Tori had seen her gaze into the eyes of the grocery store cashier with an affection no less than that which she directed to her close friends. She was not flirting, not specifically. She was simply being Sharon, simply expressing her affection and love to others without much censorship and without delineating too firmly between different forms of attraction. It all ran on the same motor for her—all the variations of love, desire and appreciation. Tori had watched Sharon watch Elena, and had seen the familiar look in her face. Elena was "in" with Sharon, and Sharon could just as easily curl up in bed with Elena tonight, caressing her hair as she fell asleep, as she would with Tori.

"Tori, it's perfect," she continued. "The feeling and connection between the two of you is perfect. I really mean it." She leaned her head back, gathered her hair into a large bundle and twisted it up onto the top of her head, holding it there with her elbows bent out. She looked back at Tori. "I know I sound woo-woo, but really.... I've been around a lot of relationships in my time—a lot of screwed up, broken people trying to figure their shit out. I look at people, mostly my clients who are in the middle of divorce or mediation, and I think *why on earth did you think you could be with that person?* The two people are so mismatched, it's unbelievable! And it's so obvious! Anyone with eyes to see can see it! But, they don't…until they do, of course, and then they have to pay me to help them get out of it. " She dropped her hair again, letting it fall in yellow cascades around her shoulders. "But, Tori—she's perfect. She's the perfect one for you. Do you see that?" Sharon smiled as she spoke, but her words popped with a serious intensity, and she did not take her eyes from Tori's while she spoke. It was as if she had a prophetic message to communicate and wanted to make sure Tori was getting it.

"I've known you a long time," she continued. "And I've loved you a long time." Her eyes began to fill. "I just have a gut feeling about this. Tori, she's the perfect one for you. You have to see that."

Tori listened to her friend and felt a rush of emotion. Any other friend and part-time lover could have been easily *anything* but loving and generous in a situation like this. Jealousy, competition, regret, sadness and overall weirdness were the norms. But, not a trace of any of these appeared in Sharon—or in Elena or even herself, for that matter. More than anything, however, a sense of fate rose up inside her as she listened to Sharon's words. It was the same feeling she had when she sat in her car outside in the dark after being with Elena that first night outside her mother's house. That sense of this being inevitable, or irresistible, or a kind of destiny. Sharon was right, and Tori knew it. She knew it as much or more than she knew anything. And hearing Sharon, her closest and most intimate friend, talk about it with such force and insistence in her words confirmed it for her.

"I love you so much," she said, dropping Sharon's feet and stretching across the couch to fall into her chest in an embrace. She tucked her head into Sharon's neck and felt Sharon's arms encircle her shoulders and back. "You're right," she said, her voice muffled by Sharon's blouse. They held each other for a while, enjoying the sound of each other's breathing and the familiar comfort of each other's bodies. Finally, Sharon stretched her back again the soft leather of the couch and yawned. Tori raised up and looked at her watch, then at Sharon.

"I'm beat," Sharon said.

Tori nodded. "You first in the bathroom. I'll go second. I want to take a shower before I go to sleep." She unfolded herself from Sharon and the couch and stood up.

While Sharon was in the bathroom, Tori walked over to the bar and got her phone out of her purse. She had a text message from Elena: *I love you. She's great.*

Tori smiled and wrote her back. *Yes. So are you. I love you too.*

# Chapter Thirteen

Tori walked to the podium and looked out at the faces peering back at her. The dining room was packed with people sitting in chairs around small tables and standing along the back walls. A few people stood outside in the courtyard near the fountain, holding their drinks in their hands, listening over the speaker system and looking in at Tori and the crowd through the large glass walls. Tori scanned the crowd, taking in the smiling faces and kind eyes. She picked out certain of the ranch staff members, their families, specific individuals from Logan city government, people from the high school, regular customers of the restaurant, contractors and vendors who had worked with the ranch in the last several months. Eugene Brooks and his wife sat at a table with a few of his foremen and their wives. She felt her heart warm as she looked at everyone. A year ago, she could count on one hand the people she knew in Logan. Now, all these people had responded to her invitation to come to Sandy Creek Ranch and celebrate the success of the first six months of operations, which coincided with the close of the major hunting seasons until the fall.

She glanced at Elena, sitting at a front table a few feet from her, next to Tori's empty chair. Letty, Jared, Dustin, and other members of the kitchen staff sat at the table with her. Luis, Ricardo, and other members of the outdoor operations staff sat at the front table next to Elena's. She took a deep breath and looked down at her small page of notes.

"Thank you all for coming tonight. I hope you enjoyed the dinner. Please join me in thanking Michael and the folks from Desert Catering in Stockdale who came down here tonight to prepare the meal. I think they did a great job." She turned and began clapping for chef Michael who stood at the kitchen door. He bowed slightly to Tori, smiled and waved at the crowd as everyone joined Tori in applauding him. Tori had met him months ago on a supplies run to Stockdale. He was a local guy whose cooking experience was limited, but he ran a good business with food that people liked. Tori was happy to hire him and his crew to come cook for this event so that ranch staff would not have to cook and clean for their own party.

"Elena, Luis, and I wanted to have this event tonight to gather everyone together and celebrate the success we've had in this first season of the ranch, and to thank everyone who's been a part of it." Tori rested her hands on the sides of the podium as she spoke and looked directly into the eyes of many people throughout the room. As she met their gaze, she felt a swell of gratitude in her heart and throat.

"An operation like this doesn't succeed without a team of committed, talented people no matter how good the initial concept is, or how successful its founders have been in the past. I came here just over a year ago and this place was a broken down hotel sitting on thousands of acres of unused land. Now, because of so many of you, we have all this…" Tori motioned with her arms to the space around her. "We've worked together, played together, struggled together, shared meals and stories with each other, and had a lot of fun together in these first months of operations, and in the months before we opened. Thank you all so much for being a part of this and for making the idea of this place a reality. None of this could have happened without you. From the bottom of my heart, thank you."

The crowd applauded and Tori smiled out at them, catching Elena's eyes again and also Luis' as he sat with his staff and a few of the vendors and most frequent local hunting customers. He grinned at her and leaned back in his chair, resting his arms on the backs of the chairs on either side of him. Tori waited for the applause to die down.

"There are two people whose contributions have been central to our success. This ranch would not be what it is without them. The first person is my business partner, Elena Rios. The second is Luis Palacios, the outdoor operations manager. I want to call each of them up to say a few words and make some presentations. Let's begin with Luis, whose knowledge of the land and of everything that goes into hunting the game on it is apparently inexhaustable. Luis, you've been a constant presence here at the ranch since the beginning really. I've learned so much from you and am so grateful to you for your leadership, for your friendship, and for everything you do around here. Thank you, Luis." She smiled down at him from the podium and motioned for him to step onto the small stage.

The crowd applauded as he rose from his chair. He smiled at everyone, waving quickly and then looked down at the floor a bit nervously as he made his way across the short distance to the edge of the stage. Tori held out her arms and embraced him as he stepped up to the podium. "Thank you," she said softly into his ear and then pulled back to look into his dark, kind eyes. She felt a pang of guilt deep in her stomach, which was made sharper by the genuine affection and appreciation she felt for him. She trusted him with so many things, and not merely with the details and logistics of the hunting operation. She had trusted him with her dreams and ideas for the entire concept, which she had shared with him at Elena's house many months ago. He had listened to her and had gotten it, almost as intuitively as Elena had, from the beginning. He had been unfailing in his work and in his friendship, and so much of the ranch's success was due directly to him. She listened to the applause die down and stepped aside to yield the podium to him, thinking that she owed him far more than the sizeable bonus check she had given him earlier in the week. She probably owed him the truth about things between her and Elena. But, she did not really know the full truth about it herself, at least from Elena's perspective. And whatever it was, it was Elena's place to tell him, not hers. She would simply have to live with the tension and guilt of it and follow Elena's lead, at least for the time being.

She watched him as he spoke to the crowd. He stood erect and solid behind the podium, wearing a black collared shirt, dark creased jeans, a sport coat and shiny black western boots. He laughed and smiled as he acknowledged Ricardo and the half a dozen others on his staff, as well as the handful of regular hunting customers in the crowd. Tori glanced out at the people in the crowd; they listened intently, laughed at Luis' lighthearted comments, and clapped for Ricardo and the other staff people. Tori watched Elena as she watched Luis. Elena smiled and laughed at him with the rest of the people, her eyes crinkling at the corners. She clapped enthusiastically for Ricardo and the others, and put her fingers between her teeth to whistle for them as Luis acknowledged them. She reached out to squeeze the hand of Ricardo's mother, who was also Luis' aunt, who sat at a nearby table. At that moment, Tori saw yet again that Sandy Creek Ranch in its short history had become more than simply a successful business venture. Sandy Creek Ranch was a hub of activity and endeavor whose spokes extended throughout Logan and beyond. It was a community institution that brought jobs and income to the local people, that brought fine dining and all the dimensions of culture and social interaction that come with it to this part of the state, and brought customers from all over the country to Logan to spend money, create memories and develop friendships. So many people were a part of the ranch, and so many people were impacted by it on a regular basis in practical terms.

And she, Elena and Luis were at the center of it all. What would happen when Luis learned about her and Elena? What would happen to the synergy of friendship and the working relationships between them? How would it affect the ranch? Tori felt a cold weight in her stomach. She focused on maintaining a pleasant facial expression as these thoughts made their way through her mind. She turned back to Luis who was finishing up at the podium. He turned to her at that moment and spoke into the microphone. "Shall we invite our culinary artist to the stage now?" he asked as he gestured toward Elena's table. Tori nodded and she and Luis turned toward Elena and began to clap. The crowd joined them as Elena quickly finished off a swallow of wine in her glass and got up from her chair to make her way to the stage. She pushed up the sleeves of her black sweater and pulled a note card from the back pocket of her black jeans. She stepped up onto the stage and opened her arms wide to both Tori and Luis. Tori heard the crowd increase its applause as the three of them huddled in a group hug. She squeezed Luis and Elena around their waists, drawing them close. Elena pulled back first and looked at the two of them, her eyes sparkling. She turned to the podium, and Luis joined Tori in standing off to the side of the stage. Elena grinned at the crowd briefly as the applause began to die down, then looked at her note card. She took a deep breath, looked back at the crowd and began to speak.

"I'm glad to see so many of you here tonight. Thank you for

coming to mark this special occasion here at the ranch." She paused for a moment. "Many of you know that I came back to Logan over a year ago after being away for, well…for a long time. I had no idea when I came back that anything like this was in store for me, certainly not here in Logan. I could never have predicted this—not in a million years. I am so grateful to Tori for the opportunity she presented to me in creating this ranch." She turned to Tori and looked deeply into her eyes. The crowd began to applaud and Elena joined them, never taking her eyes off Tori's. Tori grinned at her, but closed her eyes and held still as she listened to the applause and waited for it to die down. She opened them when she heard Elena began to speak again.

"I've worked in some of the best restaurants and hotels in the country—in the world, even—and I can honestly say that I have absolutely top-notch people working with me in the restaurant and hospitality staff here at the ranch. I could not ask for better, more committed, more talented people to work with, right here in Logan." Tori watched and listened as Elena called them all by name—Letty, Jared, Dustin, Betty and a dozen others—and asked them to stand while she told stories about them and acknowledged them for their work. Their friends and family members present in the crowd beamed and clapped for each of them while they stood there, sometimes shyly looking down at their empty plates as Elena completed her comments about them. Tori was struck again at the web of relationships and interconnections lodged at the heart of the ranch. So many families and groups of people were touched in Luis' and Elena's simple acknowledgement of the staff members.

When Elena finished her remarks, she stood back and looked at Tori, yielding the podium to her. Elena moved to join Luis as Tori took her place in front of the microphone. She looked out at the audience, finding the principal of the high school and the school board superintendent at their table in the middle of the room.

"There's one more presentation to make tonight before we clear the floor of the dining room for the band and dancing. Ms. Rinson and Mr. Taylor, would you please join us on the stage?" She stood back and waited for the principal and superintendant to make their way to the stage. Ms. Rinson, wearing black wool slacks and a red blouse that contrasted nicely with her salt and pepper gray hair, nodded curtly to people as she passed them, her face in a contained smiled. Mr. Taylor followed behind her in pressed jeans, collared shirt and a sport coat, just like Luis, shaking hands with a few people as they made their way forward. Letty and Jared emerged from the kitchen holding a large placard and walked toward the stage; they had left their seats quickly and disappeared behind the swinging door as soon as Tori has called the school administrators' names.

"This is a very special evening for me personally," Tori began as soon as everyone was gathered on the stage. "I am here in Logan because of a dear person in my life who was a longtime member of this community: my uncle—James Edward Reed—whom everyone knew as Sandy Reed. I came here a lot as a child to visit him and he was like a second father to me in many ways. I loved him and he loved me a great deal. I would not be standing here before you, nor would this ranch exist here in Logan, without him."

She turned to face the school administrators. "My uncle was very involved with the school, particularly with the sports program. I know from personal experience that he loved young people and he cared about their success, and was proud of them when they tried hard and did well." She stopped and motioned for Jared and Letty to step forward with the placard. "So, in honor of my Uncle Sandy and on behalf of Sandy Creek Ranch, which is named after him, I am happy to present the Logan High School Parent/Teacher Association this check to support the education and development of the youth here in Logan."

A gasp emerged from the crowd as Jared and Letty turned the

large placard around revealing a check written out for $20,000 to the Logan PTA. The room burst into applause and everyone stood up from their chairs. Ms. Rinson and Mr. Taylor looked stunned, their faces blank as they stared and blinked at the large cardboard check. Only when Jared placed his corner of the check into Ms. Rinson's hand did her face begin to break into a wide smile. She gazed at Tori in amazement and disbelief, and Mr. Taylor stepped forward to shake Tori's hand but ended up pulling her to himself in a giant hug. Luis and Elena stepped forward to shake hands and congratulate the school administrators, and finally they all stood in a line behind the placard as a photographer snapped their picture—all to sustained, boisterous applause. Ms. Rinson stepped to the podium to say a few words of thanks, but barely managed to get her words out. Mr. Taylor leaned in to the microphone to speak, mentioning that the funds would help the basketball team go all the way to the state championship, which caused the crowd to erupt into cheers again. After a few moments, in the midst of the cheering and applause, Elena stepped to the microphone and thanked everyone again for coming and announced a special dessert and drinks buffet out on the patio. As everyone began filing out, the band members and people from Desert Catering began moving tables and chairs to clear the space for the dance floor.

Tori, Elena and Luis stepped off the stage and greeted the dozens of people who came forward to congratulate them for their success and thank them for the ranch's donation to the school. They hugged the parents and friends of their staff members, and shook hands with customers, vendors and city officials. Tori stepped out from the rush of people to hold her arms out to Ken, who had made a beeline from one of the back tables to the front. He scooped her up in his arms, lifting her into a big hug.

"I'm so proud of you" he exclaimed, squeezing her tightly and pressing his cheek to hers. Tori breathed in the spicy clean smell of his cologne and laughed as her feet lifted off the floor. He put her down and looked into her face. "I couldn't be more proud of you if you were my own daughter," he said. "Hazel, too." He motioned to Hazel standing beside him, who stepped forward and circled her arms around Tori's neck.

"You girls have outdone yourselves here," she said. "I've said it before—you all are just what this town needed." She squeezed Tori's neck and kissed her cheek.

"Thank you both," Tori said, feeling her eyes moisten as she looked at them. They had been her first friends here in Logan and she loved them dearly. "You both are so important to me, and I'm so glad that our life paths brought us together. You've made such a difference for me out here, being new to the city and all. I can't thank you enough." She felt her throat catch and a tear escape her eye to roll down her cheek.

"Well, we're glad, too," Ken said loudly, wrapping his long arm around her shoulder to side hug her again. "Mighty glad." He turned away quickly, looking toward the distance through the glass walls, gathering himself before his own eyes began to well up.

They chatted a few more moments until Tori was pulled away by others offering congratulations and staff members wanting her to meet their friends and family. She joined the crowd of people out on the patio, enjoying the festive atmosphere and the crisp night air. People warmed themselves around the column heaters and the outdoor fireplace, and made their way through the buffet lines for dessert and drinks. Soon the band began to play and people began to move back into the dining room to dance and listen to music.

Tori felt a tap on her shoulder and turned to find Ken standing there with a grin on his face.

"May I have this dance?" he asked, extending his arm and bowing a bit at the waist.

Tori smiled up at him and looped her arm into his. "Certainly," she said as she let him lead her to the dance floor. The band was playing a moderately paced country and western song, and people were dancing in a counter-clockwise circle around the dance floor, doing a basic two-step dance. Tori put one hand on Ken's shoulder and grasped his hand with the other, and he began their two-step cadence around the dance floor. Tori had danced this pattern before, but it had been a while so she felt a bit unsure and tense for the first few steps. Within one turn of the dance floor, however, she felt the rhythm of it return to her and she relaxed into the pace Ken set for them. He laughed and spun them around so that at times she was stepping backward, and at other times forward. She held his hand and shoulder firmly, moving in mirrored lock-step to his movements. She liked the feel of her boots as they slid along the concrete floor, and the compact way her body felt attached to Ken's at the hand and shoulder as they spun and stepped around the circle. She threw her head back and laughed, singing the chorus aloud with the other dancers at the prompting of the band's lead singer. Ken sang too, loud and howling, and they both almost crashed into the wall with dizzy laughter. Hazel clapped and laughed at them each time they passed her, enjoying their dancing vicariously due to her bum knees. They had made a dozen or more turns around the dance floor by the time the song ended in a grand finale of boisterous group singing from the dancers and the band, everyone swaying their arms and braying the words out at the top of their lungs before collapsing into laughter and hugs when it was finished. The band quickly transitioned to a new song and the whole thing started over again with mostly new dancers.

Ken and Tori made their way off the dance floor and found Hazel at a small table. She had ordered drinks for them, so they took sips from their drinks and laughed and talked. A few men came over to their table, friends of Ken's mostly, and joined them in conversation and visiting. Tori was listening to one of them tell about his new horse when the band began playing a slow dance song. Ken politely excused himself from the conversation and asked Hazel if her knees could handle a slow dance. She nodded and they walked arm in arm to the dance floor. Tori excused herself from the table and went outside to get some air. Some of the crowd had gone home already and almost everyone else was inside, so she had the patio to herself for the most part. She walked out past the jacuzzi to the edge of the patio, near where she had fed a piece of her apple to that rabbit months ago. She peered out into the darkness toward the gorge, seeking out its dimensions in the blackness. She rolled her shoulders and stretched her head and neck first to the left, then to the right, then laid her head back to peer into the vast sky above. She saw only a few stars, which appeared briefly between masses of clouds. Banks of puffy clouds moved quickly across the sky, illumined by the full moon like shimmering fleece blankets. The sky was tumultuous with movement, wind and light and Tori felt its energy as she stood there taking in the view and feeling the crisp air chill her cheeks and ears. She heard quiet steps behind her and turned to see Jared and Dustin standing a few feet behind her, smiling at her.

"Are you okay out here, Tori?" Jared asked. He had grown accustomed to calling her by her first name ever since she had instructed him to do so. "Do you need anything?" His eyes were steady and his face relaxed. Dustin looked at Jared then at Tori.

Tori smiled at them. "I'm fine, thank you. I was just getting some fresh air. I got a little warm in there dancing." She looked at both of them. They were smart, dependable men whom she had grown to love in the months they had worked together. Both of them had brought family members to the event that night, and both Tori and Elena had been eager to meet them and brag to them about Jared and Dustin. She hoped they were having a good time and not feeling like they had to supervise the staff from Desert Catering.

"Are you guys actually enjoying yourselves, or are you spending your time critiquing Michael and his people," she asked, squinting her eyes a bit. "Come on…tell the truth."

They grinned at her and at each other. Dustin spoke first.

"We're having a great time. Thank you for putting this on for us and for everyone. I think everyone is really enjoying it." He stood tall and lean, his blonde hair cropped short and spiky, and his muscles bulging visibly through the sleeves of his shirt. He looked at Jared briefly then back at Tori. Jared met his glance and then turned to Tori. She sensed that they wanted to say something to her.

"It's my pleasure. I'm just glad you are here and that everyone could come to help us celebrate." She smiled and waited for a few seconds for them to pick up the conversation. Jared cleared his throat.

"Actually, we came out here to tell you something. We wanted to thank you for this ranch and for everything here. We love working here and we both feel like we're learning a lot about business, management and leadership and all…" He trailed off in a somewhat uncharacteristic way, it seemed to Tori. Jared was not a big talker and when he did speak, he usually spoke directly and clearly. It was part of his charm and contributed to his leadership style. People knew that if he spoke, he meant it and whatever he was saying was important. He was not one for idle chatter or gossip. Tori watched him now as he glanced down at his shoes, then at Dustin and then back at her again, looking directly into her eyes, his hands at his sides. Then, Dustin took his hand from his slacks pocket and touched Jared's hand, hooking his fingers inside Jared's. Tori looked down at their joined hands and then back up to their faces, first Dustin's then Jared's.

"Jared and I both wanted to say how much we appreciate working here." Dustin continued, picking up where Jared left off. "We respect you and Elena a lot and are glad to get to work with you two. Thank you." He smiled and Tori saw him squeeze Jared's fingers slightly.

She looked into their handsome faces, so strong and young. She stretched her arms out, looping one arm around each man's neck and brought them to her. They leaned in and she kissed their cheeks each in turn. She pulled back and smiled at them.

"I think the world of the two of you, and I speak for Elena as well. We love you both and would do anything for you." She took a deep breath. "I want you to be happy here at the ranch...both professionally and personally."

They thanked her again and turned to go back to the dining room. Tori watched them as they went, appreciating the trust they placed in her to reveal their relationship. As soon as she had seen Dustin grasp Jared's hand, she remembered that evening on the patio several weeks ago with Sharon and Elena. She remembered holding Elena's hand, and that Jared had seen it. And she remembered Sharon wondering aloud if Jared were gay. *Guess she was right*, Tori thought.

She watched them until they disappeared into the crowded dining room. The room was still full of people, mostly the staff and their immediate family and friends. People were enjoying themselves dancing and listening to the band. Tori stood still, her arms folded across her chest, and took it all in—the images of happy people enjoying each other's company, of laughter and music and good food—all against the backdrop of an elegantly appointed building in the middle of the spare, beautiful desert. The ranch and the people in it were like bright sparkles in an otherwise earthen darkness, sparkles that mirrored the blinking stars in the black night sky. She felt a sense of peacefulness and satisfaction deep inside her unlike anything she had remembered feeling before now. It was as if things were moving into place, settling, and stilling inside her. She was happy, not for the first time in her life, but certainly the most completely.

She stood watching the pairs of dancers through the plate glass walls of the dining room. Each pair stepped and twirled by on the arc of the circle dance floor visible to Tori from where she stood. She recognized many of them—Ken and Hazel, Mr. Taylor and a woman she did not know, the internet business couple from Geogia who lived outside of town, Letty and one of the kitchen workers, Ricardo's mother and another older woman Tori presumed to be a sister or aunt. Tori liked the Hispanic tradition of women—sisters, friends, cousins, whatever—dancing together. She had even seen a few men, mostly grown sons with their elderly fathers, dancing together at various events. She liked the intimate, family feeling of it. She had seen several such couples on the dance floor tonight and was pleased that people felt comfortable enough at the ranch to enjoy and express themselves in that way.

She watched the dancers twirl by, two by two, until she thought she was almost to the end of the circle at which point the progression would repeat, beginning with Ken and Hazel and others she recognized. She was about to turn away when Luis and Elena made the turn into her view. Luis had taken off his coat and had rolled up the sleeves of his black shirt. His strong, brown arms held Elena at the waist and by an outstretched hand. He held her close to his body and Elena's leg was nestled between his just as one of his legs was positioned between hers. They stepped in complete mirrored synchronization, gliding and turning in precise movements. Luis touched the side of his face to Elena's ear, and kept his eyes closed as they danced, as if discerning in every way but through his eyes the music, Elena and the movement of their joined bodies. Tori watched Elena as Luis twirled them in a half circle, then reversed and stepped in the other direction, easing around the arc of the dance floor. Her eyes were open and she looked out over Luis' shoulder. Her face was placid and she held her body firm against Luis, although not stiffly. She moved easily with him, gliding and turning seemingly without effort, their legs perfectly mingled, not tangled. Luis made another turn just as they neared the end of the arc visible to Tori. His back was to her now and she saw Elena's face, catching her open eyes through the glass walls. Elena held her gaze for a moment, but Tori was not sure if Elena actually saw her or if she saw her own reflection in the glass. Within seconds, Luis turned them again and they disappeared around the curve, replaced by other dancers.

Tori turned around to face the gorge again. She folded her arms tightly against herself and squeezed, taking in a deep breath and letting it out slowly. She felt her stomach convulse as the thoughts from earlier in the evening raced back into her mind. *What would Luis do when he found out? What would happen?* Now, however, other questions joined these thoughts. *How long will things go on like this? What if things drag on in this limbo for a long time?* The worst thought made Tori step over and rest her hand on the sidewall of the jacuzzi, as if to steady herself. *What if Elena never breaks it off with Luis?*

She knew as soon as she thought it that it was an irrational thought, at least for the most part. Sure, it was possible that Elena could string both her and Luis along indefinitely. But, Elena was not that kind of person, at least as far as Tori knew her. Plus, she believed Elena when she said that she was in love with her, but that she was making no moves or decisions with regard to Luis until the time of caring for her mother was passed. She trusted her instincts about people and did not think Elena was being anything but truthful about what was clearly a complex and sad situation.

She stared off into the dark night, squeezing herself around the waist and going through these thoughts several times, measuring their logic and rationale. She reached the same conclusion each time: she loved Elena, was *in love* with her. She would give Elena the benefit of the doubt, and wait for her to make the next major move. She had to trust that things would work out, and live with the tension in the meantime.

She turned around to face the dining room again. The dancers continued their constant, vibrant swirl around the dance floor.

She waited to see Luis and Elena pass again, but instead caught sight of Elena making her way through the crowd from the dance floor to a line of chairs along the near wall. She grabbed her purse and jacket from a chair back and headed toward the kitchen. She looked down into the face of her phone and seemed in a hurry. She disappeared behind the swinging door. Tori took a few steps forward and then stopped when she saw Luis follow Elena through the swinging kitchen door, his sport coat thrown over his arm.

She reached into her back pocket and retrieved her phone. She typed a text message to Elena: *Are you ok? Just saw you leave.* She put the phone back in her pocket and walked across the patio toward the dining room. She entered the room and felt the blast of warmth from the bodies hit her face. She picked her way through the crowd to the small cocktail table where she had stood with Ken and Hazel. They were still there but were about to leave. She talked with them for a few moments as they gathered their jackets. She felt the vibration of her phone on her hip as she hugged Hazel goodbye. She took out her phone to read the message from Elena: *Hospice called. Mama is near the end.*

Tori had been afraid of that. While everything in her wanted to rush over to Gloria's house to be with Elena, she knew that that was not was Elena needed right now. Luis was there and probably Tita Maria and maybe one or two of Gloria's other friends. These, along with Elena, were the people in Gloria's life, the people she loved, people she considered her family. Given time and different circumstances, Tori might have grafted herself into that group. As it was, however, she was a concerned friend of Gloria's daughter more than of Gloria herself. She knew it was best to wait on the periphery and, in this situation as well as the other one, follow Elena's lead. She texted Elena back: *I'm so sorry. I love you. You are a good daughter. I am here if you need me.*

She busied herself for the next tw hours with the party guests and with closing up the ranch. She visited with many of the guests, and walked them out to their cars as they left. She fixed a few doggie bags for people to take home to elderly or sick relatives. She helped Michael's staff in the kitchen when they did not know where to put things after clean-up. She held the doors open for the band as they wheeled their equipment out and loaded it into the back of their pick-up. Jared and Dustin stayed behind with her to help. They had no resident guests that night, so she locked up the entire building behind her as they stepped out onto the front porch.

"Thanks for helping me," she said to Jared and Dustin, who stepped off the porch and were putting on their jackets.

"No problem," Jared said. "Do you want a ride over to your cabin?"

"Yeah, we can take you—no point in you walking in the dark," Dustin added.

She actually liked walking in the dark to her cabin at night, but she sensed that they wanted to give her a ride.

"Sure, that'd be nice. Thanks." she said, stuffing her hands into her jacket pockets.

She stepped up into the back seat of Dustin's truck and closed the door. He started the engine and began to back out. She pushed a pile of stuff over to make a bit more room on the back seat. Dustin saw her in the rear view mirror.

"Sorry about all that stuff. Just push it over," he said. "I didn't clean out my gear from yesterday."

"What was yesterday?" she asked.

"I went on the quail hunt with Ricardo and the guests. Luis took the morning off and Ricardo didn't want to do the group alone." He said this casually as he clicked his headlights onto high beam. Tori was confused.

"You hunt?" she asked. "I didn't know that." She had noticed Dustin's almost obsessive attention to the details of flowers, linens, place settings and the like inside the restaurant. It surprised her that he was an "outdoor" type who hunted.

Jared turned around to face her and smiled. "We all hunt out here," he said. "You almost have to." He and Dustin chuckled. "It's part of the culture."

"But I like it," Dustin said. "I've bird hunted my whole life. I love it." He pulled up to Tori's cabin and put the truck in park. "In fact, I was going to talk to you about my job at the ranch, that maybe I could be a crossover person who works both in the restaurant and in the field. Sort of like Letty except I would help lead the hunting, too." He peered at her in the rear view mirror. Jared looked at him, smiling, and then turned to Tori.

Tori looked at both of them, meeting Dustin's eyes in the mirror.

"Well, I think that should be just fine," she said brightly. "I see no reason why that wouldn't work—in fact, that could be really great! Thanks for bringing it up. I'll put it on the agenda at the next management meeting."

Dustin's ears moved on the side of his head as he smiled. "Thank you, Tori. I really appreciate it."

"No problem. And thanks for driving me over here," she said as she opened the truck door. "You guys be careful driving home."

They waved goodbye and drove away after seeing her step safely inside her cabin door. She closed the door behind her and dumped her stuff on the bar. She took off her jacket and kicked off her boots, grabbing her phone from her hip pocket to check for messages. Nothing yet. It was past one o'clock in the morning and she had been up since just before dawn. She suddenly felt the activities of the long day and evening as a heavy weight in her bones. She shucked off her clothes right there at the bar, grabbed a towel from the bathroom and made her way to the jacuzzi outside. She sat her phone on the ledge beside her as she sank herself deeply into the hot, bubbling water. She fanned her arms and legs back and forth in the water, stretching her neck and back, squeezing her toes and the arches of her feet. She stared up into the stars, still shining sporadically through drifts of fast clouds.

She felt the cold wind brush her hair and blow it across her face.

She sat still in the hot water for about fifteen minutes, allowing herself to relax and to release some of her worry about Elena and what was happening with Gloria. She breathed in deeply the cool night air and listened to the faint sound of coyotes in the distance beyond the gorge. She could barely hear their cries above the din of the jacuzzi motor.

The phone beside her vibrated with a message. She raised a wet hand from the water, shook it as dry as possible and grabbed the phone. Her heart sank as she read the message.

*Mama is gone. Come over in the morning please.*

Tori brought her other hand to her mouth and took a deep breath. She held herself still for a moment, allowing the flashes of feeling and memory to course through her. The phone call from the sheriff that night her parents were killed. The sharp loss and stunned confusion she felt as she left the morgue that night. The profound sense of forlornness in the world she felt for weeks after their memorial service. All of it came rushing back to her in a flash, as it had so many times over the years since she lost them. She had learned that there was nothing to do but simply feel it and let it run its short, jagged course until it dissipate—until the next time it would all emerge unbidden again. She squeezed her eyes tight and steadied her breathing, sinking herself a bit more deeply into the water. After a moment, she relaxed and fresh feelings of sadness and compassion for Elena replaced her own fading memories of grief. She knew something of what Elena must feel right now—alone in the world, like an orphan. It broke her heart.

She took a deep breath and raised herself out of the water. She typed a message into the phone. *Honey, I'm so sorry. So very sorry. I love you. See you in a few hours.*

She got out of the jacuzzi, wrapped the towel around her and went back into the cabin. She dried off and got directly into the bed, sliding deep into the down comforter and soft sheets. She felt her mind begin to race with thoughts and questions about Elena and Luis from earlier in the evening, and with the flashbacks of grief about her parents. She put her hand to her chest and forced herself to breathe evenly and deeply, focusing her mind on the blowing sound of the heater in the corner of the loft. Her mind settled, her body relaxed and she finally drifted off into sleep.

# Chapter Fourteen

Elena sat at the kitchen table window and watched the gray light of morning begin its slow bathe of the mesas and mountains that rose from the sepia desert floor. She sat stilled and staring in her mother's fleece bathrobe, which she had put on as she followed behind the stretcher bearing Gloria's body down the hall and out the front door to the ambulance waiting outside. She had belted it around her waist as she stood in the yard watching them fold the stretcher's wheeled legs under it and slide it and its light load into the vehicle. She had stepped forward to place her hand on her mother's face under the sheet before they closed the doors. She felt the bony cheek of the body already turned cold and firm, already long separated from the vibrant, living woman who had been known as Gloria Rios for seventy years. The ambulance pulled away slowly and she stood in the yard and watched it until its brake lights disappeared down the main road. She stood there for a while motionless and blank-minded, and turned to go inside only when she felt Luis touch her elbow and steer her toward the front door.

She did not remember putting on the robe, but now she did not want to take it off. She sat back in the chair, her arms folded tightly around her, the robe gathered in bunches around her waist, its collar folded up and tight around her neck and its long panels draped generously over her legs. Her hands were balled into fists and tucked hidden under her arms, buried in the robe's thick cuffs. A box of tissues sat on the table in front of her next to her phone, a list of phone numbers, a cold cup of tea with bottom dregs, and several wadded, used tissues. Her eyes burned and felt swollen from crying. Her face felt itchy and stiff from dried tears she had not bothered to wipe away, instead letting them roll down to drip off her jawbone or continue down her neck to be absorbed into the fleece of the robe. Even through her stuffy nose, she could detect her mother's scent in the robe's fabric. Each time she smelled that distinct smell of powder and fragranced lotion, she breathed it in and held it until her body demanded she exhale.

She turned when she heard Luis stir on the couch in the living room. He had insisted on staying with her after the hospice people had packed their equipment and vacated the house not long after the ambulance had left with the body. Elena appreciated his presence and how he tended to her even as she knew he was breaking inside with his own grief over the loss of a friend who was like a mother to him. She had heard him gasp when the beeping monitor by Gloria's bed flatlined and went solid, indicating that she had passed from life. She was laying in the bed with her mother at that moment, and had been there for over an hour, nestled against Gloria's arm, her face on her shoulder, whispering to her about the loved ones she would meet soon who were waiting for her on the other side. People from the old country, captured in faded monochromatic photographs that Elena has seen since she was a child, people standing stiff and still in their dress clothes, their mustaches waxed and curls pinned, staring out of the picture like waxen models of living persons. People Elena had never met but about whom her mother spoke wistfully and fondly when she talked about her girlhood in a village with no running water, but bustling with goats, pigs, mule-drawn carts, shoeless children, and dotted with small houses made of handmade mud bricks prickly with straw. Elena spoke of these people into her mother's ear as Gloria labored toward death, her breaths coming easily but sporadically. She spoke their names and told their stories as she remembered them from hearing Gloria tell of them, imagining the people and speaking of them as lined up in a celestial place: on a glowing rock-rimmed butte, or among the willows beside a lively stream, all their immortal horses, mules, goats, chickens and relatives from ancestral generations past gathered behind them, waiting to receive Gloria on their side of reality. Elena did not believe in such a place really, but Gloria did. So Elena closed her eyes, sank her nose into the soft, still warm folds of her mother's neck and told their stories, chanting them like a mantra, willing those ancient loved ones to somehow reach through the ether to fetch their earthen loved one and carry her safely and easily to the other side to join them forever.

Elena felt Gloria take her last breath, a small inhalation, a faint rise of the chest, and then nothing. She heard the monitor's beep turn solid, heard Luis gasp, and heard the hospice nurse step quietly to turn off the monitor. She kept still, her eyes closed and her face buried in her mother's neck, her arm draped across her in embrace. She held the image of her own words in her mind, imagining Gloria now standing beside all those ancient beings along the creek. As tears squeezed through her eyes, and the celestial vision blurred, she felt the dull cold fingers of loss ease into her legs and up into her abdomen. Within a few minutes, the body she embraced seemed foreign and unrelated to her in any meaningful way. Her mother was gone for good.

She had gotten up from the bed and walked stiffly into Luis' outstretched arms, feeling and hearing his deep sobs as she pressed her ear into this chest. Tita Maria and another friend of Gloria's sat in the chairs against the wall, beside a small table filled with saints candles and a statue of the Virgin, their eyes reddened with tears, clasping their rosaries and fingering the open missals on their laps. A deacon from the church stepped forward and began Spanish prayers over Gloria, his sonorous voice intoning in steady, determined notes. Elena watched him but did not hear his words or even register his presence very well. He seemed to fade, along with everyone and everything else, into a blurred miasma of darkness, candles and overbearing silence that blotted out anyone's prayers, chants or tears.

Soon, the house was empty of everyone but she and Luis. They sat together at the kitchen table talking over things that would need to be done as soon as morning came. He encouraged her to try to get some sleep, but she knew that she would not. After a while, he led her to the couch where they both sat for a while, holding hands and crying, softly and intermittently, each in their own way and from within their own private grief. When he dozed off into a jerking, fitful sleep she released his hand gently, got up and came into the kitchen to make herself a cup of tea. She stood watching the water boil, feeling its steam moisten her face, and cinched the belt of the fleece robe tighter around her waist. She sat down at the kitchen table and stared out into the darkness toward Saint Elena mountain, waiting for the predawn light to illumine the jagged point of its highest peak.

Luis stirred from the couch, stretched up and turned to see her at the table. His face seemed pale and gaunt, and his eyes dulled with exhaustion. He got up and came to the table to sit with her.

"I'll make some coffee," she said as he eased himself into a chair.

"Let me do it, " he said, standing back up.

She waved him off, already up and on the way to the pantry. He sat back down and stared blankly at the items on the table and at his own hands. He rubbed his eyes and face and took a deep breath.

They sat for a while, drinking coffee and watching the morning erupt into full glow, saying only a few words here and there, mostly about funeral details and arrangements. Elena dissolved into tears when Rico rounded the corner from the hallway into the kitchen. He stood in the center of the room and looked around for a moment, sniffing the air, seeking his lost love. Finally, he moved toward Elena, reared up and jumped into her lap. She buried her fingers in the soft, orange fur of his neck and cried as she stroked him down his back and tail. He purred and kneaded her leg, butting his head against her robed arm that smelled of Gloria to him.

Elena heard gravel under tires in the driveway and hoped it was Tori. She got up and walked through the living room toward the front door. She saw Tori stepping out of her car with a pastry box and felt the urge to run out toward her. Instead, she held herself still, opened the door and stepped out on the porch. Her eyes filled and her face broke as Tori ascended the steps and circled her in a hug with one arm. She felt Tori pull her body toward her own.

"I'm so sorry, sweetie. I'm so very sorry," she heard Tori whisper into her ear. She kept her arms crossed in front of her, hugging herself tightly and leaning her whole body weight into Tori like a robed fencepost. She buried her face in Tori's shoulder and broke into choking sobs. Luis stepped to the doorway and stood watching as Tori rubbed Elena's back and kissed her head through her hair. Tori met Luis' eyes and smiled weakly in acknowledgment and greeting. Luis stepped forward, took the pastry box from Tori's hand, and they all walked back into the house.

She let Luis make fresh coffee while she sat across from Tori at the kitchen table and told the story of her mother's last hours. Tori sat still, leaning across the table toward her, peering intently at her as she spoke, listening to her story with a face slack with concern and knowing. She wanted to lose herself in Tori's light eyes, to lock onto them and bring her face so close that they blurred out of vision and she dissolved into a soft cocoon of darkness made up of nothing but Tori's body, an enveloping darkness of Tori's warmth, voice and smell. Instead, she kept her arms crossed over her waist and chest, hugging herself tightly across the cinched belt of the robe, and tried to stay focused on the matters at hand.

Luis served them all fresh cups of coffee and opened the pastry box of muffins before them on the table. He sat down and sighed, as if exhausted by the effort of it all, and listened as Elena spoke. Although she mostly kept her eyes on Tori, she felt his grief from across the table. It draped over his shoulders like a cape, tumbling over his chest and down his back, dragging his whole body downward with hard heaviness. He looked tired and confused, as if something had happened that he had not expected.

"Is there anything specific I can do to help you?" Tori asked after listening to Elena's story and taking a deep breath. Tori reached her hand toward her and let it lay there on the table in front of her. She looked at Tori's hand, unclenched her arm from around her waist and took it, holding and squeezing it on the table.

"I don't know really," she said. She smiled brokenly at her and then looked out the window toward the mountains, seeking her favorite peak again.

"We should hear something soon from the funeral home in Stockdale," Luis said, his voice low and coarse. "I think we would like the funeral to be day after tomorrow. Is that right, honey?"

She looked at him and felt her throat tighten at his use of the word "we" in this context. She felt a flash of anger at him for his presumption that he had any say in this or claim to it as his own, as if they were a couple or he were part of the family. Yes, he loved Gloria like a mother, was deeply attached to her, and was a dear friend to her. But, he was not a son-in-law and never would be, no matter how much he hoped or how patiently he waited. He needed to know that, and soon. She felt a rush of urgency and clarity, and started to say something, which would have been harsh and inappropriate given the situation at that moment. She knew that, even as she felt the burning urge of her own short fuse. She gathered herself, squeezing Tori's hand for strength. She closed her eyes, which had grown sharp with anger, swallowed and took a deep breath.

"I plan to have the funeral day after tomorrow, if the funeral home can manage it" she said, looking directly into Luis' eyes. "I'd like them to bring her back here tomorrow morning for visitation all day, vigil all night, and then have the service and the burial at the Logan cemetery the next day."

She turned away from Luis and rubbed her face with her free hand, still clasping Tori's hand with the other. She kept her hand over her eyes for a moment, and lowered it. "When I talked to them last night, they said it would take only a day to get her ready." She looked up at Tori. "Maybe you can come with me to take a suit of clothes to them for her." Tori nodded and smiled faintly.

She turned to Luis, her mind still coursing with anger and frustration, but calming a bit. His face was gaunt and drawn, and she felt herself soften toward him. "Will you help me pick out something nice from her closet?" she asked softly. "You were here when I wasn't, when she was healthy. You'll know some of her nicer clothes better than I do." He nodded blankly and looked down at his hands.

The house phone rang. Luis pushed his chair back to get up, but she stepped up from her chair quickly and went to answer it, keeping herself from glaring at him as she did. Luis watched her walk across the kitchen to the phone, then sat back in his chair and took a deep breath. Tori turned to him and patted his knee.

She received the condolences on the other end of the phone and had barely returned to her chair at the table when the phone rang again. It rang several times in the next half hour and finally she grudgingly asked Luis if he would answer it while she made other, more necessary calls on her cellphone. Almost on cue, the phone rang and he stepped away from the table to answer it. As soon as she heard him talking, she looked up at Tori.

"Thank you for being here," she said in a low voice. "I love you."

"I love you, too, sweetheart," Tori responded softly.

"I wish we could just crawl into bed together under the covers and never come out," she whispered, her voice trembling with tiredness and fresh tears. She rubbed her eyes.

"I know...I know."

She kept her eyes on Tori's face, not needing her to speak or do anything really other than to simply sit there for her to look at. As long as she looked into Tori's face, she felt she could do what she needed to do and be who she needed to be in the next few days.

"Can we leave for Stockdale soon?" she asked. "Or do you need to go to the ranch?"

"I'm yours for whatever you need today. My car is outside. We'll go whenever you are ready."

"Okay..." she whispered as if speaking to the air, not to anyone in particular. "Okay..." She felt the dual urge to sit indefinitely and stare off into nothingness or into Tori's face, or to grab her hand and race out of the house with her to disappear down the highway. She took a deep breath, and looked back at Luis talking on the phone. She looked back at Tori. "Let me go change clothes. I'll be ready in a few minutes."

Luis hung up the phone as she got up to walk toward the hallway. She turned to him and spoke before he had a chance to speak first.

"Will you go into Mama's closet to get an outfit for her? Something she wore to church maybe." She looked down at Rico standing on the floor beside her, looking up at her. "There's a red and gold brocade jacket, and a black skirt hung on the same hanger with it hanging inside the front door of her closet. That might be the best choice." She could just as easily get it herself, but she had just asked for Luis' help with this, so she felt she had to let him. He nodded and followed her down the hallway.

Thirty minutes later, she was reclined back in the passenger seat of Tori's car as they made their way out of Logan toward Stockdale. She leaned her head back and rolled to the side to gaze absently at Tori and through the front windshield alternately. She lodged her hand in Tori's lap, her fingers intertwined with hers. She listened to the soft classical music coming through the car speakers and the low hum of the engine as it carried them down the open road. The car interior smelled like leather and Tori's perfume. She felt herself sink deeper into the seat, soothed by the low sounds and by Tori's still presence. Within a few more minutes, she slipped into sleep.

The Logan cemetery was to the east of town, just off the main road on the south side. It covered several acres and was divided into Protestant and Catholic sections. Even the untrained eye could clearly distinguish them from each other. The Protestant graves were marked with square granite or marble stones that were dark gray, light gray, brown or black in color, and blended with the drab browns, yellows and dark greens of the native desert in which the graves were sunk. The stones were mostly square and were placed flat at the foot and head of the grave, or stood upright on a rectangular pedestal that left room on either side of the marker for a flower vase, flag or other such decorative element. Some graves were brick-lined in their entirety, and a few of the historical families' graves were lined up together inside ground-level brick boundaries.

The Catholic section, in explosive contrast, contained graves dressed in flowers of plastic and silk bearing colors that defied the desert landscape—turquoise, fuchia, tangerine, all manner of reds, royal purples and blues, neon greens and yellows. Stone markers identified the deceased, as in the Protestant section, but these stones were festooned with trinkets of the saints, memorabilia from the deceased's life, pictures, good luck tokens, necklaces, coins, and even paper money. Many of the stone markers stood upright, high above the head of the deceased, bearing the engraved images of the Virgin or the Crucified Christ, and were draped in jewelry, beads, garlands, and small strands holding laminated pictures of the deceased. Compared to the somber restraint of the Protestant section, the Catholic section was celebratory and divulgent. A stranger could spend a few moments at one of the Catholic graves and get a distinct sense of the resting person in the ground underneath.

Elena sat in a white folding chair under an awning and looked out over these graves and their vibrant markings. She sat still in a black suit, her glassy eyes shielded behind dark sunglasses. The rest of the funeral attendees gathered behind her, many under the awning but many also spilling out from under it into the bright sunshine. Luis, Tita Maria, and a few of her mother's closest friends sat down the row beside her to her right. Tori sat on her left. The priest had just completed the liturgy and was intoning a chant that the wind carried beyond their awning and out into the open sky. Elena had already stepped forward to kiss the casket, holding her hand on it for a moment before she let go and stepped back. She felt something give way within her as she took her seat between Luis and Tori again, as if a cord had been broken. She kept her eyes fixed on the middle distance as the casket was slowly lowered into the ground. Luis stepped forward with the pallbearers, grabbed one of several shovels placed in a line on the artificial grass rug, and began shoveling dirt into the hole. Elena heard the loose earth hitting the top of the casket. She felt a tear slip from her eye and roll down her cheek, but her face remained placid and she sat relaxed in her chair, her hands folded in her lap, and her eyes gazing out over the other graves and their myriad decorations which fluttered in the wind. She had cried more in the last two days than she had at any other time in her life, and felt that she had no more tears. But she did, of course.

She had slept a few hours last night. The house was open all day and night for vigil, and she visited on and off with the many dozens of people who came in and out the entire time. The funeral home had delivered the casket and body at mid-morning and the house was ready for visitors by lunchtime. They had pushed the large furniture to the walls, clearing the center of the living room for the casket. They placed folding chairs around the living room, kitchen and down the hallway. Gloria lay in her eternal bed, stolid and cold. Her hair was brushed back off her forehead, and her pale skin was dusted with colored powders and creams. Her eyebrows were drawn on and her hands were locked together in a clenched clasp across her abdomen. Elena stood to look at her several times, once breaking into sobs, wondering how this shrunken, wooden facsimile of a human body could actually have been her mother once. The priest had come to lead the liturgy after dark, and mariachis had led the crowd in singing when he was done. Tita Maria and the other women sang and cried at the same time, belting out the elongated Spanish words in choking, sometimes unsteady tones. The men sat at the edges of the group, along the walls, with their hands on their thighs, their shirts buttoned to the neck and their hair combed back in neat grooves. They sang, too, with restrained voices barely detectable amidst the cries of the women, their eyes closed and heads leaned back against the wall, occasionally raising an emphatic hand in the air during a crescendo of guitars.

Elena had sat with the crowd during the liturgy and the singing, but slipped away after a while down the hall to her room. She clicked the door shut, and leaned her back against it for a moment, letting it hold her weight. She closed her eyes and steadied her breathing. In a moment, she heard a tap on the door. Luis called in between the cracks to ask her if she needed anything. She did not; she just wanted to lie down, so she took off her shoes, blouse and pants and slid into the bed. She laid on her back with her arms at her sides, palms down, and stretched her legs fully, arching her back and shoulder blades into the mattress. She relaxed and looked up at the ceiling. Shadows from the cluster of saints' candles someone had put on the dresser danced on the ceiling. She followed their mesmerizing movements with her eyes until her lids became heavy and she dozed off. She slept for a few hours until she awakened to the sound of her bedroom door clicking shut behind whoever had come to check on her.

She had gotten up just before dawn and joined a deacon from the church and a few others in the living room. The deacon led the small gathering in prayers and liturgical reading. Elena sat near them, a coffee cup in her hand, listening to their prayers and chants. She did not pray or chant with them; she simply listened. She did not really believe in the saints, Christ, God or the church in the ways they did, or in any conventional way at all. She felt comforted by the ritual, however, despite her disbelief. It was something to do at a time like this, and it felt soothing.

Not long afterward, the funeral home people came to load the casket for the cemetery. The deacon and others sang as they rolled it out onto the porch, down the steps and across the gravel to the hearse. Elena walked with the casket and stood as it passed beside her into the cargo bay of the vehicle. Her eyes ran its length over the mahogany colored fiberglass draped with yellow, pink, coral, and red flowers. She knew she had seen what was left of her mother for the last time. The casket would not be re-opened for the cemetery service. As the hearse pulled away, she felt Luis' arm around her waist and he gently turned her toward the house to go back inside.

Luis had been a constant presence since Gloria's death. After those first hours, during which he seemed lost and bewildered by the very fact of death's possibility, he had gathered himself to serve as the "strong one" who was there to meet Elena's needs. She appreciated and received his care, although several times had to push back the anger and urgency she felt from the conversation about arrangements. She knew how the two of them must look to the townspeople who came in and out during the vigil and visitation. She knew that Luis was happy to have any opportunity to take charge of her through taking care of her, and for others to notice this, see them as a couple, and come to expect things to progress between them. Her lip curled at the thought of this, but she kept her contempt hidden and maintained a gracious exterior except for when the sadness of the situation overwhelmed her and blotted out every other feeling or concern. She knew that it was not fair. Luis was simply being himself—a man pursuing a woman he loved. And she being the woman in question had not given him sufficient reason to abandon his pursuit. Her reasons for allowing him to continue, for not stopping it in its tracks before his love for her sank deeper roots into his heart, made sense to her; however, in the end, they would not matter to him. And they did not matter to her in the moments when flashes of anger and resentment thrust up from her throat and into her eyes, and she had to keep herself from betraying them in her countenance or words. Just a little while longer, she told herself. Get through the funeral, the public spectacle, along with its requisite scrutiny of the two of them. Then, things would change. *She* would change them.

Now at the cemetery, she turned to watch Luis and the pallbearers scoop the last piles of dirt into the grave. His forehead beaded with sweat even though the air was cool and blustery, and a lock of hair had fallen across his face. She looked down at Tori's lap beside her. She took Tori's hand and brought it to her own lap, then looked back up at the pallbearers. She smiled faintly at Luis when he stepped back to his chair beside her and sat down with a heavy sigh. "Thank you," she said softly to him, touching his knee with her free hand. He nodded but did not look up. The priest finished the prayers and ended the service. Elena sat as a few dozen people passed in front of her to squeeze her hand or bend down to kiss her cheek or hug her. She maintained her grip on Tori's hand the whole time, letting people think whatever they wanted, now that what was left of her mother was sealed forever in a casket under six feet of dirt.

❧

A dozen or more people came back to the house after the service to visit, sit and eat from the buffet the ranch had sent over. Elena sat outside on the back porch swing talking with a few staff members for most of the time. She was glad to see them away from work, even if the situation was not a joyous one. Letty tended to her like a mother hen: freshening her tea, preparing her a plate of food, or bringing her a jacket to break the wind. Elena appreciated this affection from her young friend and protégé, and allowed herself to be served even when she did not particularly want it or need it. Jared and Dustin sat on either side of her on the swing like a pair of beautiful guardian angels in dark suits and dress boots. Tori joined them for a while as well, smiling and laughing as the staff told work stories about each other, and remembered certain customers or distinct mishaps at the ranch. Gradually, as the afternoon wore on, people left for their own homes and only Tori, Luis, a handful of ranch people, Tita Maria and a few other women remained.

"I want to come over later tonight," Elena said to Tori as they walked around the yard to the front of the house, following behind a few of the staff who were still talking and laughing. "After things clear out here. Is that okay?"

"Of course. I would like that," Tori replied, looking down at their feet as they walked. She looped her arm through Tori's and held it close to her as they walked. She hugged Jared, Dustin, Letty, and the others goodbye and squeezed Tori's hand as she opened her car door and got inside.

"Come whenever you want," Tori said, looking up at her from the driver's seat.

"Okay. In a few hours." She smiled at Tori as she shut the car door.

Inside, Tita Maria and the women were putting up the food. Elena insisted that they take plates of it home with them, that those who had given it had meant it as much for them as for her since they were Gloria's closest friends. She helped Luis slide the couch and other large furniture back into their usual places. Within an hour, the house had returned to its normal state minus the woman who had occupied it for decades. Elena looked around and sighed, feeling the finality of the last few days. The women kissed her goodbye and she took their round faces into her hands, thanking them for everything they had done for her mother and for her. They filed out, making her promise to call them if she needed anything. She made them promise to continue their lunch meetings at Galindo's so she could see them regularly. She waved goodbye to them from the front porch as they pulled away in their low-slung sedans.

Luis sat at the kitchen table holding a half-empty styrofoam cup. He still wore his black suit, but his shirt collar was open and his tie was folded and tucked into his jacket pocket. His eyes were tired and he reached a hand toward her as she walked into the kitchen. She sat down at the table across from him, squeezing his hand quickly and then letting it go.

"Do you want some more tea? I'll make it," he asked, looking into his own nearly empty cup.

"No" she said, shaking her head. "Thank you." She looked out the window across the yard and road and to the mountains in the distance. The road, the desert ground, the few houses across the road, the mesas, and the protruding peak of Saint Elena mountain had all turned various shades of dull gray. Everything was losing color in the descending dusk.

She wanted to be with Tori.

"I'm going to change clothes," she said, twisting to remove her suit jacket as she spoke. She stood up and looked at Luis. "I'm going over to Tori's for a while."

"Okay…" he said. He looked up at her blankly. She looked at him, smiled faintly and then turned to go down the hall. She scrubbed off her make-up, changed into jeans and a long sleeved black t-shirt, and pulled her hair back into its daily ponytail. She felt better immediately, as if she had shed extra weight or a superfluous skin. She snatched her jacket off the bedpost and went back to the kitchen for her purse.

Luis stood up when she came in, his face questioning and uncertain. He fished into his pocket for his keys.

"I guess I'll go home and change, too" he said, looking down at himself in his suit. He looked back up at her. "You want to just call me when you're done and I'll come back over?"

She had draped her jacket over her arm, but now she unfolded it and put it on as a physical act to help her resist the overwhelming urge to run toward the door and yell at him to go home. She knew it was irrational and cruel, but it was real nevertheless. She focused on her facial muscles as she put on her jacket, trying to keep her face smooth and her eyes mild.

"No, Luis," she said, looking up at him. "I don't know when I'll be back over here tonight, if at all." She took a breath, and stepped around him to grab her purse off the back of a kitchen chair. She reached into it, found her phone and checked the battery charge, then remembered that her mother was dead and no one from hospice would need to call her. A surge of emptiness coursed from her throat through her abdomen, down her legs and into the floor like an electric current. She again fought the urge to run out of the house and leave him standing there.

He looked into her face, then down at his boots. He took a big breath and then looked back up at her.

"Okay, then…I guess I'll see you tomorrow." His face was mostly blank, but she took no time to analyze it. She gestured toward the refrigerator and looked away.

"Take some of the food if you want. It's way more than I will eat." She turned to walk toward the front door. He did not follow her but watched her as she walked away from him. She turned to him as she opened the door. "Just lock the door behind you when you leave, okay?" And with that she left him standing there fixed in the kitchen with his hands in his pockets.

She jumped into her truck and backed out of the driveway. She glanced at the front door as she pulled forward toward the main road. She rolled down the window to get some air. Her insides felt jumpy and edgy. As soon as she passed the last cluster of low buildings on the main drag in Logan, she put her foot down on the gas pedal to accelerate herself and her truck, to catch up somehow to the speed of her roiling insides, to increase the blast of cold air on her face, to get closer and faster down the road toward the little cabin at the ranch.

She pulled in to the ranch entrance and turned into the driveway that led to Tori's cabin. She cut the headlights before she got there and coasted the last hundred yards or so in the darkness, the cabin and the sports car in front of it visible only in the faint moonlight. She eased to a stop and shut off the engine. She looked out the window at the three-quarter moon shining cold and serene above her. She took a deep breath and sat still. The five-mile drive had helped. She felt calmer and less pent up. Her breathing returned to normal and the shakiness in her stomach had subsided. She relaxed her shoulders down and stretched her neck from side to side. She rolled up her window and got out of the truck.

Tori opened the door just as she was about to knock on it, and Elena collapsed into her arms, burying her face in her neck. She breathed in deeply, sinking Tori's scent into her lungs, and opened her mouth to take in her softness. She gently turned and pushed Tori backwards into the door, pressing her full weight into Tori's body and her hands into her breasts. After a moment, Tori led Elena to the couch where they lay together, enjoying the gifts of aloneness, freedom and time. It was as if they had agreed beforehand not to rush, to move slowly and deliberately, and draw out their desire into thin, but strong threads. Elena felt as if she were at the beginning of something important and exciting. She wanted to dive into the deep end of it, but she also wanted to take care of it, to curate it and tend it.

"Can we just stay here like this for a while?" she asked. She threaded her leg through Tori's and squeezed it with her thigh.

"Of course," Tori replied in a whisper. "Why do you ask?"

She propped her head up on a crooked arm and watched her own hand as she trailed her finger down the open collar and placket of Tori's blouse. She looked into Tori's face and took a breath.

"I don't want my first time in your bed with you to be the same day I buried my mother," she said softly but frankly. She touched her fingers to Tori's face and traced its contours—the edges of her lips, the bridge of her nose, the thinly arched eyebrows. She smiled as she relished each.

Tori slid her arm under Elena, clenched her own thighs around Elena's, and wrapped her in a full body hug. Elena felt herself enveloped by Tori's warmth and the softness of the couch's leather. Exhaustion overcame her mind and limbs, and she wilted into Tori's body.

# Chapter Fifteen

I need to go home and feed Rico," Elena said as she leaned against Tori from behind and circled her arms around her waist. She kissed Tori's bare shoulder blade and then pressed her cheek against it. Tori swiveled around in her arms and leaned back against the bar in the kitchen.

Their bodies were depleted and shaky from the last several hours they had spent in the cabin loft. They had moved from the couch during the night, groggily making their way up the loft stairs and into the bed. Dawn came and sent sharp beams of light through the skylight above Tori's bed. The sunlight exploded over them as they joined their bodies, arms and legs mingled, their faces alternately clenched and slack with desire. The light moved in its slow arc over the bed, illuminating their skin and hair with shimmering halos. They tumbled and rolled, locked together in fierce embrace, hungry and feeding from each other's arched, quivering bodies. Theirs was an intuitive lovemaking, born purely of sensation and bodily instinct in the moment, not of words or instruction. By midday they were spent and ravenous, shaking inside from the physicality of their encounters as well as from the ravaging revelation of their new intimacy. They stumbled down the stairs, naked and giggling, to the refrigerator and began devouring ranch kitchen leftovers.

"Want me to come with you?" Tori asked as she swallowed a bite of quail. She wiped her hands on a dishtowel and then pulled Elena's body toward her.

"No…" Elena rested her forehead on the point of Tori's chin. "I'll probably see Luis and I need to talk to him."

Tori raised her eyebrows a bit in questioning, but said nothing.

"It's time to make a change," Elena said, taking a deep breath and looking out the window onto the patio. She looked back at Tori. "He needs to know the truth now. About me." She paused for a moment. "About us."

"What are you going to tell him?" Tori asked.

Elena looked into Tori's face, studying it as she gathered her thoughts. She grabbed a water bottle from the counter, took a drink and set it down.

"That I'm not in love with him and never have been. That I knew Mama wanted me to love him and I did enough to make her happy during her last days. Maybe that I wondered myself if I could come to love him in that way."

She paused again, reflecting, gathering her feelings and thoughts into language. She looked directly into Tori's eyes. "But, that was before you…before I knew you enough to be in love with you. Once that happened, it was done. I was done." She spoke softly, but frankly. "I just needed to hold things together like they were until Mama died. For her." She took a deep breath and continued. "I know I haven't talked to you about all this very much—at all really. I'm sorry about that. I didn't mean to leave you hanging or wondering. I just wanted to keep things mostly together until Mama died. I hope you can understand."

Tori smiled, leaned over and kissed her lightly. She pulled back and traced her finger along Elena's brown throat and down her chest between her breasts.

Elena smiled faintly and took another deep breath. "Luis won't understand…and I don't blame him."

"You think it's best to tell him about us now?" Tori asked.

Elena looked at her, closed her eyes and nodded. "Yes, because it's the full truth and he'll find out soon enough anyway," she said, opening her eyes again. "I don't want to love you in secret anymore, Tori. Life's too short and before long all of us will be in the dirt with Mama." She swallowed as felt the raspy edge of grief and rage rise in her throat and well up in her eyes "And you're the only reason I'd stay in Logan. You and this ranch we've built. Luis is not enough reason. He wasn't twenty-five years ago and he's not now."

Tori listened and nodded. She remembered the conversation with Luis that morning many weeks ago on the morning hunt, while the hunters slept off their brunch. Her stomach churned with guilt and dread. She had not told Elena about it. "What do you think he'll do?" she asked.

Elena thought for a moment. "I hope he leaves this town and goes and finds a new life for himself somewhere. He's been stuck here for too long." She looked away, out toward the gorge. "He's going to be so upset, though…" She stood still and silent for a few moments, contemplating that comment, going through everything in her mind for the thousandth time, coming to same conclusion. She was in love with Tori and never would be with Luis. And even if she had never met Tori, she would never marry Luis.

"There's no way around hurting him. I hate that, but I know it," she said quietly, her voice low with resignation.

She turned back to Tori, took a big breath and they both climbed upstairs to get dressed. Elena looked around the cabin as if seeing it for the first time.

"This really is a neat little place," she said approvingly. "And

I didn't know there was a skylight up here. That's a nice touch."
Tori smiled at her and looked up through the skylight to the clear
blue beyond it.

"I like it a lot. It meets my needs for now. At some point, I…
maybe *we*…will want something bigger," she said.

They kissed goodbye and Elena stepped out into the clear day
to drive to her mother's house, which was now hers. She glanced
at the ranch parking lot as she drove out and saw Luis' navy truck.
She knew he would come to the house as soon as he saw that her
truck was no longer parked at Tori's cabin. She wondered how long
that would be, how much time she had—a half hour, an hour, two
hours? She needed time to shower, to wash Tori's scent from her.

Rico purred and swirled around her legs as soon as she came
into the house. He ran to the back kitchen door, stood over his
bowl and meowed. Elena smiled at him as she opened the bag
of food and dropped some fishy smelling pellets down into his
bowl. "It's just the two of us now, buddy," she said as she stroked
the orange fur down his arched back and tail.

She went down the hallway to her room, stopping for a moment
to look in at her mother's bedroom. It looked again the way it had
for years, with no medical equipment or hospital bed. The tops
of the dresser and nightstands were clear, and the bed was made.
The chenille bedspread stretched tight and smooth over the bed
except for a small hollow near the pillow on Gloria's side where
Rico had slept. Elena stood in the doorway, leaning against the
doorframe, and felt the silence and emptiness of the room. She
felt tears well up in her eyes, but she took a deep breath and they
dissipated. She continued down the hall to her bedroom.

She had been home for about an hour and out of the shower for
about fifteen minutes when Luis drove up. She heard the gravel
under his tires and knew it was him before she even looked up.
She stood at the counter bobbing a tea bag up and down in her
cup and waited for him to come in. She looked up when she heard

his footsteps cross the threshold of the living room into the kitchen.

"Hey," she said. "You want some tea? I just took the water off." She put her hand on the handle of the kettle.

"No, thanks," he said. He stood in the kitchen, in jeans and a ranch shirt, watching her as she brewed the tea in her cup. She moved to the kitchen table. He stepped toward the table and sat down across from her. His boots sounded loud on the linoleum floor.

"Is everything okay," he asked. "Are you okay?" His voice was even and tense.

She took a sip of tea, frowning into the hot liquid. She set the cup down and looked at him.

"I'm fine. I slept well last night, so I feel much better." She looked into his face, which did not seem as hollow as it had the last few days. "How are you? Did you get some rest?"

He nodded, keeping his eyes on hers. "I've been at the ranch all day getting stuff together to start cutting that hiking trail along the gorge." He paused for a moment. "It's good to be busy."

She nodded. "We have that corporate group from somewhere in the midwest coming this weekend for four days." She took another sip of tea. "I'm ready to get back to work, too."

She watched him as he sat back in his chair. She could tell that he sensed something was wrong, or wanted to ask a question, but he perhaps did not know exactly what to ask. She knew she could not wait for his prompt. She would have to jump in. She took a deep breath, settling herself in her chair.

"Luis, I have some things to talk to you about," she began. "We... I should have talked with you about these things long before now, but... I've been focused on Mama and what she needed and wanted ever since I came back and, well, that just seemed the right thing to do even though some things were left undone that should have been handled." She knew she was being vague.

"What are you talking about, Elena?" he asked, his voice tight and low, his eyes trained on hers.

"I'm talking about you and me, Luis," she said, looking directly at him with both hands folded around the tea mug. "Mama wanted us to be together again. She talked to me about it a few times."

"She talked to me about it, too," he said, smiling faintly. "Even before you came back."

Elena nodded. She had not known this, but she was not surprised.

"I know—or at least I think I know—that you have wanted us to get back together as well." She looked at him and waited.

"And...?" he said, holding her gaze without blinking.

"Luis, I don't know how to say this other than to simply say it straight out." She glanced out the kitchen window toward the mountains and then looked back at him. "That's not going to happen. I'm sorry."

Luis' face tightened. He cleared his throat. "Look, I know you need some time. You've been caring for Gloria and now it's going to take a while for things to feel normal again." He put his hand out on the table toward her, softening his voice. "You can have all the time you need, Elena. I've told you that before. I've waited a long time for you. I can wait longer."

Elena listened to him, feeling her stomach drop. She looked into his dark eyes, forcing herself to look directly at him and not look away.

"Luis, this is not something that will change with time," she said simply. "I know you think it will, but it won't. I know it won't."

He took a deep breath and let it out. "Well, I don't think you can know that for sure, not really," he said, glancing out the window and then looking down at his hands on the table before looking back up at her. "I don't think you should make a decision like this in the state you're in."

"What do you mean?" she asked.

"I mean being in a state of grief after watching your mother slowly die for a year," he said sharply, his eyes widening. He took another deep breath. "I just think we need to keep going along like we have been. Give it a chance during regular life, when you're not strained with worry for your mother." He paused for a moment. "Don't they say to not make major life decisions within six months of someone close to you dying?"

"Luis...I don't want to do that. To keep going along like we have been." She tightened her grip on her mug. "That will just string you along and, regardless of what *they* say about grief, I feel certain that it's not going to work between us."

She breathed in and let it out slowly. "I think it's best if we just both move on," she said.

Luis sat back and hung his arms down the sides of the chair. His eyes dulled and his face seemed to cloud. "So, you're leaving Logan? Is that what you mean by 'moving on'?"

"No, I'm not planning to, at least not anytime soon." She started to say more, but decided against it.

He looked off for a moment and then looked back at her. He leaned forward as he spoke, his hands clasped on the table in front of him. "Look, Elena...I've loved you since we were kids. There's no secret there. I'm not saying we pick up where we left off twenty-five years ago. That's impossible. I know you're a different person. So am I." He looked intently at her, as if he were searching her eyes and face for affirmation. "So, maybe we just give ourselves a little time and then we start over fresh. Like it was the beginning." He paused for a moment. "I've never loved another woman the way I love you, Elena."

She looked down at her hands around the mug. She knew it was time to tell him about Tori, that knowing that would be the only thing that would stop his trying to convince her to give things more time. She closed her eyes and gripped her mug to keep her hands steady. She opened her eyes and looked at him, aching for him for what she was about to say.

"Luis, I'm not in love with you. I care about you deeply—I have as long as I've known you. But, I'm not in love with you." She saw his eyes sharpen and his chest rise and fall with quickening breaths. "I'm in love with someone else." She felt a bolt of heat rush from her abdomen to her throat and up into her face.

He sat back into his chair with his mouth slightly open, staring at her. She thought she detected a sneer, but was not sure. He crossed his arms over his chest and swallowed. "Someone back in California, I guess. Are they planning to move here or something? You said you weren't planning to leave." He looked out the window, waiting for her answer.

"No. I'm in love with someone here." She looked at him, waiting to see if he would turn to face her, or if he would guess the person she loved. She saw his jaws clench as he pressed his lips together. "Luis…it's Tori. I'm in love with Tori. And she's in love with me." She held still, bracing herself for his response.

He continued looking out the window and began shaking his head slowly. He licked his lips, pursed them again and swallowed. He looked down at his boots, still shaking his head, and then looked at her with a strange, lazy smile. "You're more messed up than I thought, Elena. This grief has got you thinking you're a *lesbian* or something." He snorted and shook his head again. "I read about it on the internet. It can make people do crazy things. You gotta admit, this is pretty crazy." He laughed incredulously and looked at her with raised eyebrows.

She sensed the rage coming before it even hit her fully. She felt it well up at the base of her neck, at the very back of her throat. As she heard his words, she felt it expand into her ears and fill her skull. Her mouth and eyes watered, and she felt her chest begin its own rapid rise and fall as she struggled to breath in and out without spewing fire across the table to burn him up.

"Leave now," she said in a low, strained voice. She pressed her hands flat onto the table. "I mean it, Luis. Leave this house now."

He looked surprised and backed his chair away from the table, but he did not stand up. He leaned forward and looked at her, still wearing that detached smile. "Elena, you should get some help for this. They probably have somebody up in Stockdale who can help you. Not the gay part—I mean, really, you're not a lesbian, anyone can see that." He chuckled. "I mean the grief and this craziness you're feeling and talking. I mean, you gotta let yourself grieve— that's natural. But, you can't let it totally mess up your life like this."

"Get out!" she barked. Her chair scraped loudly against the linoleum floor as she forced herself back. She stood up and glared at him and, for the first time in her life, felt a physical urge to hit another person. She clenched her fists, restraining herself from leaping across the table to slap him. Rico startled from the sunbeam on the living room floor where he had been lounging and disappeared down the hall.

"Elena, wait a minute…calm down," he said as he stood up and took a step back from the table and her. He held his hands up, palms out facing her. "Just hold on…" He patted the air with his hands. "Just hold on, calm down. We're both adults here." He lowered his voice and spoke in even, measured tones, as if calming a scared horse.

"Then be an adult and leave my house like I've asked," she said, matching her tone to his. As she heard her own voice, lowered and steeled, she felt herself retreat inside herself and harden. She had kept her heart open earlier, feeling for Luis and hating his pain. Now, that softness hardened into a knot and she felt as if she were inside it, looking out at Luis from within its encased confines.

Luis lowered his hands and stood there staring at her. His odd smile dissipated and he seemed puzzled by her words and reaction. After a moment, his brow relaxed and he sighed. He threw his hands up slightly in resignation, turned and started walking toward the front door. She did not follow him but stood still in her spot in the kitchen and watched him walk away. She felt a molecule of violence release its hold on her as he moved further away from her.

He opened the front door and turned back to her. "We can talk more later. Tonight or tomorrow." He paused and then added. "I'm here for you, Elena. We can get through this."

She felt her lip slightly curl and wanted to scream at him, but instead she held still and said nothing except through icy dark and glaring eyes. He turned and walked out, clicking the door shut behind him softly.

She bent over and braced herself on the kitchen table, letting her head hang down between her shoulders and opening her mouth to breathe. Her legs felt shaky and warm, and were tingling like they did when she curled them under her for too long in her office chair. She raised one leg off the floor and shook it a bit, then lowered it and raised the other. "Oh my God…" she said, as a bundle of emotions coursed through her shaking body. She reached over and took a swallow of the tepid tea.

After a few moments, she stood up straight and went to the bathroom. She sat on the toilet for a long time, lost and glazed over in a kind of empty nothingness, as if all capacity for thought and feeling within her had been used up and needed replenishing, like a cellphone battery. She looked absently down at Rico as he swirled around her legs and head-butted her limp fingers. Finally, she got up, went into the living room and fell asleep on the couch.

❧

She awakened as dusk began its daily swaddling of the town and the surrounding mesas in grays and browns. She stretched her legs and back, got up and went to check her phone on the kitchen table. Tori had sent a text message an hour ago: *Luis left and then came back to the ranch. Did you see him?*

She took a deep breath and texted her back: *Yes. Bad*

*conversation. I had to take a nap. Dinner? Come over?* Within a moment, Tori texted back: *Be over soon. Don't cook anything.*

She stood in the kitchen and stared out the window at the descending darkness. She texted Tori: *Come around to the back.* She put on her jacket and went out through the back door to the yard. Within a little while, a fire roared in the chiminea and she sat in front of it with a glass of red wine. An empty chair, the wine bottle and an empty glass waited for Tori. Elena held her wineglass with one hand and held the other out to receive the heat. Her legs stretched out in front of her. She could already feel the warmth coming through her jeans. She sat, mesmerized by the flames, embraced by the dark sky and its bright band of galaxy overhead. She leaned her head back against the chair and looked up into the gaudy sky. New stars emerged from the thickening darkness each minute, it seemed. She followed the fiery, descending arc of several shooting stars. She listened to the crackle of the pine in the fire, and breathed in the warmth emanating from the chiminea's ceramic. She felt herself relax and settle into her chair. The conversation with Luis seemed far away although it had happened only a few hours before.

Soon she heard a car in the driveway. It dawned on her that it could be Luis, returning to talk. She turned her head on her chair and smiled a sigh of relief when Tori rounded the corner of house. She watched her as she came toward her and the fire, growing more visible in the light of the flames with each step. She had zipped her leather jacket to the top and the collar was flipped up. Her hands were stuffed in her pockets. She stood in front of her chair, looking down at Elena.

"This was a good idea," she said, smiling at her.

Elena nodded. "Sit down. Pour yourself some wine. There's your glass and the bottle," she said, pointing at the ground under the chair.

Tori bent down, kissed her softly, and sat down to face the fire.

She poured her wine and put the bottle on the ground between their chairs. She looked into the flames and took a sip, swallowed and sat back in her chair. They sat there together in silence, enjoying the quiet and each other's presence. After a little while, Elena stretched her hand over to Tori, palm up. Tori looked at it and placed her fingers through Elena's. They held their clasped hands in the space between them as they drank their wine, watched the flames, and let themselves be nourished by the elements of earth, sky, air and fire.

After a while, Elena looked over at Tori and felt a wave of relief that Luis knew the truth now. Even if he did not believe her, or respect the love between her and Tori, at least he knew. She was not concealing or hiding anymore.

Tori looked back at her and smiled faintly, raising her eyebrows in a question.

"It was bad. Mainly because I got so angry. I had to work really hard not to hit him," Elena said. She looked into the fire. "I don't remember when I've felt that angry."

"What happened?" Tori asked softly.

Elena recounted the story and the conversation to her. Tori listened intently and kept her grasp on Elena's hand. Elena felt Tori squeeze her hand when she quoted Luis saying that she should get some professional help because "anyone can see" that she is not a lesbian.

"I felt violent, Tori. I'm not kidding," she said. "I'm not a violent person, at least not normally. But, my eyes and mouth started watering, and I tasted this mineral taste in my mouth, and all I could think of was to yell at him to get out because…I don't know….I was so close to hitting him or throwing something at him." She shook her head and continued staring into the fire. "It scared me a little bit, how angry I got. And then, I just cratered and had to sleep for a while."

Tori listened and nodded. "I can imagine…" she said.

"What? That I had to sleep?"

Tori nodded again. "Yes, that and you getting so angry and feeling so violent." She paused for a moment, as if choosing her words carefully. Elena turned to look at her. "I remember, after my parents were killed, I had flashes of very strong anger. Sometimes over things that probably wouldn't have upset me as much at any other time." She looked into the fire. "I didn't have a situation, at the time, like you have with Luis, but I can imagine how angry and violent I would have felt if I had, and if I'd had the conversation you had with him."

Elena looked back at the fire. "Do you think I should apologize to him for getting so angry?" she asked after a moment.

Tori looked at her and squeezed her hand. "I don't think there's a *should* or *shouldn't* here. I think it's understandable you got angry." She thought for a second and then chuckled. "I'm probably not the best one to ask since I'm not exactly a *neutral* party in this whole situation."

They sat quietly for a moment looking into the fire.

"He says he wants to talk more, but I don't have anything else to say about it really," Elena said. "I could tell him details of our relationship, how it all started between us far before Mama died, but…." She felt her face shift into a scowl as she said these words. Tori looked over at her. "It feels like I'd be telling something precious to someone who doesn't understand it or believe it, or even want to get it or believe it." She felt an ember of anger begin to stir within her again.

"Deal with that when the time comes," Tori said, detecting the emerging anger inside Elena. "Whatever you need to say will come to you in the moment. Don't think about it now. Just let it be." She paused for a moment. "Just let him be."

Elena looked over at Tori.

"He's grieving, too" Tori added softly. "He loved your mother." Again, she seemed to choose her words carefully. "Now he's losing you, too." She looked back at the fire. "He's a good person, but he's probably going to do and say things that are out of character for a while. We both probably should brace ourselves to hear some cruel things from him."

They sat for a while longer, enjoying the early evening and their time together. Elena felt herself settle and as she sat holding Tori's hand, she knew even more than she already did that she belonged with Tori and would make her life with her, or with no one at all.

Tori finished her wine and looked over at Elena. "I thought maybe we could drive into Stockdale for dinner. There's a new fish place up there I hear is really good. You want to go try it?"

Elena took a deep breath, as if breaking a spell on herself, and looked over at Tori. "Sure, that sounds great. Just give me a few minutes to get things together." She got up, turned the water hose on the embers of the fire, and then followed Tori into the house to change her blouse. She put more food and fresh water down for Rico, cleaned his litter box, grabbed her phone, jacket and purse, and then stood in the middle of the kitchen. "Alright, I'm ready."

Tori stepped over to her and put her arms around her waist. Elena felt Tori's hands on her back, and placed her own hands flat against Tori's hips and slid them down her thighs. She looked into Tori's face without blinking.

"Thank you," she said, and kissed her lightly.

"For what?" Tori asked softly.

"For being you and for being here for me during all this." Elena said. "For being patient with me."

"You're quite welcome," Tori said. "I love you."

"I'm so glad," Elena replied, grinning slightly as she pressed her lips more firmly to Tori's.

The stood in the middle of the kitchen for a little while, kissing and holding each other. Finally, Elena pulled back and looked at Tori. "A *fish* place? Really? In Stockdale?"

Tori laughed and nodded. "That's what I thought, too. We should probably reserve our judgment until we try it out."

"I don't know…" Elena said, raising her eyebrows in doubt and grinning as Tori turned around and she followed her out the door and to the car. Elena sat in the front seat looking down at her phone while Tori backed out of the driveway and pulled out onto the main road. Neither of them saw Luis' navy truck parked on the dark street a few dozen yards past the driveway where, sitting inside with his hands tightly clenched around the steering wheel, he had watched them through the large, open kitchen window as they held each other.

# Chapter Sixteen

Tori quietly unfolded herself from around Elena, pulled on fleece pajamas and went downstairs to make coffee. She looked out her back window toward the gorge as she waited for the brew, listening to the gurgling and steaming of the coffee-maker. The sun was a few minutes from breaking over the horizon. The desert was still the brown of winter—drab, dull and brittle. Soon, however, its browns would take on sheens of vibrancy, shifting from drab colors to rich, glossy caramels, olive greens, cinnamons and almonds. The greens would plump and brighten as the buds and blooms of prickly pear, Spanish dagger, purple sage, Indian paintbrush and desert rose swelled beyond their stalks and exploded into brash color. The winds of March, which were just beginning, would blow away all that had died during the winter, and pollinate and seed the living. Soon the desert landscape would break out in all its thorny, flowery glory—the sharp emerging with the soft, the deadly with the delicate, all enmeshed and interwoven into a terrible tangle of beauty and mystery.

When the coffee was ready, she poured a large mug full, and stepped outside to the back patio. She sat her steaming mug on the edge of the jacuzzi, slipped her pajamas off into a pile at her feet, and entered the warm, bubbling water. She sank to her ears and eased herself into the submerged seat. She reached for her coffee and settled in to greet the sunrise.

She thought about Luis, and how things might change at the ranch. She felt unsure of how to proceed. She had never been in this situation before, certainly not professionally with an employee or colleague. Luis was an employee, technically, but she had always viewed him not so much as a subordinate, but as a colleague. He was also a friend. She had not seen him much since the funeral and now, at least in his world, everything had changed for the worse for him, and she was in the middle of it. She wondered if they should simply sit down and talk about it, like adults. That did not seem feasible, however, given what Elena had said about her conversation with him. Nothing about this seemed *simple*, period.

She brooded about this as the sun peeped over the eastern horizon and its orange glow began to enliven the desert ground in deep gold and tangerine. She heard the patio door open and turned to watch Elena step forward wearing Tori's robe, her arms crossed over her chest and her shoulders hunched to ward off the morning chill. Her eyes were squinting and sleepy and her hair knotted in a disheveled, bound ball on the back of her head.

"Get in," Tori said, smiling at her. "It's warm."

"Let me get coffee," she mumbled, turning back inside.

Tori scooted over in her underwater chair to make room, and in a moment Elena returned with her coffee. She quickly undressed and submerged herself in the steaming water. She kissed Tori's wet shoulder as she settled in beside her and grabbed her coffee. She looked out toward the gorge and the rising sun.

"Beautiful morning," she said, blowing into her cup. Tori agreed, and leaned in to Elena's body, caressing her smooth thigh under the warm water. They sat together in silence, watching the sun's glow expand over the desert.

"That corporate group comes in today, right?" Elena asked, wiping the sleep out of her eyes with wet fingers.

"Yeah, for four days. They've got the whole place booked," Tori said. "I've got paperwork to do this morning and then I'm going over to the ranch to be there when they arrive sometime after lunch. I guess I'll just hang out, visit, have dinner with them. You know, the usual. What's your plan today?"

"Do lunch at Galindo's and then come to the ranch in the afternoon to get ready for the dinner service, I guess," Elena said.

Tori leaned forward in her chair, curling her back and stretching her legs out in front of her. She turned to Elena. "How do you think things are going at the ranch with Luis?"

Elena sighed and shook her head slightly. "I don't know...I've haven't seen him too much. He's hasn't been around the hotel—I guess he's been out on the property." She looked off into the distance and took a sip of coffee. "I don't know what to expect from him." She looked at Tori. "You know?"

Tori nodded and looked down at the water and her shimmering legs below its bubbling surface. "Yeah..." she said. "I'm not really sure what to do about anything—not really," she said after a moment. "I guess we can just keep going along as normal until the situation demands something different." She looked up at Elena.

Elena nodded. "I can always just stay at Galindo's for a while, too—let Letty run things at the ranch. Give Luis some space."

Tori began shaking her head in disagreement before Elena even finished her sentence. "No..." she said. "You're a partner in this operation. Plus, we're transitioning into the non-hunting season of business. I don't know that it will be so completely different, but still, it's the first time we're doing it and you should be on site as much as you need or want to be."

They both were quiet for a moment. "Let's just see how things go," Tori said. "Are you okay with that?"

"Sure," Elena said. "I can be civil and professional. As long as he doesn't tell me again I need to go get therapy for my *lesbian grief phase*." She grinned wryly.

Tori smiled back at her. "Let's both try really hard not to throw anything at him if he says something like that."

"Agreed," Elena said, swishing her fingers across the burbling surface of the water.

Tori sat in the ranch dining room going over spreadsheets on her laptop. The outside stucco of the buildings shone bright and clean in the midday sun, and the gentle splashing of the fountain reverberated throughout the courtyard and into the dining room through the slightly opened door. She could hear a few of the staff people in the kitchen loading supplies through the heavy delivery door, and beginning preparations for the next several days of full occupancy. Letty and Jared had come in a while ago to set up for the guests who would arrive soon by bus from the airport in San Angelo. Jared had prepared the meeting rooms and was now on the patio, wiping down the wrought-iron tables and chairs, and setting up the column heaters to cut the chill that remained in the emerging spring air. Tori watched Letty stock the portable bar from the permanent bar in the corner of the dining room and roll it out to the patio to its position in the center of things. She would roll out another unit soon with crackers, cheeses and iced hor d'oeuvres.

She had learned from Betty that Luis, Ricardo and Dustin were out cutting the trail along the bottom of the gorge. A team of workers had come in a few weeks ago with heavy equipment to cut staired switchbacks down both sides of the gorge directly behind the hotel, and in one- or two-mile increments down its length on either side of the hotel. The stairs were minimalist, merging with the natural slope and curvature of the gorge's sides, meandering around large rocks and established plants. The workers had used small explosives to blast out sections of the stony earth and had embedded chunks of limestone and sandstone to make steps. At other points, they stabilized the natural rocks with mortar and other bracings, making sure to disturb the natural landscape as little as possible while making a safe, identifiable way to enter and exit the gorge. Tori had sat in a lawn chair on the edge of the gorge behind the hotel when they had first begun the work, watching them carefully level rocks, spread mortar and lock in support mechanisms. Luis and Ricardo had begun then to walk the gorge floor in both directions, determining the best path through the rocks and brush, crossing back and forth over the dry creek bed that ran the length of the gorge like a sandy vein. Often the best path was an animal trail, visible through the desert fauna as a worn-down sliver of openness amidst the sharp brambles and cacti, dotted with scat and occasional leavings of bones bleached white by the desert sun.

Tori felt a mixture of satisfaction and dread as she sat in the dining room of her own ranch and looked over the projected financials for the next quarter and the rest of the year. She felt strong satisfaction at having dreamed up a business concept for her land and executed it with such success. She knew, almost in her bones, when she first met her that Elena was the right person to be her business partner, that she had gifts and vision to match her own, but in ways that were complementary, not duplicative. And as she gazed at the water dripping from the ledges of the fountain the courtyard, she felt an intense pleasure deep within her in the new relationship with Elena. Now, it was as if everything they did and would do together at the ranch—the hunts, the trail rides, the hikes, the meals, the brunches in the field, all of it—was but one more indication of their love for each other and the synergy of their connection. All of it was its own manifestation of their desire, as real and as expressive as anything they did with each other's bodies, having come from the same source and been nourished by the same currents.

Dread sat alongside the satisfaction, however, like a cold heavy stone in her stomach. She dreaded what she intuitively knew was coming from Luis, even though she had no idea of the details or how it would take shape. She dreaded not only whatever it was in itself, but also the reverberations it would create throughout the ranch and the larger community. She just had a bad feeling about it all, and she wondered if Elena felt it as well, or if she were too mired in grief to sense anything but loss and emptiness punctuated by moments of rage and sexual desire.

Lost in these thoughts, she heard the noise of footsteps and turned to see Dustin and Ricardo on the patio. They stopped to talk to Jared and, as they helped him move one of the heavy tables and its chairs into another position on the patio, she saw Luis step onto the patio as well. They all wore jeans, ranch shirts, jackets, broad-brimmed hats and high snake boots. As soon as the table was put into its new place, the three of them turned and began walking toward the dining room door. Tori looked up at them as they came in.

"Hey," Dustin said brightly as he stepped into the dining room. His smile was broad and beaming, and Tori smiled back at him, sensing his pleasure at having been out with Ricardo and Luis on the land working on the trails instead of working inside with linens, flowers and flatware. He took off his cowboy hat and ran his fingers through his hair. "It's really nice outside today."

"Yes, it is," she responded. "If I could see my laptop screen in the sun, I would sit outside on the patio and work." She closed her laptop and sat back in her chair. She looked at Ricardo and then at Luis. Luis did not meet her glance but stepped past her toward the bar in the corner. He bent down to retrieve cold water bottles from the refrigerator and set two of them on the counter, opening a third one for himself and drawing a long drink from it. Tori watched him, but then looked back at Ricardo and Dustin as they both stepped forward to get a bottle.

"How did it go out there? How's the trail coming?" she asked.

Ricardo nodded at her as he held the bottle to his mouth and drank. He lowered the bottle, swallowed and wiped his mouth. "It's coming along good," he said. He pushed a stray lock of dark hair back from his forehead. He set his water down and took off his jacket, tossing it onto the back of a nearby dining chair. "There's not a lot of brush to clear. I think it helps that we're doing this in a time of year when everything's not already bloomed out." He took another long drink. "The animal trails are easy to see. We just kind of follow them."

Tori glanced at Luis again as Ricardo spoke, but Luis still did not look at her. He drank his bottle empty, tossed it into the recycling bin, and then just watched Ricardo as he spoke. Tori turned back to Ricardo and Dustin.

"The switchbacks are nice," Dustin said. "They did a good job on them. The steps really blend in with the natural landscape." He glanced at Luis, as if waiting for Luis to add a comment, and then looked back at Tori. "We installed some basic signs and markers—little ones, not big glaring ones—that will help people see the steps when they get near them. Otherwise, they might miss them because they blend in so well."

"That's good," Tori said. "I'm excited to walk the trail myself. Maybe I'll walk a little of it this afternoon." She watched as Luis stepped from behind the bar and disappeared into the kitchen. She looked back at Ricardo and Dustin. They watched him, too, then looked at each other. Tori noticed Ricardo shrug slightly and then turn to sit down. Dustin pulled out a chair and sat down as well, taking off his jacket and laying it across his lap with his hat.

"When do you think it'll be ready for guests?" Tori asked. She wanted to ask about Luis, about Ricardo's shrug, but she didn't want to involve Dustin and Ricardo in the situation unnecessarily.

"The part right here behind the hotel in either direction until the next set of steps is ready now," Ricardo said. "They probably shouldn't go past that for another week or two."

Tori nodded and smiled. "That's great—I'm really glad to hear this. Thanks for all the work you guys have put into it recently. I think it's a nice addition to what we offer here, especially during non-hunting periods."

"Yeah, we should tell people to be extra careful and to stay on the trail during hunting season," Ricardo said. "We don't want anyone to get hurt."

"Good point," Dustin added.

Tori nodded in agreement and turned as Luis returned to the dining room. He looked at her briefly with a blank, distracted expression, and looked away toward Ricardo and Dustin.

"I'm going to get lunch. You coming?" he asked them without breaking his stride toward the dining room door that led to the patio.

Ricardo and Dustin looked at each other and then back at Luis.

"Ya'll go ahead. I'm going home for a while and then coming back for the dinner service tonight," Dustin said.

"I'll come with you," Ricardo said, getting up and grabbing his jacket. "See you later, man," he said to Dustin. "Bye, Tori" he said as he moved toward the door.

"Bye. Thanks again," she said to him as he stepped out to follow Luis. She watched them cross the patio and disappear around the corner of the east wing. She looked back at Dustin. He looked at her, raised his eyebrows, and stood up to put his empty water bottle in the recycling bin.

"Is everything okay?" she asked in a calm, even voice.

"Yeah..." he said, walking back over to the table where she sat. "Luis was just in a bad mood today, I guess."

She nodded and smiled at him, waiting to hear whatever else he wanted to say about things. She did not want to ask for anything more. Dustin looked out onto the patio. Jared was wiping smudges off the stainless steel of the portable bar. Dustin looked back at Tori.

"I heard him say something to Ricardo about Elena," he said. She nodded again slightly. He looked into Tori's eyes and held her gaze. "I figure he knows now, right?"

Tori simply nodded her assent, keeping her eyes on his and making sure her face retained a pleasant, neutral expression. She felt her heartbeat quicken, and felt the surprising urge to blurt out all the details to Dustin. But, she knew that probably was not a good idea, so she managed her facial muscles and measured her words.

"Yes," she said, again in a calm, even tone. "Elena spoke with him. I'm sure he's upset and will be for a while." She smiled up at Dustin and took a deep breath. "We should all probably just give him some room."

Dustin nodded in agreement. He looked down at his boots, then back out to Jared on the patio, then back at Tori. His cropped hair was bent in multiple directions from being smashed under his hat, and his cheeks were red from the wind and sun. His eyes were bright, the clear highlight of his open, kind and handsome face. He reached out and put one hand on the back of Tori's chair.

"Let me know if you or Elena need anything. Any help or whatever...I don't know the situation, of course, but Jared and I are here for you two." He stepped back a bit, but not before Tori reached up to squeeze his hand perched on the chair back at her shoulder.

"Thank you," she said, her face breaking somewhat. "That

means a lot to me. To Elena, too." She took another big breath and let go of his hand. She smiled up at him. "Things will be rough for a little while, I think, but it'll all be okay."

"Okay," he said as he patted the back of the chair and let go of it. He reached for his jacket and hat. "I'm going home to clean up. I'll be back later to work the dinner service. We're full tonight, right?"

"A full house in the hotel for the next four days and a full slate of reservations in the restaurant," she said. "Business is good."

"Awesome," he grinned. "See you in a while then."

She watched him walk out onto the patio. He stopped to talk to Jared. The two of them stood for a moment. Tori could not hear their conversation but smiled when she saw Jared reach up and thump the edge of Dustin's hat brim. Dustin put the flat fingers of his fist into Jared's chest and gently pushed him back, grinning at him as he stepped away to disappear around the east wing. She watched Jared watch him go, and then smiled as Jared turned to catch her eye. He smiled back at her and then both of them returned to their work.

Tori stood by the courtyard fountain the next evening, drinking a glass of merlot and watching the ranch guests. The corporate group was loud and giddy, and had moved outside to the portable bar and jacuzzi as soon as they had finished dinner in the dining room. Most of the local restaurant guests remained inside and the dinner rush continued well past nine o'clock. She had milled around the tables, greeting people and chatting. Elena had come out from the kitchen from time to time as well, checking to make sure people were pleased with their food and bringing extra off-the-menu items to a few special guests. The atmosphere was alive and vibrant, and everyone seemed energized by the cool spring air that smelled verdant and ripe, even though the desert's blooms remained hidden still in their casings and stalks.

Tori moved to a table near one of the column heaters and nodded quickly at Jared. He nodded back at her and disappeared into the dining room. He emerged a few moments later with fresh table linens, flatware, plates and cups. Tori stood back as he set the table for four. When he finished, he pulled a chair out for her.

"I'll just send them over when they arrive, okay?" he asked.

"Sure, they should be here any minute." She looked at her watch. "You can always count on Ken Honeycutt to be on time, especially when there's *tres leches* involved."

Jared laughed and nodded. "I'll tell Elena when they get here, so she can come out."

"Perfect," she said, taking another sip of her wine. She sat back and faced the dining room and the sidewalk that led from the lobby entrance.

Within moments, Ken and Hazel came through the lobby doors that open out onto the courtyard. They smiled and waved as they caught sight of Tori at the far end of the patio. She stood up, waiting to greet them as they made their way down the sidewalk past the fountain.

"How are you?" she asked as Ken bent down to hug her.

"We're doing just fine," he said. She kissed his cheek and then turned to Hazel, hugging her and holding her hand for a moment.

"Hazel made us a big pot of chili for supper and now we're here for desert," Ken said, pulling a chair out for Hazel. "So, life is good!" He laughed and looked at Hazel, who grinned at him.

"It's always so nice out here with the heaters and the lights and the fountain and all," Hazel said, looking around at everything as she sat down. "And the tables always look so pretty." She placed her fingertips lightly on the surface of her desert plate and then smiled up at Tori.

"Thank you," Tori said. "Jared and the staff do a great job keeping everything looking nice." She looked at Jared across the patio. "Would you like coffee? I'm going to have some. I think Elena's got some deserts set aside for you, too."

"Oh how nice!" Hazel said as they both nodded in favor of coffee. Tori motioned to Jared and in a moment he returned and filled their cups.

"So how's business?" Tori asked, first to Hazel. "How're things at the crafts store?"

Hazel talked excitedly about two new artists who had placed their work in her store on consignment. One of them painted cow skulls with religious images—crosses, ohms, stars of David, and the like—and then decorated the skulls with beads and other colored paint and patterns. He called the series "Sacred Cows." Another artist did origami and made all sorts of things with the intricately folded paper—brooches, hair clips, binder clips, mobiles for children, and other things.

"Are they selling well?" Tori asked a bit incredulously.

"Yes, especially the Hindu cow heads and the origami baby mobile," Hazel said. "I've had to ask the artists twice already for new stock to replace what has sold." She took a sip of coffee. "People really like this stuff, for some reason." She laughed and shrugged. "I mean, you know, it's not my style, but that's not the point, is it?"

They all laughed and continued talking and visiting, enjoying each other's company and friendship. After a little while, Elena walked out from the dining room to join them.

"Well, hello!" Ken boomed, standing up to hug her. "How's the chef this evening?" She hugged him back, then caressed Hazel's shoulders in greeting as she stepped around the table to take her seat next to Tori. She smiled and winked at Tori as she sat down. Jared stepped up beside her and poured her a cup of coffee.

"How is everyone?" she asked, smiling at Ken and Hazel across the table. "It's nice out here tonight." She glanced at the sky and looked around the patio. She sat back in her chair and took a deep breath.

"Busy night, huh?" Ken asked. He looked into the dining room and back at Elena. "It looks like it's nearly full even this late in the evening."

Elena nodded. "Yeah, we're busy tonight. That corporate group has the whole hotel rented, and then we've had lots of local customers, too, so…" She held up her coffee cup toward them. "Here's to being busy with lots of customers."

"Here, here!" Ken said, holding his cup up and clinking it to Hazel's and the others'.

The four of them sat together, swapping stories about the goings on of the town, the various people they knew in common, the achievements of the high school basketball team, and whatnot. Tori listened and chimed in alternately, enjoying the feeling of belonging she felt not only with Ken and Hazel and, of course, with Elena, but also with the town at large. Logan was her home now, she felt. She cared about the town and its people and their successes and failures. She was a part of it and them, and they were a part of her.

After a while, Jared and another waiter came with food and refills on coffee. Four plates sat in the middle of the table, each containing a different desert—a traditional *tres leches*, a glistening flan, a tall wedge of dark chocolate cake, and a bread pudding. Ken and Hazel sampled all of them, mock swooning with each bite, closing their eyes to savor the rich flavors on their tongues. Elena and Tori sampled them as well, nodding and grinning at each other in approval.

"These are fantastic, Elena," Tori said. She wiped her mouth with her napkin, took a sip of coffee and sat back. "Really great."

"Thanks. I'm pleased with how they turned out." She cut her fork into the dark chocolate cake and took another bite. "I switched brands on the chocolate and I think I like this one better. And it's not as expensive, which is good."

"It sure tastes expensive, I'll tell you that right now," Ken said, taking another bite. "This *tres leches* is something else, too. It's my favorite."

"You've always liked *tres leches*, even when it's not any good. It's always your favorite," Hazel teased, elbowing him in the ribs.

"I am not ashamed of being a fan of *tres leches*," he drawled dramatically, and they all laughed.

"But this is really, really good, Elena," Hazel added.

They talked more, sharing the deserts and shaving them away bite by bite until very little was left of any of them. The dining room had cleared out for the most part and just a few other people remained on the patio with them. A few hotel guests were in the jacuzzi and two couples were at a table in the far corner, still having coffee and desert. Just as Ken plopped his napkin on the table and sat back in his chair, signaling that he had eaten enough, the lobby door opened. Tori and Elena both looked up when they heard the noise and watched as Luis strode toward them. His boots sounded firm on the walkway and he walked with purpose, his back straight and his eyes focused on Tori. He neared the table and stopped, just behind Ken and Hazel. He stood with his hands in his jacket pockets.

"May I talk to you for a minute?" he said to Tori. He glanced at Elena briefly, but then returned his eyes to Tori.

"Sure, Luis," she said, getting up and placing her napkin on her chair. "Excuse me for a moment, please," she said to everyone at the table. As she stood up, Luis turned and walked away from them back toward the lobby door. Tori turned to Elena for a moment before following him down the walkway. Elena shrugged her shoulders and shook her head.

She joined Luis in the dim light near the lobby. He had stopped and turned around, waiting on her. He watched her as she stepped closer and stopped in front of him. She looked up into his placid face.

"What's going on?" she asked. "Has something happened?" She thought it conceivable that something other than the matter of him, her, and Elena might be the reason for his visit to the restaurant in the late evening, something he rarely ever did.

Luis looked at her for a few seconds, not saying anything. His face did not change and his eyes did not move from hers. She thought he seemed detached, remote, too calm.

"I'm taking some time off, " he said finally. "A couple weeks or more."

Tori nodded. "That sounds fine. Like a good idea actually." She looked at him and waited to see if he anything else to say.

"Ricardo can handle things while I'm away. He and Dustin. He can show Dustin what needs to be done," he said, his voice calm and even.

"That sounds fine, too," Tori said. "It'll be good for Dustin to learn more about things." She stood for a moment, looking at him. "Is that all you wanted to tell me?"

He looked over at the table where Elena sat with Ken and Hazel. As soon as he did, Ken turned away to face Hazel. Elena kept her eyes fixed on Ken and Hazel as she sat relaxed in her chair, sipping from her coffee cup.

Luis looked back at Tori and took a deep breath. "It's been a tough few weeks, Tori. In lots of ways." He took one hand out of his pocket, rubbed his face, and put it back in his pocket. "I know about this thing with you and Elena. I see it as part of her grief. I mean, anyone can see she's not a lesbian." He turned and looked back toward the table at Elena, who still kept her eyes fixed on Ken and Hazel, then looked back at Tori. "I don't know about you, I mean…that's your business. But I know Elena. I've known her my whole life."

"Luis, I don't think now's the time to talk about this," Tori began. "Why don't we meet…"

"I don't want to meet and talk about it," he interrupted, his voice still low. "I'm just going to take some time away. Give me and Elena both some space. Let this thing run its course." He took his hands out of his pocket and stepped toward the lobby door to open it. "And it will run its course, Tori. I hope you know that."

Tori shook her head and shrugged. "Luis, I don't think…"

"It doesn't matter what you think, Tori. I know what I know." He stepped inside the lobby, held the door open and turned back to her. "I'll be in touch with Ricardo. I'll be back in a few weeks or so."

"Okay," she said, as the lobby door swung shut and he disappeared. She looked at her dim reflection in the glass of the door. She stood for a moment with her arms crossed, then turned and walked back to the table to join the others. As she sat down, they stopped their conversation and looked at her.

"Is everything okay," Ken asked. "Has something happened?"

Tori took a deep breath and sighed. "No, nothing's happened, not like an emergency or anything." She took a sip of lukewarm coffee and nodded for Jared to bring a refill. She looked at Elena and back at Ken.

"Luis came to tell me he's decided to take some time off. Get away for a few weeks or so," she said. She watched Jared pour the hot liquid into her cup. "I think it's a good idea. He's worked a lot of long hours in the last few months, and it's been a tough few weeks."

"Did he say where he's going," Elena asked.

Tori shook her head. "No. He said he'd stay in touch with Ricardo."

She looked at Elena, then at Ken and Hazel, who sat respectfully silent, as if listening to a conversation they thought they were not meant to hear. She looked into their faces and, for a moment, thought of her parents.

"I guess it's time for me—or for us—to tell you something," she said, looking at Ken and Hazel. She turned to Elena and saw a softening in her eyes and felt Elena place a gentle hand on her knee under the table. She looked back at Ken and Hazel.

"Elena and I are more than simply business partners. We, of course, have been close friends for a while now, but now we're even more than that." She smiled quickly at Elena. "We're a couple now…we've fallen in love with each other. I would have said something sooner, but it just wasn't the right time until now."

Ken began grinning before she even finished her last sentence. He reared back in his chair, crossed one arm over his chest and covered his mouth with his hand. As soon as she finished speaking, he turned to Hazel, whose face was breaking into a soft smile.

"Didn't I tell you Hazel," he whispered, almost gleefully. "I was right!" His face turned red and his eyes sparkled.

Hazel looked at him and shook her head, in mock exasperation at his gloating. She looked back at Tori and Elena. "You girls…well, I just think you're great together. I've already told you that a bunch of times. And this just makes it even better."

"I knew it!" Ken said, louder now. "I knew it months ago! I had a feeling! I have a knack for these things, you know. Don't I Hazel?" He looked at her expectantly, seeking her confirmation. "I knew about our son long before he ever told us. I just had a feeling. And he, you know, he doesn't *look* gay—you know what I mean, I'm not trying to use an ugly stereotype, but sometimes you can get a hunch. Not with him. But I knew. What do they call that, Hazel…we heard Ray say it once…it's like gay radar." He searched for the term in his mind.

"Gaydar?" Elena asked weakly, smiling as if she could hardly believe what she was hearing or watching.

"That's it! Yeah!" Ken said, laughing aloud. "Gaydar!" He draped his arm around Hazel's chair, smiling with glee. "I have it," he said proudly. "So, I knew…*I knew*. And I'm so happy for you both. You girls are like two peas in a pod."

Tori laughed a bit and sat back in her chair. She glanced at Elena, raised her eyebrows in a "whaddaya know" sort of way, and looked back to Ken and Hazel. "Well, I don't really know what to say." She paused for a moment. "Thank you. You both mean so much to me. You were the first friends I had here, and I love you and think of you as my second parents, sort of. I know I've never told you that, but it's true." She stopped and looked at Elena.

"Me, too," Elena added. "I mean, not in exactly the same way as Tori, but I love you both and consider you some of my closest friends here. It means a lot to me—to us—to have your support. Thank you."

Hazel smiled at them, and looked at Ken. "We love both of you, too," she said softly, looking back at them. Her kind eyes misted slightly and she grabbed Ken's hand sitting on the table. "Our Ray is about ya'll's age, and he's not around for us to fuss over and things, so I guess we can do that with you two."

Ken nodded and smiled, but then his face turned more serious. "What about Luis?" he asked. "How is he with this?"

"He's not pleased," Elena said. "I'm sure that's why he's taking some time off. Or at least, that's part of the reason." She turned to Tori. "Don't you think?"

"I do," Tori said, nodding and taking another sip of coffee. "He said he needed to get some space." She left it at that. She would tell Elena the rest of it later.

"Well…" Ken said, "That's probably a good idea. It'd do him some good to get out of Logan for a change."

Everyone nodded, suddenly quiet for a moment.

"He's a good person," Elena said. "I hate that this hurts him so much, but I didn't see any way around it."

Ken nodded and took a sip of coffee. "Yes, he's a good man. Everyone likes him." He set his cup down. "He's a strong man, too, I think. He'll be fine. It's part of life, you know. Things don't always work out like you want or plan. You just have to make peace with it and move on the best you can. He'll figure it out."

"I hope so," Elena said.

Again, they all nodded and were silent. Ken looked at his watch and then at Hazel. "Shall I take you home, my bride?" he said. "It's about past our bedtime." She grinned at him, nodded and backed her chair away from the table.

Tori and Elena walked with them through the courtyard and lobby and out the front door to the parking lot. Everyone hugged goodbye. Tori felt Ken close his arms around her as she hugged him. "Love you, sweetie," he said in her ear as he squeezed her tight.

"Love you, too, Ken" she said, squeezing him back. "Thanks for everything."

Tori and Elena waved and watched Ken's red truck turn onto the main road and its brake lights disappear into the darkness. Tori turned to Elena and they both let out big sighs simultaneously.

"Good Lord, that was exhausting for some reason," Elena said. "I mean, in a good way, but still…"

"No kidding. I felt like I was coming out all over again." Tori put her hand on her hips and stretched from side to side. They walked back into the hotel and out to the table on the patio where they had been sitting.

"Did Luis say anything else?" Elena asked.

"Yeah…he told me that he knew about us and that he thought it was part of your grief." Tori paused and looked at Elena's face, to gauge her reaction and choose her words accordingly. "He said he's known you all his life and that he knows you aren't a lesbian. That this will run its course. He's taking some time away to give him and you some space."

Elena held her arms crossed over her chest and looked at Tori plainly and intently. "Is that all he said?"

"Yeah, that's all…other than what I already said at the table."

Elena took a breath and looked up at the sky for a moment, her arms still crossed over her chest. She blew out the breath. After a moment, she looked back at Tori.

"Well, I guess it's good you talked to him instead of me," she said flatly. "I would have likely thrown one of the garden rocks at him." Her face betrayed a slight smile, and Tori saw one hand clench and unclench inside her chef's coat sleeve.

Tori stepped close to Elena and pushed a stray strand of dark hair back over her ear. "Well, you know…" she grinned at Elena. "Glad I could help."

Elena's face was still for a moment as she held Tori's gaze, then she relaxed into a slight grin. She unfolded her arms and turned toward the building. "Come on, little helper," she said. "Help me close this place up for the night."

# Chapter Seventeen

Tori stopped her car and clicked her headlights onto high beam to see exactly what was blocking the driveway of the hotel near the entrance. She inched the car toward the sandy brown colored object that lay stretched out across the asphalt about twenty-five yards from the main road. As she got closer she recognized the texture of hair on the object and realized it was a dead deer.

"Oh no…" she said softly as she eased her car around on the asphalt to the right of the carcass. She stopped when she thought she was even with it and opened her car door to peer out. In the dim glow of the interior lights, she saw the awkwardly bent neck of the animal and its broken face. Its legs were under it and a dark shadow of what Tori's presumed was blood leached out from it.

She grimaced and put the car in park. She stepped out of the car and bent down over the deer, looking at it. She touched its cold body lightly and then just sat there for a moment, squatting on the asphalt beside it. She stood up, got back in the car, and texted

Ricardo: *Dead deer at the driveway entrance. Will you take care of this asap? Call or txt either of us later. We'll be on the road. Thx.*

Hers was the only car on the road in Logan. A few pickup trucks were parked at the big gas station, and a few men wearing hardhats stood outside the building under fluorescent lights drinking coffee in the predawn darkness. She cruised past them and past the darkened buildings near Hazel's crafts store and Galindo's. She turned onto Elena's street and into the driveway, and parked behind the silver Tahoe.

"Good morning, sunshine," Elena said, opening the front door as soon as Tori stepped onto the porch.

"Good morning yourself," she answered. She stepped into the doorway and kissed Elena. They stood for a moment and then Elena closed the door and Tori followed her into the kitchen.

"I'm ready," Elena said. "Just let me put out food and water for Rico. Letty's coming to check on him every day but today." She dumped the bowl out into the sink and filled it to the brim with fresh water. Rico came running when he heard the pellets drop into his dish. He circled Elena's legs with his orange back arched and his tail quivering. Tori could hear him purring all the way from where she stood at the kitchen table.

"See you in a few days, buddy," Elena said to him, bending down to scratch him under his chin. "Don't tear anything up." She gave him a final pat and stood up. "Ok, let's go!" she said brightly. "Oh wait, should I make coffee for us?"

"I have a thermos in the car. Let's roll."

The inky black of the night sky was paling to gray as they drove east out of Logan on the way to Houston. Tori's car purred smoothly along the black highway that ran through the desert, sometimes cutting right through rocks mesas and small mountains. They watched the eastern sky brighten with each mile until the rich orange of the sun's curved edge finally appeared over the horizon. The desert fauna awakened with the day, curving their blooms to face it, arching their leaves to soak in its energy, their colors and contours suddenly visible yet again in the increasing glare.

They stopped at a picnic area overlooking Lake Amistad with its high limestone cliffs and deep clear water fed by three rivers. Mile-long beams of sunlight sparkled across the lake, highlighting the wondrous wet resource in the middle of desert dryness. Small whitetail deer walked quietly in the brush forty yards from the concrete picnic table on which they sat, and a long-eared rabbit came within twenty feet and stopped, craning its neck and flaring its nostrils to pick up the smell of the peanut butter sandwich Elena ate. She looked at him as she ate, smiling slightly, and finally threw him the last bite of bread crust. He darted forward, grabbed it, and disappeared into the thorny bushes nearby.

Tori called the real estate manager who was handling her townhome in Houston, to confirm that they were arriving later today and would be staying for three nights. The place had been rented to the same tenant nearly the entire time Tori had been in Logan, but he had moved out two weeks ago. Tori needed to go back to Houston to meet with Vincent to discuss her leave of absence, which was almost up. Plus, she wanted to see Sharon, and she wanted to show Elena her favorite big city and former home. So, they decided on a road trip. Luis was not the only one who stood to benefit from some space and a change of scenery.

As the landscape changed and they entered the urban and suburban expanse of south central Texas that stretches from San Antonio to the eastern border of the state, Tori remembered the feeling of sadness she used to have driving back to Houston, before she lived in Logan. Sadness at leaving the desert, leaving Logan, leaving some part of herself back there to return "home" to Houston. Now, she felt a tinge of that sadness, but it was overshadowed by excitement of seeing her friend, and of showing Elena her favorite haunts and her former home. Indeed, it was *former*. Logan was her home now, and she would be happy to be back there in a few days.

"Nice skyline," Elena remarked late that afternoon as they neared the dazzling cluster of skyscrapers whose polished and smoked glass reflected the western sun that boiled in Tori's rearview mirror. They neared downtown Houston and glided onto the bayou level parkway that led to Tori's neighborhood. The parks that flanked the bayou were full of people—runners, walkers, people walking their dogs or playing with their kids. Cyclists pedaled past pedestrians and a few kayakers paddled in the murky green water that was home to carp, crayfish and nutria.

"Are you glad to be back in your city?" Elena asked, caressing Tori's arm.

Tori smiled and nodded. "It's a big city with lots of big-hearted people who accomplish big, ambitious things."

"In short, it's big," Elena teased.

"Exactly," Tori said, grinning. She sped her sports car through the knots of intersecting freeways, threading it through the traffic, and gliding onto the street that led to her townhome. She pulled into the parking garage, found her same old assigned space, and killed the engine.

"Here we are," she said brightly.

Elena leaned over and kissed her. "I'm really glad to be here with you," she said, smiling.

The townhome looked just as Tori had left it many months ago—open, spacious, sparsely and elegantly appointed—except for the big gift basket that sat in the middle of the bar. Oranges, apples, bananas, crackers, assorted cheese wedges and small bags of nuts crowded around three bottles of wine. The whole collection was wrapped in glossy cellophane and tied with a glittery gold ribbon. Tori took the note that was taped to it and read it aloud: *Wash that desert dust off and meet me at Qi for sushi at 8. I'm eager to see you two. Text me when you get here. XOX Sharon*

"How sweet," Elena said, dropping her purse on a barstool. "God, that sounds fantastic! I haven't had good sushi since I left San Francisco."

"Qi is a great place too, or it used to be at least," Tori said. She texted Sharon and then walked over to the floor-to-ceiling windows and drew open the curtains. She stood with her hands on her hips and looked out at the dusk settling over downtown. Elena walked over and stood beside her. Tori pointed out various buildings, including the one that held her old office, all of which were beginning to sparkle against the darkening sky with the fluorescent light coming from their windows. After a moment, Elena left and returned with a bottle of wine and two glasses she retrieved from the kitchen. She handed the glasses to Tori, opened the wine and poured it. She took her glass and held it up to Tori.

"To a safe drive here, to seeing good friends, to Houston...and to being together," she said.

"Cheers," Tori said as she clinked her glass to Elena's.

Tori showed Elena around her place and they got settled. They showered and, for what seemed like the first time in ages, got dressed up to have a nice dinner whose menu neither of them had planned and whose success was not their responsibility.

'Well, aren't you two a sight for sore eyes," Sharon said as they walked toward her at a table in the center of the restaurant. She stood up to hug and kiss both of them, and motioned for the waiter to come open the champagne that sat chilling in an ice bucket beside the table. Her blonde hair was pulled back in a French twist, which opened up her clear face and eyes, and revealed her long neck. She wore black trousers, black stilettos, and a tailored blouse of gray silk with the collar open and the sleeves pushed up. Diamonds sparkled at her ears and at the end of a delicate chain that draped into the shadow between her breasts.

"I'm so glad to see you," Tori said as she sat down and reached over and squeezed Sharon's arm. Seeing her now—so beautiful, energetic and fun—Tori felt how much she had missed her best friend since her visit to Logan months ago.

The three of them talked and caught up with each other's news.

Sharon updated Tori on current events in Houston, and news about people they knew in common. Sharon wanted to know how everything was going at the ranch. She asked about Ken and Hazel, and about others she had met during her short visit.

"I'm so sorry to hear about your mother," Sharon said, touching Elena's hand.

"Thank you," Elena said. She turned her hand over to grasp Sharon's fingers and squeezed them. "I miss her."

Tori and Sharon both nodded and were quiet for a moment.

"Gloria was well-loved in Logan," Tori added. "So many people came to the house during the vigil, and then to the service. People really showed their love. For her and for Elena."

Elena nodded. "It was a special time. Devastating, but also very special."

Sharon reached for her champagne flute and held it up. "To Gloria," she said quietly.

"Salud" Elena and Tori said in turn, clinking their glasses to Sharon's. Elena's eyes began to well. Tori grabbed her hand.

The waiter came to take their order, which shifted the mood away from sadness about Gloria. Sharon asked for everyone's preferences and then ordered an assortment of sushi rolls and sashimi. Tori and Elena sat back and let her take charge of things, smiling and enjoying being taken care of and waited on. Soon the waiter returned with the first round, and they dug in with their chopsticks as if they had not eaten in days.

"This is good," Elena said after a few minutes. "I mean, *really* good." She sat back in her chair, put her hands on her lap and looked around the restaurant. She looked at Tori and then at Sharon. "Thank you for choosing this place. And for being with us here tonight."

"Are you kidding?" Sharon said, finishing off a bite of soft shell crab. "I wouldn't be anywhere else—unless I were being paid a lot of money. You two are my people." She grinned. "So, update me on things between the two of you. What's up? Are we in the closet or out, or under the radar, or what?"

Elena and Tori took turns telling the story of Luis and his reaction to Elena's breaking things off with him. They told her about Jared and Dustin, how supportive they had been and how much leadership they were taking at the ranch. Tori told about the evening with Ken and Hazel, the night Luis came to say he was taking time off, and they all laughed when Tori mentioned Ken's "gaydar" comment.

"He is the dearest man," Sharon said, shaking her head and laughing.

They continued eating, then talking and drinking until late in the evening. The dinner crowd had mostly left and was replaced by a late-night crowd that was beginning to squeeze into the upscale piano bar on the other side of the restaurant. Just as the waiter brought the ticket to their table, a group of women walked in and asked to be seated at the bar near the piano. As the hostess began to lead them back, one of the women recognized Sharon and turned to walk toward their table. She smiled at Elena and Tori as she came near and waited for Sharon to look up from her wallet and notice her. Sharon pulled out a credit card, and then looked up and around. Her face shifted into a sly smile when she saw the tall brunette standing next to her.

"Hey," the woman said, smiling down at Sharon. "What a nice surprise to see you here." She touched Sharon's shoulder lightly. She wore a cream suit coat style leather jacket over a black silk shell with cream trousers. She towered over their table in high black heels. Her skin was smooth and light, and her dark hair was pulled back into a jeweled clip. Wispy strands of it fell attractively around the sides of her face and neck. She turned her green eyes to Tori and Elena. "Excuse me for interrupting. I just wanted to say hello." She extended her hand across the table. "I'm Deborah Meeks."

"These are my dear friends, Tori Reed and Elena Rios," Sharon said as they extended their hands to greet Deborah. "They are in town for a few days so we are catching up." She looked at Tori, winked and then turned back to Deborah. "So, you're here with friends as well, huh?"

Deborah turned back to Sharon and smiled down at her. "Yeah, we came for drinks and dessert. Mostly friends from law school." Tori watched her as she turned to look absently in the direction of her friends, and then looked back at Sharon. "Why don't you join us when you're finished here?" She looked at Tori and Elena. "All of you—come join us."

Tori looked at Elena, then at Sharon. "I think we're finished for the night. Thank you, though. It's sweet of you to invite us," she said.

Deborah looked at Sharon. "You then…you'll at least come have a drink with me, won't you?"

Sharon looked up at her and smiled. "Sure, as soon as we're done here. I'll come find you."

Deborah's face broke into a wide grin. "Excellent. I'll see you soon." She turned to Tori and Elena. "Have a wonderful visit. Pleasure to meet you." She turned and walked away to join her friends.

Sharon picked up her water glass to drain it and looked over the rim into Tori's eyes. Tori could see the mischievous grin on her face as she crunched her ice.

"And who is Deborah?" Tori asked suggestively. Elena pressed her lips together in a smile and raised her eyebrows.

"She's another divorce lawyer in town. We represented the two sides in a case not long ago." Sharon sucked another ice cube from her glass, crunched it and swallowed it. "I'm glad to see she's not still mad at me for my ravaging of her client's assets."

"No, she doesn't seem mad at you. Not at all." Tori teased.

"She's a nice person. We had dinner once after the case was over. I think I was supposed to call her for another date, but I got busy and didn't do it." Sharon sat back in her chair, relaxed and confident in the way that only people comfortable in their own skin can be. "I guess I can make it up to her tonight," she said.

She walked them to the door and stood with them as they waited for the valet to bring the car. She made them promise to see her again before they left. They hugged each other tightly and said their goodbyes as the valet stood at the open door.

"Let us know how things go with Deborah," Elena said as she eased into the seat.

"Sure," she said, winking at Elena. "But, I already know how things are going to go." She stepped back and blew them a kiss as they drove off into the dark gray night of the city.

❧

Tori leaned against the elevator wall as it glided slowly down the shaft, passing forty-seven floors before settling softly at the bottom. She had no idea how many times she had ridden this elevator up and down from the company office suites. She felt a little sad, but mostly relieved that this might be one of the last times.

Her meeting with Vincent had been more of a formality than anything. They had already talked on the phone a few times and he knew that she was not returning to the company. He wanted to meet anyway, though, just to visit and make a formal ending. In typical Vincent style, he had ordered a continental breakfast for the two of them delivered to his office, and they sat at the conference table eating and catching up on company business as well as the details of Tori's ranch. Vincent's gray eyes beamed in intensity as she told him about Sandy Creek Ranch—the concept and the execution of it—and the success it had achieved so far. He smiled slightly and nodded as the story unfolded, his legs crossed and his elbows resting on the arms of his chair. She knew he respected her and was happy for her success.

They hugged goodbye and she thanked him for all he had done for her, the opportunities he had given her over the years. He was gracious and self-effacing as always and told her he was the lucky one who managed to snap her up before someone else did. After a few more awkward moments of goodbye, his assistant came in with a pile of contracts for him to sign. The meeting was over and Tori's time there was done.

She stepped out of the elevator into the crowded lobby and made her way to the front entrance and out onto the sidewalk. She looked up toward the sky, which was visible as a patch of blue high above her between the tops of the tall columnar buildings that surrounded her. She looked across the expanse of the intersection nearest where she stood. The metro train hummed through the intersection on its embedded tracks, avoiding by mere inches the dozens of cars and buses that waited in multiple lanes. Pedestrians rushed the crosswalks, their briefcases and tote bags bulging. Messengers on cycles weaved in and out between cars stopped in their lanes. The breeze swirled between the buildings and created mini tornados of leaves, small paper debris and plastic bags that twisted and careened through the streets and esplanades like a broken auger.

Tori breathed it all in, the energy of the city and its people, with all their plans, ambitions, deals and projects. She felt the pulse of it all deep within her, almost instinctively, having been a part of it for so many years. Now, though, she felt appreciation for it as an outsider of sorts—as someone who knew the drill, but who had mastered it and moved on to other lessons. She knew that she would always feel a level of comfort in the fast-paced world of big deals and big money, and that maybe her life would intersect with it again at some point in the future. For now, however, she was glad to have carved out a new path for herself, one not quite so grand, flashy or as lucrative, but one that was far more satisfying and had come with utterly unexpected joys.

She turned to the row of shops diagonally across the intersection from where she stood, scanning the clusters of tables and chairs on the sidewalk in front of them. In the middle of them, Elena sat reading a newspaper and drinking from a cup the size of a small goldfish bowl. She sat in her jeans, t-shirt and leather jacket and peered at the paper through dark sunglasses. A wide swath of sunlight bathed that particular strip of tables in blazing spring light, and Tori saw the sheen on Elena's hair and the glint of her hoop earrings even from across the street. She smiled and started walking toward the crosswalk to join her.

"Hey! How'd it go?" Elena asked as Tori sat down across from her at the café table.

"Well," she said, smiling at her. "He was great. I was glad to see him." She turned to the waiter who stood near her waiting for her to finish her sentence before asking for her order. "Good morning. May I have a large latte please?" She turned to Elena. "Do you want tacos? I ate with Vincent, but they are really good here—I could eat one." Elena nodded enthusiastically. "Also, a small plate of assorted breakfast tacos. With extra salsa—hot, not mild." The waiter smiled, nodded, and hurried away.

"Anyway, we had a good visit. He wanted to know all about the ranch and how we've targeted our niche." Tori took off her jacket and draped in on the back of her chair. The waiter sat her own fish-bowl coffee in front of her and she took a sip. "He said he wanted to come out sometime, at least have dinner, maybe stay the night. I told him he was welcome anytime—we'd make sure to give him the *premium treatment*." She laughed as she said those last words.

Elena laughed with her and watched Tori settle in to her chair and enjoy her coffee. "How do you feel now?" she asked Tori after a minute. "Does it feel weird to be officially finished with that job after all these years?"

Tori looked around her at the buildings and took a deep breath. She looked back at Elena. "I don't feel any sadness really. I feel…complete with it all, I guess. Like it's finished or completed. Not just it, but me—I'm finished and completed with it. And now I've moved on." She took a sip of her coffee and set the gargantuan cup back onto the table. "I like that I'm leaving all this on good terms."

Elena nodded. "That's a good feeling." She folded the newspaper in front of her and set it aside. "It's odd, I felt that way sort of when I left San Francisco. I hadn't planned on leaving, but when it became clear that Mama needed me to move back to Logan, I didn't feel sad really." She fingered the handle on her cup. "Maybe part of me was done with that, too, sort of like you are with all this here. I didn't think it consciously, but when the time came to leave, I didn't feel like I was leaving anything undone or unfinished, or like anything in my life had been interrupted in any way. It was just clear that it was time to leave. And when I did, I wasn't sure I would ever come back to live—certainly not to the same job or even the same city."

Tori listened and nodded. The waiter came with their food and they began to eat. The soft tacos were made from tortillas made on site and they each brimmed with a variety of fillings— scrambled eggs, *chorizo*, potato, cilantro, avocado, pork *carnitas*, onions, beans and herbed rice.

"Wow, you were right. These really are good," Elena said after taking a few bites. She opened the folded tortilla to inspect its contents and added a string of extra salsa. "I like the tortillas—they're different. A cross between a regular tortilla and a soft flatbread. Almost like pita bread." She pinched a piece of the soft bread off, fingered it, and then ate it. "Interesting. I bet we could make these. They'd be perfect in the field service." Tori smiled and watched her face shift into its now familiar look of making a mental note.

They finished the morning in downtown, people watching and

walking along the wide sidewalks that led to expansive courtyards and small, landscaped parks lined with shallow pools and fountains. They took the train into the museum district and had lunch at the fine arts museum, and then walked a few blocks to the long reflecting pool at the sprawling, inner city public park. They walked along its wide banks in the mottled shadows of towering oaks, smiling at young parents pushing toddlers in strollers and elderly couples sitting on the park benches feeding breadcrumbs to fat ducks and squirrels. They meandered through the Japanese garden and on around the park's main lake to the paddleboat landing. They rented a boat and paddled out to the middle of the lake, enjoying the warmth of the sun on their faces and shoulders, and taking in the spectacular views of the towers of the nearby medical center.

Tori liked showing Elena her hometown and all the things she loved about it. She showed her the house where she grew up, a tidy nineteenth century cottage in the Heights, a historic neighborhood that overlooked one of the bayous. She took Elena to the university and showed her the Hilton School where she had studied. The next day, they drove to Galveston and she showed Elena the beach house her parents had bought a few years before they were killed. Tori had sold it not long after inheriting it, finding it too painful to enjoy any time there. They sat on the seawall near one of the many rock jetties, their legs dangling out over the rocks and sand. They watched groups of serene pelicans skim the surf in tight formation. Dolphins occasionally broke the water's surface, their curved backs and lone fin appearing then disappearing again into the dark green waves. Noisy gulls fluttered and sailed overhead, begging for tourist gifts of sandwich crusts or french fries. Black and brown grackles joined them in the never-ending search for food scraps. Their long tail feathers were scraggly or missing altogether, and they jumped from rock to rock along the jetties, balancing on forked feet hardened by the heat, salt, and concrete.

By the end of their second full day, Tori had shown Elena nearly everything she loved about her city and they flopped onto the living room couches with the tiredness that comes from relaxation and pleasure. They watched a movie and ate their Vietnamese takeout from each other's plates, devouring the lettuce-wrapped spring rolls and char-broiled pork slices that floated in a savory broth of noodles, vegetables, spices and sprouts. As they were eating their fortune cookies, Elena's phone rang. It was Letty.

"Hey, what's going on," Elena said. Tori continued eating and watching the television, not really listening to the conversation.

"What was it—a dead dog?" Elena said after a moment. Tori turned to her and waited. She could hear Letty's voice through the speaker of Elena's phone, but could not make out the words.

"It probably got hit on the road during the night or something," Elena said, and listened as Letty continued talking. Tori turned back to the television.

"Luis is back?" Elena asked. Tori turned to her and Elena looked at her, raising her eyebrows slightly as she listened to Letty.

"What else is going on, anything? How are reservations?" Elena asked. Tori got up, gathered the styrofoam containers and used napkins and took it all into the kitchen to the trash. She listened to Elena's side of the conversation as she and Letty talked about menus, ingredients, deliveries and whatnot. Elena was ending the call by the time she came back into the livingroom.

"So?" Tori asked as she sat back down on the couch. She muted the volume on the television.

"Luis is back. She said he came back to work the morning we left," she said. "She said he seems fine, the same as he's always been. He and Ricardo have been out fixing windmills on the ponds. One of them blew over, I think, or somehow got messed up—she didn't really know what happened." Elena took a long drink from her Vietnamese iced coffee, wincing as she swallowed. She looked into the glass, as if questioning what she was drinking.

"This stuff is really strong. Really good, but really strong. I can already feel my heart racing. I may not sleep for days."

"Yeah, it's really strong. I love it," Tori said as she reached for her own glass and took a swallow. "What was that about a dead dog?"

"She said when she went to check on Rico this morning, there was a dead dog in the driveway. I told her it probably got hit on the road during the night." She looked up at the television. "She called Luis and he came and got it and took it to the county incinerator."

"That's odd," Tori said after listening and sitting quietly for a moment.

"What?"

"A dead dog."

"It happens sometimes, especially there on the main road."

"Yeah, I'm sure that's true. I don't mean that…" she trailed off. Elena looked at her with a questioning look.

"I forgot to tell you. As I was driving out of the ranch the morning we left, on my way to pick you up, there was a dead deer in the driveway just at the entrance." She looked at Elena. "I texted Ricardo and asked him to take care of it. I'm assuming he did. Did he mention it when you talked to him when we were on the road? I forgot to ask about it."

"No, he didn't mention it." Elena took another drink of her coffee and looked back at the television. "It's pretty common—dead deer on the roads. I'm surprised we haven't had them on the ranch before now."

"Is that what you do with dead animals out there—take them to an incinerator?" Tori asked. "Here, a city department will come pick them up for you."

Elena nodded. "Yeah, if you do anything at all. Usually, the buzzards will clean them up in a day or two if you just leave them. But, you can load it yourself and take it to the county dump. A few times a week they start the incinerator." Elena screwed up her nose as she spoke. "They have a little bulldozer there they use to scoop up all the carcasses and dump them into it."

"How do you know all this?" Tori asked.

"Luis told me, one day when he borrowed the bulldozer to do some work at the volunteer fire department. Plus I remember it from when I was a kid." She slid from the couch onto the floor, leaned back against the couch and stretched her legs out in front of her. "I remember this girl in school once, her horse died and her dad managed to get it loaded onto a trailer and they took it to the dump. For some reason, they didn't start the incinerator for a long time, so that girl—I forget her name—was upset for weeks about her horse out there rotting at the dump. It was terrible."

"Jeez…" Tori said, wincing. She slid down onto the floor next to her and draped one leg over Elena's. She hooked her foot onto Elena's and rocked it back and forth slightly. They sat for a while, watching television and talking about nothing in particular. Finally, when Tori saw Elena's head begin to drift backward in a doze, she turned off the television and stood up.

"Sweetie, let's go to bed. You're falling asleep out here." She bent down over Elena and kissed her lightly.

Elena startled a bit, then slowly raised herself from the floor and started toward the bedroom. Tori checked the door, turned out the lights, grabbed a bottle of water and her phone, and followed her down the hall.

As they were settling into bed, Tori saw her phone light up with a text message. It was Sharon: *Breakfast at Chez Sharon in the morning. Get here at 9. You'll be on the road by 11.*

Tori smiled as she read the text, and then leaned over to show it to Elena, who read it, grinned and plopped down onto her pillow. "She's the only person I've met who gets away with bossing you around," she said, her voice muffled in the sheets.

"I don't know, you do a pretty good job of it sometimes." Tori said as she turned off the lamp on the nightstand.

"Well, someone's gotta do it if Sharon's not around." Elena opened her arms as she spoke and Tori nestled into the crevice between her neck and shoulder. They were quiet for a moment. Elena took one of Tori's legs between her own, sliding her foot up and down Tori's smooth calf.

"Hey, I meant to ask you something," Tori said suddenly. Elena stopped her foot and held still as Tori continued. "Remember our opening night at the restaurant? When you had me come taste a sauce for the fish? Do you remember that?"

"Sort of. Why?"

"I asked you what was in the sauce and you made some crack about it being a secret ingredient, that you'd have to kill me if you told me."

Elena grinned into the darkness. "Yeah, I remember."

"What is it? The ingredient?"

"Anchovy paste." Elena paused for a moment. "But you *cannot* say anything about it to the customers."

"Anchovy paste? *Really?*" Tori's voice communicated suspicion and distaste in the darkness.

"See…that's why you can't tell people! You tasted it and loved it, and even you can't believe it was anchovy paste." Elena said in a mocking scold. "People won't order anything if they know it has anchovy in it."

"Wow," Tori said after a moment. "Who knew?"

"Don't make me have to kill you," Elena said as she resumed stroking Tori's calf with her foot.

"I won't. I promise."

❦

Sharon answered the door of her Mediterranean style townhome wearing red silk pajamas and flip flops. She wore no makeup and her hair was pulled back into a rough ponytail. She flung open the door with one hand and held a half-filled highball glass with the other.

"Good morning, beautiful women!" she exuded brightly. Her eyes danced and crinkled at the corners with the wideness of her smile. She opened her arms to embrace Tori and Elena as they stepped into the foyer.

"Come this way," she said, beginning the climb up a large wrought iron spiral staircase. "We're up here on the third floor patio enjoying the spring sunshine." She took the stairs quickly and by the time Tori and Elena caught up with her, she was standing at the top waiting for them with one hand on her hip.

"We, you said?" Tori asked in a low voice. She grinned at Sharon and raised her eyebrows in question.

Sharon smiled widely again and turned toward the small bar in the corner of the room just beside the opened glass door that led out onto an expansive balcony. Deborah Meeks stood at the bar putting crushed ice into two highball glasses. She looked up as Elena reached the top step behind Tori.

"Good morning," she said, smiling and looking at them from behind a pair of red horn-rimmed glasses. Her long dark hair hung loose and tousled around her shoulders, and she wore a pair of black silk pajamas that Tori recognized as belonging to Sharon.

"You remember Deborah, don't you?" Sharon asked.

"Of course. It's nice to see you again," Tori said as she walked over to shake Deborah's outstretched hand. Elena and Sharon moved to join them at the bar.

"What would you two like to drink?" Deborah asked. "We have a variety of juices as well as sparkling water, sparkling wines and some other stuff. Sharon is drinking a screwdriver. I'm drinking mimosas. But, you all have a long day of driving ahead, so…what'll it be?" Her glasses moved slightly on her face as she smiled.

"I'll have some sparkling water for now," Tori said.

"Grapefruit juice for me," Elena said.

"Come outside," Sharon said as soon as Deborah finished pouring their drinks. "It's so nice out here." They all followed her out into the dazzling spring morning. The patio was decorated sparsely, but in grand fashion. Two twenty-foot palm trees sunk into planters the size of kitchen stoves stood like sentinels on the patio's west end. A large built-in masonry fireplace as well as a tall urn fountain occupied the east end. Long rectangular concrete planters stretched the entire length of the northern railing and held a variety of pink, yellow, purple, and white blooming flowers. Tori could see the cluster of downtown buildings a few miles away. The breeze brushed her face and she felt the sun's warmth through her dark blouse. Elena moved to the edge of the patio and looked down onto the surrounding houses in the neighborhood.

"Nice view," she said, turning to Sharon. "And what a great outdoor space, both for cold and warm weather. I really like the fireplace.

"I know, I like it too! I didn't think I would use it that much—I've never had one before," Sharon said. "But, I've used it a lot. We have so many months here with cool evenings. And it's almost always breezy up here even when it's hot and muggy in the summer." She walked over to a glass table and sat down next to Deborah. Tori and Elena followed. "I spend a lot of time out here."

"So, how've the last few days been?" Sharon asked. She looked at Tori. "Did you show Elena all your old haunts and favorite places?"

They went through the rundown of their days. Deborah listened and smiled, nodding in recognition as they described various things they had seen and done.

"I'm listening, keep talking," Sharon said as she got up and stepped inside the house to retrieve a large fruit tray from the refrigerator by the bar. She set it in the middle of the table between them all. She went back inside and returned with a stack of plates, flatware, napkins, and a basket of various pastries.

"Houston has a lot to offer," Deborah said after listening for a while. "I moved here from Dallas almost five years ago. Growing up there, I had the impression of Houston as mostly a big industrial city that was the oil capital of the world and NASA. I wasn't too excited about moving here, in fact." She set her glass down on the table. "Now, though, I don't want to leave. It's got so much stuff—so much more than anything Dallas has to offer really, in term of the arts, culture, the diversity…"

"The food scene," Sharon interrupted to add. "Houston's got world class restaurants, and no one on the other coasts really knows that apparently."

"It's true," Elena said. "People in the food world forget about Houston but it's a great food town. I've always heard that from other chefs even though I'd never visited myself before now."

They doled out the plates and began filling them with fruit and pastries. The sun bathed them in light and warmth, and the balcony filled with the sounds of conversation, laughter and utensils clinking on ceramic plates.

"So, Sharon's told me about your ranch out in West Texas," Deborah said after a while. "It's very impressive. Congrats on your success." She held up her glass in salute, smiling at Tori and Elena.

"Thanks," Tori said, looking first at Elena and then at Deborah. "We've had fun with it, I think. Would you say that?" She turned to Elena.

"Definitely," Elena said, swallowing a bite and laying her fork down. "It's always fun to have an idea or concept that you think'll work, then execute it and then—*viola*—it works!" She looked at Tori. "The concept, of course, was Tori's. I had a gut feeling it would work when she shared it with me." She grabbed Tori's hand and smiled. "I feel lucky to be a part of it."

"We make a good team," Tori said, smiling at Deborah.

They talked more about the ranch and about Logan, telling stories about the people and the culture. Sharon chimed in with details she remembered from her visit a few months before.

"How is it for the two of you being together, as a couple?" Deborah asked after a while. "Is the culture okay for gay people?"

"Yeah, I was going to ask about that, too," Sharon said. "You all haven't had any problems, have you?"

Tori pushed her plate away and sat back in her chair. "It's been fine so far. No problems at all." She looked at Elena.

"It is a traditional culture out there in many ways," Elena said. "Rural, ranching, lots of Hispanics. I'm from there, so I know it well. That's part of what I was getting away from when I left years ago."

"But, there's also a *live and let live* sort of ethos as well, don't you think?" Tori asked Elena.

"Yeah, I think so. It's very freedom-loving in that wild west, open country, *don't mess with me* kind of way," she said. "So, if you're a good citizen, you treat people okay, you work hard, pay your taxes—you know, just be a decent person—people may think being gay is weird or wrong, but they're not going to mess with you about it."

Deborah and Sharon nodded as they listened.

"It helps that neither of you wear it on your sleeve," Sharon said. "I don't mean staying in the closet, but….you don't have *lesbian* tattooed on your forehead and aren't trying to drape the whole town in a rainbow flag."

"Right," Tori said. "I've never been that way—not that there's anything wrong with that—it's just not my personality."

"Yeah, it's like being left-handed for me. It's just one fact among many facts about me, and not one that I feel like making a big deal about," Elena said. "I think that helps people a lot in Logan, especially the traditional types. If you're not making a big deal about it, they come to see all the other things about you that they appreciate and like. Those things come to have more weight than the one fact of being gay." She took a drink from her glass. "At least, that's my experience. Of course, I haven't been out and proud in Logan, not yet at least. " She grinned at Tori.

"Yeah, you've been the high school beauty who left her town and sweetheart behind, but who's now come back and established herself again—and may marry her old flame," Tori said, grinning back at her.

Elena rolled her eyes and took a deep breath. "We'll see how things work out as the change in that narrative becomes clearer to people." She leaned her head back to take in the bright sunshine on her face. "I think it's already getting clear to people."

"Me, too," Tori said. She turned to look at Sharon and Deborah. "I think it'll all be fine. We have a great group of people who work with us at the ranch. The town has embraced the ranch as it's been successful. I think it'll be fine."

"And you gave that big check to the school. Don't forget that," Sharon added shrewdly. "Never underestimate the power of money to change people's longheld convictions and deepest values. I count on it every day." She looked at Deborah and raised her eyebrows. "Am I right, or am I right?"

"You're right," Deborah said, nodding. "We've both done pretty well operating on that simple truth of human nature, haven't we?"

"You sound so cynical!" Tori said, sharpening her eyes in mock indignation at Sharon.

"It's simply the truth, my dear desert romantic friend," she said as they all laughed.

"On that note, we should probably hit the road," Elena said after a moment. She looked at Sharon, smiling into her vibrant eyes. "Thank you for having us here and for dinner the other night. Seeing you has been one of the highlights of the last few days."

"You are quite welcome, beautiful one," Sharon said. "I wouldn't miss seeing you and this one here for anything in the world." She reached over and grabbed Tori's hand.

The carried everything back into the bar and then made their way down the stairs. Deborah hugged them both as they left and Sharon handed off a bag of snacks and a bundle of water bottles for the road.

"Come out to see us again, sometime soon," Tori said quietly to Sharon as Elena was getting in the car. "I miss you so much sometimes."

"I will. I miss you, too. A lot." Sharon said. She grasped Tori's face between her hands and gave her lips a light kiss. "I love you."

"I love you, too," Tori said, covering Sharon's hands with her own and looking deeply into her eyes.

The sun was only a third of the way up the sky as they began the drive toward home. They drove west with the sun, its rays finally overtaking the car and beaming into the windshield as they entered the desert terrain past Del Rio in mid-afternoon. Tori felt herself ease into the wide expansiveness of the landscape, feeling her own spirit expand and spread with each passing mile. She enjoyed the glide of her car's tires on the black ribbon of road, and the sound of the car's body cutting through the fresh air as it made its way around the mesas and over rivers and creek beds. She looked over at Elena from time to time, who drowsed for much of the way. Tori remembered her own seemingly random bouts of exhaustion in the weeks and months after her parents died, symptoms of the searing strain of grief working its way through the heart and mind. She gently lowered the passenger side sunvisor to cover Elena's face from the glare as they drove the last few hours into the late afternoon sun.

Dusk had turned to dark when they drove into Logan. They first passed the high school, on the east side of town, whose parking lot was filled with cars.

"Must be a basketball game tonight," Tori said.

"It's a playoff tournament, I think," Elena said. "I remember Letty saying something about it on the phone."

"Looks like the whole town is there." Tori slowed the car and they both looked at all the cars as they passed.

"Why don't you stay with me tonight?" Elena said. "Rico will be glad to have us both there with him."

Tori looked at her and grinned. "You love that cat."

Elena smiled. "He's a sweet boy." She looked off. "He sure loved Mama."

"He did," Tori said, caressing Elena's thigh lightly. She was quiet for a moment. "Let's just drive to the ranch for a minute, I'll drop some stuff off, then we'll come back, okay?"

"Sure," Elena said. "Do we have guests in now? I didn't remember to check with Betty before we left."

"Just a few," Tori said. "Tourist types, I think. Retirees."

They drove through Logan and sped the five miles down the highway toward the ranch. They saw the spotlights on the stone and stucco entrance a half-mile before they reached it. The dark, chiseled letters of the ranch name grew larger and more legible as they neared.

"I still feel so happy every time I drive through this entrance," Tori said.

"I know, me too."

Tori turned into the driveway and then veered onto the drive that led to her cabin. They noticed a few cars in the parking lot and could see the lights of the lobby. A dim glow from the patio lamps emerged from the back of the building. Tori pulled to a stop in front of her cabin and started to turn off her engine when something on the porch caught her eye. She stopped in mid-motion and looked.

"What is it?" Elena asked, noticing Tori's sudden stillness.

"What's that on the porch?" she asked. She clicked her headlights onto high beam. They both looked at a dark mound the size of a duffel bag on the porch just above the top step.

"Keep your lights on it—I'll go take a look," Elena said. She got out of the car and walked toward the porch. She put one foot on the lowest step, and leaned forward to see the mound more closely. She turned and came back to her seat in the car.

"It's a dead dog," she said gravely, looking at Tori.

# Chapter Eighteen

W hen did you see the dead deer in the driveway?" asked Sheriff Winston Banks. He stood with one hand on his pistol handle and the other leaned against the dark green of his patrol car. Lonnie Welch, his young deputy, stood beside him, taking notes as Tori and Elena answered the sheriff's questions. They all stood in the shade of Tori's cabin, just a few steps away from the front porch where the dark, swollen dog carcass still lay.

"Four days ago, on Thursday, early in the morning," Tori said.

"And then a dead dog was in my house driveway two mornings later on Saturday," Elena added. The sheriff nodded and watched as Lonnie scribbled these details down into his notebook.

"And then you came up on this one here last night when you got back into town, right?" he asked.

"Right," Tori said.

The sheriff sighed deeply and stared off into the blue sky. "So…three dead animals in the course of just over four days…" he mused. He tapped his boot toe in the gravel mindlessly. His thin, graying hair was combed back from his forehead in neat grooves, and his skin was wrinkled from the sun and age. His eyes were brown and calm, the eyes of someone who had seen many things, and who was no longer very easily surprised. He turned to look out at the road, as if expecting someone, and then turned back to Tori and Elena.

"What'd you have done with the other carcasses?" he asked. They told him that Ricardo and Luis had come to pick them up and disposed of them.

"Do you know that for sure?" he asked, lowering his face and looking at them over the top rim of his glasses.

Tori and Elena looked at each other and then back at him. "Well, I think so…as far as we know," Tori said. At that moment, a movement in the distance toward the road caught her eye, and she looked to see Luis' truck driving in to the ranch from the front entrance. "There's Luis right there, you can go ask him."

The sheriff and the deputy turned to watch Luis' truck slide into its usual space on the parking lot. Tori looked at Elena, and then they both looked back at the truck. Luis got out of the driver's side and then Ricardo stepped out of the passenger side.

"That's Ricardo," Elena said.

"Yeah, I know him," the deputy said. "We were in school together."

Luis turned toward them as he walked along the side of his truck toward the back. The sheriff raised his arm in a wave. Luis waved back, and turned his back on them to lower the tailgate of his truck. He and Ricardo stepped up to the hotel porch and disappeared inside.

"Let's go talk to 'em," the sheriff said, glancing at the deputy. "Ya'll going to be around for a while? I may need to come talk to you some more."

"Sure," Tori said. "I'll be over at the hotel probably, in the dining room at one of the tables doing paperwork." She looked at

Elena, and back at him. "We'll both be over there most of the day."

The sheriff and deputy eased out of the driveway and drove to the main parking lot. They parked next to Luis' truck. Tori watched them as they walked up the steps of the porch and into the hotel. She turned to Elena, who was looking at the carcass on the porch.

"Does this have to stay here, or can we get rid of it now?" she asked. Tori turned to the carcass. She had not thought to ask the sheriff about it.

"I'm going over to the hotel in a minute. I'll ask about it," she said. She turned to Elena. "What are you up to this morning?"

"I'm going over to Galindo's for a while, then I'll come back here. Letty and I need to go over quarterly stuff." She stretched her hand out to Tori absently. Tori grabbed her hand and stepped closer to her.

"Okay, well, I'll be over there," she nodded toward the hotel. "See you later." She leaned forward to kiss Elena lightly. "Love you."

"Love you, too," Elena said. "Text me with any news from the sheriff."

Tori watched as Elena stepped up into her truck and backed out of the driveway. As Elena's truck made it to the asphalt headed toward the main road, she turned and started waking around to the back of her cabin. As long as the carcass was on the front porch, she would use the back door.

A half hour later, she had her briefcase packed and was on her way to the edge of the gorge to pick her way down the trail to the hotel. The sun was up and the air was dry and warm. A westerly breeze caressed her cheeks and blew her hair back off her face as she made her way. She felt the brightness of the day even behind dark sunglasses and held her hand over her eyes the cut the glare and see more clearly where she stepped between the rocks and small, thorny bushes. Halfway between the cabin and the hotel, she heard a small tumult of rocks in the gorge to her left. She stopped and craned her neck to see over the side a bit. Two white rumps bounded down at an angle behind her, disappearing into the shade of some large boulders near the bottom of gorge. She waited for a moment to get another glimpse of the deer, but they did not appear again. She blinked her eyes, thinking maybe they were right there in front of her, disguised in their natural camouflage of desert browns, greens and drab grays. Still she saw nothing. After a moment, she turned and continued toward the hotel.

She walked up the trail from the gorge to the hotel, stepping up onto the patio beside the jacuzzi. The sheriff and deputy sat at a table near the fountain, talking with Luis and Ricardo. They all had coffee cups in front of them and seemed to have concluded the official part of their business. The sheriff leaned back in his chair, one leg crossed over the other. Luis sat with his chair turned slightly toward the sheriff's, and listened with interest to a story the sheriff was telling. Tori smiled at them as she stepped toward them. The sheriff looked at her, smiled and leaned forward.

"This sure is a nice place you got here, Ms. Reed," he said. "This is my first time out here to see the inside. I've heard about it, though. Everybody talks about how nice it is, and it sure is." He smiled broadly and stood up as Tori stopped at their table.

"Thank you, Sheriff. I'm glad you like it." She looked at Luis and Ricardo, smiling slightly. "I've had lots of good help with it, as you know." She paused for a moment. "May I get you all some more coffee?"

"Oh no," the sheriff said, nodding quickly to the deputy. "We've got to be going." He looked at Luis and Ricardo as they stood and began gathering up the coffee cups. "Thank you boys for the information. We'll be in touch."

"Anytime. Always glad to help," Luis said as he extended his hand to the sheriff. Luis caught Tori's eye for a moment, then looked back down at the table, gathered two cups and started walking toward the dining room door.

"I'll start loading the stuff into the truck," Ricardo said as he followed Luis into the building.

"Walk with me to the car, Ms. Reed?" the sheriff asked. Tori nodded, plopped her briefcase down in the chair, and began walking up the sidewalk toward the lobby. The deputy followed behind. The sheriff waited until they stepped from the lobby out onto the hotel porch to speak.

"Well, they both tell the story the same way you and Ms. Rios do, so that checks out at least." He took a deep breath. "Here's what I want you to do. Sit tight for a few days, and let's see if anything more happens. I don't think this is a coincidence, but let's just give it another chance. If another incident happens, we'll see about setting up some kind of surveillance. In the meantime, I'll have Lonnie here and the other night deputies keep an eye out on things around here and around Ms. Rios' house."

Tori nodded. "Okay, that sounds fine. Do you want us to keep our routine, or should we do anything differently?"

"Just go about your business," he said, looking at her again over his glasses. "Don't act different or anything. Just take the normal precautions anyone would take in terms of driving at night, being safe and so forth." He paused for a moment. "This could just be kids playing pranks for all we know."

"What about the carcass on the porch? Can we take it to the dump?"

"Sure. Go ahead. Lonnie got pictures on his phone. Didn't you?" He looked back at Lonnie, who was standing in the open door of the passenger side of the patrol car. Lonnie nodded.

"Call me if anything else happens," he said as he stepped into the patrol car. "I can be out here in nothin' flat."

Tori watched the car drive away, and turned to go back inside.

The high school gymnasium was filled to near capacity as the Logan Javelinas prepared to take on their opponents in the regional basketball championship. Nearly all the residents of Logan were there, stacked shoulder to shoulder in the bleachers on the home side, wearing the maroon and gold colors of their team. Tori and Elena sat with them, right in the middle about ten rows back from the scorer's table, eating popcorn and cheering. Jared, Dustin, Letty, Ricardo, and several others from the ranch filled out the bleacher beside them. A few of the Galindo's staff sat behind or in front of them. The teams were shooting warm-up drills on the court, and the cheerleaders and school band conducted the crowd from the sidelines in the school fight song and other chants.

"It looks good," Elena said, holding the game program open for Tori to see the full- page ad they had bought for the ranch. Tori looked at it, smiled and nodded, and then jammed her hand down into the red and white striped bucket in her lap for more popcorn.

"There should be another one," Tori said, her words garbled from the popcorn in her mouth. "The one for the PTA scholar-ship." She turned from the program and looked back out at the court. Elena thumbed through the program, found the page with the second ad on it, and then held it over to Tori, who looked at it and nodded.

"We should do something at the ranch if they go all the way to the state championship—win or lose," Elena said. She put the program aside and picked up a cup of root beer nearly the size of the popcorn bucket. She took a drink from the straw, held it absently as Tori took a drink, and set it down again.

"Yeah, I was thinking that too, maybe a dinner or a reception. Something like that." She put another handful of popcorn in her mouth. "Maybe the coaches want to give out team awards or something. We could host the awards dinner."

"That's a good idea," Elena said, reaching over to grab some popcorn.

"Take it. I'm going to make myself sick with this stuff," Tori said and she sat the bucket in Elena's lap and wiped her hands on her jeans. Elena took a big handful, and passed it on to Letty next to her.

The gymnasium went dark and a spotlight danced in large circles around the court floor. One by one, the players for both teams were introduced and ran through billows of illuminated smoke blowing from the dark corners. The crowd applauded and whistled as each player's name was called, and then erupted into explosive cheers when the lights came back on and the band struck up again. People who had come into the gymnasium while the lights were down now made their way across the front and up the aisles, looking for the few empty spots in the bleachers.

"That was a pretty fancy introduction for a high school game," Tori said, smiling and gazing around at the residual smoke. "That was like a pro team."

Elena looked around. "Well, we gave them that big check. Guess they spent some of it." She raised her eyebrows and shrugged.

"Look," Tori said, elbowing Elena lightly and nodding to her right. Elena turned and they both watched a smiling Luis make his way across the gym along the front row of bleachers. He stood tall and relaxed, wearing a maroon collared shirt, pressed jeans, and boots. As he walked, he held the hand of the woman who walked with him. She had long dark hair that she had pulled up into a ponytail near the top of her head. Large hoop earrings dangled from her ears, and she wore an oversized Logan Javelinas football jersey. Her jeans were tight around shapely legs and bunched around her ankles over the top of her boots. She held on to Luis with one hand, and to the shoulder strap of her oversized purse with the other.

"Do you know her?" Tori asked. Elena shook her head and reached over to Letty's lap for another handful of popcorn.

"Her name is Juanita," Letty said. "Her son is on the team…"

Letty scanned the Logan team players as they gathered at their bench for final instructions from the coach. "Right there, the little one. Number twelve. I forgot his name. But he's her son."

Luis and Juanita stopped at the scoring table and talked with a man sitting there. Luis shook his hand vigorously, and they both talked and laughed for a moment. Juanita stood nearby, saying hello to a few people in the front rows and glancing often toward the team bench and her son. After a moment, they stepped away slowly from the scoring table and began scanning the crowd in the bleachers for people they knew and for empty seats. Luis stood facing the incline of bleachers, allowing his gaze to make its way slowly through the rows of people. His eye caught Tori's and stopped. His face barely shifted from its pleasant smile. He glanced at Elena on Tori's right for a moment, and moved his eyes onward down the row and behind them, searching for friends and seats. He leaned toward Juanita and pointed toward a section in the bleachers behind Tori and Elena. Juanita nodded and they began to make their way up the aisle toward the empty seats. Juanita led the way and Luis trailed behind her with one hand still clasped in hers. He looked over at Tori and Elena as he walked past their row in the bleachers. Elena kept her eyes fixed on the court, but Tori turned slightly and smiled as they passed. Luis looked past her to Elena, and turned his face upward toward the high bleachers.

"Well…that was weird," Tori said as soon as they had passed. She stretched her arm and open palm across Elena's lap toward Letty and the popcorn. Letty leaned the bucket toward her and held it while she grabbed another handful.

Elena rolled her eyes and reached down for the giant cup of root beer. "So *high school*," she muttered before taking another giant swallow. She sat the cup down and looked forward toward the players on the court.

Tori looked at her for a moment, and leaned into Elena's

shoulder, giving her an affectionate bump. Elena kept her face still, gazing forward. Tori bumped her again gently. Elena grinned and moved her eyes to Tori's, without moving her head, and then leaned into Tori's arm.

"You're right," Tori said quietly. "It does seem sort of juvenile. It's like he wanted to be sure you saw them."

"Whatever," Elena said, almost under her breath. "I hope he's happy. I'm happy for him, if he is." She uncrossed her legs and re-crossed them in the other direction. At that moment, one of the star players, the son of one of the ranch kitchen workers, ran out onto the court to prepare for the opening jump. "Let's go, Morris! Let's go Javelinas!!!!" Elena yelled, jumping to her feet with the rest of the crowd to cheer the start of the game.

The game began and the players ran seemingly non-stop from one end of the court to another for over a half hour. Very few fouls were called, so the only stops in action were for timeouts. During those few breaks, people made their way quickly down the aisles to the vending stands or to the restrooms, cheering and clapping all the way until they made it back to their seats. Tori saw Luis cross in front of them and exit the court to their right. He returned a while later, carefully climbing the stairs with a big bucket of popcorn and two drinks wedged inside a cardboard carry box.

At the half, the score was tied. Elena, Letty and a few others went to the restrooms while Tori threaded her way through the bleachers into the next section to visit with Ken and Hazel. She walked with them onto the court and out into the hallway pavilion to buy nachos. Ken stood in line while Hazel and Tori stood off to the side near him, chatting about the goings-on of the town and commenting on the game. Ken surveyed the crowd as he stood in line. His face was red with excitement and he called out greetings to friends and acquaintances as they passed. Finally, he stepped to the counter, fished his money out, buried his wallet back into his hip pocket, and walked toward Hazel with two drinks and a big plate of cheesy chips.

"That cheese looks neon, Ken," Tori teased. "You think it glows in the dark?"

He laughed. "Well, if it does it'll get the chance in just a minute, as soon as I swallow it down."

Tori reached and picked a piece of jalapeno off one chip and popped it into her mouth.

"Have some more," Hazel said. "We sure don't need to eat all this!"

Tori shook her head. As she did, she saw Sheriff Banks walking slowly across the other side of the pavilion toward the court. She wanted to catch him before he went inside.

"No thanks. Lord knows I don't need it either," Tori said. "I'll catch up with you two later. I need to run talk to someone right quick."

They waved Tori off and she strode across the pavilion toward the sheriff. He saw her as she got a third of the way to him. He stopped, turned toward her and smiled. He was in uniform, but he wore a Logan Javalinas baseball cap and one of the maroon and yellow plastic bracelets the team had sold as a fundraiser.

"It's a tight game, isn't it Ms. Reed," he said. His brown eyes were bright with excitement. He shook Tori's hand and then hooked his thumb into a belt loop that was barely visible under the bulge of his belly.

"It sure is," she replied. "I hope they can pull it out in this last half."

"Me, too," he said. "Me too!" He suddenly looked past Tori and motioned to someone behind her down the hallway. She turned and saw a deputy down the hall standing near the restrooms. He looked at Sheriff Banks, moved further down the hall, then looked back at the sheriff and nodded, slightly bewildered. She turned back to the sheriff and he looked at her, shaking his head slightly.

"Sorry," he said. "That's one of our new deputies. This is his first time doing a big game like this. He doesn't know exactly where he needs to be all the time."

"Gotcha…" Tori nodded and smiled. "Well, things have been pretty quiet the last few weeks since you came out to the ranch."

"I was going to ask you about that as soon as I saw you. No new incidents, huh?" He shifted his weight and leaned toward her a bit, his tone turning serious as he put his excitement for the game aside.

"Nothing," she said. "Everything is going along well. Totally normal."

"Well, I'm glad to hear it. I hoped as much when I didn't hear from ya'll again. The night deputies increased their patrols in the general area, as I told you they would, so maybe that helped." He turned aside to sneeze suddenly. He covered his mouth with both hands, then retrieved a white handkerchief from his back pocket and wiped his mouth and nose. He carefully folded over the used portion of the limp cloth and placed it back in his hip pocket. He looked at Tori again with a red nose and watery eyes that seemed sharp in contrast to the gray hair that protruded from underneath his cap.

"Excuse me," he said as he inhaled deeply. "It's those smoke machines they use at the beginning of the game. Those particles stay in the air for days, seems like. I guess I'm allergic." He cleared his throat loudly and sniffed again.

"You know, now that you mention it, my eyes burned a little at the beginning of the game. I wonder if that stuff got on my contacts?" Tori said. She touched the edge of her eye.

"Could be," he said, nodding and wiping his nose again with the back of his hand. "Anyway, I'm glad to hear things've been quiet down your way. You all are running a nice outfit out there. Hate to see anything go on that would mess up ya'll's business or anything."

"Right. Thank you," she said, smiling. "Thanks for all your help, yours and the deputies'. I'm sure you all being involved made a difference."

The buzzer from inside the court echoed out into the pavilion, and the school band began its traditional song for the start of the second half.

"Well, I guess we better get this thing settled," the sheriff said. "Go Javelinas!"

"Go Javelinas!" Tori chimed in agreement as they both turned and began walking toward the court. The sheriff held the heavy door open for her as she passed through. "Thank you again, Sheriff Banks. I really appreciate it. You and your family be sure to come have dinner with us at the ranch sometime. We'll be happy to treat you."

"We'll do it, Ms. Reed. Thank you. Ya'll call me if there's ever any trouble." He smiled and shook her hand again as soon as he released the door, then turned to take his position at a small table a few feet away from the doorway. Lonnie Welch sat in uniform at a swivel chair at the table, but stood when the sheriff approached. The deputy glanced at Tori, smiled and waved briefly before she began walking toward her seat in the bleachers. A few minutes later, as she sat in her seat, she saw him leaned against the gymnasium wall near the entrance, his cowboy hat pushed back off his forehead, watching the game and eating from a tub of popcorn as big as his head.

The game resumed and the crowd got louder with each minute. The teams pounded the court and pushed the score higher and higher, but no team took a lead greater than a few points. With five seconds left in the game, the clock was stopped and Juanita's son, number twelve of the Javelinas, stood at the free throw line to take two shots after having been fouled. The score was tied. All he had to do was make one shot and then, if the Javelinas prevented their opponents from scoring, they would win the game.

Tori turned back to Luis and Juanita in the stands behind her as the player bounced the ball preparing to shoot. Juanita leaned into Luis with her arm tightly looped through his. She covered her mouth with her hand and sat quietly as the crowd roared all around her. Her son took the first shot. The ball hit the backboard, then the side of the rim and bounced away. The crowd groaned and then began to cheer again.

"Oh God, I hope he makes this," Elena said, taking a deep breath. "Poor kid." She clapped her hands and cheered with the rest of the crowd. Tori stuffed her hands in her jeans pockets and dug her fingers into the denim. The crowd's cheering went silent as the second shot arched toward the basket, hit the backboard and plunged through the net. The crowd erupted into a roar and the opposing team called a time-out. Tori cheered along with everyone else, and then looked back at Juanita, who was wiping tears from her cheeks. Luis had his arm around her and was smiling broadly.

Play resumed on the court and the crowd held its collective breath as the opposing team lobbed a last second shot from mid-court. When it bounced off the top of the backboard out of bounds, it seemed the roof would blow off the building. The band struck up its most raucous song with blaring horns and pounding drums. Tori and Elena raised their hands and arms in high fives with the people near them in the bleachers. Everyone hugged each other, shrieking and whistling for the team. Tori could feel the vibration of the bleachers under her as people jumped and danced in the stands.

Tori and Elena stood and watched as people made their way down the aisles and onto the court to greet the players. Before long, people started making their way toward the exits.

"Ready?" Tori asked.

"Sure," Elena said. They picked their way down the aisle, stepping over popcorn buckets and drink cups. They greeted a few people as they left, saying hello to regular customers and other people they knew from around town. Everyone's faces, including their own, were frozen in beaming smiles.

They meandered with the slow crowd out into the pavilion

hallway and then out into the parking lot. The clear night air felt clean on Tori's cheeks and she took a deep breath. The band's music faded into the background as they made their way across the parking lot to her car.

"That was fun," she said. "This is my first high school basketball game in a long time. I don't even remember the last time. Maybe my own high school's games."

"Yeah, it's a big deal out here. I guess we'll find out tomorrow when the next game is," Elena said, reaching out to squeeze Tori's fingers briefly, and then letting them go. "Once we find out, we can decide what we want to do for the team."

"Yeah, or we could also just call the coach tomorrow and ask what their plans are," Tori said. She looked straight ahead and found her car at the end of the row. "See if they have an awards ceremony or something."

"That's a good idea," Elena said, waving at two people on the next row, who waved at her. She recognized them as regulars at Galindo's.

Tori slowed to a stop a car or two away from hers as she fished in her purse for her keys. She found the keys and began to step forward, but then suddenly froze.

"Stop!" she said to Elena, grabbing her arm to keep her from going any closer to the car. Elena looked back at her, then at the car. She, too, froze. There, stretched in the trench between the hood and the windshield, lying on top of the wiper blades, was a headless rabbit carcass.

"Thanks for staying," Elena said, looking at Luis. They stood in the parking lot with Tori and Letty watching Sheriff Banks and

Lonnie Welch dust the hood and windshield of Tori's car for fingerprints. Luis looked at her and shrugged slightly.

"Of course," he said softly. "Anything I can do to help." He stuck his hands in his pockets and looked back at the sheriff. He and Juanita had come walking up the parking lot aisle just a few moments after Tori and Elena had seen the rabbit on the car. He saw Elena's face and stopped to see what was wrong. When he saw the rabbit, he told Juanita to get a ride home with some friends, and loped off to get the sheriff from the gymnasium.

Tori stood quietly on the other side of Elena with her arms crossed over her chest. She slowly tapped her foot on the pavement and stared at her car with a blank look. She had never been in a situation quite like this, and did not know what to make of it. Whoever was doing this clearly was targeting her and Elena. But was it the two of them personally? Was it the ranch as well? Only one of the carcasses had been in the ranch driveway; the others were on their personal property. She could not believe that someone would target the ranch. It had been such a success and had so many people in the community connected to it. So, maybe this was personal.

She felt her stomach drop as the thought ripened in her mind. Not once in her life had she dealt with overt homophobia—not in school, college or at work. She had worked hard, played by the rules, and been a responsible colleague, neighbor and citizen. The companies she owned, worked for or managed had been good corporate citizens. Seemingly, no one had cared that she was a lesbian. She had been praised for her accomplishments and appreciated for her contributions. But now, standing here in the chilly parking lot of a West Texas town, she wondered if her years-long streak of good luck and good standing had come to an end. It seemed obvious to her that, although Sheriff Banks had not yet mentioned it, whoever was leaving carcasses for her and Elena to find had an issue with the two of them. What other issue could be so bothersome but that they were two women in love?

Sheriff Banks stepped away from the car and put his hands on his hips. He watched Lonnie intently as the deputy carefully lifted strips of tape from the car's surface and placed them on cards. They had dusted much of the hood and all but one side of the windshield. While Lonnie dusted, the sheriff had searched the immediate area for other clues, like the head of the rabbit, or something with blood on it, but found nothing. He stepped away from the car and walked toward Tori.

"We'll send in the prints first thing in the mornin'. It shouldn't take more than a few days to get something back, if there's anything to report." He brushed his hand across his head, stilling a few gray strands that had come loose from their grooves in the breeze. He reached into his back pocket, retrieved his Javalinas ball cap and placed it back on his head. "In the meantime, the four of you come down to the station in the morning and let's get you printed. Then we'll have your prints on file to cross-check with whatever else shows up. Anyone else ridden in your car or touched it in the last few days that you know of? A mechanic or gas station person, or anyone from the ranch?"

Tori looked into the sheriff's eyes and thought for a moment. She nodded. "Jared took my car to Stockdale yesterday to pick up some clients." She turned to Letty. "He went alone, right? Dustin didn't go with him, did he?"

Letty shook her head. "He went by himself." She stood with her hands stuffed into the hip pockets of her jeans, leaning in toward Elena.

"Should we get the clients' fingerprints too?" Tori asked, looking back at the sheriff.

"Yeah, probably—just to make it easier," he said. "Can't hurt. I'll send Lonnie out with the remote kit if you want. In fact, let's just do this—ya'll stay put in the mornin' and I'll send Lonnie out to get everything." He looked into Tori's eyes. "Just tell your clients that you've had some vandalism done on your car and we need prints in order to eliminate them from the equation. That usually does the trick."

Tori nodded. "Okay," she said quietly, still looking intently into the sheriff's eyes. "May I call you in the morning to talk over some things?"

"Of course, Ms. Reed. Call me anytime." He reached into his shirt pocket and fished out a handful of business cards. He gave one to each of them. "My cell and the office numbers are on there. But, I'll probably come out with Lonnie, or thereabouts. I want to talk with you both about next steps." He looked at Elena, then back at Tori.

They all turned as they heard Lonnie snap off his latex gloves. He stuffed them into a plastic bag and closed up the dusting kit. He turned toward the sheriff and nodded curtly.

"Okay, well, we'll see you folks in the mornin'. Thanks for your patience." The sheriff stuck his hand out first to Tori and then to the others.

"Thank you, Sheriff. I really appreciate it," Tori said.

He nodded and stepped away with Lonnie toward the patrol car parked near the front of the gym.

Tori turned toward Elena, and then looked at Letty. "Come on, we'll take you home." She turned toward her car and held out the key fob to unlock it. The lights blinked once and the locks clicked open. She stood with her arm outstretched for a moment before dropping it and walking slowly toward the drivers' side. Elena and Letty followed toward the passenger side.

"Thank you, Luis," Tori said, turning back to face him as she stood in front of her open car door. "I really appreciate you staying around."

He nodded slowly, looking at her then at Elena as she lowered herself into the car. He looked back at Tori. "No problem," he said. "Ya'll be careful on the way home." He dug his truck keys out of his pocket and stood twirling them on his finger as he watched them pull out of the parking slot. Tori waved to him in her rearview mirror as she drove away slowly. He waved back at her and stepped toward his truck.

Tori turned the car onto the main highway. Letty lived in small house with her family about four miles west of the ranch. The three of them were quiet as they drove past the low buildings of town and out into the dark desert beyond them.

Elena reached over for Tori's hand resting on the gear shifter. She laced her fingers through Tori's and brought their joined hands to her lap. "What are you thinking," she asked softly, turning to Tori.

Tori shook her head, took a deep breath and let it out slowly. "I'm not sure what to think exactly, but…" She trailed off, her eyes fixed on the illuminated road ahead.

"But what?" Elena asked. She squeezed Tori's hand.

Tori shook her head again slowly. She paused for a moment. "I can't help but think this has to do with us. That we're together."

"Yeah," Elena whispered as she turned away from her and stared at the road. They all sat quietly for another few miles, turning to look at the ranch as they passed its entrance on the main road.

"What do you think?" Tori asked, looking at Letty in the rearview mirror.

Letty met her gaze, raised her eyebrows and took a deep breath. She shifted in her seat and looked out the window into the passing darkness. "It's possible," she said finally. "I mean, there's people out here who don't like gay people. Mostly they just keep to themselves and, you know, live and let live. But…" She paused for a moment, then looked back at Tori in the mirror. "I don't know what they would have against you personally—either one of you. And I don't know how many people even know about ya'll's relationship. And even if they do, I mean, so what? Everyone who knows you likes you, especially if they work at the ranch or know anyone who does."

Tori listened and then looked away from the mirror when Letty finished speaking.

"We don't know yet what's going on, not exactly," Elena said after a moment. "Let's see what the sheriff thinks tomorrow." She softly caressed Tori's forearm in her lap. "Okay?"

Tori nodded slightly and kept her eyes fixed on the road.

❧

"Excuse the mess in here, Sheriff," Elena said as she scooped up a stack of food magazines from the seat of the extra chair in her kitchen office. Tori cleared a space for herself on one corner of Elena's desk and sat down on it, her back to the window that opened onto the kitchen. Elena stacked the magazines atop another stack already piled up precariously on the far end of her desk. "Someone will be here in just a minute with some coffee," she added, settling into her own office chair.

"Thank you, this is fine," the sheriff said. He looked out at the kitchen and sat back in his chair. "This is a nice little set-up you got here, huh? This way, you can do your office work but also keep an eye on things." He smiled knowingly, as if he had discovered a secret.

Elena smiled and nodded. "Yeah, that's pretty accurate." She looked out toward the kitchen, as if to prove the point. She looked at Tori then back at the sheriff.

Sheriff Banks pulled a small spiral notepad from his front shirt pocket. He flipped over the cover and a few pages, touching the tip of his thick thumb to his tongue to moisten the page corners until he got to a clean one. He retrieved a pen from the same shirt pocket, dropped his hands to his knees, and looked up at them with an open face.

"So," he said somewhat loudly. "Let's talk about what might be going on here." At that moment, a light tap came through the door and it eased open. Jose, one of the new young kitchen helpers stood holding a coffee service tray. He smiled nervously as he stepped forward, gripping the tray tightly.

"Here," Tori said, sliding over on Elena's desk to make space for the tray. Jose set it down carefully and stepped back. He put his hands together as if in prayer.

"Anything else, Ms. Rios?" he asked, looking at Elena. His voice was nasal and worried.

"No, Jose. That's fine," she said, smiling at him. "Thank you so much."

"Yes, thank you Jose," Tori added. He smiled, nodded and backed out of the door, clicking it shut behind him.

"He's new, right?" Tori asked, turning her head to Elena as she mindlessly grabbed the carafe and held it aloft in the air ready to pour the sheriff a cup.

Elena nodded. "He's...well, let me get this straight...he's the nephew of the sister of Jared's stepfather." She closed her eyes and held still, making sure of her facts. "Yeah, that's right." She opened her eyes and reached for a coffee cup.

"Well, it's good to keep things in the family," Tori said lightly. She poured steaming liquid into the sheriff's cup, which he held in mid-air toward her. "Take anything in it?"

"Just black," he said. "Yeah, everybody's connected to everybody out here, seems like." He sat back in his chair and blew into his cup before taking a short sip. He set the cup on his knee and looked back at them.

"Tell me, who do you know who might be upset enough with you to do this with these animal carcasses? Have you fired anyone recently? Any disgruntled employees or upset clients? Customers mad at you? Vendors you haven't paid? Upset boyfriends or girlfriends? Anyone?"

Tori and Elena looked at each other, searching each other's faces. They both caught the sheriff's phrase *upset boyfriends or girlfriends.*

"Surprisingly, we've had no employee or vendor issues here at the ranch—at least none that we know of," Tori said. "We've actually not fired anyone."

"We had two people quit, but that was because they moved out of town—they weren't upset or anything," Elena added.

The sheriff nodded and waited for more details. He took another sip of his coffee.

Elena looked at Tori and back at the sheriff. "We've been thinking, Sheriff, that maybe this has to do with our relationship." She paused for a moment, her hands resting on her thighs. "That maybe someone is upset that Tori and I are together in a romantic relationship."

The sheriff nodded slowly and looked from Elena to Tori, then back at Elena. He took another sip of coffee and swallowed it. "Well, that could be," he said. "You know of anyone who'd be upset about that around here? I mean, has anyone said anything ugly to you about it or treated you in an ugly way because of it?"

They both shook their heads. "No, not at all. In fact, it's been just the opposite. The people who know have been really supportive, for the most part," Tori said.

"We haven't taken out an ad or anything," Elena added with a chuckle. "We mainly just go about our business everyday, but the people close to us—at work and our friends in town—know about us."

"Who have you told for sure? I mean, directly?" he asked. "Of course, things like this spread to all sorts of people, but who are the people you yourself have told or talked to about it?"

Tori and Elena looked at each other as they listed off the names: Ken, Hazel, Jared, Dustin, Letty, Ricardo and Luis. The sheriff set his cup on the floor and wrote down the names, asking for last names. After he finished scratching on his small notepad he looked up at them.

"Any of these people upset about it?"

Tori and Elena were quiet for a moment, and then Elena spoke.

"Luis was upset," she said, looking directly into the sheriff's eyes. The sheriff made a note on his pad. "He was really upset about it right after I told him, but he seems okay now."

"Yeah, he really does," Tori added. "I guess that time off helped him."

"Why exactly was he upset?" the sheriff asked.

Elena took a deep breath. "He and I dated in high school, but I moved away for nearly twenty-five years. I came back last year to take care of my mother, who died not long ago. Luis thought that we would get back together, but I didn't want to." She paused and looked at Tori. "And I fell in love with Tori," she said simply. "I told him that and he was upset. But, like we said, he took some time off, and has been fine since he came back."

"He's got a girlfriend, it seems," Tori said. "Juanita—is that it?" She looked at Elena, who nodded.

The sheriff watched and listened to the two of them, and then reached for his cup on the floor. He set it on his knee and looked at it. Then he looked back up at them.

"Was he upset in a jilted lover kind of way, or was it more because of you being gay?" he asked. "Do you know what I mean? I mean, maybe it's hard to tell, but those are two different things."

"I know what you mean," Elena said. "I think he was upset because I ended his hopes for our relationship. I think that was the gist of it." She looked up at Tori. "Would you agree?"

Tori looked down and nodded. "Yeah, he's always been respectful to me and treated me as a friend. A close friend even. And he knew I was gay long before Elena ended it with him and told him about us." Elena nodded in agreement. "He's a good person. He was just very upset about losing Elena, as anyone would be."

The sheriff wrote a few more notes and then looked up at them. "Anyone else upset about that or about anything else that you can think of?"

They thought for a moment then shook their heads. Tori turned to the sheriff.

"What do you think? Do you have any ideas?" she asked.

He took a deep breath and put his notebook back in his pocket. "Well, we're just at the beginning still, so it could be anybody really." He looked up at the ceiling, and out into the kitchen, collecting his thoughts, then looked back at them. "You know, we've got all kinds of people out here in this part of the state. Some people are real interesting and have strong opinions about things, if you know what I mean. Strong political and religious views. They get real strident and they hole off by themselves out here on a mountain or a small ranch and you never hear from 'em until something happens that upsets them. Could be that word traveled about ya'll and they got it in their head that, you know, the homosexual agenda has come out here to West Texas, or something such as that." He graveled his voice a bit and arched his fingers in quotes around the words *homosexual agenda*.

He took a swallow of coffee and set the cup on his knee before continuing.

"It's just hard to know at this point. So, let's get the prints done off your car. See what we have there. Then, let's focus on some basic surveillance of this ranch and both ya'll's houses. Set up some simple cameras maybe, unless you already have those installed. Do you?"

"No, but I can get them installed this week," Tori said, shaking her head. She looked at him with a resigned smile. "I had thought we might not need them out here. I was wrong, I guess."

# Chapter Nineteen

Do you have confidence in this sheriff?" Sharon asked over the phone. "I mean, does he seem to know what he's doing and take it all seriously?"

"Yeah, I do," Tori said. "He's an old-timer out here, but he's responded really well to every incident. He's been really professional." She paused for a moment. "He and his deputy both."

"Well, that's good." Sharon was silent on the other end of the phone. Tori sat at her kitchenette table looking out over the patio and toward the gorge. A gentle haze muted the mid-morning sun, which dulled the glare off the hard desert ground and would prevent the temperature from reaching triple digits. The June temperatures had soared in the last few weeks, breaking monthly records seemingly every day, driving people indoors as much as possible except during the morning hours and at dusk. Shade was an increasingly valuable commodity. Under an eave, awning, umbrella or tucked against a wall or into the dark side of a mesa, the temperature dropped by twenty degrees and it was possible to even feel cool if a breeze blew the clear, dry air.

"He seems to get it," Tori added, fingering the corner of the some papers on the table in front of her. "And he likes the ranch a lot, and likes us. He even brought his wife to eat dinner at the restaurant last week."

"Did you give him the *law enforcement* discount?"

Tori smiled. "Of course, and I'm sure Elena sent them out something special." She stood up, put on her sunglasses and walked outside to dip her fingers into the jacuzzi. She had turned the heater off and had been leaving the cover on it during the day to keep the sun from warming the water. She slid the cover to the side with her hip, touched her fingers to the cool water, shook them off, and nudged the cover back in place. "So what's going on with you? How's Deborah?"

Sharon launched into a meandering summary of her current cases, the oddities of her clients and their break-up situations, the most recent goings on of friends she and Tori had in common around town, new restaurant openings and closings, museum exhibits, the speaker at a recent gala event, and whatnot. Tori heard commotion in the background at one point in the conversation.

"Where are you?" she asked, sitting back down at the kitchen table and raising her sunglasses to the top of her head.

"In downtown, in the tunnel. Why?"

"I hear a lot of noise."

"Oh, yeah, that's some sort of protest or something…" She trailed off and Tori heard her greet someone she knew who was passing by, then she returned to the phone. "I don't really know what the issue is. I should have used the ATM in the other direction."

"They let people do protests in the tunnel now?" Tori asked, annoyed. She immediately thought of the Chinese food place directly under her office building where she used to order lunch a few times a week. Sometimes she would order take-out and then stroll through the tunnel system that winds its way underground and connects many of the downtown buildings, window-shopping and people watching. During the steamy, tropical summer months, the tunnel system was a godsend, a way to move around downtown—attend a meeting in another building, grab a bite to eat, go to the ATM or the gym, buy a quick gift—without having to step out into the weather and ruin a perfectly nice set of dress clothes.

"I guess so," Sharon answered. "Anyway, I think you would have liked that speaker at the Alliance gala the other night. He was longwinded and the wait staff had to stand off to the side for a half-hour watching the ice cream melt before they could serve dessert, but nobody minded I don't think. It was really interesting."

"Hmm, it does sound interesting," Tori replied. "And how is Deborah?" she asked after a moment of silence. "You didn't say anything about her."

"She's fine," Sharon said cheerfully. "Really good. She just finished up a big case that stretched on for months, and she got what she wanted for the client, so she's pleased. Big payload. She's taking some time off. Taking her mother and aunt to Italy and Greece on a cruise."

Tori sensed there was something Sharon was not telling her and waited for more details, but Sharon did not offer them.

"Are you still seeing her?" she finally asked.

"Yeah, actually, I'm going with them on the cruise," she said nonchalantly.

Tori's face broke into a gaping grin. "Don't tell me you've become the *family* type now. Going on vacation with the mom and the aunt?! I didn't think it was possible," she teased and giggled into the phone.

"Please, you are so lame…don't start with me…." Sharon said in voice equally tinged with threat and sheepishness.

"I'm so proud of you! Are you actually getting serious with someone after all these years?" Tori leaned back in her chair and smiled.

"Oh, you're one to talk, *Miss I'm Too Busy Being a Rock Star to even have dinner, much less a relationship!*" Sharon giggled at herself as she heard these words come out of her own mouth. "How many plants died in your house over the years because there wasn't enough *room in your life* for them—a hundred?"

"You're right, you're right. I admit it," she laughed. "I just thought you'd be forever *the player*, right up to the end." She emphasized the word "player" pronouncing it "playah."

"Well, you know…we're all gettin' old, so you gotta start making adjustments," Sharon said in a drawl, clearly trying to sound tough and cynical but not doing a very good job of it. "Things are startin' to fall down all around me, if you know what I mean, and I'm not payin' for the plastic surgery to keep 'em all up. So, I gotta get what I can while the gettin's good."

Tori guffawed so loud she startled herself. "Oh my God, you are ridiculous!" she squealed.

"Whatever…I'm just being realistic about things," Sharon said.

Tori finished laughing, and they both went quiet for a moment.

"I'm really happy for you, sweetie," Tori said finally, in a more serious tone. "Really happy. Deborah Meeks is a lucky woman."

"Well, thanks," Sharon said quietly, shifting away from her earlier joking persona. "She's a good person, and her mom and aunt are really nice people. They've come down to visit a few times. We all get along well."

"That's good. The cruise will be fun."

"Yeah, it will be. I'm excited about it." Sharon paused. "Deborah and I will have some time to ourselves. We got a penthouse cabin on the ship and it looks really nice online."

"Of course you did," Tori smiled. Sharon always sprang for the nicest amenities in travel and entertainment.

"I'm going to ask her to move into my house with me," Sharon said after a moment.

"Wow. Who are you and what have you done with my dear friend Sharon?" Tori said with only a bit of teasing in her voice.

"Don't start up again!" Sharon said loudly.

"Okay, okay, okay! I'm just so surprised—and I'm thrilled and happy for you." Tori sensed her friend wanting her blessing or affirmation. "She seems perfect for you, Sharon. Elena and I both really liked her. I got a great feeling from her and everything you've said about her bears it out."

"She's good, right?" Sharon asked somewhat tentatively. "I mean, you don't think I'm making a mistake, do you?"

"No, not at all. You don't make mistakes, right? Not in relationships. You love yourself too much—in the best way." Tori said. "Yeah, she's good."

"You would tell me, right?"

"Yes, I would tell you. Just like you would have told me if Elena wasn't right for me."

"Right."

"We've got each other's backs."

"Right."

"Right."

They were quiet for a moment. Tori heard the echo of Sharon's footsteps and the din of background noise through the phone.

"Sharon, are you in love with her?"

"Yeah, I am," she said.

"Is she in love with you?"

"I think so…yeah, she is. She said so."

"Well, then that's all you really need to know, isn't it?"

Sharon sighed. "Except she and I both spend our days separating the assets of people who were once in love with each other."

"Well, then, you'll both know good lawyers to do that for you it if it ever comes to that."

Sharon gasped into the phone. "Don't say that! Why would you say that?" she exclaimed.

"Come on, Sharon, you know better than this," Tori chuckled. "I've known you longer than any of your friends, and I've never heard you say you were in love with someone. You are not going to let, you know, *all the bad in the world I see from my job blah blah* get in the way of that." She cleared her throat. "Really. One, you can't live like that and, two, it's not you."

"I hate you, especially when you're right," Sharon said softly, with a resigned voice.

"I know, but with you it's so rare, I have to take advantage when I can."

They were quiet for few moments. Tori heard the ding of an elevator.

"Am I about to lose you in the elevator?"

"Yeah. One more thing and then I gotta go."

"Yeah?"

"Don't stay out there if this thing doesn't get resolved. Come back to Houston. Bring Elena with you."

Tori went quiet and felt a small knot form in the pit of her stomach. The thought of turning her back on everything she had built in Logan had come close to the edges of her conscious mind, but she had pushed it back because she did not want to think it. But now Sharon spoke it aloud and she could not avoid it.

"Did you hear me?" Sharon asked.

"I heard you."

"I mean it, Tori. You're not obligated to stay out there and carry the rainbow flag. Just walk away from it if it's not safe or if you're always going to be wondering when the next incident's going to happen. Like you just told me, *you can't live like that.* You shouldn't have to. Elena either. Just walk away and come back home. Start something new here. Make another big pile of money."

Tori swallowed and fingered the corners of the papers on the table. "Okay," she said finally. "I'll think about it. Elena and I need to talk about it."

"I"m just sayin'…"

"I know. I know what you're saying. You're right."

"Okay."

"I love you."

"I love you, too, sweetie. I gotta go."

"Me, too. I'll talk to you next week. Give Deborah my love."

"Elena, too. And Tori…thank you."

"You're my best friend in the world."

"Okay, bye," Sharon said and kissed into the phone.

Tori put the phone down on the table and stared blankly across the patio. A wave of emptiness washed over her at the thought of leaving all this behind. It had only been a year and half or so since she had inherited it all, but in that short period her whole life had transformed. She felt settled, at home and complete in her life in a way she had never experienced before now. Could she walk away from all this? Was this physical place—Logan, her ranch, the desert—so central to her experience that to leave it would mean leaving her sense of satisfaction? Or was it all, or mostly, tied up in Elena? She had walked away from dozens of projects and developments in her life, things into which she had put her talent, energy, creativity and passion. Maybe she could walk away from Sandy Creek Ranch in the same way, or at least try to, if necessary. Maybe not, though. Maybe it would tear her heart out.

She rubbed her eyes, took a deep breath and stood up. She would just have to talk it over with Elena. They would figure it out together.

Elena stood aside as Sofia Diaz helped her mother, Urleen, slide into the booth by the window at the cafe. The lunch crowd was gone, except for a husband and wife team of truck drivers who stopped in every week during their run from El Paso to Beaumont and back. They sat at their usual table against the back wall. A pile of papers and receipts were spread out in front of them, and the wife looked over her reading glasses into the laptop screen as she typed. They used Galindo's as their bi-weekly office space, so to speak. Elena always saw to it that the wait staff kept their drinks filled throughout their working afternoons and sent them off with to-go boxes for the road.

Sofia slid into the booth next to her mother. Elena stood beside the table looking down at them. Urleen wore a turquoise house-dress with a white scarf draped around her shoulders that she used while outdoors to shade her head and face from the sun. Her weathered skin was brown and dry. Sofia had her mother's dark eyes and high cheekbones, but the gray tinge in her pulled back hair was covered by a rusty red tint instead of the jet black dye that colored her mother's hair. Long, jangling earrings hung from her ears and several rings glittered on her fingers. Her capri pants matched her mother's housedress, and her pink blouse matched the flush in her cheeks and the gloss on her lips.

"What would you both like to drink or eat?" Elena asked, smiling. "We still have our lunch menu items on the stove, if you're hungry."

Sofia smiled and looked at her mother. "Mama, do you want something?" she asked the old women, speaking a bit loudly and slowly. Urleen looked at Sofia, listening intently and following the movement of her daughter's lips as she spoke. She nodded when Sofia finished speaking and looked up at Elena.

"*Tres leches* and Nescafé, please," she said, her voice quiet but steady. Her watery eyes blinked and she sat back in the booth with her hands folded across her lap.

"Do you have that?" Sofia asked Elena in a voice too soft for her mother to hear.

"Of course," Elena said to Urleen after winking in acknowledgment to Sofia. "Shall I bring two?" she looked at Sofia, who broke into a wide smile.

"Sure," she said. "Thank you."

Elena left them and returned to the kitchen. She had no idea why they had wanted to meet with her. Sofia had called the day before and asked to bring her mother over to "talk about some things." Elena assumed it had to do with the café, but beyond that she had no idea. Things had done well—spectacularly well, in fact—with the restaurant ever since she had begun to manage it not long after she returned to Logan over a year and a half ago. Initially, Urleen Galindo was paying her only a token amount to run the restaurant, which was fine with Elena. At the end of the year, though, Sofia had come in bearing a sizeable bonus check written in Urleen's scrawling, aged handwriting. "Mother is so happy that the café is doing so well," Sofia had said. "She knows it's all because of you." Sofia had dropped off bonus checks every few months ever since then, all written in her mother's handwriting and with a tiny orange post-it note stuck on them that said *"Gracias."*

She gathered the two desserts, flatware, and three coffee mugs filled with boiling water onto a serving tray. She served brewed coffee in the restaurant, but kept jars of Nescafé for the older customers and a few others who preferred it. She grabbed a large jar of the dark granules, plunked it onto the middle of the tray and walked back out with it all to the women at the booth.

"Look, Mama! This looks so good," Sofia exclaimed as Elena sat the tray on the edge of the booth and began unloading it onto the table. The old woman smiled, unfolded her hands and held them aloft above the table as the dessert and coffee mug were placed in front of her. Elena sat down across from them, opened the Nescafe jar and slid it across the table to Urleen. The old woman dug her spoon down into the dried coffee grounds and carefully lifted a delicate heap of them into her mug, slowly stirring it into the hot war. Elena watched her and smiled when, after a moment, she dug another spoonful out and dissolved it into her cup. She sat back and smiled back at Elena, who then slid the coffee container to Sofia.

Elena prepared her own coffee as the two women began eating their desserts. Sofia chatted about her grandkids and a recent camping trip they had taken to a wilderness area near the Llano River. She bragged on their preschool exploits and how the oldest one was "gifted and talented" in several elementary school subjects. Elena listened politely and asked questions when appropriate, to keep the conversation going. She stirred her coffee, waiting for it to cool so she would not burn her tongue for the second time that day.

Urleen ate slowly while Sofia talked, and put her fork down after she finished half her dessert. She sat back and looked at Elena. When Sofia finished her sentence about the youngest grandchild being in the top percentile of toddlers who could feed themselves, Urleen spoke to change the subject.

"I want to talk to you about the restaurant," she said plainly, looking directly into Elena eyes.

"Of course," Elena said, nodding and taking a sip of her coffee. "I assumed as much when Sofia called yesterday."

Sofia looked at her mother and then down at her own empty dessert plate. She had managed to eat all of it, even while talking. She fingered a drizzle of milky sauce on the plate, popped it into her mouth, and looked back at her mother.

"You have done a good job with the restaurant," Urleen said. "You remind me of myself when I was young." She swallowed and placed one hand on the edge of the table, as if to steady herself from the very act of speaking.

"Thank you," Elena said. "I've been pleased with how business has grown here in the last year or so." She looked at Sofia and back at Urleen, smiling and waiting.

Sofia looked at her mother, who had reached for a napkin and was slowly and deliberately wiping her mouth with it. Sofia looked back at Elena.

"Things in our family are changing," Sofia said. "My daughter's husband has a great new job in El Paso and they're moving there the end of the month." She glanced back at her mother, who was sitting still now with her hands in her lap, staring at Elena.

"Well, my husband and I, you know, we're retired and Mama lives with us," she continued, smiling at her mother and then looked back at Elena. "And we just love those grandbabies so much and can't stand the thought of them being so far away from us out in El Paso." She looked back at her mother, as if waiting for the old woman to pick up the conversation.

Urleen looked directly at Elena. "I would like to sell Galindo's to you, Elena Rios," she said softly but matter-of-factly, as if there were no question implied in her words, just a simple statement of fact and eventuality.

Elena felt her stomach lurch. She swallowed the mouthful of coffee she had just sipped and sat the mug down on the table quietly. She placed her hand on the table beside it and looked first into Sofia's face and then into Urleen's dark watery eyes.

"I am honored that you say that, ma'am," she said. "Very honored. This restaurant has been in your family and borne your name for a long time."

Urleen nodded slightly and smiled. "Yes, we've had it a long time. It's almost, how do you say it…an *institution* in Logan." She paused for a moment. Just as Sofia was about to speak, Urleen continued. "But, it was going down until you came. And now, we are leaving and it is right for you to have it."

Elena had not thought about buying Galindo's, although now that the idea was presented to her, it made a certain sense. She had spent only minimal time there on a daily basis in the last months, or even year. She went there mainly to interact with customers and to keep tabs on things, but the daily operations went along smoothly without her being there every open hour. She had thought about proposing a more formal relationship between the ranch and Galindo's—maybe some kind of partnership that involved meals at Galindo's as part of an all-inclusive package for Sandy Creek Ranch customers. But, she had not sketched it out enough, or talked it over with Tori enough to actually propose it. The thought of buying it outright had not occurred to her, especially lately in the wake of the incidents with the animal carcasses. Only when that was solved—if it were ever solved—would she think of taking on another business responsibility besides the ranch in Logan. For all she knew, she would have to walk away from the one she already had if Logan could not deal with two lesbians owning it.

"You all are moving to El Paso to be with your children and their family?" Elena asked.

Sofia nodded. "Yes. We want to stay close to them, and my daughter needs help with the kids. They are excited to move to a bigger city with more things to do, more opportunities…you know, for them and for the kids. They both have been here their whole lives."

Elena listened and was quiet. She looked at both women, especially at Urleen who had not taken her eyes off Elena's since she had first said that Elena should have Galindo's.

"Not trying to pry, but just out of curiosity, what will you do if I don't buy it from you?" she asked.

The old woman took a deep breath but did not move her eyes from Elena's. "We may try to sell it to someone else, or else just close it down for good, but…*mija*, you should buy it. It is right for you to have it."

Elena's throat tightened as she heard Urleen call her by the endearment her own mother had always used for her. She dropped her eyes and brought her hand to her face to push a stray strand of hair back across her head.

"You have done well since you came back, even with Gloria's illness. This is your home. You should stay here now," Urleen said. She spoke in soft, commanding tones that belied her seeming frailty. As she spoke, she seemed to gain clarity and focus. "You should have your life here now with your business," she said. "You and your friend."

Elena looked up at Urleen at the mention of her "friend." Did she mean Tori? Or was she thinking of Luis? So many in the town, she figured, still expected her and Luis to eventually be together.

"The ranch has done really well, hasn't it?" Sofia asked. "You two have done such a good job. Everyone says so." She paused for a moment. "Maybe Galindo's could be an extension of the ranch there somehow…I don't know. You could talk to your friend about it—Tori, right? That's her name, isn't it?"

Elena nodded and smiled faintly. "I could talk with her about it." She took another sip of coffee, trying to settle herself and stay focused on the business of the conversation instead of the emotion she was suddenly feeling.

"You have made Galindo's a success again, like in the old days," Urleen said. "We will sell it to you for a low price. You have already earned the right to own it."

"Our family lawyer is in Stockdale. He will send you the proposal and the other forms," Sofia said. "We already told him that we wanted you to buy it, so the materials are ready. I just need to call him to tell him you are interested."

Elena looked into their eyes and swallowed. "Okay…well, I'll certainly be glad to look it over. Thank you again for thinking of me. It's an honor, really." She stretched her hand out to Urleen across the table. The old woman touched her fingers to hers and Elena felt the warm, thin skin of the woman's hand.

Urleen smiled broadly and her eyes brightened. "Did you make this *tres leches* yourself?"

Elena smiled and shook her head. "No, but it's my recipe. I taught the staff to make it."

"It's very good. It's like I used to make." Urleen smiled and looked at Sofia, indicating that it was time to leave.

Elena walked them out to their car in the parking lot and shook Urleen's hand again as she settled herself in the passenger side of the car.

"Thank you for coming over, Ms. Galindo," she said. "And for your offer."

"You will see the offer soon. It's a good one," she replied, pulling the heavy door shut. She waved a frail hand and watched Sofia round the front of the car toward the driver's side.

"Thanks for the coffee and dessert," she said. "We'll talk again soon."

"Sure," Elena said. "I look forward to it."

She stood in the parking lot and watched them drive out onto the main road and glide away. She put her hands on her hips and took a deep breath, held it and let it out. She looked at her watch. It was almost time to go to the ranch to get ready for the evening's dinner service. Letty would already be there.

She pulled her phone from her back pocket as she walked back into the restaurant. She typed a text message to Tori. *Leaving Galindo's soon. I have news for us to talk about. xox*

❦

Elena walked across the ranch patio, past the jacuzzi and out onto the desert ground. She meandered down the path that led to the edge of the gorge. What had been an animal trail was now a tended, widened path of crushed granite. Tori had hated doing away with the animal trail—it had been one of the first intimate details of her land that she had come to love—but something better was needed for guests and visitors to walk down to the gorge to enter the trail that now ran along its sandy bottom. Elena looked ahead and saw Tori sitting on a bench underneath one of several sunshade structures Luis, Ricardo and Dustin had built along the length of the gorge's rim near the exit and entrance stairs to the trail. The sun was an hour or more from setting, but its heat and glare were still enough to warrant shade if it were available.

Elena stopped in the path for moment to watch Tori. She sat with her back to Elena and the hotel, facing the gorge to the south. Her arms stretched out and rested across the back of the bench, and her legs were straightened and crossed in front of her. She wore sunglasses and the breeze tousled her auburn hair. She turned her head slightly to the west and Elena saw her distinct profile—the strong jawline and chin, the straight nose and the high forehead. She felt her insides grow warm and fluid as she watched her. Tori just sat there, doing nothing but watching the sun and the living desert all around her, but her simple presence—the very fact that she existed in the world, and in Elena's world—created a shudder deep inside Elena. She felt it and knew that her love for Tori caused it, and that she would do whatever was in her power to never live without this woman in her life. If they had to leave Logan, they would.

She took a deep breath and stepped forward on the path. Tori heard her and turned to see her. Her face opened into a smile.

"Hey, you," she said, taking off her sunglasses as Elena stepped forward from the path to the bench. Elena removed her own sunglasses, grabbed Tori's outstretched hand, and bent down to kiss her.

Tori smiled into Elena's lips. "I missed you today," she said.

"Me, too," Elena said, sitting down beside her and throwing one leg over Tori's. Tori kept one arm stretched on the bench behind Elena and ran her fingers lightly over her neck and shoulders and through her dangling ponytail.

"Is everything okay out here?" Elena asked.

"Yeah, I was just sitting out here enjoying the weather," she replied with a chuckle. "It's actually nice under this shade with the breeze blowing."

Elena looked around her, as if to take in the climate and nodded. "It's always so quiet," she said. "That's what I like about it."

"Me, too."

They sat for a moment, holding each other, enjoying each other's presence amidst the silence, allowing the dry air to brush and cool their skin, and rustle their sleeves and pants' legs.

"Is anyone down there?" Elena asked, sitting up a bit to peer down into the gorge.

"I don't think so. I think a few of them hiked around earlier this afternoon, but they're already back and in the pool." Tori put her sunglasses back on and leaned back against the bench. She looked at Elena. "So, what's your news? What happened?"

Elena took a deep breath and blew it out. "Well, I told you that Sofia called yesterday to say her mother wanted to come by the café today, right?"

"Yeah."

"So, they both came by after the lunch service and we had coffee and dessert." She paused for a moment, and put her sunglasses on top of her head. "Urleen wants me to buy Galindo's from her. She is moving to El Paso with Sofia and their family, to stay close to their kids and grandkids. Their family lawyer is sending me the proposal and other paperwork." She looked and Tori and raised her eyebrows.

"Wow! Well…that's definitely *news!*" Tori said, taking her sunglasses off again and putting them on her head. She looked into Elena's eyes. "How do you feel? What do you think about it?"

Elena shrugged a bit. "I'm not exactly sure," she said. "Well, I take that back," she added hastily. "I think it makes a certain kind of sense, if things stay the way they've been for us here."

"What do you mean?"

"I mean, I'd thought about not so much buying it outright, but about incorporating it more officially into the offerings of the ranch—sort of like a formal partnership or something—so that we could offer service at Galindo's as part of the price of a stay at the ranch. Sort of our in-town partner, if you will. Buying it outright would certainly accomplish that, and more." She became animated as she spoke and explained her idea, loosening her grip on Tori's hands so her hands and arms were free to enhance her words. Tori smiled slightly as she watched and listened.

Tori nodded. "That sounds like a workable idea. Even without that, though, it could be a good idea—to just own it on its own regardless of any relation it had to the ranch." She mindlessly ran her thumb across Elena's shoulder blade. "You could do completely what you wanted with it, even more than you do now."

Elena looked at her and nodded, then looked back out at the gorge. They were silent for a moment.

"Do you know how much she wants for it?"

Elena shook her head. "She says she'll sell it to me for a low price. That it was going down before I came and that in bringing it back I've earned the right to own it." She looked at Tori and then turned back to the gorge. "It was an interesting conversation. I've not talked to her very much before, just on a few occasions. But, she became very focused on me, very…I don't know…almost like an aunt or my mother or something."

Tori furrowed her brow. "What do you mean?"

"She said I'd done well here in Logan and that I should stay here—that this is my home and I should stay here and run my business." She turned to Tori. "Actually, she said that about both of us."

"She mentioned *me*?" Tori asked incredulously. "I don't think I've ever met her."

"She said 'Elena, you and your friend should stay here'," Elena explained. "Well, she didn't say *Elena*. She called me *mija*." Elena stopped talking and stared out at the gorge. Tori saw her swallow and blink her eyes a few times.

"Like Gloria," she said quietly. Elena nodded and Tori grabbed her hand again. They sat for a moment in silence.

"It sounds like she's already decided that you're the one," Tori said after a little while. "What do you mean about things staying the way they are here for us?"

Elena turned and looked at her blankly, as if returning to Tori and her presence beside her from a long distance. Her own comment from a moment ago came back to her within a few seconds, and her face grew somber.

"I mean that if things continue on with us and the ranch as they have in this first year of operations." She paused for a moment. "I mean if this dead animal thing doesn't drive us out of town."

Tori leaned her head back over the back of the bench and sighed deeply. She rubbed her eyes and rested her hand on her forehead.

"It's been in the back of my mind for a few weeks now, even though there've been no new incidents," Elena said.

"Yeah…mine, too." Tori lowered her hand and raised her head back upright. She stared out at the gorge. "I talked to Sharon this morning and she mentioned it."

Elena turned to her. "Yeah? How's she doing? What did she say?"

"We didn't talk about it very much—just at the end of our conversation before we hung up. She had asked me if I trusted the sheriff and the job he was doing. I told her I did. And then we talked about other stuff, things going on with her. At the end, she said for us to move to Houston if things didn't get resolved here."

"What did you say to that?"

"I told her I understood her point, and that you and I needed to talk about it." She turned to look at Elena.

"That would break your heart, wouldn't it," Elena said.

Tori looked out at the gorge. Her mouth was slightly open, but her face was placid, almost blank. "Yeah, pretty much," she said quietly, but definitively. "But, if it's what we have to do, then we do it. That was Sharon's point. Let's see...her exact words were that we aren't *obligated to stay out here and carry the rainbow flag*."

Elena chuckled. "That sounds like something she would say." She rubbed the backs of her fingers against the soft fabric of Tori's t-shirt between her breasts. "She loves you a lot."

Tori nodded. "She doesn't want us to get hurt out here. She'd love it if we moved to Houston. She said for me to come back, bring you with me and make another big pile of money." She grinned along with Elena as she said this, thinking of her friend.

"She and Deborah are going on a cruise with Deborah's mother and aunt," Tori added.

"What?! That doesn't sound like a Sharon thing to do."

"It's not—at least, not typically. Sharon's never really been serious about anyone, at least in the ten years I've known her. But...she's serious about this. She says she's in love with her." She turned to Elena and smiled.

"Well, whaddaya know." Elena said. "Good for her. Is Deborah in love with her?"

"She says so."

Elena smiled. "Good for them."

Tori nodded and grinned. "I think it's great. I'm really happy for her. Of course, I had to tease her about it, going on a cruise with the mother and the aunt, like it was some sort of Disney family affair or something."

Elena laughed and slapped the side of Tori's leg with her own that was draped across Tori's. "That's terrible!"

They sat quietly for a little while, thinking and reflecting on all they had said. The sun had moved further down in the western sky to their right and they could feel it warming their cheeks and arms exposed to its rich golden pre-dusk rays.

"I just want to be with you, no matter where we are," Tori said finally. "I mean, I'll grieve to leave all this out here. It'll hurt." She took a deep breath. "But, my life is with you. Wherever that is."

Elena leaned over and kissed her. When she pulled back, she took Tori's hand in her own and looked into her eyes. "I've left Logan before, I can leave it again—as long as we're together."

Tori sat back and sighed. Her face was tight and pale. "I really hope we don't have to leave. Maybe this will get resolved. They'll find who's doing this and it'll be over."

Elena nodded.

Tori looked off across the gorge for a moment and then pulled her phone from her back pocket. She looked at it and back at Elena.

"It's that time."

"Customers await." Elena stood up and held out her hand. Tori grabbed it and they walked back up the path to the hotel.

# Chapter Twenty

Elena slammed on the brakes and threw her arm out unconsciously across Tori in the passenger seat. Her truck skidded in a straight line on the hot asphalt, slowing just enough for the antelope to race across the road in front of the vehicle. She lifted her foot off the brake and they coasted down the highway at a low speed until they caught their breath.

"Good Lord…" Tori said, after a few seconds. "That was close."

"No kidding," Elena said, putting her hand to her heart as if to still it.

"I didn't see it at all before we were right on top of it."

Elena shook her head. "Me either." She pulled the seat belt out and repositioned it across her midsection. She rubbed her chest a bit where it had locked into place when she hit her brakes. She accelerated the truck and continued down the highway to the sheriff's office just a few miles out of town on the main road between Logan and Stockdale.

"I wonder why he wanted us to drive my truck instead of your car," Elena said after a few moments.

"I don't know," Tori said. "He didn't give any clues when you talked to him?"

Elena shook her head. "None at all. He just said for us to come see him in the office and to drive my truck. That he had an idea he wanted to talk over with us. And to not say anything to anybody."

"Well, we'll see."

Ten minutes later they walked up to the entrance of the beige stone building. A big star with the state of Texas in it was mounted on the rock wall above a landscaped rock bed dotted with labeled cactus plants. A blast of cold air hit them as they pulled open the glass doors and stepped into the lobby.

"We're here to see Sheriff Banks," Elena said to the receptionist, a plump middle- aged woman with frosted hair.

"Okay, what are your names, please?" the woman asked. She smiled up at Elena.

"Elena Rios and Tori Reed from Logan. He called yesterday and asked us to come over this morning."

"That's right—I remember him telling me," she said. "Let me buzz him."

They waited in the lobby, standing on the shiny linoleum floor. In a few minutes, Sheriff Banks appeared through a gray metal door.

"How're you two doin'?" he said as he stuck his hand out to each one of them. "Glad to see ya'll." He smiled widely and looked at each of them directly in their eyes as he shook their hands and they all greeted one other. They stepped from the lobby into a hallway as he held the gray metal door open for them. He closed the door, stepped ahead of them and they followed him down the hallway to the last office on the left. He stood aside and motioned them inside to sit in two dark leather chairs in front of his desk.

"Can I get ya'll anything to drink? Coffee or water or cokes or something?" he asked as he walked around to the side of his desk to face them.

"Water would be great, " Elena said.

"Me, too," Tori said, smiling.

"Alright. I'll have Barbara bring some in to ya'll. I'll be right back. I need to get something to show you." He left the office and within a minute the receptionist walked in with two chilled bottles of water wrapped in paper towels. She sat the bottles down on the sheriff's desk in front of them. She nodded and smiled when they thanked her, and hurried out of the office.

"He likes to hunt, I guess," Tori said, bringing the bottle to her mouth and nodding toward several deer and antelope heads mounted on the walls around the office.

"Looks like it," Elena said, swallowing a mouthful of water. "I wonder if he hunts birds? We already had him for dinner. We could invite him out to hunt, too. You know, grease the wheels."

Tori nodded, and then they sat quietly.

Sheriff Banks returned and sat down at his desk across from them. He placed a cardboard box in front of him on the desk. He sat back in his chair, smiled and sighed.

"So, I guess there haven't been any more incidents, right?" he said, rocking a bit in his chair.

They shook their heads. "No, not since the night of the basketball game," Tori said.

"That's been over two weeks ago," the sheriff said in a way that seemed to both confirm his memory and also state the facts of the case.

They nodded. He nodded back at them.

"How are ya'll holdin' up?" he asked.

They looked at each other and then back at him. "I think we're okay," Tori said simply.

"It's scary sometimes," Elena said, "But I try not to think about it or dwell on it."

"We don't do things by ourselves much lately. We're together or with other people," Tori said.

"I just wish we could find out who did it and resolve it one way or the other," Elena said, folding her arms across her abdomen.

"Alrighty then. On that note, I've got a plan I want to talk to you about. Here's my thinking on this." He leaned forward, rested his forearms on the desk and clasped his hands together. He looked at them directly, paused a moment and then continued.

"This may be just a prankster or someone who had a beef with you all who's played out. You know, they made their point, expressed themselves or what have you, and now they've moved on and we'll have no more instances. And if we do, the cameras would most likely catch 'em and we'd be able to make an arrest. So, from now until then—if and when another incident happens, which it might not—we just proceed as we've been. Go on with life."

They nodded, listening intently. He paused, rubbed his forehead briskly for a second, and put his hand back on the desk.

"But, here's my thought: I have a hunch about this, and I want to try something to see if we can push this person out into the open one more time. Get one more incident to happen and see if we can get it on camera." He looked down at the box on the desk in front of him and began to open it. He opened the lid, set aside the documentation and instructions, turned it around and nudged it toward them for their inspection. A tiny square box about the size of a book of tear-off matches sat in its indented foam slot next to a thin, neatly coiled power cord.

"This is a little night vision camera I'd like to install in your vehicle, Elena. It can run on the cigarette lighter and clip up onto the sun visor or someplace. It's activated by motion. It's got a wireless signal that we can monitor from our computers. Lonnie can set it up so that we get a nice wide-angle view of the entire front of the vehicle and part of the sides. That way, if somebody steps near the vehicle and throws a carcass up on the windshield like they did Tori's car, we'd get 'em on camera." He sat back in his chair and began to rock again.

"Why my truck instead of Tori's car?"

"Well, like I said, I have a hunch about this and I think your truck might give us a better shot." He smiled and continued to rock.

"Do you have an idea who's doing this?" Tori asked.

He looked at her and registered her question only by continuing to rock.

"I'll keep to my own counsel for now, with your permission. I *will* say that I have a theory about it, and I want to try this out to see if my theory's right." He stopped rocking and leaned forward on the desk again suddenly. "Here's the thing though. Two things actually. I don't want you to say anything to anybody about this. No one. No one at all. Just keep it between you two, and me and Lonnie. Okay?"

They both nodded. "What's the second thing?" Elena asked.

He looked at her. "You put cameras at your house, right? Around the front and the back?"

She nodded.

"But not at Galindo's—only at the ranch, at the cabin and at your house, right?"

They both nodded again.

"Okay, well, I want you to park your truck overnight behind Galindo's for a few nights. Enough for you to establish it as a pattern for anyone who's watching. You normally park in the front, right?"

"Yes, if I drive at all. Often I walk from my house," Elena said. "So, just park there by the back loading door?"

"No, back away from the building a bit—toward the back of that gravel area. By the dumpster." He sat back again. "Just start parking back there for a while instead of in the front, and then leave it there when you leave the cafe. Get Tori or someone to give you a ride home or to the ranch or what have you. Just for a few days."

They were all silent for a moment. Tori wanted to press the sheriff on his theory, but decided against it.

"Try it this week. Leave your truck at Galindo's a few nights, on and off. Let's see if anything happens. If not, we haven't lost anything." He waited for any comments or questions from them.

"Okay, well, that sounds easy enough," Elena said, looking at Tori and then back at the sheriff.

"Sure, no problem," Tori added.

"Good," he said, swiveling in his chair to peer out his office window into the parking lot. "I see Lonnie's car, so he's here. Let's get him to install this camera." He grabbed the box, put everything back inside, closed it and got up. They stood when he did and followed him out and down the hallway to the lobby.

"I think it's probably just some crank who's doing it," Ken said with a note of disgust in his voice. He scraped up the last bite of cake from his plate, put it in his mouth, and pushed the plate aside. He wadded his napkin up and tossed it to the side. He looked at Tori with eyes fierce and intense.

Tori sat back in the booth at Galindo's with her arms crossed over her chest. She nodded slowly.

"You may be right, Ken. Whoever it is, though, is still out there." She looked out the window onto the parking lot and the road. Only a few cars remained in the lot even though it had been nearly full an hour ago when she had driven up to meet Ken for lunch. This was her third time eating lunch at Galindo's in the last week since their meeting with Sheriff Banks. She would eat lunch, hang out at the restaurant, work on her laptop, then she and Elena would drive to the ranch or to the cabin, leaving Elena's truck in the back parking lot with its camera ready to capture any activity. Nothing had happened for it to capture so far, except for a stray cat jumping onto the hood of Elena's truck the first night and sprawling out to bathe itself for a half-hour before bounding off into the darkness.

"Part of me is glad nothing more has happened in the last three weeks, but another part of me wishes something would happen so maybe there could be a chance at catching whoever's doing it," she said. "I mean, I hate just going along with it in the back of my mind all the time." She looked back at Ken.

"Does the sheriff have any ideas?"

Tori shrugged. She didn't want to break her promise to not tell anyone about the camera in Elena's truck even though she was sure Ken was safe to tell. "He's hoping he still might be able to get something on one of the cameras," she said. "It's only been a few weeks since the last incident, so..." she trailed off.

They were silent as they both sipped their coffee. Ken's face was drawn and Tori sensed that he took this personally, not only for her sake, but also because of his son.

"Just seems like there oughta be more they could do to find out who it is," he said. He looked up at her. "You know? I mean, do you just have to wait to see how far they'll go? Wait to catch them in the act?" Tori heard the frustration in his voice, but his questions were rhetorical. Of course, there *was* really nothing else to do but try to catch the person in the act. The camera in Elena's truck would hopefully do exactly that, but she could not say anything about that right now to make Ken feel any better.

"It's frustrating," she said and looked back out onto the road. "It's not a situation I want to have to deal with indefinitely."

"What'll you do if they don't catch anyone?"

Tori took a deep breath and looked at Ken. His eyes were as kind and earnest as they had been the first time she met him out at the run-down hotel a year and a half ago. She loved him and hated the thought of leaving him and all the people and things that had become her life in Logan.

"I'm not sure…Elena and I've talked about it some." She grabbed the handle on her coffee cup and turned the cup in its place slightly. "We talked about just selling out and going to back to Houston, if it comes to that."

Ken sat back and sighed. He shook his head and looked out the window. "God, I'd sure hate that," he said after a moment. "So many people would hate that."

"We'd hate it too. I love it out here," she said. "And I love the people out here, especially you and Hazel." She smiled weakly. "But, I don't want to live somewhere where I'm going to be afraid all the time, or worried about being harassed for being who I am."

"I understand."

"I'm not someone who walks around advertising my sexuality to people, but I expect to be respected and allowed the freedom to live my life the way I want to. I'm a good person, a good citizen and a good neighbor. That should be enough for people, I think. But, if it's not, then I have to make a choice."

"I don't blame you," he said simply. "I still hate it."

"Yeah, me too," she said softly. They both stared blankly out the window and were silent again. After a moment, a Sandy Creek Ranch truck pulled into the parking lot. Luis, Ricardo, and Dustin got out and walked into the restaurant. Tori watched them as they took a seat at a table on the opposite wall. Luis nodded a greeting to her as he sat down, then looked away. She smiled at him and also at Dustin and Ricardo who had turned to see her when they saw Luis nod in her direction. Ricardo sat down, but Dustin put his hat down and began walking over to her.

"Hey," he said to her, standing at the table in a ranch shirt, jeans and boots. His sunglasses hung on a lanyard around his neck. "Hello Mr. Honeycutt," he said, extending his hand to grasp Ken's. Ken grabbed his hand and pumped it, smiling up at him.

"What are ya'll up to?" Tori asked, smiling up at him.

"We're just having a late lunch. We've been out on the southwest corner checking the windmills and also the food plots. Luis said he thought maybe the deer ate all the winter grain plots we planted for the quail, but it looks like they're okay. We didn't see a lot of deer tracks around them." He spoke excitedly and seemed eager to continue with the details of the morning.

"These food plots, these are plans he got from the state wildlife management people, right?" she asked.

Dustin nodded. "The guy came out a few weeks ago and went with us on a check of some of the plots. He wasn't sure a lot of them would grow in a desert climate, but we kept them pumped and watered and it seems like it worked."

"Well, that's good," she said, smiling. "We gotta have quail— fat ones."

Ken laughed and took another sip of coffee. At that moment, Elena emerged through the swinging kitchen doors into the dining room, followed by another staff person who stepped over to the table where Luis and Ricardo sat. She smiled at Tori, Dustin and Ken as she walked toward them dousing a tea bag up and down in the mug she held.

"Hey everybody!" she said, sitting the mug down onto the table and scooting into the booth beside Tori.

"We're just having coffee and hearing about the quail habitat out on the ranch," Tori said. "Dustin here's become quite the expert in winter quail food plots. He assures us that there'll be plenty of quail for dinner service at the restaurant—both here and at the ranch—once the season starts this fall." Elena nodded approvingly and looked up at Dustin.

"I'm very impressed," she said, only half teasing. "Who knew we had a quail expert on our hands?"

Dustin grinned and shook his head. "Whatever…" He looked back toward Luis and Ricardo at their table. Their heads were buried in menus. He looked back at Tori and Elena. "Well, good talking to ya'll. I'm going to go order lunch. Will you be at the ranch later?"

They both nodded and watched him walk back to his table after he said goodbye to Ken.

"Nice kid," Ken said.

"Yeah, really nice," Tori agreed. "He and Jared both."

"The two of them and Letty," Elena added. "Thank God for them. I mean, all our people are good, but those three are the core."

They sat and talked for a little while, each of them finishing their coffee or tea, enjoying each other's company and easy friendship.

"I sure hope this thing gets resolved with whoever's leaving these animals around everywhere," Ken said to Elena after a while.

"Me, too," she said, looking at Ken and then at Tori. She braced her head in her hand, propped on an elbow.

"Ken and I were talking about it earlier," Tori said. "About what the plan is if they don't end up catching anyone."

Elena looked at Ken, sighed and raised her eyebrows. "I don't know…" She was quiet for a moment. "It's a hard decision. And it's not something to decide in a hasty way…we've worked too hard to build the ranch and all to just walk away from it in a hurry. But, it's like I told Tori—I've left Logan before and I can leave it again. It was a hard decision then, too, but…" She shrugged again and fingered the string on the teabag in her mug.

"Well, maybe something'll turn up here soon," Ken said loudly and definitively, as if willing something concrete to happen. "Let's just see how it works out and hope for the best." He looked at his watch and put his hands flat on the table. "I gotta get going. Hazel's waitin' on me to take her to Stockdale to get some new shelves for the crafts store."

They said goodbye to Ken, and Tori waited in the dining room while Elena finished up in the kitchen and got her stuff from her kitchen office. Tori ambled over to the table where Luis, Ricardo and Dustin sat.

"Dustin told you about the food plots, huh?" Ricardo said, wiping his mouth with his napkin as she walked up. She nodded, smiling.

"It's really good if we can be successful doing that out here in a more desert climate. Usually, the food plot thing is done in more wooded areas." *He's become an expert, too,* she thought, smiling at his excitement.

"Well, this is good to know," she said, trying to match and honor their enthusiasm. "We definitely need systems to manage and preserve the quail population in a way that supports the business, so this is all good news." She looked at Luis, who sat sideways in the booth with his back against the wall. He had finished his food and was drinking a cup of coffee.

He looked at her and nodded. "The state wildlife guy says that if we have them do the counts for us, and the numbers are good, they could do a white paper with us as the case study and put it on the state website." He reached over and grabbed one of the last chips from the basket, dunked it in the salsa and put the whole thing in his mouth. He looked back at Tori, chewing.

"That's great, Luis," she said. "Really great." She had grown accustomed in the last month to being cordial to Luis, despite the tension she felt. Since he had come back from his vacation, he had been cool to her and somewhat evasive. He did not hang around at the ranch as much as he used to, before Elena told him about her and Tori. But, he had done his job as well as he always had, and had been professional in his behavior toward them. He simply avoided them a good deal of the time.

Elena appeared through the swinging doors again holding her sunglasses and with her big purse slung across her chest and shoulder. She walked toward them all at the table.

"So, are ya'll coming back to the ranch after this?" she asked. "Betty says reservations are almost full for dinner tonight. Are you on?" She looked at Dustin.

He nodded. They all nodded.

"We're going back out to check the water hole and windmill in the south/southeast section," Luis said. "Me and Ricardo." He looked at Dustin. "This other one here's gotta go home and get cleaned up to change into his fancy dinner clothes." Tori detected a hint of teasing and mischief in Luis' eyes, and felt a spark of gladness that at least he was making a joke of some sort in her presence.

"Okay, well, we're taking off," Elena said. "See you over there." They started out the door and Elena stopped. "Wait…let me make sure I have my keys." She fished around in her purse until she found them. She looked at Tori. "Pick me up around back? I wanna make sure I locked my truck before we leave."

"No problem," Tori said. Elena disappeared back through the swinging doors. "See you guys in a little while," she said, and then stepped out into the parking lot.

The restaurant ended up being filled to capacity. What few tables not taken by advanced reservations or by hotel guests were snapped up by walk-ins almost as soon as dinner service opened. Elena and Letty managed the kitchen while Tori helped Betty seat and greet everyone. The crowd was the usual mixed bag of customers—hotel guests from out of state dazzled by the exotic desert and the rugged expanse of West Texas, Logan locals who liked a nice meal out for a birthday or anniversary, drive-ins from Stockdale and the surrounding area who appreciated a restaurant of such quality out in the middle of nowhere, and friends and family members of the ranch staff who came to support their loved one and to take advantage of the employee family discount.

Elena and Tori moved among them all with a casual elegance that fit the entire motif of Sandy Creek Ranch. Tori walked among the tables holding a wine glass or a sparkling water, saying hello and introducing herself to customers. She asked after family members, jobs, school, grandchildren and whatever else she remembered from the last time they visited the restaurant. She brushed her hair back with her fingers and stood with her hand on her hip listening to their stories. She looked compassionately into their eyes and touched their shoulders when they told of an aging parent or a sick relative. She wore black linen pants and a cream linen blouse that hung loosely on her tallish, slim frame and made her auburn hair seem, in contrast, even richer in color than it usually did. She was at ease and in her element, engaging people, seeing to their needs, making sure they enjoyed more than just the food.

Only Elena, emerging from the kitchen periodically to talk to specific guests, rivaled Tori in natural grace in the dining room. She wore her standard uniform—dark jeans, a black t-shirt and her white chef coat, with her dark hair pulled tight into a ponytail. Her dark eyes gleamed as she laughed at guests' jokes or asked about their business or family. She knew many of the family members of the staff, and always gave them an extra bit of attention, sending out a bottle of wine or a special appetizer, something she insisted she was "trying out" and for which she needed to use them as guinea pigs.

Occasionally, the two of them stood together at a table talking to guests or off to the side, surveying the expanse of people and tables spaced across the dining room and out onto the patio. They checked in on people's reactions to certain dishes—a sauce, or spice level, or a particular dessert—and they made verbal notes with each other about things to change or repeat or never to do again. As the months had progressed, they had become fused as a team, reading each other's minds and finishing each other's sentences—alone just the two of them or standing together at a table with guests. People saw it, appreciated it and came to expect it. Their respective expertise in the operation was evident, as was their joy in doing their work and accomplishing their vision for the place.

It was nearly midnight when they walked along the gorge to the cabin after closing the restaurant. Guests had lingered after their meals out on the patio, enjoying visiting with their friends and feeling the dry breeze on their skin. The night sky grew gaudier with each passing hour, as more and more stars glittered from the black canopy above. The three-quarter moon shone clear and bright above them and lit the way along the gorge's rim. The moonlight bathed the desert in a gray paleness that enlivened the normal inky blackness of night. Tori had walked it so often, she thought she could walk it even in total darkness. She liked the way the moonlight kindled the desert stillness somewhat. It was as if the plants and rocks and animals were saying *we are here, living and real, even when you cannot see us.*

They entered the cabin through the back door and dumped their purses and briefcases onto the bar. They peeled off their clothes, Tori grabbed two towels from the bathroom and they went back out the patio door to the jacuzzi. They immersed themselves into the cool, bubbling water and eased their way to the sides to sit down.

"God, this feels good," Elena said, squeezing her leg muscles and holding each foot in turn against a jet. Tori agreed and sunk down in the water to her earlobes, moving her head from side to side, stretching her neck and shoulder muscles.

"At some point, maybe we won't have to work these late nights as much," Tori said, waving her arms back and forth in the water in front of her.

"Maybe," Elena said, bending her leg to massage her foot underwater. "We'd miss the customers, though."

"Yeah, I always think the night will go slowly, that I'll be counting the hours to get through the reservation list, but then I end up enjoying it so much I don't even feel the time pass."

"You even forget to eat, I've noticed lately," Elena said in a slightly scolding voice. "I sent that salad out to that one table—when you were sitting with the car dealer guy and his wife—and you got up to go to another table and didn't even eat it. The one you ate was a second one I sent out an hour later." She leaned her head back to peer at the glittering sky. "I think Dustin ate the first one you didn't eat."

"Good for him," Tori said, smiling as she bobbed up and down slightly in the water. "Thanks for thinking of me, though." She moved through the bubbling water and found Elena's hips under the water. They joined their bodies, enveloped by the warm water and the cool desert air. They held each other fiercely, surfing the sensations of their mingled pleasure and the caress of the water.

They dried themselves with the towels on the way up the loft stairs and fell into the bed naked. They wrapped themselves around each other and were barely able to kiss their goodnights before sleep grabbed them both and pulled them deep within itself for the night.

Neither of them stirred until Tori's phone rang on the bar downstairs just after daylight. Tori let it ring and go to voicemail, but then roused after a few minutes and went downstairs. She started the coffee pot and then grabbed her phone. She hit the button to return the call.

"Hi, Sheriff Banks? This is Tori Reed. I'm sorry I missed your call a moment ago."

"Ms. Reed, good morning. I hope I didn't wake you. I called Ms. Rios as well, but didn't get an answer."

"Not at all, not at all. And Elena's here with me." She looked up at Elena, who appeared at the top of the stairs and sat on the top step to listen. Tori turned the phone on speakerphone.

"Well, I thought you'd both want to know first thing that we got something on camera. Lonnie checked the feed early this morning when he came in off night patrol." He paused for a moment.

"I'll see the judge in a minute—I'm driving over to his house right now with an arrest warrant. Then I'll take a deputy with me to go make the arrest." Tori thought she heard his car police radio in the background.

"So, you have a clear identification? You know who it is?"

He sighed into the phone. "Yes ma'am. I do. It's clear who it is. The video is very clear."

"Is it someone we know?"

"Yes ma'am, I'm afraid so." He was quiet. Tori said nothing but instead waited for him to speak. She looked up at Elena on the stairs above her, who sat with her knees together and her arms folded across her abdomen.

Finally, the sheriff spoke. "It's Luis Palacios."

# Chapter Twenty-One

They drove silently in Tori's car down the highway toward the sheriff's station. Elena sat with her elbow propped on the window staring straight ahead behind dark sunglasses. She rested her head in her hand at a slight angle to ward off the glare of the mid-morning sun beaming in through the window. Tori stared out from behind her own dark glasses, her eyes locked on the road ahead, one hand in her lap and the other clenched onto the steering wheel.

Very few words had passed between them since Tori ended the call with Sheriff Banks. When he hung up, Tori had simply dropped her arm to her side and stood there naked in the kitchen looking up at Elena at the top of the stairwell. When the sheriff said Luis' name, Elena's mouth had slowly fallen open, and her face seemed to drain of life and color as she stared down at Tori. She looked into Tori's eyes, but Tori felt and saw the stunned blankness in her expression before she propped her elbows onto her knees and silently covered her face with her hands.

"He says we can come down there later this morning to discuss things. He'll be back at the station in an hour or two." Tori had said placidly, feeling whipsawed from shock. She watched Elena, who sat motionless on the stairs, and felt her stomach churn with dread and disbelief.

They had dressed in silence, and sat for a little while drinking coffee at the kitchen table before heading out. "I don't even know what to think," Elena had said quietly, staring out the kitchen window, her eyes fixed and emotionless.

"Me either," Tori said, looking over at Elena's face which now seemed gaunt and drawn.

They pulled into the station parking lot, parked and walked into the lobby. Barbara looked up from her desk and smiled. Without speaking, she buzzed the sheriff on the intercom. "He'll be out in just a minute," she said to them. "Ya'll need some coffee or anything?"

"No thanks," Tori said. Elena shook her head.

They waited near the large front window, standing beside a row of multicolored plastic chairs. After a moment, the gray metal door opened and Sheriff Banks motioned them into the hallway. They followed him to his office and sat down.

He sat down across the desk from them, looked at them and sighed. They looked at him blankly.

"Well, I wish it hadn't come to this, but…I'm glad we caught who's doing it anyway," he said, rubbing his forehead with his hand and then dropping his hand onto the desk. His eyes were kind and soft.

"What did he do?" Elena asked simply.

The sheriff turned to her and swallowed. "Well, what we caught on tape was him putting a carcass across the front hood of your truck at 2:18am," he said matter-of-factly. "After we made the arrest, Lonnie and another deputy went over to Galindo's to get pictures, gather evidence and whatnot." He paused for a moment. "It was a rattlesnake carcass. A long one. Stretched nearly the whole way across the hood. He laid it out real careful."

Tori and Elena listened transfixed, forcing themselves to take in and believe what seemed incredulous to them. Elena's face was slack, her lips together but teeth apart. Tori sat rigidly with one hand covering her mouth and the other arm crossed tightly over her abdomen.

Sheriff Banks sat still and watched them while they registered his words. "Do you want to see the video?" he asked after a moment.

Tori lowered her hand from her mouth and shook her head. "I don't, thank you." She turned to Elena. "Do you?"

"No, I don't need to see it," she said. "But, may I see him?"

Tori felt her stomach lurch. The sheriff rocked slightly in his chair and looked at Elena.

"I'll ask him if he's willing to see either of you," he said. "He's under no obligation to see you, of course. But, I'll ask him."

Elena looked at the sheriff blankly, not responding to his words.

"If he consents to see you, one of us will need to come in with you," he continued. "You can stand in the walkway and talk through the bars. There's nobody else in the cells, so it'd be private, as far as that's concerned." He turned to Tori. "Do you want to see him too?"

She paused for a moment and then nodded. "I suppose so."

"Okay, well, let me go see about it." He got up and started out the door into the hallway. He turned back to them. "Ya'll need anything? Coffee?" The shook their heads and he disappeared.

He returned after what seemed to Tori like an eternity but which really was only about ten minutes. He sat down across from them, placing a fresh cup of coffee on the desk in front of him.

"He says he'll see you both, but not right now," the sheriff said. "Later this afternoon or evening."

Tori and Elena looked at each other and then back at the sheriff.

"That's fine with me," Elena said. Tori looked questioningly at the sheriff.

"He didn't say exactly why he wanted to wait to see you," he said. "He's pretty upset, though, as you might imagine." He looked at them both with a neutral expression.

"What are the charges on the arrest?" Tori asked.

"Right now, the charges are trespassing, harassment and vandalism. But, we should talk about that at some point today or tomorrow." He leaned back in his chair. "We have forty-eight hours after the arrest to amend the initial charges when we file it with the state. The current charges—if he confesses, pleads no contest or is convicted in a trial—carry mostly fines and maybe some prison time. Given who he is—upstanding person in the community, no priors, this being perhaps a *heat of passion* type thing—he probably won't serve any time at all. Probably get fines and probation, community service, things of this nature."

He paused for a moment, taking a sip from his coffee cup.

"Of course, it could be escalated," he said, looking at them directly as he sat his cup down again. "We can keep this relatively local and at the level we have it now. Or we could shift it up to federal and move it into the category of hate crimes." He rocked slightly in his chair and waited for their response.

"Do we have a say in that?" Tori asked.

The sheriff continued to rock, considering his words before he spoke.

"My responsibility is to file the appropriate paperwork to the relevant offices based on the initial charges and the evidence that supports them." He paused for a moment, looking at them both intently. "I'd want to know what you two think before I took any action other than that," he said simply.

Tori understood his meaning, or at least thought she did. He would shift this to a hate crime if they wanted him to; otherwise, he would leave things as they were.

"Okay…well…" she turned to look at Elena, who sat still, her face still slack, taking in all the sheriff said. Suddenly, she turned to Tori as if waking from a trance.

"I guess we'll be back later, then," Elena said, first to Tori then to the sheriff.

"Alright. I'll probably be here, or Lonnie will," he said. "I'll let you know at that time if there's any new developments."

They walked out of the lobby and donned their sunglasses to face the blinding glare of the sun.

"What do you think?" Tori asked as she accelerated the car back down the highway to Logan.

Elena rubbed her eyes and then rolled her head back against the seat's headrest. She took a deep breath and blew it out.

"I don't know what to think. I'm just so mad." Her voice was calm and quiet, and betrayed nothing of her anger. But Tori looked at her and saw the fury that bubbled underneath her placid face and calm voice. She looked the same as she did the night she told Luis about their love and he had not believed her or taken her seriously.

"Are you sure you want to see him?" she asked.

"Oh yeah, I'm sure," Elena said simply and quietly. "I want him to tell me to my face why the hell he did this to me. To both of us."

Tori took a deep breath and stared at the road. "He may not know the answer to that," she said after a moment.

"Well, maybe he can figure it out if he sits in jail long enough," Elena snapped, her voice now slightly tinged with the rage that burned inside her.

Tori turned to look at her and then looked back at the road. She thought about saying something in response, but decided to keep quiet.

"Let's go to my house. I need to feed Rico," Elena said after a moment. She had turned her face away from Tori to stare blankly out the window at the passing desert landscape dotted with scrub brush and patchy spots of pasture grass. After a moment, she turned back to Tori, reached over and took Tori's hand.

Tori looked at her, squeezed her hand and then looked back at the road.

❧

"We're going back to the station in a little while," she said, tracing a pattern through the condensation on her glass of iced water that sat on the table in front of her.

"I don't guess you need me to go with you, although I'm happy to do it," Ken said quietly.

"I know. Thank you. Really." She took a deep breath. "I think we'll be okay. The sheriff's been really great about everything. He'll probably be there." Her glass sat on a napkin that had soaked up some of the moisture. She pulled a wet corner of it off, balled it up and rolled it between her fingertip and the table.

"Elena's really mad," she said. "I am, too, but not in the same way she is I don't think."

"Well, I guess that's understandable. She's got a long history with him, of sorts. And then in the recent year with her mother and all."

"I just hope she can hold herself together."

"Yeah." He paused. "She'll probably be okay. Don't worry about it."

They were quiet for a moment.

"How do you feel about seeing him?"

"I feel okay. I mean, it's almost like I want to see him to ask him to confirm what the video shows. To hear him tell me that he actually did this. It seems so out of character for him. At least from how I've known him in the last year and a half." She sat back in her chair and looked out the kitchen window to the gray ridge of mountains in the distance. She picked out a peak she thought was the one Elena had shown her from this window before, the one atop Saint Elena mountain.

"It does. It really does seem out of character," he said. "Although grief makes people do crazy things sometimes."

"Yeah, I know. That's what I told Elena weeks ago. But this…I didn't expect anything like this from him." She felt herself gesture into the air with her free hand, surprised at her own vehemence. "I don't really know what to make of all this. If it's even about grief, you know? I have no idea what to expect him to say."

"It crosses a line, that's for sure. A big line."

They were quiet again.

"Well, let me know how it goes and if I can do anything to help," he said. "I'm sure you have legal contacts galore, but I know a few good lawyers out in this part of the state. I can make an introduction if you think you need one."

"Thanks, Ken. I really appreciate it." She leaned forward in her chair and put her elbows on the table. "I'll call you later tonight or in the morning, let you know what's going on."

"Okay, you take care. Love you."

"Love you, too."

She put the phone down and sat quietly for a moment, gazing out the window toward the mountains. Her stomach still churned, but now she felt a sense of dread and sadness settle deep inside her. She knew that whatever Luis said or did later, it would be sadder and more tragic than she or Elena could prepare for. How could it not be? This was not some stranger holed up in an isolated ranch somewhere who had come into town to do ugly things to make a point. This was a friend. A colleague. Someone she and Elena both had loved and trusted, like a family member in Elena's case. For Elena, he was a former lover, if history were traced all the way back to high school. How could he do this? What could have driven him to act in such a way? What depths of hurt or loss or anger? He was not a weak man. He was not a bad man. He was a good, respected man whom everyone loved and trusted. What had broken him? As she thought these things, she felt her own anger, confusion and sadness along with a measure of his, at least as she imagined it. Her stomach convulsed with nausea and dread at the thought.

She heard Elena in the hallway and turned to her as she rounded the corner into the kitchen. Elena's eyes were sleepy, her hair hung long around her shoulders and her t-shirt had stark creases across the front of it where she had slept on it.

"How was your nap?" Tori asked, smiling at her and extending her hand toward her. Elena walked forward and leaned her hip into Tori's shoulder. Tori buried her face in her abdomen and kissed her through her shirt.

"I feel better," she said. "I slept hard." She looked around for her phone. "What time is it?"

"It's 5:30. We can go whenever you're ready."

"Let me make some tea for the drive," she said, moving away toward the stove.

Tori sat staring out the window while Elena disappeared down the hallway again while the water boiled on the stove. After a while she returned wearing a fresh blouse. She had brushed her hair and put it up in a ponytail high on the back of her head. Silver earrings hung from her earlobes and Tori smelled the faint scent of lotion as she came near her and stood at the stove.

"Want some?" she asked, holding the kettle aloft. Tori shook her head. Elena poured her tea into a large travel mug, dropped a tea bag inside, and brought the mug over to the table where Tori sat.

"What have you been doing?" she asked, mindlessly blowing into the mug.

"Just thinking about everything," she said, sighing deeply. "Ken called. He'd heard through the grapevine. I guess half of Logan knows by now."

Elena raised her eyebrows and looked down into her mug, nodding slightly.

"I told him what the sheriff said about the charges and all," she said.

"What did he say?"

"Nothing really—at least about that. He just asked me how I felt about it all, and how you were doing." Tori looked out the window toward the mountains, then back at Elena.

"How do you feel about it?" Elena asked.

Tori looked at her and grimaced slightly. "Sad mostly. Nervous about how he'll be, but mainly sad. Because no matter how he is, it's just sad. Sad that he's come to this." She paused. "Does that make sense?"

Elena stared at the steaming tea in her mug. "You can be sad for him on my behalf, at least for now," she said looking up at Tori. "I'm mad. Really mad."

"I know. I told Ken that, too. And that I hoped you could hold yourself together when you saw him at the jail."

Elena looked back down at her tea, then out the window. Her face had regained its color and form, and she no longer wore a look of stunned disbelief. She looked back at Tori. "I'll be fine. I just want to talk to him. I want to hear his explanation for this."

Tori nodded and looked down at her hands. "What do you think about the charges?"

"I think I'm too mad at the moment to think about it," she said simply. "I want to hear what he says."

"Okay."

They were mostly quiet on the drive to the station. Tori turned on classical music to calm her grinding stomach and to fill the silence, which suddenly seemed oppressive. A few miles from the station, she turned to look at Elena who had leaned her head against the window. A wet streak ran the length of her cheek and Tori saw the small drop of tear about to fall from her jawbone.

"Sweetie…" she whispered, reaching over to touch her arm. Elena wiped her face and kept her gaze directed out the window.

"I never would have believed he could do this. To either of us, really. But especially to me," she said after a moment.

They drove the rest of the way in silence. The parking lot was mostly empty when they pulled in except for patrol cars and one white pick-up truck. They walked into the lobby and were greeted by a young deputy who sat at the reception desk. Tori recognized him as the one who had been confused working the high school playoff game.

"I'm Tori Reed and this is Elena Rios," she said walking toward him and extending her hand. "We're here to see someone you have in custody. We were here earlier this morning and arranged it with Sheriff Banks."

"He told me ya'll were coming," he said. He smiled and stood up. "Let me go get him. Wait right here." He disappeared through the gray doorway. A few minutes later Sheriff Banks appeared and motioned for them to follow him. He led them into his office, but turned around to face them before they sat down.

"Okay, are ya'll ready?" He spoke calmly and looked at both of them with concern.

They both nodded.

"Like I said, there's nobody else in the cells so your conversation will be private except for I'll be standing off to the side with the deputy. That's standard procedure. It'll probably be best to stand back away from the bars a bit. I can give you all about fifteen minutes or so, give or take." He looked at both of them. "Alright?"

They both nodded again.

"I told you this morning that he was upset. He still is. And I imagine you are, too, to some extent. So, we'll just see how it goes. If it gets volatile at all, we'll end the visit right quick. Okay?"

"Okay," Tori said, looking at Elena.

The sheriff walked between them and turned around to face them as he stood in the doorway. "Leave all your belongings in here—purse, car keys, anything in your pockets. Just set it all there on my desk or in the chairs." He watched as they unloaded their stuff onto his desk.

They followed him through a door across the hall and down another small hallway to the end. The deputy from the reception area emerged from an adjoining hallway, meeting them in front of a large metal door. He sorted through several keys on a large hoop ring, found the one he wanted, and opened the large door. They all stepped inside and the deputy closed the door behind them with a loud, echoing clang. He fastened the keys onto a strap on his service belt. They took a few steps forward down yet another hallway, and the sheriff motioned for them to stay put. He walked past them, almost to the end and turned to face someone. "You ready?" he asked, then nodded curtly and turned to face Tori and Elena. He motioned for them to come forward.

Tori followed Elena as they walked toward the sheriff, their shoes echoing on the hard floors. Pale light from skylights along the top of the wall seeped into the hallway and the cells that lined it. Tori turned to peer through the bars of the empty cells they passed. Each cell had a twin bed, a toilet and a small sink with a single faucet. They passed three cells before they met the sheriff standing in front of Luis' cell. As they approached him, he stepped further down the hallway to give them the entire space to stand directly in front of Luis.

Elena turned to face him first, before Tori had passed the adjacent cell and could see into where Luis stood in his cell. Elena backed away from the bars and braced herself against the whitewashed cinderblock wall across from Luis. She placed one palm flat on the wall behind her, as if to make sure she could hold herself there. Her other hand came to her face. She stood for a moment with her hand over her eyes, her mouth gaping open in a gasp. Then she lowered her hands and glared into the cell, tears streaming down her cheeks.

"Oh, Luis…" she hissed in a fierce whisper.

Tori stepped to her side and turned to look into the cell. Her stomach dropped as she saw Luis. He stood in the middle of the cell. A shaft of light from an overhead encased spotlight beamed down on him, illuminating the top of his head, his cheekbones, shoulders and chest in a fluorescent glow. His eyes were swollen and small, and he looked at them with a dull expression as if from a great distance. His face was dark with day-old beard growth, and his hair was unkempt and greasy, and to Tori it seemed grayer than she remembered. He wore faded jeans, boots, and a wrinkled collared shirt with the tail untucked. He seemed old and exhausted, completely different than he had been at Galindo's yesterday. There, he had seemed "normal" and mostly himself. Now, he looked undone, to the point that Tori wondered later if she would recognize him immediately had she seen him on the street. He stood unmoving and looked at Elena as she leaned against the wall. As Tori came into his view, he turned to meet her gaze briefly before raising an arm to wipe his face with his sleeve. He then lowered his arm and just stood there looking down at the floor.

"What have you done?" Elena demanded. "Explain it to me!" She stood with her hips against the wall still, but leaned her upper body forward and thrust her chin toward him as she raised her voice. "Look at me, you coward!"

Tori felt herself lean against the wall beside Elena and watched as Luis raised his head slowly to look at her, as she commanded him to do. His mouth was open and Tori could see his chest beginning to heave. He put his hand to his head, grabbed a handful of hair and squeezed his fingers into a fist. He squeezed his eyes tight as he clenched his own hair. Tori could not tell if he was wincing from the pain on his scalp or the pain of looking into Elena's face. Finally he opened his eyes.

"Say something!" Elena yelled. She now placed both her palms flat on the wall behind her and jutted her upper body forward as if ready to spring from the wall toward the cell bars.

Luis dropped his hand from his hair heavily, letting it flop to his side.

"I can't explain anything," he said. His voice was low and raspy, barely recognizable as his.

Elena stomped her foot one time, which sent an echo resounding through the hallway. Tori saw the sheriff take one step toward them then stop, waiting for a sign to come further and end the meeting. Tori met his gaze quickly then turned back to Elena. She gently reached over and covered Elena's hand nearest to her on the wall with her own, feeling the trembling inside it. Tori looked down at the floor, waiting to hear if Luis would speak.

"I don't know what to say," Luis stammered, his voice breaking. "I can't explain anything." He coughed and wiped his eyes with his sleeve again.

Elena looked down at the floor and back at him. "Why did you do this? What did you think you would accomplish?" Hearing this, Tori looked up again at Luis.

He shook his head and looked down. After a moment, he put his hands on his hips and bent down at the waist, as if resting his back from the weight of his actions. As if all his strength was being used up in simply standing there, facing them. Tori looked at him directly now, and felt herself engaged by Elena's question. She spoke to him for the first and only time.

"That's what I want to know," she said, trying to keep her voice calm and even. "What were you trying to accomplish?"

Luis stayed bent over, but brought his hands from his hips to his face. He covered his eyes and cheeks, rubbing them slightly and then just holding them over his face. Finally he straightened up and lowered his hands. He looked at both of them directly through swollen, watery eyes.

"I've been so angry," he said. "Just so angry and...I don't know...hurt." He looked up at the ceiling and back at them. "I guess I wanted to hurt you."

Elena listened to him intently and stared at him as he spoke. "You wanted to hurt me," she repeated. "Is that all? Is that it?"

He looked at her, then looked down again and shook his head. "I thought maybe something in the situation would change." He grabbed his hair again, wincing at his own words. "Why did you have to come here?!" he yelled at Tori, gripping his hair and glaring at her. "Everything was fine until you came! We would have been fine without you!" His black eyes were small, but fierce, and his voice had strengthened almost into a roar.

Tori listened, horrified, and could barely breathe. Before she could say anything, Elena spoke.

"So, what…this was to punish us? Punish Tori for coming here? Is that it?"

"I don't know, " Luis said, dropping his hand from his hair and turning his back to them. Tori could see his shoulders shaking.

"Turn around! Look at me!" Elena was relentless and her voice matched Luis' in desperation. He turned around and looked at her.

"Were you punishing me for loving her and not loving you? Is that it?" she demanded. "Oh, no, wait…maybe this is it…" she said in a voice dripping with deadly sarcasm. "Since I'm not *really a lesbian*, then maybe you thought this would scare me off of her and I'd come running to you. Is that it? Is that it?!"

He stared at her and dropped his head. "I guess I knew that wouldn't happen," he said after a moment. He put his hands on his hips and looked back at them. "But you two just went on like normal, though, like nothing had happened—just *carefree little lovebirds* going about your business, not caring how it impacted anybody else!" His words were sharp and accusing, although his sarcasm did not match Elena's venom.

"What were we supposed to do, Luis—*ask your permission!?*" Elena glared back at him as if daring him to answer her.

Luis bent at the waist again, clearly unable to stand still or upright for any length of time. Tori saw his shoulders begin to shake and his chest heaving again.

"Who have you become, Luis? " Elena's voice was low and steely now.

His shaking intensified and he began to sway slightly. He slid one foot to the side, to keep his balance, and stepped to the wall to brace against it. He rested his forearm on the wall at eye level and leaned his forehead on it. He began struggling to catch his breath and Tori realized he was sobbing. She felt tears well up in her own eyes, not so much from compassion for him personally, but from the sheer terribleness of the whole situation in that moment. She felt awful—for herself, for Elena, for Luis, for the sheriff and deputy watching this, and for the world in which people did things like this to those they loved.

She looked at Elena, who straightened her body and leaned her back against the wall. Elena wiped a quick tear from her eye and took a shaky breath. She blew it out.

"I'm just glad Mama's not alive to see this," she said finally. As the words came out of Elena's mouth, Tori knew their devastating effect. Luis's body softened and bent toward the wall. He raised his other arm to cover his face and his sobs became louder. Slowly, he slid down the wall to the floor until at last he knelt on the concrete floor with his face buried and turned away from them. They saw only his heaving shoulders and heard his broken, choking sobs.

Elena watched him as he slid down the wall and collapsed into a heap in his cell. She pushed herself away from the wall and took a step so that she stood in the center of the hallway facing the cell. Tori followed, standing slightly behind her. Elena wiped her eyes and squeezed them shut with her fingers. She lowered her head, as if thinking or absorbing everything she had heard and seen in the last few minutes. She raised her head, opened her eyes and looked at Luis.

"Luis, I've loved you nearly my whole life," she said, her voice steady, low and determined. "You were like family to Mama, and I will always appreciate the help you gave me and her in her last year." She paused. "But, I want nothing to do with you ever again for the rest of my life. Do you understand me?"

Luis continued sobbing.

"*Do you understand me?*" Elena said again, more loudly now, demanding a response. He nodded his head against his arms braced on the wall.

"I'm not leaving Logan," she continued. "Tori and I have built something here that we don't want to leave. And you've been a part of it. But, that's over, Luis. Do you understand?"

His sobbing subsided a bit, but when he did not acknowledge her words, she yelled out at him. "*Do you hear me, Luis?! You can't stay here!*"

Tori saw him startle when she yelled, and his sobbing resumed. Finally, after what seemed like an eternity, he spoke. "I know," he said into his shirt sleeve. "I know."

Sheriff Banks stepped forward and looked at Tori, indicating that it was time to end the meeting. Tori took one step toward Elena and put her hand on her back. Elena turned her head slightly in acknowledgement and then looked back at Luis. He leaned against the wall silently shaking and sobbing, his face still buried. Elena looked at the sheriff and then back at Luis.

"One more thing," she said. "I want you to know that you succeeded."

He brought his face from his arm and turned it slightly toward her.

"You said you wanted to hurt me," she said. "Well, you have. You've broken my heart." Her voice cracked for the first time as she said those last words, and she raised her hand to cover her mouth. She turned abruptly and walked away from the cell, heading back toward the hallway entrance. The sheriff stepped forward, looked into the cell at Luis and then waited for Tori to follow behind Elena. Tori looked at the broken man inside the cell and felt a wave of sickening nausea wash over her. She sucked in a hard breath to stave off the urge to throw up, then turned to follow Elena.

The next afternoon, Tori startled out of a hard sleep and looked around her cabin for a few seconds to get her bearings. Slowly she eased herself up on the couch, and leaned her arms and head on her raised knees. Neither she nor Elena had slept well the night before. They had tossed and turned, and even Rico had been up and down on the bed all night. Finally, Elena had gotten up a few hours before dawn, made tea for herself and sat in the kitchen reading a magazine. When Tori saw the pale light of dawn begin seeping through the bedroom curtains she got up to join her.

Now, she looked at her phone on the coffee table beside her. Elena would be coming over soon. They would walk over to the staff meeting together. She got up and walked to the kitchen. She put on a pot of water, dumped a few scoops of coffee into the french press, and stood staring blankly out the window toward the gorge.

She no longer felt the roiling in her stomach, but all she had to do was imagine Luis in that cell last night, with Elena pressed against the wall yelling at him, and a tinge of nausea would return and she would have to take a deep breath to fight it off again. She wondered if she would ever forget the image of him standing in that cell and eventually sliding to the floor in uncontrollable sobs. It was an image that seemed, in an odd way, as violent as a crash scene comprised of maimed bodies and mangled limbs. Everything about it—about Luis—was profoundly broken, perhaps permanently so. There was no recovering from it, not really. Elena's words had been harsh and harrowing, but they had been true. Tori knew Elena had spoken from her heart and did not regret one word of what she had said, no matter how searing and painful. Yet, the words were painful indeed, and not only to Luis. Tori felt her own heart ache as Elena accosted him, and she knew that Elena's heart was torn and would be permanently scarred, too.

She turned when she heard the water begin to boil and saw out her front window the reflection of the sun off Elena's truck. She poured the water over the grounds and smiled as Elena came through the front door. Elena stepped to the bar, laid her sunglasses on the countertop and shrugged her purse off her shoulders onto a barstool. She rounded the bar and leaned in to Tori from behind, hugging her around the waist and pressing her cheek into her shoulder blades. Tori leaned her head back to feel Elena's, and ran her fingers over Elena's forearms at her waist.

"Did you get a nap?" Tori asked. She felt Elena shake her head.

"No, I stayed at Galindo's." She released Tori and leaned against the counter and watched Tori press the plunger down on the coffee.

"Maybe Letty can cover for you tonight and you can take off after the meeting. We have only a few hotel guests in the restaurant tonight."

Elena shook her head, reached for a coffee mug from the cabinet above the counter, and slid the mug toward Tori. "She covered for me while we were at the jail last night, so I told her to take tonight off."

"I'm happy to make you some tea," Tori said before pouring coffee into Elena's mug.

"Coffee's fine. It's stronger, especially when you make it." She held her mug still as Tori filled it and they sat down at the table.

"Do you still feel okay about the meeting? About what we talked about?" Elena asked after a moment.

"Yeah, I think so." Tori said. "Do you?"

Elena nodded, took a sip of coffee and looked out the window.

"I mean, it's right that we tell them what's happened. That they hear the facts from us and get our take on it. It's already spread through town, of course, but still…It'll mean something for them to hear about it all from us," Tori said. "Don't you think?"

"Of course. It's the right thing." Elena said, looking back down at her cup.

Tori watched her for a moment and then spoke. "I keep thinking of him sliding down that wall," she said softly. "It was horrible. It was like he'd become someone I didn't know. Maybe even that he himself didn't know."

Elena swallowed and looked up into Tori's eyes. Her eyes filled with fresh tears. Tori saw the effort in her face to steel herself and keep from crying. She also saw remnants of rage at the corners of Elena's mouth and down into the tendons of her neck.

"He just needs to leave Logan," she said simply, turning away from Tori and back to the window.

They walked along the gorge, picking their way along the trail which by now was well-worn and widened enough for two people to walk together, side by side, instead of only in single file. Tori felt her spirits rise slightly as she took in the wide expanse of desert sand, rocks and brush she had seen hundreds of times in the last year and a half, and had grown to love and depend on as somehow vital to the very core of her happiness. She moved her eyes along the pieces of the horizon that she could see between the flattened mesa tops, tracing its contours in the far distance. She breathed in the clean, dry air and squinted into the afternoon sun that illumined everything in stark highlight. She felt her muscles relax and her shoulders lower as she walked. She felt a calmness begin to settle within her, replacing the dread that had been there for weeks. And she felt her soul open, expanding to match the undulating desert around her with its miles and miles of space and silence. *The world is big enough,* she thought, *for all of us. For me and Elena. For our love and our work together. And for Luis, too. For all of us.* She looked at Elena, who peered out over the middle distance from behind dark glasses. She had pulled her hair loose from her ponytail and it blew free in the breeze. Tori grabbed her hand.

Most of the staff had arrived when they stepped up onto the patio, still hand in hand, and walked toward the glass doors leading into the dining room. Several were standing near the bar drinking from the soda and water bottles lined along its length. Others were sitting at scattered tables, talking and laughing with each other. All eyes turned to them when they walked in, but most people continued talking and visiting even as they kept an eye on the two of them. Tori felt people observing her as she gathered a few chairs near the center cluster of tables. Elena disappeared into the kitchen. Tori glimpsed Letty through the window of the swinging door. She saw Letty embracing Elena when the door swung back a second time.

Letty, Elena, and a few others emerged from the kitchen a few moments later. Elena walked toward Tori and everyone else planted themselves in chairs. Suddenly the room became quiet as all the chatter died down, and Tori and Elena stood together near a front table. They looked at the group, then at each other, and then Tori began.

"I appreciate you all coming on short notice, especially those of you who are off today. We felt it was important, or we wouldn't have asked you to interrupt your day and your plans." She looked down at the table in front of her, as if to look at her notes, but she had no notes. She looked back up at the group.

"Many of you know that the sheriff's office has been trying for several weeks now to catch the person who's been placing animal carcasses on our property—both here at the ranch and at our homes. I'm sure most of you have heard by now that Luis Palacios was arrested for this yesterday morning. He was caught on video putting another carcass on Elena's truck." She heard murmurs throughout the group but continued on. "We have met with the sheriff a few times, and we met with Luis last night." She stopped and looked down for a moment. She felt a lump in her throat, and then she felt Elena's hand on her back. She looked back at the crowd. "It goes without saying that he will no longer be working here at the ranch. And from what we understand, he will be leaving Logan as soon as his case is finished."

Tori paused for a moment and looked into their faces. Some of them had been at the ranch since the very beginning, before they served their first meal or hosted their first hunts. Others had come recently, as late as last month. Seeing them all gathered, listening to her with stark faces, she felt her responsibility to them—as their employer, as the one who signed their checks, as someone who had established something in the community that made a difference for them, that helped them support their families and make their lives into what they wanted. She felt a moment of guilt, for having considered leaving them and the ranch behind, for the very idea of turning her back on them and walking away because of adversity. But it was only a moment. In the next moment, the guilt was overcome with relief. There was now no hard decision to make. There was now only the easiest, most obvious choice. She was staying. Elena was staying. The ranch would go on and, with any luck, continue to prosper, along with her and everyone else involved with it.

She turned to Dustin and Ricardo, who sat to her right about halfway back. Ricardo's face was somber and looked a bit scared. Tori had called him earlier to talk to him about taking Luis' place at the ranch. He had seemed surprised that Tori still wanted him at the ranch, presuming that she would want him to leave since Luis' was his cousin. She had learned from the sheriff that Ricardo had known nothing of Luis' crimes and was just as shocked as everyone else. She felt bad for him. She knew he would miss Luis even as he felt deeply betrayed by him.

"Ricardo will take over the position of Manager of Outdoor Operations. He has worked alongside Luis since before the ranch opened and knows everything that needs to done here. Dustin will step into the position of Associate Manager, into Ricardo's former slot. They have already worked together for the last several months. Elena and I have every confidence in them and are happy to have them in their new positions, although…" She turned to Elena. "I think you're not too happy to lose Dustin as a point person here in the dining room." Elena shook her head and smiled slightly.

"He's still a crossover person, as far as I'm concerned. If Letty can do it, so can you." she said, looking directly at Dustin now, her face widening into a full-blown grin. Letty laughed and looked at Dustin with raised "I told you so" eyebrows. Tori was glad to feel the mood brighten a bit in the room, and relaxed a bit as a few people chuckled at Elena's teasing.

Tori felt Elena's hand on her back again, and turned to her as she began to speak.

"This has all happened very quickly, " Elena said in a determined, but slightly shaky voice. "And it's quite shocking, for lots of reasons." She paused. "At least, it is for me, and I know it must be for many of you, too. Luis is well-known in Logan and, well, everyone has always loved him." She was quiet for a moment and Tori saw her swallow to keep herself together.

"I guess what I want to say is that Tori and I are relieved that this episode of the last month or so is over, even though we feel devastated by what's happened. And we wanted to meet with you about it and tell you the facts about it ourselves, instead of you hearing it from other people." She stopped and looked out at the group. She took a deep breath and continued. "We don't want there to be any questions or uncertainties or rumors about anything, so in that spirit we are happy to take any questions you have about any of this. Any of it. We'll answer them as best we can."

She reached down for a water bottle on the table in front of her. She looked out at the group as she twisted off the cap and took a long drink. As she drank, Omar, a member of the kitchen staff, raised his hand. She nodded in his direction.

"Why did he do it?" he asked.

The room fell still and everyone turned to Elena and Tori. Tori reached for her water bottle and began twisting off the cap. She looked up at Elena, who swallowed and swirled the remaining water in her bottle.

"I'm not really sure, not exactly," Elena said, in a voice more bold and direct than a few moments before. "We both asked him that when we saw him last night. He didn't give a coherent answer." She looked past them all, over their heads, out the glass doors toward the distance. Then she looked back at Omar. "I don't think he knows why himself exactly." She paused and took another drink before continuing.

"But, I'll tell you the situation that led to this. Some of you already know this, but some of you don't and it's time for it to be out in the open so we can be done with it and move on." She sat the water bottle down and put her hands on her hips. "Luis and I were high school sweethearts, but I left Logan after high school and didn't come back until about a year and a half ago to take care of my mother. Luis helped me a lot with her, up through when she died not long ago. Many of you remember that." She paused for a moment. "Luis hoped that we would get back together. We didn't. There was no chance of it, really. I didn't want to...for lots of reasons." She turned to Tori and back to the group. "One of which is that I fell in love with Tori."

Tori crossed her arms over her chest, as if protecting herself from a cold wind, and looked out at the group. A few of them smiled at her—Jared, Letty, Dustin, a few others—and others kept their eyes focused on Elena, their faces still and expressionless, riveted by what Elena was telling them.

"Luis didn't take this news very well," Elena continued. "So, as I say, I can't really explain what went through his mind to have him do what he did, but that's the situation in which it happened." She finished and looked at Omar. He nodded at her and smiled slightly, seemingly satisfied with what she had said to answer him.

Tori watched as several people shifted in their chairs and busied themselves by drinking from their soda or water bottles, as she and Elena had done earlier.

"What would've happened if they didn't catch him? I mean, if they never found out who was leavin' the dead animals everywhere?" asked Nancy, a red-haired woman who sat next to Betty and whom Betty supervised in housekeeping.

Elena and Tori glanced at each other before Elena answered. "Well, we were in the process of deciding what to do about that. We didn't feel that we—the two of us—could stay in Logan if it didn't get resolved somehow. We didn't want to live with the worry in the back of our minds all the time that another incident would happen, or that something even worse would happen. So, we were considering our options. One option was to leave Logan and move back to where either of us came here from—either San Francisco or Houston. Probably Houston."

"You're not still thinking that, are you?" asked another person from across the room. Tori heard a few people murmur their concern at the idea.

"No, not anymore," Elena said firmly. She turned to Tori.

"I love it here and don't want to leave. I've made good friends. I love this ranch and everything about it, including all of you. I love my life here with Elena," Tori said, picking up the story from Elena. "But, we don't want to live somewhere if we're going to be harassed. There are plenty of other places to live where that doesn't happen as a matter of course, so we were prepared to leave here if we had to."

"You should tell us if something like this happens again," said Nancy. "That way, we can know what's going on and can help out." Many in the group nodded and gave their assent.

"We didn't know this was going on really," said Andrew, a new waiter whom Jared had hired only a month ago. "If we'd known, we could have, you know, supported ya'll in some way, or helped out. This isn't really about ya'll being gay—that's ya'll's business and everybody has their own view about that, you know? Some people here may not believe in it, and others are okay with it, but that's not really the point." He looked at both Tori and Elena with an earnest face. "I mean, from what I heard, he put those dead animals onto the ranch, not just at your personal homes. That affects all of us. We all work here, and eat here and bring our families and friends here for nice occasions. I don't want anything bad happening to this place any more than ya'll do. I mean, I don't own it like ya'll do, but still . " he trailed off, shrinking back suddenly as if he thought maybe he had said too much.

"He's right," Nancy said. "We all like working here and don't want anybody messing that up for us regardless of what any of us thinks about you being gay. That's a separate issue. Lots of us, well, I'll speak for myself…I didn't have a good job until I started working here for Betty." She reached over and touched Betty on the shoulder. "Everybody here is real nice and it's a nice environment, and the customers are mostly really classy people. I don't want to lose that. I'd be devastated if ya'll came in here and announced that ya'll were closing it down because somebody was doin' sick stuff like that. Whoever's doin' it needs to hear from all of us first. They need to know it's not just you two here in this operation. There's lots of us here that it impacts." She sat back in her chair and clasped her hands together over her crossed legs. Her face was worn, too worn, for her age, but her eyes were bright and fiery, like her hair, and she seemed to come alive as she spoke. Betty patted her on the leg, smiled and turned to look up at Tori and Elena, smiling more widely as she found their gaze.

Elena and Tori looked at each other, stunned a bit at what had just been said. Elena turned to the group. "Well, I hadn't thought about it that way exactly, which is my fault. I should have. Thank you for saying all that." She looked directly into Nancy's eyes. Nancy nodded back at her.

"Me, too," Tori added. "Thank you for saying this. It means a lot to me. More than you know. Hopefully, we don't have any more bad situations like this in the future, but if we do, we'll be sure to communicate with you about it so we can deal with together as a team." She felt herself start to choke up and immediately flashed back to the last time she stood in this room in front of a group making a presentation—back when she gave the big check to the school—and how she felt overwhelmed by the ranch and all the people it embraced and impacted through its operations. She felt a tinge of guilt again for even thinking of leaving. She vowed to not make that mistake again, at least to not make the decision without the input of the community it would impact the most—the people who sat in front of her.

The meeting ended as it had begun, with people standing around in groups. Some people lingered to talk and visit, others jumped into action to get things ready for the dinner service, and others left to continue their plans for the day and evening. More than a few stepped up to Tori and Elena to shake their hands or hug them. Outspoken, red-haired Nancy thanked them for not closing or selling the ranch and for letting Betty hire her. Betty told them later that Nancy was the most exacting and hardest working person she had ever seen except her own late husband, and that actually Nancy should be supervising Betty instead of the other way around.

The group thinned and a few hotel guests appeared on the patio to get drinks from the portable bar that Jared had just rolled out and stationed near the pool. Everyone on duty slipped into their usual roles and routines, and ranch business returned to normal. Tori sat down at one of the dining tables and watched Elena tie her hair up in a ponytail and tear the plastic off her freshly dry-cleaned chef coat.

"Well, I guess that's that," Tori said, looking around at everyone and everything continuing as usual. "We carry on, I guess."

Elena ran her arms through her coat sleeves and then began rolling the sleeves into cuffs up to her elbows. She looked around as she rolled, and then looked at Tori. "I guess so. I guess there's really nothing else to do really." She shrugged and smiled. "Would you like a drink? I could certainly use one myself and we've got some mighty fine spirits in this cabinet over here." She turned and headed to the built-in bar in the corner of the dining room.

Tori sighed deeply, slapped her hand on her thigh and got up to follow her. "That sounds fantastic."

# Chapter Twenty-Two

Y ou've got a full house at the ranch this weekend, I bet," Ken said jubilantly as he sat across the table from Tori at Galindo's. He dunked a large corn chip into a bowl of red salsa and put the whole thing in his mouth, crunching down loudly with his teeth.

"Yep, we're full up," Tori said, smiling and reaching for her own chip from the basket. "Come on, it's opening weekend of dove season! What kind of hunting ranch would we be if weren't full on opening weekend?"

Ken laughed. "You feel good about Ricardo stepping into Luis' spot?"

Tori nodded. "Yeah, he's good. He's as knowledgeable as Luis about most of the work that comes with that job." She stared out at the street and then looked back at Ken. "He's sad still. He loved Luis."

Ken nodded. "Is he in touch with him at all?"

"Yeah, he says Luis is in northeast Texas, somewhere near Paris,

I think. Working on a horse ranch or something." Tori folded her arms across the table in front of her. "Letty keeps her ear on the grapevine around here. She said Juanita—the woman he was dating—is moving up there to be with him. Or maybe she already has. I don't know the details."

Ken sat back as the waiter sat two longneck beers topped with limes down in front of them. Tori squinted as she squeezed the lime into her bottle. Ken took his off and laid it on her napkin.

"Well, I'm glad to hear that," Ken said. "It was a bad situation, for everyone involved. Lot of hurt feelings." He slid his beer from one hand into the other. "I hope he can get his life together up there. A new life."

"Me, too," Tori said, taking a deep breath and smiling into Ken's kind face.

Ken held his bottle up and waited on Tori to do the same.

"Cheers! To opening weekend!" he said loudly with a big smile.

"And to good friends," Tori added, clinking her bottle to his and taking a long draw from the neck.

They resumed eating their chips and talking about various things around town and the ranch. Soon the waiter returned with their entree plates piled with sizzling meat, tortillas, herbed rice, and grilled mixed vegetables. Ken unrolled his fork and knife and dug in, without waiting on Tori, who noticed a message alert on her phone and picked it up to take a look.

"It's Elena. She's back from Stockdale. She stopped at the ranch but she's on her way here now," Tori said, putting her phone down on the table beside her and grabbing her napkin roll.

"Good! I'll be glad to see her and congratulate her on her new title." He grinned as he spoke and Tori grinned back at him. They ate their lunch, alternately talking and watching people outside the front window. New, wide sidewalks had been poured throughout much of Logan's main drag, including along the buildings that housed Galindo's and the surrounding businesses. More and more people were now walking from Hazel's crafts shop all the way down the row of small businesses and shops, several blocks away, which now included a little art gallery and a coffee bistro that had opened recently. On the other side of Galindo's, on the next block, an old warehouse had been gutted to get ready for a combination antique/Texas novelty store that was opening within the next month or so. The sidewalk stretched well past that warehouse, and between it and Galindo's were several commercial spaces that had "For Rent" signs in them. Ken represented some of those building owners and said he expected them to lease fairly quickly, that the Logan real estate market was picking up a bit.

"I think the energy's building in this little town," he said, sitting back to take a breather after finishing off half his plate in just a few minutes. "We've always had tourists coming through here on the way to the big parks further west along the border, but I don't think the town ever really took advantage of that traffic. Now, it seems people are waking up and taking notice."

Tori nodded and wiped her mouth with her napkin. "It's a perfect set-up, really. And all this growth in the town just helps us out down at the ranch, not to mention here at the café."

They talked for a while longer, trading stories and news of business deals in the area, and relating things they had read or heard about on the news. Tori liked these lunches with Ken. The new gallery owner from down the street, an older woman named Theresa with long gray hair wearing a sand-colored flowing linen outfit, came in to place a take-out order. She nodded to Tori and Ken and they called her over. Tori had met her once at the ranch when she came to the restaurant for dinner with some new friends.

Theresa was standing beside their table telling them about a gallery she used to run in Sante Fe when Tori saw Elena's truck pull into the front parking lot. She tried to stay focused on Theresa, but saw Elena from the side of her eye get out of her truck, grab a briefcase and make her way across the gravel to the front door. She came through the front door, pushed her sunglasses to the top of her head, and smiled as she spied Tori and Ken and started toward them.

"Look who's here!" Ken called to her as she stepped to the table beside Theresa. He scooted out of his seat, stood up and gave her a bear hug. She laughed and circled her arm around his neck and kissed his cheek. After he put her down, she turned to greet Theresa quickly and then leaned down to kiss Tori's cheek. Theresa seemed taken aback by all the fuss.

"Elena, this is Theresa. She owns the new little gallery on the next block. Ken and I were just chatting with her while she waits on her order."

"Nice to meet you, Theresa," Elena said, grinning uncontrollably. "I think Tori mentioned to me that you came to the ranch restaurant a week or so ago. I'm sorry I didn't get to meet you that night."

"Oh! You're the chef there! I didn't make the connection at first," Theresa said, clasping her hands together at her chest. Her eyes got big and her voice grew serious. "Oh, the food is very, very good there." She nodded as she spoke, as if making a solemn pronouncement. "Very good."

"Thank you. I'm glad you like it," Elena said, turning to Tori. "We try to make it a special experience for people."

"She's not just the chef *there*, though," Ken said. "She's been the chef here for even longer than she's been at the ranch. And now…" he raised his eyebrows in utter glee, stretching the sentence out for maximum dramatic effect. "Now…she's not just the chef here at Galindo's…" His voice got louder with each word of the sentence, and Tori made the sound of a drum roll on the table and started clapping her hands.

"Oh my," Theresa exclaimed. "How wonderful! What's the new title?" Ken stepped away from the table and into the center of the cafe.

"If I can have everyone's attention, just for a minute, please," he said loudly. "We have a special occasion to commemorate here in the cafe." He turned to Elena and stretched out his hand for her to come forward. A waiter who had been serving the table next to the kitchen door stuck his head into the kitchen to call the staff to come out into the dining room.

Ken waited until most of them had come out to stand along the wall in their stained white aprons, wiping their hands on towels draped across their shoulders. Then he continued, looking around the room, his voice loud and official. "I'm proud to announce that our acclaimed local chef, Elena Rios, who has put this place on the map for the last year and a half now has a new title here at Galindos—the title of *owner*! Let's give her a round of applause and congratulations."

The three dozen or so customers, along with the staff, clapped their hands and began holding up their water glasses and beer bottles, calling out her name and saying "Salud!" She laughed and waved at the customers she recognized, receiving their cheers and well wishes. The kitchen staff whistled and swirled their towels in the air.

"Thank you! Thank you all!" she said, turning to try at least to glance at everyone in the restaurant. She waited for their cheers to subside. "Thank you for making the restaurant a success with your business and with your help. I could never do it without you. I'm proud to be the new owner and proud to continue the tradition that Urleen Galindo started several decades ago." She glanced at Tori and winked, then turned to the crowd again. "Let's celebrate this new chapter in the café together. Everybody, order a drink— it's on the house!"

The crowd applauded and cheered again, laughing and banging the tables with their hands. Elena went from table to table, greeting everyone and thanking people for being at the café. She turned at one point to receive a ribboned bouquet from a delivery driver. She opened the little card, smiled and found Tori across the room. She mouthed the word "Sharon" and Tori smiled and nodded in return. Ken sat back down at the table with Tori. Theresa got her order and stopped to congratulate Elena on her way out. The waitstaff hustled from table to table, taking everyone's drink orders and bringing them back out quickly—longneck beers, icy margaritas, and tall, fruity, frozen concoctions. Elena grabbed a red, frozen drink off a tray a waiter was returning to the kitchen and brought it to the table with her. She plopped down next to Tori and put the drink on the table in front of both of them. Her face was beaming and Tori did not know when or if she had ever seen her that visibly happy.

"Drink some of this with me," Elena said, sliding the tall glass toward Tori. Tori took a sip of it and pushed it back to Elena, who took a long drag of it from the straw. She sucked in her cheeks and held the slushy mixture in her mouth for a few seconds before swallowing.

"Wow, that's strong," she said, blinking her eyes and looking at the glass as if she might be able to detect the alcohol content simply by looking at it.

"Yeah, and I'm getting freezer head from it already," Tori said, rubbing her forehead and breathing through her mouth.

"Let me try that," Ken said, grabbing the glass and drinking straight from the lip of it. He swished it around in his mouth and then swallowed. His eyes sparkled and he grinned at the two of them. "These girly-looking drinks will deceive you, won't they!" He laughed and sat back in his chair.

"So, everything went well?" Tori asked after a few moments, when the atmosphere had settled down a bit.

"Yeah, it's done," Elena said. "The lawyers had it all drawn up and were waiting for me at the bank when I got there. They walked me through it all. Sofia brought Urleen by, they signed their part of everything, I signed my part, gave them my check, we shook hands and it was done. The bank manager came and took a picture of me and Urleen. She's sending me the file of it. I'm going to print it and put it in a frame and hang it in here some-where. You know, just to commemorate the history of the place."

"That's a good idea," Tori said, smiling at her. She put her arm on the back of Elena's chair and caressed her shoulder with her fingertips. "I'm really proud of you. And so happy for you."

"Thanks, sweetie," Elena said softly. "I'm happy too."

"Well, I'm proud of you both," Ken said. "Between the two of you, you're gonna take over this whole town if given enough time. And that would probably be a good thing." They laughed together and finished their drinks, turning from time to time to watch the people outside—tourists, road trippers, kayakers, truck drivers, locals—who milled about along the new sidewalks, stroll-ing in and out of the shops, the West Texas sun reflecting off their cheeks and shoulders.

❧

Ricardo and Dustin had left an hour earlier with two trucks full of hunters. Tori had met them all well before dawn, when the guests had sleepily made their way from their rooms across the patio to the fresh coffee and muffins waiting for them in the din-ing room. She told them about the flocks of whitewings she and the other ranch staff had seen in the days and weeks leading up to this morning. By the time they loaded themselves and their gear into the trucks, they were as giddy and giggling as schoolgirls at their first school dance.

Tori reclined on a chaise lounge on the patio with a cup of coffee and waited for the sun to rise. She remembered this exact morning a year ago, when she sat in the same spot and fed a rabbit a piece of her apple before falling asleep to the lulling sound of the jacuzzi. So much had happened in the year since. So many good things. Some bad things, too—sad, confusing and tragic things—but mostly good things. She leaned her head back and sighed, feeling glad that she was here, that she had not left when things got tough, and that she was not nearly as nervous on this day as she was on this morning a year ago.

Elena appeared on the patio almost on cue, just as she had a year ago. "Scoot over," she said, as she stood beside the chaise where Tori sat. Tori sat her coffee on the ground and scooted over, shifting her body to its side. Elena wedged herself into the space, cradling her head in the crook between Tori's neck and shoulder.

They held each other for a while, silent and drowsing, until pale light began to show itself over the eastern horizon. The eerie *hoot-hoot* of an owl emerged from the darkness of the gorge in front of them, urging them from their stillness. They both sat up and stared toward the gorge and into the lightening sky.

"I think it's that time," Tori said finally, almost whispering, not wanting to break the stillness any more than the owl already had.

"Yes, it is." Elena got up first and Tori followed her into the kitchen to help her get things ready and packed for the field brunch.

The sun was well up and the morning coolness had disappeared by the time they reached the camping area where they would serve the brunch. Tori was relieved to hear volleys of shots every few minutes as they set up the tables and chairs. At least there would be fresh meat for the brunch. It had been a long spring and summer without it.

They worked in tandem, as if they had been doing it for years and knew instinctively what to do themselves as well as what the other one would do. By the time Tori had the chaise lounges set out, the table linens and servings in place, and the buffet tables arranged and decorated with freshly cut sage, Elena was already grilling vegetables and had rice in a large wok ready to stir-fry.

Tori, holding to tradition, grabbed a champagne bottle from the ice bucket, popped the top and filled two glasses to overflowing with the frothy liquid. She brought the glasses over and handed one to Elena.

"To our second season," she said, looping her arm through Elena's.

"Indeed, to our second season, the most successful one yet!" Elena took a long sip from the glass and closed her eyes as she swallowed. "You know, the older I get the more I like this stuff. I didn't used to like it too much."

"Really? I've always loved it," Tori said, taking another sip after her initial one. She looked at the wok and the grilled meat. "What's this?" She didn't remember seeing a brunch dish, or any dish at the ranch, prepared in this way.

"It's a surprise," Elena said flatly. "I can't tell you about it, or I'll have to kill you." She smirked at Tori and bent down under the cooking table to dig through a bin. She came out with a bottle of sesame oil. She opened and drizzled a few tablespoons of it out into the wok with the rice.

"I've kept the secret about the anchovy paste," Tori said with mock indignation. "You can trust me."

"This is different," Elena retorted. "But, you can stand and watch. Just don't ask me to explain anything, or else…"

"I know, you'll have to kill me." Tori leaned against the table and watched as Elena continued working on the dish. By the end of it, she had a wok full of rice, pieces of grilled vegetables, pieces of marinated grilled quail, various herbs and spices. An egg fried in an adjacent pan, and when she had doled out a portion from the wok onto small plate, she lifted the perfectly fried egg out of the pan with a spatula and placed it squarely on top of the mound of rice, meat and vegetables. She grabbed a sprig of cilantro from the bunch standing in a nearby glass and delicately laid it in the center of the egg's yellow. She inspected the plate, placed a fork on its edge and handed it to Tori.

"Here." She stood back with her hands on her hips, smiling slyly. "Cut into the egg first, mix some of the yolk around into the rest of it, and eat a bite that has a little bit of everything in it," she instructed.

Tori did as she was told and looked at Elena over her plate as she put the first forkfull into her mouth. She did not know what she was expecting, but whatever it was, the food in her mouth far outstripped it in taste and sophistication. It was as if the comfort foods of parts of Asia had fused with that of the natives of West Texas into a simple, but nuanced concoction of earth and life. The rich texture and flavors of the egg yolk mixed with that of the sesame oil to form the backdrop against which the quail and vegetables exploded in sharp, but pleasing contrast. The rice served as the soft threading that drew and tied it all together into a coherent, simultaneously complex and simple dish. It was perfect for the field and perfect, as a symbol, for the casual elegance of the ranch and its entire approach.

"Oh my God…" Tori said, as she swallowed part of the first bite. She stared at Elena first, then at her plate. She took another bite and chewed it, savoring the flavors on her tongue and feeling their comfort as she consumed them. "What is this?"

"You like it, I see." Elena smiled and looked over the plate to Tori's eyes. "I think it will be one of the ranch's featured dishes. Our signature field dish. It will be even better with fresh wild birds. These are farm-raised and new, but they've been frozen." She watched Tori gather her third bite.

"It's very simple," Elena continued. "It's quail fried rice, basically."

Tori continued eating and shook her head slowly. "Elena, this is out of this world. I can't say exactly what's so special about it because everything in it is rather common and normal, but…" She lowered the plate a bit and grinned slightly. "I feel like I want to wallow in it, or smear it all over me and you both." She laughed aloud as she heard herself say this.

Elena smiled and raised her eyebrows. "Well…" she said, as she slipped off her coat and stepped toward Tori.

# The End

# About the Author

Jill Carroll is an author, speaker and public scholar in the area of world religions. Her first career was as a university professor and corporate trainer. She now works as a freelance journalist, an organizational consultant, and a fiction writer. *Quail Fried Rice* is her first novel. Visit her website at http://www.jillcarroll.com

1015328R00236

Made in the USA
San Bernardino, CA
21 October 2012